3 4/0

D1447399

PROGRESS · RUSSIAN CLASSICS SERIES

IVAN TURGENEV

FATHERS AND SONS
A NEST OF THE GENTRY

Novels

PROGRESS PUBLISHERS
MOSCOW

C. M. Grenville

Translated from the Russian by *Bernard Isaacs*
Illustrated by *Konstantin Rudakov*

ИВАН ТУРГЕНЕВ

Отцы и дети. Дворянское гнездо.
Романы
На английском языке

First printing 1951
Second printing 1974
Printed in the Union of Soviet Socialist Republics

T $\frac{70301\text{-}285}{014(01)\text{-}74}$ 123-74

CONTENTS

IVAN TURGENEV

by *Yari Mann*

Speaking of the principles of his work, Turgenev once said: "...To achieve a reproduction of the truth, the reality of life accurately and powerfully is the greatest happiness for a writer, even if this truth does not coincide with his own sympathies." This statement was not just a declaration, for in striving for the truth Turgenev sometimes came up against his "own sympathies"—both political and social—and overcame them. Below, we shall see a confirmation of this.

The words quoted above are interesting in another respect as well. This statement, made by a mature writer already renowned in the European world, clearly shows the traditions which Turgenev adopted for his own, and the school he had gone through in his youth. What we have in mind is the so-called *natural school*.

The 1840s were a time of important changes in Russian literature. Interest in the social environment, in the hidden motives of people's behaviour, in the laws and norms of community life became manifest. The conventional pattern of literary characters was changing quickly as well: a motley and picturesque mob of characters burst into the foreground to share the stage with the higher classes, if not to crowd them out. These were clerks, craftsmen, merchants, servants, serfs, strolling musicians, and actors. The topography and geography were changing too: the scene was shifted more and more often from drawing rooms, artists' studios, aristocratic mansions and the landed gentry's estates to city squares, to the poverty-stricken outskirts of a large town, to an artisan's workshop, a pub, the wretched quarters of a caretaker or a clerk, to the market place, to a post chaise

---

setting out on a long journey, or to a city omnibus. Central Russia with her quiet colours, unspectacular landscapes, and her gentle and simple lyricism, now became an artistic object on equal terms with St. Petersburg, Moscow, and Russia's exotic fringelands which had inspired the romantics—the Caucasus, Crimea, Finland, the Baltic states, and Siberia. It was not only the themes, characters and objects of representation that changed, as we have seen, but the very tone of artistic expression. From the romantically spectacular, striking and extraordinary, literature was turning more and more to the common-place, discovering hidden poetic sources in the humdrum prosiness of life, seemingly devoid of any artistic interest. Big changes also took place in the matter of genres: although several first-class poets were very active in the 1840s, it was essentially a time of prose writing, when the novel and the short story resolutely pushed the lyric and epic poems into the background, and when the feature story, satirical sketch, or a story of mores and manners became the most popular genres in Russian journalism, as widespread as the elegy and the friendly epistle had been in the times of yore.

Turgenev had a hand in all these far-reaching changes, together with other representatives of the "natural school", among whom we find practically all the outstanding Russian mid-nineteenth century writers: Herzen, Goncharov, Dostoyevsky, Nekrasov, and Grigorovich. Each one of them could have subscribed to Turgenev's statement.

It is obvious from the aforesaid that the natural school was a realistic school. Interest in de-poetised, everyday reality, in life's social foundations, in ordinary heroes, as well as the tremendously expanded sphere of literary representation, and the democratisation of genres and means of poetic expression—all this shaped that particular, realistic manner of artistic thinking within the framework of which our major Russian writers developed their individual creative styles.

"The natural school has now come to the forefront in Russian literature," Belinsky wrote in 1848. In the language of modern literary categories this means that the new realistic school held almost undivided sway among the front-ranking Russian writers.

* * *

The circumstances of his life prompted Turgenev to devote his first books to a problem that was especially acute and important at the time.

Ivan Sergeyevich Turgenev was born on October 28 (Old Style), 1818 in Orel, and spent his childhood in the family seat of Spasskoye-Lutovinovo.

This family seat was typical for Central Russia estates with their spreading fields, water-meadows, shady parks, linden-lined walks, lilac, honeysuckle and acacia thickets, and nightingale trills at night. All this, seen and heard in his childhood, was later to occupy such a large place in the writer's artistic world.

But there were also childhood impressions of a different kind. The Turgenevs enforced the law of serfdom on their estate unreservedly. Their serfs were whipped or recruited for the most trifling offence. Varvara Petrovna, the future writer's mother, supervised the "disciplining" herself. A cruel and despotic woman, she once had all the gardeners whipped because somebody had plucked a tulip of an expensive variety from the flower bed.

And yet this same Varvara Petrovna—such were the incongruities of Russian serf-owning society—loved Russian and French literature, and knew it well. It was she who first cultivated a taste for literature in her son. When Turgenev's poem "Parasha", one of his first works, was published, his mother wrote to him: "I really see talent in you. It's splendid, I mean it seriously.... I've just been served some strawberries. We, country folk, love everything real. Your poem, it smells of strawberries." Thus, in her peculiar fashion, Varvara Petrovna defined the fragrance and artlessness of her son's realistic writing.

When Turgenev was 9 years old, the family moved to Moscow. In 1833, he was enrolled in the philology department of the Moscow University, and a year later transferred to the St. Petersburg University from which he graduated in 1837 at the age of 19.

Whereas most of the young men of his age would have been quite satisfied with such a sound education, Turgenev was inclined to regard it as merely a preparatory stage, and the year after his graduation he joined the Berlin University to perfect his knowledge of ancient languages, history, and especially modern philosophy, Hegel's among it. Fortunately for Turgenev, among the external students of the University there were such outstandingly gifted Russians as Stankevich who headed the Moscow philosophical circle, Granovsky the historian, and Bakunin who was to become a well-known revo-

lutionary anarchist. Talking and arguing with these people stimulated
Turgenev's thought and imagination, and provided him with that
precious material which later helped him to describe the intellectual
and spiritual life of Russian society.

Turgenev had another reason for going abroad, beside his desire
to further his education, and it may well have been the main reason.

He left Russia of his own free will, we know. He had not been
persecuted by the tsarist government, he had not emigrated like
Herzen. Nevertheless, Turgenev later spoke of his departure as a
step made of necessity, as almost an escape, as a deliberate breaking
away from his milieu. "I could not breathe the same air with what
I had come to hate.... It was absolutely essential for me to withdraw to a distance from my enemy in order to attack it all the more
powerfully from there. In my eyes this enemy had a concrete image
and wore a well-known name: my enemy was serfdom. Under this
name I collected and concentrated everything that I was resolved
to fight against till the end, everything I had sworn never to reconcile myself to.... It was my Hannibal Pledge. It was the better to
carry it out that I moved to the West." We do not know precisely
when Turgenev made his pledge, but it is obvious that it reflected
the hatred of serfdom and the compassion for the oppressed serfs
that he had carried in his heart since childhood, and that the resolve had been maturing for many long years.

In the 1840s, having published several poems, short stories and
articles, Turgenev already had the reputation of a gifted and highly
promising writer. But real fame came with the publication of works
that were connected in one way or another with the fulfilment of
the "pledge". We are speaking of his *A Hunter's Sketches*.

In 1847, the progressive magazine *Sovremennik (Contemporary)*
whose chief editor was Vissarion Belinsky, published "Khor and
Kalinich", the first story from this cycle, to be followed by "The
Steward", "The Freeholder Ovsyanikov", "The Counting-House"
and others.

In 1852, *A Hunter's Sketches* came out in book form. Its success,
both literary and social, was something Russian readers had not seen
for a long time. Mikhail Saltykov-Shchedrin, the democratic writer,
in a later review said that *A Hunter's Sketches* had started "a new
literature dedicated to the people and their needs".

However topical the theme, and however trenchant Turgenev's
condemnation of serfdom, these factors alone could not have explained the effect produced by the book, which was not even the

most striking example in this sense. There were already books like Radishchev's *A Journey from Petersburg to Moscow* and Pushkin's *Village*, where the barbarity of the serf owners was wrathfully exposed and the slave traders were branded with infamy. The narrative tone of Turgenev's stories is much calmer, more reserved and the manner of narration more thorough. But it was this thoroughness and reserve that gave the stories their irresistible strength.

Wandering about Central Russia, in Kaluga and Orel gubernias, with a rifle and a hunting dog, the narrator could not help observing the mores and manners of the serfs, their everyday life, and their relations with the landowners and the authorities. In one place the "hunter" saw a serf being whipped, in another—a contest between two singers in a village pub. Here, he overheard the conversation of peasant boys on night watch; and there he happened upon a lovers' tryst. The life of the peasants revealed itself to him in its natural course, disclosing its intimate side, as it were, that was not for show.

And as he observed this life, the narrator arrived at conclusions that were worth a major discovery. Here is one of these conclusions. Speaking of his meetings with Khor, a shrewd and prudent peasant, the author concludes: "...From our conversations I carried away one conviction, which my readers will certainly not anticipate ... the conviction that Peter the Great was pre-eminently a Russian—Russian, above all, in his reforms. The Russian is so convinced of his own strength and powers that he is not afraid of putting himself to severe strain; he takes little interest in his past, and looks boldly forward." By drawing a parallel between a common peasant and a tsar, Turgenev elevated the peasant in the most important sense— the moral sense, and by so doing deprived the champions of serfdom of their strongest argument.

Karamzin, the author of one of the first stories about peasants, declared long before Turgenev's time: "...Peasant women can truly love, too." The word "too" is used defensively here. In Turgenev's *A Hunter's Sketches* it is dropped. It is said simply, without any reservations, that peasants can truly love. Just as they can feel any other human emotions.

Vissarion Belinsky who had known Turgenev personally since 1843, wrote that in *A Hunter's Sketches* Turgenev had approached the people from a side they had never been approached from before. Belinsky was the biggest Russian critic, a recognised leader of Rus-

sia's progressive democratic forces, and Turgenev very aptly called
him the "central figure" of his day.

A Hunter's Sketches was to become the favourite book of many
generations of Russian readers. It became a source of knowledge
about Russia for readers abroad, beginning from Turgenev's contemporaries—Mérimée, George Sand, and Flaubert, to our own
contemporaries—Galsworthy, George Moore, and Hemingway who
in his *A Moveable Feast* recalled wandering about Russia with the
author of *A Hunter's Sketches*.

After the publication of this book, the tsarist authorities turned
hostile to Turgenev. When Gogol died in 1852 and, defying the
censors' prohibition, Turgenev published his obituary in *Moskovskiye
Vedomosti*, they arrested him and banished him to his Spasskoye-
Lutovinovo estate. In a letter to Louis and Pauline Viardot, he explained: "...They have long been looking askance at me. And so
they took their first chance."

* * *

Belinsky who, to quote Turgenev, possessed "infallible aesthetic
discernment", nevertheless made one mistake in assessing the author's
talent. And it was a happy mistake.

In his article "A Look at Russian Literature of 1847", written in
1848 when Turgenev was mainly known for his poems and several
stories from *A Hunter's Sketches*, Belinsky said: "Apparently, he has
not the gift for pure creativity, as he cannot create characters and
place them in such relations with one another from which novels
and stories become formed of themselves. He can portray reality,
seen and studied by him, and create too, if you like, but only from
ready material provided by reality."

Turgenev's creative manner was always based on a profound and
thorough study of reality and a reliance on facts. But in the 1850s
and the following decades he strove for precisely such a grouping
of characters from which "novels and stories became formed of
themselves". He wanted to "create characters" and disclose their
psychological evolution. "I have tried long enough to draw *triples
extraits* from human characters in order to pour them into tiny phials
afterwards," Turgenev once said. "Enough, enough! But the question
is—am I capable of something big, something sedate?" Thereafter,
he switched his entire attention to big forms.

He had written several plays early in the 1850s—*The Bachelor*, *A Month in the Country*, and *Hanger-On*. These plays, combining a simple plot with involved psychological revelations, and a straight-forward dialogue with a deep lyrical undertow, made a major event when they first appeared. Critics quite rightly see in them a harbinger of Chekhov's dramaturgy.

In the 1850s and in subsequent years, Turgenev devoted himself wholly to big epic forms—stories and novels. One after the other he published his novels *Rudin* (1856), *A Nest of the Gentry* (1859), *On the Eve* (1860), *Fathers and Sons* (1862), *Smoke* (1867) and somewhat later *Virgin Soil* (1877). It was these works that brought Turgenev world recognition as one of the founders and classics of the Russian realist novel.

His two masterpieces *A Nest of the Gentry* and *Fathers and Sons* will best acquaint readers with Turgenev the novelist. And we feel certain that readers will appreciate the author's skill in disclosing the socially significant characters of his personages.

As a matter of fact, Turgenev created a whole gallery of related types belonging to the category of the so-called "superfluous men". For all their individual psychological distinctions, these characters had the following traits in common: estrangement from the official life of Russia, awareness of their superiority over their native milieu (the nobility or the landed class, more often than not), singular abilities, a striving towards lofty aims, a desire for fruitful activity—and, at the same time, profound skepticism, spiritual lassitude, and a constant quarrel between word and deed. It is an interesting point that the expression "superfluous men" which was extremely popular in Russia came from Turgenev's story "Diary of a Superfluous Man" written in 1850.

Far from following a pattern, Turgenev endows his characters with a psychology all their own, and these variations are truly infinite. Take Lavretsky, the main character in *A Nest of the Gentry*. It would be natural to expect a western orientation from a man of his convictions, yet Turgenev makes him a Slavophil, and compels Panshin, his opponent, an effective speech-maker and careerist, to extol European progress as a reproach to backward Russia. And does Lavretsky look like a person tortured by morbid reflection? A huge fellow with a ruddy face and powerful hands who can easily lift several poods? However, he has the blood of a serf woman in his veins, so no wonder. But in his heart he carries all the family illnesses of a "superfluous man": a craving for useful activity, a striving for lofty ideals, combined with an increasing spiritual lassitude and anemia of the will.

For Turgenev, the antithesis Lavretsky-Panshin had yet another meaning. "I am a radical, incorrigible westerner, and I never made a secret of it," Turgenev wrote. "And yet, in spite of this, I took particular pleasure in describing the shabby aspects of occidentophilism as well. I made Lavretsky the Slavophil defeat all of Panshin's arguments. Why did I do it? Because, above everything else, I wanted to be sincere and truthful." Here is an example of how Turgenev suppressed his personal sympathies of which we spoke at the beginning of this article.

Important historical events took place in the period between the writing of the first and second novels, included in the present volume. In the early 1860s a revolutionary situation developed in Russia, and there was a general social upsurge.

In *On the Eve* which came between *A Nest of the Gentry* and *Fathers and Sons* Insarov, a fighter for the liberation of Bulgaria, a strong personality with a clear purpose in life, is placed in opposition to the "superfluous men" like Shubin and Bersenev. This novel, whose very title sounded like a promising symbol in those years, was Turgenev's response to the social upsurge and the mood of great expectations. However, when the critic and democrat Dobrolubov drew far-reaching conclusions from this novel and wrote in his article "When Will the Real Day Come at Last?" of the much needed emergence of Russian Insarovs, in other words, Russian revolutionaries, Turgenev severed relations with the magazine *Sovremennik* which was headed by Dobrolubov and Chernyshevsky.

The novel *Fathers and Sons* which appeared shortly after this was perceived in the light of the recent happening, and this light, it must be said, was much to the disadvantage of the novel. In the main character, people saw a malicious caricature of the revolutionary youth, and a desire to stultify their aims and ideals. Pisarev was one of the few in the democratic camp who thought highly of Bazarov and appreciated his sharp mind and his plebeian hatred of deceit and oppression.

Time has sifted away many of the prejudices against this novel, and today we can say that its artistic purpose extended far beyond the topical problems of a long past day. Needless to say, like Turgenev's other works, this novel also tackled contemporary, sore subjects. When Turgenev ridiculed the epigons and chance people in

the revolutionary movement (like Sitnikov and Kukshina), or when
he said, having in mind such people like Arkady or the Kirsanov
brothers, that his whole story was aimed against the nobility as the
foremost class, he was being topical, of course. But the gloomy
figure of the main character, towering over circumstances and time,
raised the novel as a whole to a different, a philosophical plane, we
would say.

Turgenev used to say that his idea was best understood by Dostoyevsky who commented, very briefly but most expressively, on the
main character: "...the restless and anguished Bazarov (a sign of
a big heart)."

Bazarov was by no means against the progressive ideas of his
time, as some readers imagined. But the standards he set were so
high and his nature was so restless that he was always finding himself in the position of a maximalist whom no concrete political
slogans could satisfy: neither the liberal's hope in reforms (he saw
the narrowness and emptiness of liberalism), nor the idea of peasant
communes (he saw what was behind this, and knew that a commune
was anything but a cell of socialism, as the Utopists believed), nor
enlightening propaganda (which he considered insufficient). Max-
imalism doomed Bazarov to idleness (as far as social activity was
concerned) and most unexpectedly brought him into close relation
with a "superfluous man", although these two characters had an
entirely different psychology and philosophy.

As a literary type, Bazarov was not the last in Turgenev's gallery.
As though to prove to the revolutionary youth how unbiased he was
(and actually suppressing his class prejudices and sympathies) Turgenev readily and with great feeling portrayed revolutionaries, for
example, in his last novel *Virgin Soil* and in "The Threshold", a
poem in prose.

Here is one more evidence to the point. In 1876, Turgenev wrote
about this new novel: "Perhaps I should have outlined the figure of
Pavel more sharply, Solomin's factotum, the future revolutionary ...
in time he'll become the central figure in a new novel. In the meantime I have barely outlined him."

In his later years Turgenev lived mostly abroad, in Western
Europe, where he did a great deal for the propaganda of Russian
culture.

Turgenev died on August 22 (Old Style), 1883 in Bougival, not far
from Paris. His body was brought to St. Petersburg and laid to rest
in the Volkovo cemetery.

Ernest Renan, the French scholar, said in his funeral speech: "Honour and glory to the great Slav race whose emergence on the avant-scene is the most amazing phenomenon of our age. Honour and glory to it for so early finding its spokesman in this incomparable artist. He belongs to the whole of mankind."

Translated by *Olga Shartse*

FATHERS AND SONS

To the memory of
Vissarion Grigorievich
Belinsky

I

"Well, Pyotr? No sign of them yet?"—a gentleman a little over forty in a dusty coat and checked trousers, emerging hatless onto the doorstep of a little country inn on the X— Highway, enquired on May 20th, 1859 of his servant, a plump-faced youth with a whitish down on his chin and lacklustre little eyes.

The servant, in whom everything, including his pomaded head of varicoloured hair, the turquoise earring in one ear, and polite manners, bespoke a product of the modern progressive generation, vouchsafed a glance down the road and retorted, "No sign yet, sir."

"No sign?" his master repeated.

"No sign," the man reiterated.

The gentleman sighed and seated himself on a little bench. Let us introduce him to the reader, while he sits there with his legs tucked away, gazing around meditatively.

His name was Nikolai Petrovich Kirsanov. Within fifteen versts of the inn he had a good estate of two hundred souls, or—as he preferred to call it since he had granted his peasants the right of tenure and set up a "farm" of his own—a property of two thousand dessiatins. His father, a general who had seen active service in 1812, a coarse uneducated but not ill-natured Russian had been in harness all his life, commanding first a brigade, then a division, and had always lived in the provinces, where, by virtue of his rank, he had been a person of importance. Like his brother Pavel, of whom more anon, Nikolai Petrovich was born in the south of Russia and was educated at home until the age of fourteen, surrounded by cheap tutors, swaggering but obsequious adjutants

and other regimental and staff gentlemen. His mother
(née Kolyazina), called Agathe as a girl and Agafokleya
Kuzminishna Kirsanova as a general's wife, was one of
those "officer ladies" who wear the breeches in both
marital and military affairs; she affected ornate caps and
rustling silk gowns; in church she was always first to
come up to the cross; she spoke loudly and volubly; permitted her children to kiss her hand in the morning and
gave them her blessing at night—in fine, she enjoyed life.
Being the son of a general, Nikolai Petrovich, who far
from being distinguished for bravery had even been
dubbed "craven-heart", was to have entered the military
service like his brother Pavel, but he broke a leg the very
day the news of his commission arrived, and after being
laid up for two months, he retained a slight limp for the
rest of his life. His father gave him up in disgust and
launched him on a civil walk. As soon as the boy turned
eighteen he took him to St. Petersburg and placed him in
the university. At about that time his brother became an
officer of the guards. The young men took up quarters
together under the distant surveillance of Ilya Kolyazin,
a maternal uncle and a high government official. Their
father returned to his division and his wife and once in
a while sent his sons large quartos of grey paper scrawled
over, in a bold clerkly hand, graced at the bottom with
many a flourish and curlycue: "Pyotr Kirsanov, Major
General." Nikolai Petrovich graduated from the university in 1835 *cum laude*, and the same year General Kirsanov was placed in the retired list following an unfortunate review, and went to live in St. Petersburg with his
wife. He had just rented a house in Tavrichesky Gardens
and become a member of the English club when he suddenly died of a stroke. Agafokleya Kuzminishna soon
followed him: she could not get used to the loneliness of
metropolitan life; the misery of a retired existence got
the better of her. Meanwhile, Nikolai Petrovich had contrived during his parents' lifetime and to their no small
chagrin to fall in love with the daughter of his former
landlord Prepolovensky, a man in the civil service. She
was a pretty girl of what is called advanced views—she
used to read the serious articles in the science columns.

He married her as soon as the period of mourning was over, and quitting the Ministry of Appanages where he had procured a post through his father's influence, was blissfully happy with his Masha, first in a summer villa near the Forestry Institute, then in a pretty little flat in town with a tidy staircase and a chilly parlour, and finally in the country, where he settled down for good and where a son, Arkady, was shortly born to him. The young couple lived very happily and quietly: they were practically inseparable, read together, played together on the piano and sang duets. She planted flowers and looked after the poultry; he occasionally went out shooting and attended to the affairs of the estate, while Arkady grew and grew—in the same happy quiet way. Ten years passed like a dream. In 1847 Kirsanov's wife died. The blow all but crushed him; his hair turned grey in a few weeks; he was on the point of going abroad for the sake of distraction when the year 1848 intervened. He was obliged to return to the village and after a rather prolonged period of idleness devoted himself to improving his estate. In 1855 he took his son to the university in St. Petersburg, where he spent three winters with him, hardly ever going out and trying to make friends with Arkady's young chums. The last winter he had not been able to come— and so we find him in the month of May, 1859, already quite grey and chubby, with a slight stoop, waiting for his son, who had taken his degree as he had once done.

The servant, from a sense of decorum, or perhaps to escape his master's eye, withdrew to the gateway and lit his pipe. Nikolai Petrovich, his head bent, studied the rickety steps: an overgrown mottled young chicken strutted on the porch steps, its big yellow feet pattering loudly; a grimy cat, perched demurely on the banister, watched it with a hostile look. The sun was scorching; from the dim shadows of the passageway came a smell of warm rye bread. Nikolai Petrovich fell into a reverie. "My son ... a graduate ... Arkasha ..." kept revolving in his mind; he tried to think of something else, but would inevitably come back to the same thoughts. He recalled his dead wife. "She did not live to see the day!" he whispered sadly. A fat pigeon alighted in the roadway and hastily steered for a puddle by the well to take a drink. Nikolai Petrovich was preoccupied with this scene when his ear caught the sound of approaching weels.

"I think they're coming, sir," the servant announced, popping out of the gateway.

Nikolai Petrovich jumped to his feet and stared down the road. A tarantass drawn by three posting horses abreast came into view, he caught a glimpse of the blue band of a university cap, the familiar lineaments of a dear face. . . .

"Arkasha! Arkasha!" Kirsanov shouted, breaking into a run and waving his arms. A few moments later his lips were pressed to the beardless, dusty, tanned cheek of the youthful graduate.

II

"Let me shake the dust off first, Dad," Arkady said, in a slightly travel-husky, but fresh boyish voice, as he gaily responded to his father's caresses: "I'll get you all dusty."

"Never mind that, never mind," Nikolai Petrovich kept repeating with a beatific smile, giving his son's coat collar and his own a couple of slaps. "Let's have a look at you," he added, stepping back, then hurried towards the inn, interjecting all the while: "This way, this way, we'll hurry those horses up!"

Nikolai Petrovich seemed to be much more excited than his son; he looked a bit bewildered, nervous as it were. Arkady checked him.

"I want to introduce to you a good friend of mine, Dad," he said. "Bazarov, the one I wrote you about so often. He has been so kind as to consent to be our guest for a time."

Nikolai Petrovich turned round quickly, and going up to a tall man in a long travelling coat with tassels, who had just stepped out of the tarantass, he warmly shook his red ungloved hand, which the latter did not immediately extend.

"I am delighted," he began, "and grateful to you for your kind intention of paying us a visit; I hope. . . . May I ask your name and patronymic?"

"Yevgeny Vassilyevich," Bazarov answered in a lazy but manly voice, and turning back the collar of his coat, revealed to Nikolai Petrovich his whole face. Long and lean, with a broad forehead, a nose flat at the bridge and tapering towards the tip, large greenish eyes and sandy drooping whiskers, his face was enlivened by a calm smile and self-confidence and intelligence.

"I hope you will not find it dull with us, my dear Yevgeny Vassilich," Nikolai Petrovich proceeded.

Bazarov's thin lips stirred slightly, but he made no reply, and merely raised his cap. His tawny hair, which was long and thick, did not conceal the protuberances of his capacious skull.

"What do you say, Arkady," Nikolai Petrovich resumed, turning to his son, "shall we have the horses harnessed right away? Or would you like to have a rest?"

"We'll have a rest when we get home, Dad; have the horses harnessed."

"Very good, very good," his father assented. "Hey, Pyotr, d'you hear? Look alive, my dear fellow, hurry up."

Pyotr, who, being the model servant he was, had not kissed his young master's hand and had merely bowed to him from a distance, disappeared once more through the gateway.

"I have my carriage here, but we can get a relay of three horses for your tarantass too," Nikolai Petrovich said in a bustling manner, while Arkady was drinking water out of an iron dipper which the innkeeper's wife had brought him, and Bazarov lit his pipe and went up to the driver, who was unharnessing the horses, "only the carriage is a two-seater, and I don't know how your friend. . . ."

"He'll go in the tarantass," Arkady interrupted him in an undertone. "Don't stand on ceremony with him, please. He's a wonderful chap, quite simple—you'll see."

Nikolai Petrovich's coachman led the horses out.

"Stir your stumps, greatbeard!" Bazarov said to the driver of the stage horses.

"Hear that, Mitya!" cried his mate who was standing by with his hands thrust into the slits of his sheepskin coat; "hear what the gentleman called yer? Greatbeard—it's what you are all right."

Mitya merely shook his head and pulled the reins off the heated shaft horse.

"Look sharp, my lads, look sharp," Nikolai Petrovich cried. "There will be a tip coming!"

In a few minutes the horses were harnessed; the father and son got into the carriage; Pyotr clambered up on the box; Bazarov jumped into the tarantass, and sank back on the leather cushion—and both carriages rolled away.

III

"Well, so you've got your degree and have come home at last," Nikolai Petrovich was saying, touching Arkady now on the shoulder, now on the knee. "At last!"

"How is uncle? Is he all right?" asked Arkady, who despite the genuine, almost childish delight that filled his heart, was eager to turn the conversation from things emotional to more matter-of-fact topics.

"He's quite well. He wanted to come with me to meet you, but changed his mind for some reason or other."

"Have you been waiting long?" asked Arkady.

"About five hours, I should say."

"Good old Dad!"

Arkady turned impulsively towards his father and gave him a hearty kiss on the cheek. Nikolai Petrovich laughed softly.

"What a splendid horse I've got for you!" he began. "You wait and see. And your room has been freshly papered."

"Is there a room for Bazarov?"

"We'll find one for him too."

"Please be nice to him, Dad. I can't tell you how I value his friendship."

"Have you known him long?"

"No, not very."

"Ah, I thought I didn't see him last winter. What does he go in for?"

"His chief subject is natural science. But he knows everything. He intends to take his doctor's degree next year."

"Ah! So he's studying medicine," observed Nikolai Petrovich and fell silent. "Pyotr," he said presently, pointing his hand, "aren't those our peasants?"

Pyotr looked in the direction his master was pointing. Several carts drawn by unbridled horses were howling swiftly along a narrow country lane. In each cart there sat one, at the most two, peasants, their sheepskin coats thrown open.

"They are, sir," replied Pyotr.

"Where are they going—to town?"

"I suppose so. To the pub," he added scornfully, inclining his head towards the coachman, as though calling him to witness. But the latter did not stir; he was a man of the old stock and did not accept the modern views.

"I'm having a lot of trouble with the peasants this year," Nikolai Petrovich went on, turning to his son. "They don't pay their quitrent. What's a body to do?"

"Are you satisfied with your hired hands?"

"Yes," Nikolai Petrovich muttered. "The trouble is they're being tampered with; they haven't buckled down to the job properly yet; they spoil the harness. They ploughed fairly well, though I suppose things will come right in the end. But you aren't interested in farming now, are you?"

"It's too bad you haven't got any shade here," Arkady said, leaving the question unanswered.

"I have had a big awning put up over the balcony on the north side," Nikolai Petrovich said. "Now we can dine in the open."

"Won't that be a bit in the bungalow style? But that doesn't matter. My, but the air here is wonderful. How delicious it smells! Really, I don't think it smells so sweet anywhere else in the world! And the sky here, too. . . ."

Arkady suddenly broke off, stole a look behind him and said no more.

"Of course, you were born here," Nikolai Petrovich said, "and everything is bound to strike you as remarkable."

"Really, Dad, it makes no difference where a man is born."

"But. . . ."

"No, it makes absolutely no difference."

Nikolai Petrovich cast a sidelong look at his son, and the carriage travelled on for half a mile before the conversation was resumed.

"I don't remember whether I wrote you or not," began Nikolai Petrovich, "but your old nurse, Yegorovna, is dead."

"Is that so? Poor old thing! But Prokofich is alive, isn't he?"

"Yes, and not a bit changed. Still the same old grumbler. In fact, you won't find many changes at Maryino."

"You still have the same steward?"

"Well, that's about the only change I here made. I decided not to keep any of the freed serfs in my employ —those I used to have in the household—or at any rate not to give them any jobs of responsibility." (Arkady motioned in Pyotr's direction.) *"Il est libre, en effet,"* Nikolai Petrovich remarked in an undertone. "But then he is only a valet. My new steward is a townsman, he seems to know his business. I am giving him two hundred and fifty rubles a year. But," he added, rubbing his forehead and eyebrows, which with him was always a sign of inward embarrassment, "I told you just now that you would not find any changes at Maryino. . . . That's not quite so. I ought to warn you, though. . . ."

For an instant he faltered and then continued in French.

"A strict moralist would find my candour misplaced; but, firstly, the thing can't be concealed, and, secondly, you know I have always had my own ideas about what the relations between a father and a son should be. Still, you have every right to disapprove of me. At my age, you know.... In short, this ... this girl, of whom you have probably heard already...."

"Fenichka?" Arkady asked carelessly.

Nikolai Petrovich reddened.

"Please don't speak her name out loud. Well, yes—she is living with me now. I have put her up in the house ... there were two small rooms there. Of course, all that can be changed."

"Heavens, Dad, what for?"

"Your friend will be staying with us ... it's rather awkward...."

"As far as Bazarov's concerned, please don't worry. He is above all that."

"What about you though," Nikolai Petrovich continued. "The little outbuilding is such a poor place—that's the trouble."

"For goodness sake, Dad!" Arkady interposed. "Anybody would think you were apologising; you ought to be ashamed of yourself!"

"I really ought to be ashamed," Nikolai Petrovich said turning redder than ever.

"Oh, come, Dad, what nonsense, really!" and Arkady smiled affectionately. "What a thing to be apologising for!" he thought to himself, and a feeling of indulgent tenderness for his kind, softhearted father, tinged with a sort of secret superiority, filled his heart. "What nonsense," he repeated, involuntarily revelling in a sense of his own development and freedom.

Nikolai Petrovich glanced at him through the fingers of his hand with which he continued to rub his forehead, and felt a pang in his heart. But he instantly pulled himself up.

"This is where our fields start," he said after a long silence.

"And that is our forest in front, I believe," Arkady said.

"Yes. Only I've sold it. It's coming down this year."

"What made you sell it?"

"I needed money; besides, that land is going to the peasants."

"Who don't pay you quitrent, by the way?"

"That's their lookout; still, they must pay some time, surely."

"I'm sorry about the forest, though," Arkady said, and began to look round him.

The places through which they were passing could hardly be called picturesque. Field after field stretched away to the horizon, dipping, then rising again; here and there were patches of wood and winding ravines overgrown by low scanty brush, which put one in mind of their own counterparts as depicted on the old-fashioned maps of the time of Catherine the Great. They passed streams with beetling banks eroded at the base, tiny ponds with rickety dams, and little villages with squat huts under dark roofs half-bare of thatching, and ramshackle little threshing barns with walls of wattled brushwood and gaping doorways opening on deserted threshing floors, and churches, some brick-built with the plaster peeling off in places, others built of wood with lurching crosses and moldering graveyards. Arkady's heart slowly contracted. As luck would have it the peasants they met were all a shabby lot on miserable nags; the roadside willows, with trunks stripped of bark and branches broken, stood like ragged beggars; gaunt, scraggy, rawboned cows hungrily nibbled the grass growing along the ditches. They looked as though they had just wrenched themselves from the fell clutches of some death-dealing monster,— and the dismal sight of these emaciated creatures in the midst of that lovely spring day evoked the pale spectre of a cheerless, endless winter with its blizzards, its frosts and its snows. "No," thought Arkady, "this is not a fertile region, it certainly does not impress one as being prosperous or industrious; things mustn't, they mustn't go on like this, reforms are essential ... but how are they to be brought about, how is one to begin?"

Thus Arkady mused ... and while he mused, spring was coming into its own. Everything around was golden green, everything—the trees, the bushes, the grass—throbbed, and stirred, and shone under the warm breath of a soft breeze; everywhere the larks trilled in gushing rivulets of song; the lapwings emitted their wailing cry as they flapped over the low-lying meadows or flitted noiselessly over the hillocks; the rooks made a pretty showing, strutting darkly among the tender green of the half-grown spring corn; they disappeared in the already whitening rye, their heads alone bobbing up at intervals amidst its misty waves. Arkady gazed long upon the scene, and his thoughts, relaxing, grew dimmer and faded. He flung off his coat and looked at his father with such a gay young-boyish look that the latter gave him another hug.

"We haven't far to go now," Nikolai Petrovich said. "We'll see the house as soon as we get up that hill. We shall make a fine job of life together, Arkady; you'll help me about the farm, if you won't find it dull. We should become close friends, get to know each other better, shouldn't we?"

"Of course," said Arkady. "But what a marvellous day it is!"

"To welcome you, my dear. Yes, it's spring in all its glory. I agree with Pushkin though—you remember that bit from *Eugene Onegin*:

> *"How sad to me thy coming is,*
> *Spring, spring, the time of love!*
> *What...."*

"Arkady!" came Bazarov's voice from the tarantass. "Send me a match; I've nothing to light my pipe with."

Nikolai Petrovich broke off, while Arkady, who had begun to listen to him in some astonishment though not without sympathy, hastily drew a silver matchbox out of his pocket and sent it to Bazarov by Pyotr.

"D'you want a cigar?" Bazarov cried again.

"All right," answered Arkady.

Pyotr came back with the matchbox and a thick black cigar which Arkady promptly lit, spreading around him such a strong acrid smell of rank tobacco that Nikolai Petrovich, who had never smoked in his life, was obliged to turn his nose away, albeit imperceptibly, so as not to hurt his son's feelings.

A quarter of an hour later both vehicles drew up before the steps of a new wooden house, painted grey, with a roof of red sheet-iron. This was Maryino, also known as New Hamlet, or as the peasants called it, Lonely Farm.

IV

No crowd of house serfs poured out on to the porch to greet the masters; the only one there was a girl of twelve, followed by a lad greatly resembling Pyotr and dressed in a grey livery jacket with white armorial buttons—the servant of Pavel Petrovich Kirsanov. He opened the door of the carriage and unfastened the apron of the tarantass in silence. Nikolai Petrovich together with his son and Bazarov entered a dark and almost empty hall, through the door of which they caught a glimpse of a young woman's face, and proceeded into the drawing room furnished in the latest style.

"Well, here we are at home," Nikolai Petrovich said, taking off his cap and tossing back his hair. "Now for supper and a rest."

"Not a bad idea, something to eat," Bazarov said, stretching himself and sinking into a sofa.

"That's right, supper, let's have supper," said Nikolai Petrovich, and for no apparent reason, stamped his feet. "Ah, and here's Prokofich."

A man of about sixty entered, white-haired, lean and swarthy, in a brown swallowtail with brass buttons and a pink neckerchief. He grinned, went up and kissed Arkady's hand, then bowed to the guest, retreated to the door and placed his hands behind his back.

"Well, Prokofich, here he is," Nikolai Petrovich began. "He's come at last. Eh? How do you find him?"

"The young master is looking fine, sir," the old man said, and grinned again, only to cover it up promptly by drawing his bushy eyebrows together in a frown. "Do you wish to have the table laid, sir?" he added impressively.

"Yes, yes, please. But don't you want to go to your room first, Yevgeny Vassilich?"

"No, thanks, there's no need to. Just tell them to bring up that old suitcase of mine and these togs here," he added, taking off his travelling coat.

"Very good. Prokofich, take the gentleman's coat." (Prokofich with a kind of puzzled air took Bazarov's "togs" in both hands and holding them aloft went out on

tiptoe.) "And what about you, Arkady, will you go up to
your room for a moment?"

"Yes, I must get a clean down," Arkady said, making
for the door; but at the same moment a man of medium
height, dressed in a dark English suit, a fashionable low
cravat and patent leather shoes, entered the drawing
room. This was Pavel Petrovich Kirsanov. He looked
about forty-five; his close-cropped grey hair shone with
a dark lustre, like new silver; his face, saturnine but free
from wrinkles, had remarkably clear-cut finely chiselled
features, and bore traces of unusual good looks; especially attractive were his clear, dark, almond-shaped eyes.
The whole aspect of Arkady's uncle, so refined and well-
bred, still retained a youthful shapeliness and that air
of aspiring upwards, away from the earth, which usually
disappears after a man's twenties.

Pavel Petrovich drew his hand out of his trouser pocket
—a beautiful hand with long pink nails, looking all the
more beautiful against the snow-white cuff fastened with
a single large opal,—and extended it to his nephew.
After a preliminary handshake in the European manner,
he kissed him Russian style, or rather brushed his cheek
three times with his perfumed moustache and said: "Welcome."

Nikolai Petrovich introduced him to Bazarov; Pavel
Petrovich greeted him with a slight inclination of his
supple body and a faint smile, but did not give him his
hand, which he restored to his pocket.

"I was beginning to think you weren't coming today,"
he said in a pleasant voice, rocking on his toes, shrugging his shoulders and revealing beautiful white teeth.
"Did anything happen on the way?"

"No, nothing happened," Arkady replied, "we were
held up a bit, that's all. But we're as hungry as wolves
now. Tell Prokofich to hurry up, Dad, I'll be back in a
moment."

"Wait a minute, I'm coming with you," Bazarov exclaimed, starting up from the sofa. The two young men
went out.

"Who's that?" Pavel Petrovich asked.

"Arkady's chum, a very clever fellow, he says."

"Is he going to stay with us?"

"Yes."

"What, that hairy fellow?"

"Why, yes."

Pavel Petrovich drummed his finger tips on the table.

"I think Arkady—*s'est dégourdi,*" he remarked. "I'm glad he's come back."

Little was said at supper. Bazarov especially spoke very little but ate much. Nikolai Petrovich related various incidents from what he called his farmer's life, dwelt on impending government measures, talked about committees, deputations, the necessity of introducing machines, and so on. Pavel Petrovich paced slowly up and down the dining room (he never had supper), taking an occasional sip from a glass of red wine and still more rarely uttering a remark or rather an exclamation such as "Ah! aha! hm!" Arkady recounted several items of St. Petersburg news, but was conscious of a slight embarrassment such as usually overcomes a young man when he has just grown out of childhood and returns to a place where he had always been looked upon as a child. He dragged his speech out needlessly, avoided the word "dad" and even once used "father" instead—true he mumbled rather than said it, and with a too free and easy manner poured himself out much more wine than he really wanted and tossed it off. Prokofich did not take his eyes off him, his mouth working and mumping all the time. As soon as supper was over they all separated.

"Queer fellow, that uncle of yours," Bazarov said to Arkady, sitting by his bedside in his dressing gown and sucking a short pipe. "Fancy all that foppery out in the country! And talk about fingernails—they could be placed on exhibition!"

"Of course, you don't know," answered Arkady, "he was a society lion in his day. I'll tell you his story some day. He was awfully handsome, you know, and the women were crazy about him."

"Oh, I see. So it's for old times' sake. There's nobody to charm down here though, more's the pity. I kept looking at that marvellous collar of his, stiff as a board, and

that clean-shaven chin. Don't you think it's ridiculous, Arkady Nikolaich?"

"Well, I daresay! But he's a good sort, really."

"He's an archaism! But your father's a fine chap. He could do better than read poetry though, and I don't think he knows much about farming, but he's a good old soul."

"My father's a regular brick."

"Did you notice—he seems to be a bit nervous?"

Arkady nodded as though he were not nervous himself.

"Funny thing these romantic old fellows," Bazarov continued. "They work their nervous systems up to a state of excitation—and, naturally, the balance is upset. However, good night! There's an English washstand in my room, but the door doesn't lock. Still, they should be encouraged—English washstands I mean—they stand for progress!"

Bazarov went away and Arkady gave himself up to a feeling of joy. How sweet it was to fall asleep in your own home, in a familiar bed, under a quilt which fond hands had fashioned, perhaps the hands of his dear nurse, those kind, tender, tireless hands. Arkady thought of Yegorovna and sighed and blessed her. He said no prayer for himself.

Both he and Bazarov soon fell asleep, but there were others in the house who did not go to sleep for quite a time. His son's homecoming had excited Nikolai Petrovich. He went to bed but did not extinguish the candle, and with his head propped up on his hand, lay thinking long thoughts. His brother sat in his study until well after midnight, in a roomy armchair before the fireplace, in which a coal fire had burnt itself down to smouldering embers. Pavel Petrovich had not undressed; only red Chinese bedroom slippers had replaced the patent leather shoes on his feet. He held in his hands the latest issue of *Galignani's Messenger*, but he was not reading; he stared into the grate where a bluish flame flickered on and off. Heaven knows where his thoughts strayed, but they did not stray into the past alone; his face looked grim and concentrated, unlike that of a man absorbed in recollections only. And in a small back room, sitting on a big chest in a blue sleeveless jacket with a white kerchief thrown over her dark hair was a young woman, Fenichka, now listening, now dozing, now glancing at the open door through which she could see a child's cot and hear the regular breathing of a sleeping baby.

V

The next morning Bazarov woke up before any of the others and went out of the house. "Hm!" he thought, looking around, "a pretty poor place this." When fixing the bounds between his own and his peasants' lands Nikolai Petrovich had had to set apart four dessiatins of absolutely flat bare land as a site for the new manor house. He had built his house and outbuildings, laid out a garden, dug a pond and sunk two wells, but the saplings did not thrive, there was very little water in the pond, and that in the wells turned out to be brackish. Only one arbour of lilac bushes and acacia had done fairly well; here occasionally tea or dinner was served. It did not take Bazarov more than a few minutes to explore the garden, the cattleshed and the stable and come upon two small boys, whom he immediately made friends with and took along with him to a small swamp within a mile of the house to hunt for frogs.

"What do you want the frogs for, sir?" one of the boys asked.

"Well, I'll tell you," answered Bazarov, who possessed a peculiar knack of inspiring confidence in the lower orders, though he was never ingratiating and treated them off-handedly. "I cut the frog open and have a look to see what's going on inside of him, and as you and I are just the same as frogs, except that we walk on two legs, I'll get to know what's going on in our insides, too."

"What do you want to know that for?"

"So as not to make a mistake if you get ill and I have to treat you."

"Why, are you a doctor?"

"Yes."

"Vaska, d'ye hear that, the gentleman says you and me's the same as frogs. Ain't that funny!"

"I'm scared of frogs," observed Vaska, a barefooted boy of seven with a flaxen head, dressed in a grey coat with a stand-up collar.

"What's there to be scared of? They don't bite!"

"Well, into the water with you, philosophers," Bazarov said.

Meanwhile Nikolai Petrovich awoke too and went to see Arkady, whom he found up and dressed. Father and son went out on the terrace under the awning; the samovar was already boiling on a table near the balustrade, among great bunches of lilac. A little girl appeared—the one who had been the first to meet them when they arrived —and said in a shrill voice:

"Fedosya Nikolayevna ain't well and she can't come and she told me to ask you to pour the tea yourself or should she send Dunyasha?"

"That's all right, I'll pour it myself," Nikolai Petrovich put in hurriedly. "What do you want in your tea, Arkady—cream or lemon?"

"Cream," replied Arkady, and, after a short silence, interrogatively: "Dad?"

Nikolai Petrovich looked up in some embarrassment. "What is it?"

Arkady dropped his eyes.

"Excuse me, Dad, if my question strikes you as being out of place," he began. "But your own frankness yesterday seems to call for equal frankness on my part ... you won't be angry, will you?"

"Say what you wanted."

"You give me the courage to ask you.... Isn't the reason Fen.... Isn't it because of my being here that she doesn't want to come to pour the tea?"

Nikolai Petrovich turned his head away slightly.

"Perhaps," he said presently. "She thinks ... she's ashamed...."

Arkady raised his eyes quickly to his father's face.

"She has nothing to be ashamed of. In the first place you know what my ideas are on that score" (Arkady rel-

ished the words he spoke) "and, secondly, I wouldn't interfere in your way of living and your habits for anything
in the world. Besides, I'm sure you couldn't have made an
improper choice; if you let her live with you under one
roof she must be worthy of it: in any case a son can't be
his father's judge, and particularly I, and particularly a
father like you who has never restricted my liberty in any
way."

Arkady had started with a tremor in his voice; he felt
magnanimous, while at the same time realising that he
was reading his father something in the nature of a lec-
ture; the sound of his own speeches, however, has a strong
effect upon a man, and Arkady uttered the last words
firmly and even strikingly.

"Thanks, Arkady," Nikolai Petrovich said in a low
voice, and his fingers strayed once more to his eyebrows
and forehead. "What you say is quite right. Certainly,
if the girl was unworthy. . . . This is no frivolous whim of
mine. It's awkward for me to talk to you about it; but, you
understand, she feels shy in your presence, especially on
the first day of your coming here."

"If that's so, then I'll go to her myself!" cried Arkady
under a fresh surge of magnanimity and jumped up from
his chair. "I'll make it clear to her that she has no reason
to be shy of me."

Nikolai Petrovich also rose to his feet.

"Arkady," he began, "please don't . . . really . . . there
is . . . I should have told you that. . . ."

But Arkady was no longer listening and ran out. Nikolai Petrovich looked after him and sank back into his chair
in confusion. His heart throbbed. Did he at that moment
realise how singular his future relations with his son
would necessarily be? Did he realise that Arkady would
perhaps be showing him greater respect by keeping out
of this business? Did he reproach himself for being too
weak? It is hard to say. He was experiencing all of these
emotions, but merely in the form of sensations, and even
these were vague. The flush was still on his face, his heart
still palpitated.

There was a sound of hurrying footsteps and Arkady
came on to the terrace.

"We've become acquainted, Father!" he exclaimed
with an expression on his face of tender and benign tri-
umph, as it were. "Fedosya Nikolayevna is really not
quite well today and will come out later. But why didn't
you tell me I've got a brother? I'd have kissed him last
night, as I did just now."

Nikolai Petrovich wanted to say something, wanted to
get up, to open his arms. Arkady flung himself on his
neck.

"Hullo! Cuddling again?" they heard the voice of
Pavel Petrovich behind them.

Father and son were equally relieved at his entrance
at that moment; there are touching situations from which
one is nevertheless glad to escape.

"Does it surprise you?" Nikolai Petrovich cried gaily.
"I've been dreaming of Arkady's homecoming for ages.
I haven't had a good look at him since he has arrived."

"I am not surprised at all," observed Pavel Petrovich.
"I wouldn't mind giving him a hug myself."

Arkady went up to his uncle, and again felt the touch
of his perfumed moustache on his cheeks. Pavel Petrovich
sat down to the table. He wore a smart morning suit of
English cut, with a small fez on his head. The fez and a
carelessly tied small cravat suggested the untrammelled
ways of country life; but the stiff collar of his shirt—a
coloured one this time, which was the proper article of
wear for that time of day—propped up the clean-shaven
chin as inexorably as ever.

"Where's that new friend of yours?" he asked Arkady.

"He's gone out; he's usually up and about early. The
main thing is not to pay any attention to him; he doesn't
like ceremony."

"Yes, that's obvious," and Pavel Petrovich began
leisurely to butter his bread. "Will he be staying here
long?"

"It all depends. He's stopping over on his way to his
father's."

"And where does his father live?"

"In our gubernia, about eighty versts from here. He
has a little estate there. He used to be an army surgeon."

"Tut, tut, tut. And I've been wondering all the time

where I'd heard that name—Bazarov! Nikolai, if I am
not mistaken, there was a medical chap in our father's
division by the name of Bazarov, wasn't there?"

"I think there was."

"Why, of course. So that medical fellow is his father.
Hm!" Pavel Petrovich twitched his moustache. "Well,
and what about Mr. Bazarov himself, what is he?" he said
slowly.

"What is Bazarov?" Arkady looked amused. "Shall I
tell you what he really is, Uncle?"

"Please do, nephew."

"He is a nihilist."

"A what?" Nikolai Petrovich asked, while Pavel Petrovich stopped dead, his knife with a dab of butter on
the tip arrested in mid-air.

"He is a nihilist," Arkady repeated.

"A nihilist," Nikolai Petrovich said. "That's from the
Latin *nihil*, *nothing*, as far as I can judge; does that mean
a person who ... who believes in nothing?"

"Say: 'who respects nothing'," put in Pavel Petrovich,
applying himself to the butter again.

"Who regards everything critically," Arkady observed.

"Isn't that the same thing?" asked Pavel Petrovich.

"No, it isn't. A nihilist is a person who does not look
up to any authorities, who does not accept a single principle on faith, no matter how highly that principle may
be esteemed."

"Well, and is that a good thing?" Pavel Petrovich
broke in.

"It all depends, uncle. It may be good for some people
and very bad for others."

"I see. Well, this, I see, is not in our line. We are men
of the old school—we believe that without principles"
(he pronounced the word softly, in the French manner,
whereas Arkady clipped the word and accentuated the
first syllable), "principles taken on faith, as you put it,
one cannot stir a step or draw a breath. *Vous avez changé
tout cela*, God grant you good health and a generalship,
but we'll be content to look on and admire, *Messieurs
les* ... what do you call them?"

"Nihilists," Arkady said distinctly.

"Yes. We used to have *Hegelists*, now we have nihilists. We shall see how you manage to live in a void, in a vacuum; and now please ring the bell, brother Nikolai Petrovich—it's time for my cocoa."

Nikolai Petrovich rang the bell and called: "Dunyasha!" But instead of Dunyasha, Fenichka herself appeared on the terrace. She was a young woman of about 23, all daintily soft and fair-skinned, with dark hair and eyes, childishly full red lips and delicate little hands. She wore a neat print dress; a new blue kerchief lay lightly upon her rounded shoulders. She carried a large cup of cocoa and having placed it before Pavel Petrovich, stood overcome with bashfulness: the hot blood spread in a deep blush under the delicate skin of her pretty face. She dropped her eyes, and stood there by the table, leaning lightly on her finger tips. She seemed to be ashamed of having come, yet looked as though she felt she was within her rights in coming.

Pavel Petrovich knit his brows sternly, while Nikolai Petrovich felt embarrassed.

"Good morning, Fenichka," he mumbled.

"Good morning, sir," she answered in a clear yet quiet voice, and with a sidelong glance at Arkady, who gave her a friendly smile, she quietly withdrew. She walked with a slightly waddling gait, but even that was becoming to her.

Silence reigned on the terrace for some seconds. Pavel Petrovich sipped his cocoa, then suddenly looked up.

"Here comes Mr. Nihilist," he murmured.

Indeed, Bazarov was striding down the garden, stepping over the flower beds. His duck coat and trousers were muddy; a clinging marsh weed was twined round the crown of his old round hat; in his right hand he held a small bag with something alive squirming in it. He quickly approached the terrace and said with a nod: "Good morning, gentlemen; sorry I'm late for tea; I'll be back in a moment; must fix up a place for these captives."

"What have you got there, leeches?" asked Pavel Petrovich.

"No, frogs."

"Do you eat them or breed them?"

"I use them for experiments," Bazarov said indifferently and went into the house.

"He's going to dissect them," Pavel Petrovich said.
"He doesn't believe in principles, but he believes in frogs."

Arkady glanced regretfully at his uncle, and Nikolai
Petrovich furtively shrugged his shoulders. Pavel Petrovich perceived that his joke had fallen flat, and began
talking about the farm and the new steward, who had
recently come to him complaining that Foma, one of the
hired labourers, was a "rowdy customer" and had completely got out of hand. "That's the kind of Aesop he is,"
he had said, among other things; "he's earned himself a
disgraceful 'reputation'; he'll come to a bad end, he will,
you mark my words."

VI

Bazarov reappeared, sat down at the table and began
hurriedly drinking his tea. The two brothers regarded
him in silence, while Arkady's eyes travelled stealthily
from uncle to father and back again.

"Did you go far?" Nikolai Petrovich presently asked
Bazarov.

"You've got a little swamp here, close to the aspen
wood. I flushed five snipe; you can shoot them, Arkady."

"Don't you go in for shooting?"

"No."

"You're studying physics, I understand?" Pavel Petrovich asked in his turn.

"Yes, physics; the natural sciences generally."

"The Deutschländer are said to have made considerable progress in this field."

"Yes, the Germans are our teachers in that subject,"
Bazarov answered casually.

Pavel Petrovich had used the word Deutschländer
instead of Germans for the sake of irony, but this had
passed unnoticed.

"Do you have as high an opinion of the Germans as
all that?" enquired Pavel Petrovich with studied suavity.
He was beginning to feel a secret irritation. His aristocrat-

ic nature was up in arms at Bazarov's sheer insouciance. This son of an army sawbones, far from being diffident, answered bluntly and reluctantly, and there was something rude, almost insolent in the tone of his voice:

"Their men of science are a practical lot."

"So, so. Well, I suppose you have no such flattering opinion about Russian scientists, have you?"

"I suppose so."

"That's very praiseworthy selflessness," retorted Pavel Petrovich, drawing himself up erect and throwing his head back. "But Arkady Nikolaich has just been telling us that you recognise no authorities. Don't you believe them?"

"Why should I recognise them? And what am I to believe in? When anyone talks sense, I agree—that's all."

"Do the Germans all talk sense?" Pavel Petrovich murmured, and his face assumed an expression so impassive and detached as though his thoughts had gone woolgathering.

"Not all of them," Bazarov said stifling a yawn. He was obviously unwilling to continue the word-play.

Pavel Petrovich glanced at Arkady as much as to say: "A polite fellow, this friend of yours, I must say."

"For my part," he went on, not without some effort, "I must plead guilty to disliking the Germans. I say nothing of the Russian Germans: we know that type. But I can't even stomach the German Germans. Those of the old days well—one could put up with in a pinch; they then had their—well, Schiller, Goethe, you know.... My brother, for instance, thinks a lot of them. Now they've all become chemists and materialists...."

"A decent chemist is twenty times more useful than any poet," broke in Bazarov.

"Is that so?" commented Pavel Petrovich with a slight lift of his eyebrows, looking as if he were going to doze off. "You don't believe in art then, I suppose?"

"The Art of Making Money, or No More Piles!" Bazarov said with a sneer.

"So, so. You are having your joke, I see. You repudiate everything then, is that it? All right. Does that mean you believe only in science?"

"I've already told you that I believe in nothing; and what is science, science in general? There are sciences, as there are trades and callings; but science in general does not exist at all."

"Very good, sir. But what about the other conventions, those accepted in human society—do you maintain the same negative attitude here as well?"

"What's this, a cross-examination?" Bazarov said.

Pavel Petrovich paled slightly. Nikolai Petrovich deemed it necessary to intervene.

"We shall discuss this matter more fully with you some day, my dear Yevgeny Vassilich; we shall learn your views and let you know our own. For my part, I'm very glad to know you are studying natural science. I hear that Liebig has made some surprising discoveries in soil fertilisation. You might help me in my agricultural pursuits; you might be able to give me some useful advice."

"I am at your service, Nikolai Petrovich; but it's a far cry to Liebig! A person has to learn his *a b c* first before he can begin to read, whereas we haven't set eyes on our alphabet yet."

Well, you certainly are a nihilist, I see, thought Nikolai Petrovich.

"Still, I hope you won't mind me bothering you in case of need," he added aloud. "And now, brother, I think it's time for us to be seeing the steward."

Pavel Petrovich stood up.

"Yes," he said, looking at nobody in particular. "It's a sad thing to live five years in the country as we do, enjoying no intercourse with the great minds of the age! You become a silly ass before you know it. Here you are, trying not to forget what you've been taught, when—lo and behold!—it turns out to be all tommyrot, and you're told that sensible people no longer waste time on such trifles and that you yourself are an old dunderhead, if you please. Ah, well! The young people are cleverer than us, it seems."

Pavel Petrovich turned slowly on his heel and slowly walked out; Nikolai Petrovich followed him.

"Is he always like that?" Bazarov asked coolly, as soon as the door had closed behind the two brothers.

"Look here, Yevgeny, you handled him rather roughly, you know," Arkady said. "You've insulted him."

"I'll be blowed if I'm going to humour these rustic aristocrats! It's nothing but conceitedness, swell habits, foppery! Why didn't he carry on in St. Petersburg, if that's the way he's made. Well, enough of him! I've found a water beetle, a rather rare specimen—*Dytiscus marginatus* —do you know it? I'll show it to you."

"I promised to tell you his story—" began Arkady.

"The beetle's?"

"Come, come, Yevgeny. My uncle's story. You'll see he's not at all the man you think he is. He deserves sympathy rather than sneers."

"I'm not denying it, but what makes you harp on him?"

"One must be fair, Yevgeny."

"What's the implication?"

"No, just listen. . . ."

And Arkady told him his uncle's story. The reader will find it in the next chapter.

VII

Pavel Petrovich Kirsanov received his early education at home, like his younger brother Nikolai, and afterwards in the Corps of Pages. He was extremely handsome from childhood; in addition to this he was self-confident, and had a droll sarcastic sense of humour—he could not fail to please. He began to appear in society as soon as he received his officer's commission. He was made a fuss of, and indulged his every whim, even to the extents of playing the fool and posing; but even this was becoming to him. Women lost their heads over him, men called him a fop and secretly envied him. As has already been said, he shared lodgings with his brother—whom he loved sincerely, though he in no whit resembled him. Nikolai Petrovich had a slight limp, his features were small, pleasing but somewhat melancholic; his eyes were small and black, his hair soft and thin; he liked to take things easy, but he was fond of reading and shunned society. Pavel Petrovich never spent an evening at home, was famed for

his daring and agility (he set the fashion for gymnastics
among society youth) and had not read more than five or
six French books. At twenty-eight he was already a captain; a brilliant career was before him. Suddenly everything changed.

At that time a woman used to appear on rare occasions
in St. Petersburg society, a Princess R—, whom many still
remember. She had a well-bred, respectable, but rather
stupid husband and no children. She had a way of suddenly going abroad and suddenly returning to Russia,
and, in general, led a queer life. She had the reputation
of being a frivolous coquette, plunged avidly into the
whirl of pleasure, danced to exhaustion, and laughed and
joked with young men, whom she entertained before dinner in her dimly-lit drawing room, while at night she
would weep and pray, unable to find peace, and often
feverishly pacing her room till morning, wringing her
hands in anguish or sitting, pale and cold, over a psalm
book. Day would come and once more she would be the
lady of fashion, making her round of calls, laughing, chatting and throwing herself headlong into anything that
could afford her the slightest distraction. She had a magnificent figure; her heavy braids, like spun gold, reached
below her knees, but no one would have called her beautiful; her one good feature was her eyes, and not so much
the eyes—they were grey, and not large—as their look,
which was swift and deep, with an almost devil-may-care
defiance, and wistful to the verge of despondency—an
enigmatic look. They had a strange light in them, those
eyes of hers, even when her tongue was babbling inani-
ties. She dressed exquisitely. Pavel Petrovich met her at
a ball, danced a mazurka with her, in the course of which
she had not uttered a single sensible word, and fell passionately in love with her. Accustomed as he was to easy
conquests, he soon attained his object here too; but the
case of success did not cool his ardour. On the contrary:
he became still more strongly and agonisingly attached
to this woman, in whom, even at moments of complete
surrender, there still remained something sacrosanct and
inaccessible, something no one could reach. What lay hidden in that soul was a mystery to all save God alone. She

seemed to be a prey to some occult forces, unfathomable
even to herself, that played their will upon her and for
whose whims her poor mind was no match. Her conduct
was a chain of incongruities; the only letters that might
have aroused her husband's legitimate suspicions she
wrote to a man who was practically a stranger to her,
while her love was freighted with sorrow: she never
laughed or joked with the person upon whom her choice
had fallen, but she would listen and gaze upon him in perplexity. Sometimes, and for the most part suddenly, this
perplexity would give way to chill horror; her face would
become deathlike and wild; she would shut herself up
in her bedroom, and her maid, putting an ear to the key-
hole, would catch the sound of her smothered sobbing.
Time and again when returning to his room after a tender rendezvous, Kirsanov would suffer the bitter pangs
of mortification which wring the heart with a sense of
utter failure. "What more do I want?" he would ask
himself, while his heart was numb with pain. He once
gave her a ring with a sphinx engraved on the stone.
    "What is this?" she asked. "A sphinx?"
    "Yes," he replied, "and that sphinx is you."
    "I?" she queried, and slowly gave him that inscrutable
look of hers. "That is very flattering, you know!" she added with faint mockery, while her eyes still held the same
odd look.
    Pavel Petrovich suffered torment even while Princess
R— loved him, but when she cooled towards him—and
that happened fairly soon—he nearly went mad. He was
distraught with love and jealousy, he gave her no peace,
trailed after her everywhere; she grew tired of his im-
portunities and went abroad. He resigned his commission, despite the pleadings of his friends and the remon-
strances of his superiors, and followed in the Princess'
wake; he spent four years abroad, sometimes following
her about, at other times intentionally losing sight of her;
he felt ashamed of himself, despised his own weakness,
but it was no use. Her image, that baffling, almost senseless, but fascinating image had become too deeply embed-
ded in his heart. At Baden chance threw them together again on the old footing; never, it seemed, had she

loved him so passionately ... but a month had hardly elapsed when it was all over; the flame had flared up for the last time and was then extinguished forever. Realising that separation was inevitable, he wanted at least to remain her friend, as though friendship with such a woman were possible. She gave him the slip at Baden and henceforth steadily avoided him. Kirsanov went back to Russia, and tried to resume his former life, but he could not get back into the old groove. He roamed like one stricken from place to place; he still went out in society, still retained his man-of-the-world habits and could even boast two or three new conquests; but he no longer expected anything from himself or from others, and did nothing. He grew older, his hair turned grey; to sit in the club of an evening, bitterly bored or listlessly arguing with bachelor cronies, had become a necessity for him— and that, as we know, is a bad sign. Of course, nothing was further from his mind than matrimony. Ten years passed in this wise—colourless, barren, swift, terribly swift years. Nowhere does time fly so quickly as it does in Russia; in prison, they say, it flies still more quickly. One day, during dinner at the club, Pavel Petrovich heard of Princess R—'s death. She had died in Paris in a state bordering on insanity. He left the table, and for a long time he paced up and down the club rooms, coming to a stop near the cardplayers and standing there as if rooted to the spot, but going home no earlier than usual. After a while he received a small parcel containing the ring which he had given the Princess. She had drawn a cross over the sphinx and asked him to be told that the answer to the riddle was the cross.

This took place at the beginning of 1848, just when Nikolai Petrovich came to St. Petersburg after the death of his wife. Pavel Petrovich had seen practically nothing of his brother since the latter had settled down in the country: Nikolai Petrovich's marriage had coincided with the early days of Pavel Petrovich's acquaintance with the Princess. After his wanderings abroad he had gone to his brother's place with the intention of spending a few months there in enjoyment of his brother's domestic bliss, but he had not been able to stand more than a week of it.

Too great had been the difference in the positions of the
two brothers. In 1848 this difference was less marked:
Nikolai Petrovich had lost his wife, Pavel Petrovich had
lost his memories; after the death of the Princess he
tried hard to banish her from his thoughts. But whereas
Nikolai enjoyed the sense of a life well spent, with his
son growing up before his eyes, Pavel, on the contrary,
was a lonely bachelor, entering upon that dim twilight of
life, filled with regrets akin to hopes and hopes akin to
regrets, when youth has gone and old age has not yet
come.

This period of life was more trying to Pavel Petrovich
than to any other man, since in losing his past, he had
lost everything.

"I'm not inviting you to Maryino," Nikolai Petrovich
had once said to him (he had given his estate that name
in honour of his wife). "You found it dull there when my
dear wife was alive, and now, I am afraid, you'll be
bored to death."

"I was silly and restless then," answered Pavel Petrovich. "I have now grown sober, if not wiser. Now, on the
contrary, I'd like to stay with you for good, if you don't
mind."

By way of reply Nikolai Petrovich embraced him; a
year and a half passed after this conversation, however,
before Pavel Petrovich resolved to carry out his intention. But once he was settled in the country he did not
leave it, not even during those three winters which Nikolai Petrovich had spent with his son in St. Petersburg.
He took to reading, mostly in English; his whole life, in
fact, had been built on English ways; he seldom saw his
neighbours and only went out at election time, when he
hardly opened his mouth, unless it was to tease and star-
tle the landed gentry of the old school with his liberal
sallies, yet holding himself aloof from the younger generation. Both sets considered him proud; but both respected him for his air of distinction and aristocratic manners, for the fame of his conquests, for the exquisite way
he dressed, and for the fact that he always stopped in
the best room at the best hotel; for the fact that he dined
well and had once dined with Wellington at Louis Phi-

lippe's table; for always carrying about with him a real
silver dressing case and a portable bathtub; for the wonderful "gentlemanly" scent he used; for his excellent game
of whist and the fact that he always lost; and lastly, they
respected him for his scrupulous integrity. The ladies considered him a charmingly melancholic person, but he did
not cultivate their society.

※   ※   ※

"So, there you are, Yevgeny," Arkady said, as he finished his narration. "Now you see how unfairly you judged
my uncle! To say nothing of how many times he has helped
my father out of difficulties, given him all his money—
you may not know it, but the estate is not divided up—
yet he is always ready to help anybody, and always takes
the part of the peasants; true, when he speaks to them, he
grimaces and sniffs Eau de Cologne. . . ."

"To be sure—nerves," Bazarov interposed.

"Perhaps, but his heart's in the right place. He's by
no means a fool, either. He's given me no end of good
advice . . . especially . . . especially as regards women."

"Aha! Blowing somebody else's cold water after scald-
ing himself on his own milk. We know all about that!"

"In short," Arkady went on, "he's terribly unhappy,
believe me; it's a shame to despise him."

"But who despises him?" Bazarov protested. "I must
say, though, that a man who has staked his whole life
on the card of a woman's love and who, when that card
is beaten, falls to pieces and lets himself go to the dogs—
a fellow like that is not a man, not a male. You say he's
unhappy: you know best; but all the nonsense has not
been taken out of him yet. I'm sure he really believes
he's a smart fellow just because he reads that rag of a
Galignani and once a month saves a muzhik from a
flogging."

"But remember the kind of education he's had and the
time he lived in," Arkady said.

"Education?" Bazarov broke in. "Every man must edu-
cate himself—like me, for instance. As for the time, why

should I depend on it? Better let it depend on me. No, my dear chap, that's just sheer lack of discipline, futility. And what, I'd like to know, are these mysterious relations between man and woman? We physiologists know all about these relations. You just study the anatomy of the eye: where's the enigmatic look you talk about? It's all romanticism, piffle, rot. Let's rather go and have a look at the beetle."

And they both went off to Bazarov's room, which was already permeated with a peculiar medico-surgical odour, mingled with the smell of cheap tobacco.

VIII

Pavel Petrovich did not stay long at his brother's interview with the steward of the estate, a tall skinny man with a sweetish consumptive voice and roguish eyes who, to all his master's remarks, replied: "Why, certainly, sir, to be sure," and tried to make out that all the peasants were drunkards and thieves. The farm, which had recently been remodelled on new lines, creaked like an unoiled cart wheel and cracked like homemade furniture of unseasoned wood. Nikolai Petrovich was not disheartened, but he frequently sighed and brooded: he realised that he could not go on without money, but nearly all his money was gone. Arkady had spoken the truth: Pavel Petrovich had helped his brother out more than once; very often, when he saw him floundering and racking his brains to find a way out of his difficulties, Pavel Petrovich would walk slowly up to the window, thrust his hands into his pockets, mutter: *"Mais je puis vous donner de l'argent,"* and give him some money; but that day he had none himself and so he preferred to withdraw. Business worries bored him to death; moreover, he had a constant suspicion that Nikolai Petrovich for all his zeal and activity was not handling things the right way, though he could never himself suggest where he erred. "My brother is not practical enough," he would debate with himself. "He's being cheated." Nikolai Petrovich, on the other hand, had a high opinion of his brother's acumen and always sought

his advice. "I'm a soft, weak-willed fellow, I've spent
all my life in the backwoods," he would say, "whereas
you've been about a lot and know people well: you have
an eagle eye." Pavel Petrovich by way of reply would
merely turn away, but would not disabuse his brother's
mind.

Leaving Nikolai Petrovich in his study he went down
the passage which separated the front part of the house
from the back and stopped thoughtfully before a low
door, plucked at his moustache and knocked.

"Who's there? Come in," sounded Fenichka's voice.

"It's I," Pavel Petrovich said, opening the door.

Fenichka jumped up from the chair on which she had
been sitting with her baby boy. She placed him in the
arms of a girl who promptly carried him out of the room,
and hastily adjusted her kerchief.

"Pardon me if I have disturbed you," Pavel Petrovich
began, without looking at her. "I just wanted to ask
you. . . . I believe somebody is going to town today . . .
would you order some green tea for me, please."

"Yes, sir," Fenichka answered. "How much do you
want?"

"Oh, half a pound will do, I think. You've made a
change here, I see," he added with a swift look round,
which glided over Fenichka's face in passing. "Those curtains," he murmured, seeing she had not understood him.

"Ah, yes, the curtains. Nikolai Petrovich gave them to
me, but they have been up a long time."

"Yes, and it's a long time since I've been in your room.
It's very nice here now."

"Thanks to Nikolai Petrovich's kindness," Fenichka
murmured.

"Are you more comfortable here than in your old
room?" Pavel Petrovich enquired politely, without the
trace of a smile.

"Oh, yes, sir."

"Who is in your old room now?"

"The laundry maids."

"Ah!"

Pavel Petrovich fell silent. "He's going now," Fenichka thought, but he did not go, and she stood before him

as if rooted to the spot, nervously fiddling with her fingers.

"What made you send the baby away?" Pavel Petrovich said at length. "I am fond of children: let me see him."

Fenichka blushed with confusion and delight. She was afraid of Pavel Petrovich: he hardly ever spoke to her.

"Dunyasha," she cried, "please bring Mitya in here" (she never used the familiar "thou" to anybody in the house). "No, wait a minute; get him dressed first."

Fenichka started for the door.

"It doesn't matter," observed Pavel Petrovich.

"I shan't be a minute," Fenichka said, and was gone.

Left by himself Pavel Petrovich made a careful survey of the room. The small, low-ceiling chamber was very cosy and clean. It smelt of freshly painted floorboards, camomile and melissa. Chairs with lyre-shaped backs were ranged against the walls; they had been purchased by the late general in Poland during the campaign; in one corner stood a bed under a muslin canopy next to a clamped chest with an arched lid. In the opposite corner a little image lamp was burning before a large dark icon representing St. Nicholas; a tiny porcelain egg suspended by a red ribbon attached to the nimbus hung down over the saint's breast; glinting greenly on the window sills stood jars of last year's jam, on the carefully tied paper lids of which was inscribed in Fenichka's own sprawling hand: "goozberry"; Nikolai Petrovich was particularly fond of that jam. Suspended from the ceiling by a long cord hung a cage with a hobtailed siskin; it chirped and hopped about incessantly and the cage constantly shook and swayed; the hemp seeds dropped to the floor with a patter. On the wall between the windows, over a small chest of drawers, hung some rather poor photographs of Nikolai Petrovich in sundry poses, taken by an itinerant photographer; next to them was a bad photograph of Fenichka herself—a sightless face with an unnatural smile looked out of a dark little frame—the rest was simply a smudge; and above Fenichka, General Yermolov in a Circassian felt cloak scowled at the Caucasian mountains looming

in the distance, from under a silk pincushion in the shape
of a boot dangling over his eyebrows.

Five minutes went by; there was a rustling and whispering in the next room. Pavel Petrovich picked up a well-
thumbed book from the chest of drawers, an odd volume
of Massalsky's *Royal Streltsi*, and turned over several
pages. The door opened and Fenichka came in with Mitya
in her arms. She had dressed him in a red little shirt with
an embroidered collar, and had combed his hair and
wiped his face; he was breathing hard, wriggling his body
and waving his little arms the way all healthy babies
do; the spruce shirt obviously impressed him: delight was
written all over his plump little person. Fenichka had put
her hair in order too and changed her kerchief, but she
could have spared herself the trouble. For what can be
more fascinating in the world than a pretty young mother
with a healthy baby in her arms?

"What a chubby little fellow," Pavel Petrovich said
indulgently, and tickled Mitya's twin chins with the tip of
his long fingernail; the child stared at the siskin and began to crow.

"It's Uncle," Fenichka said, bending her face down to
him and giving him a little shake, while Dunyasha quietly
placed a lighted pastille on a copper coin on the window
sill.

"How old is he?" asked Pavel Petrovich.

"Six months; going on seven, come the eleventh."

"Won't it be eight, Fedosya Nikolayevna?" Dunyasha
put in timidly.

"No, seven, to be sure!" The baby chuckled again, fixed
his eyes on the chest and suddenly clutched his mother's
nose and lips with all five fingers. "Naughty, naughty,"
Fenichka said, without drawing her face away.

"He looks like my brother," Pavel Petrovich remarked.

Who else should he look like? Fenichka thought.

"Yes," Pavel Petrovich went on, as though talking to
himself, "a decided resemblance."

He regarded Fenichka attentively, almost sadly.

"It's Uncle," she repeated, this time in a whisper.

"Ah! Pavel! So this is where you are!" Nikolai Petrovich's voice sounded suddenly.

Pavel Petrovich spun round with a frown; but his brother was looking at him with such unfeigned delight and gratitude that he could not help responding with a smile.

"It's a fine little fellow you have," he said and glanced at his watch: "I dropped in about some tea for myself."

And assuming a matter-of-fact air, Pavel Petrovich immediately left the room.

"Did he come in on his own?" Nikolai Petrovich asked Fenichka.

"Yes. He just knocked and came in."

"Well, and has Arkady been in to see you again?"

"No. Hadn't I better move back to the wing, Nikolai Petrovich?"

"What for?"

"I was thinking it would be best for the time being."

"N-no. . ." Nikolai Petrovich said hesitatingly, fingering his forehead. "We should have thought of it before. Hullo, dumpling," he said with sudden animation, and going up to the baby, kissed him on the cheek; after which, bending slightly, he put his lips to Fenichka's hand which lay creamily white against the baby's red shirt.

"Nikolai Petrovich! What are you doing?" she faltered, dropping her eyes then slowly looking up again. Charming was the look in her eyes as she gazed from under her lowered lids, smiling tenderly and a little foolishly.

*   *   *

Nikolai Petrovich had met Fenichka under the following circumstances. One day, some three years ago, he had had occasion to spend the night at an inn in a remote provincial town. He had been agreeably struck by the cleanliness of his room and the freshness of the linen. "The mistress must be a German," he had thought; but she proved to be a Russian, a woman of about fifty, well-spoken and neatly dressed, with a pleasant, intelligent face. He had a talk with her over his tea; she took his fancy. Nikolai Petrovich had at that time just moved into his new house, and as he did not want to keep serfs about the place he was on the lookout for hired servants.

The landlady of the inn, for her part, complained about the scarcity of travellers and the hard times; he offered her a position as his housekeeper; she accepted. Her husband had died a long time ago, leaving her an only daughter, Fenichka. Within a fortnight Arina Savishna (that was the new housekeeper's name) arrived with her daughter at Maryino and moved into the small wing of the house. Nikolai Petrovich's choice had proved a happy one. Arina soon had everything in the house shipshape. Fenichka, who was seventeen at the time, was rarely seen and never mentioned; she lived unobtrusively and quietly, and only on Sundays would Nikolai Petrovich catch a glimpse of the delicate profile of her milk-white face in some corner of the parish church. A little over a year passed in this wise.

One morning Arina had come into his study, and with her usual low bow asked whether he could help her daughter who had got a spark from the stove in her eye. Like all stay-at-homes Nikolai Petrovich practised domestic doctoring and had even acquired a homeopathic medicine chest. He ordered the patient to be brought to him at once. On hearing that the master had sent for her, Fenichka was terrified, but went with her mother nevertheless. Nikolai Petrovich drew her to the window and took her head in both his hands. Having carefully examined her inflamed eye he prescribed a lotion, which he made up himself, there and then, and tearing his handkerchief into strips showed her how to apply it. Fenichka heard him out and turned to go away. "Kiss the master's hand, silly child," Arina said. Nikolai Petrovich did not hold out his hand, and, thrown into confusion himself, he implanted a kiss on the parting of her bent head. Fenichka's eye soon got well; but the impression which she had made on Nikolai Petrovich did not pass so soon. That pure, sweet, timorously upturned face haunted him; he felt the touch of her soft hair on his palms, saw those innocent, slightly parted lips through which the pearly teeth glistened moistly in the sun. He began to watch her more closely in church, tried to draw her into conversation. At first she had been very shy, and one evening, when she met him on a narrow footpath running through

a rye field, she had stepped into the tall dense grain overgrown with wormwood and cornflowers to avoid meeting him face to face. He had seen her head through the
golden latticework of rye, peeping out at him like some
wild little creature, and had called her kindly:

"Good evening, Fenichka! I don't bite, you know."

"Good evening", she had whispered, without coming
out of her hiding place.

Gradually she grew accustomed to him, but was still
shy in his presence. Suddenly her mother Arina died of
cholera. What was she to do? From her mother she had
inherited a love of order, common sense, and staidness;
but she was so young, so lonely, and Nikolai Petrovich
was so kind and modest.... The rest requires no telling....

*   *   *

"So my brother actually came in to see you?" Nikolai
Petrovich asked her. "Just knocked and came in?"

"Yes."

"Well, that's fine. Let me play with Mitya."

And Nikolai Petrovich began tossing him up almost to
the ceiling, to the huge delight of the infant and the no
little anxiety of the mother who, every time he flew up,
reached out her arms to his exposed little feet.

*   *   *

And Pavel Petrovich returned to his luxurious study,
papered in elegant grey, and hung with weapons against
a colourful Persian rug, with walnut furniture upholstered
in dark green mock-velvet, a renaissance bookcase of
old black oak, bronze statuettes on a magnificent desk,
and a cosy fireplace. He threw himself on the sofa, his
hands clasped behind his head and lay motionless, gazing with a look almost of despair at the ceiling. Whether
it was to conceal from the very walls, what his face betrayed, or whatever it was, he got up, drew the heavy
window curtains and flung himself on the sofa again.

IX

That day Bazarov, too, made Fenichka's acquaintance. He was strolling about in the garden with Arkady, trying to explain to him why some of the trees, particularly the young oaks, had not taken root.

"You should plant more white poplars and fir trees and perhaps some limes and give them some loam. That arbour has done well," he added, "because acacia and lilac are adaptable fellows and don't need much tending. I say! There's somebody in here."

Fenichka, with Dunyasha and Mitya, were sitting in the arbour. Bazarov stopped, while Arkady nodded to Fenichka as to an old acquaintance.

"Who's that?" Bazarov asked him when they had passed by. "What a pretty girl!"

"Who?"

"It's plain enough: only one pretty girl there."

Arkady, not without embarrassment, told him briefly who Fenichka was.

"Aha!" Bazarov said. . . . "Your father knows a good thing when he sees it. I like him, by Jove! He's all there. However, we must get acquainted," he added, and retraced his steps to the arbour.

"Yevgeny!" Arkady cried out in dismay: "For God's sake be careful!"

"Don't you worry," Bazarov said. "We're no greenhorns, we city folk."

Coming up to Fenichka he took off his cap.

"Allow me to introduce myself," he began with a polite bow, "Arkady Nikolayevich's chum, and a harmless person."

Fenichka got up from the bench and looked at him in silence.

"What a fine kiddie!" Bazarov went on. "Don't worry, I haven't got an evil eye. Why are his cheeks so red? Is he cutting his teeth?"

"Yes, sir," Fenichka murmured. "He's cut four teeth already, and now his gums are swollen again."

"Let me have a look . . . don't be afraid, I'm a doctor."

Bazarov took the baby in his arms; to the amazement of both Fenichka and Dunyasha, he did not show the slightest resistance or fear.

"I see, I see.... Everything's all right: he's going to have a fine set of teeth. If anything happens, let me know. And how do you feel?"

"Quite well, thank God."

"Thank God—that's the great thing. And you?" he added turning to Dunyasha.

Dunyasha, who was a very prim maid indoors but a very mischievous one out of them, merely giggled by way of reply.

"Splendid. Here, take this strapping fellow of yours."

Fenichka took the baby from him.

"How quiet he was in your arms," she murmured.

"All children are quiet with me," Bazarov answered. "A little bird told me the secret."

"Children have a feeling of those who love them," remarked Dunyasha.

"That is so," confirmed Fenichka. "Now Mitya won't go to some people, not for anything."

"Will he go to me?" Arkady said. He had been standing at a distance for a while, and now joined them.

He held his hands out invitingly, but Mitya threw his head back with a wail, much to Fenichka's distress.

"Next time—when he gets to know me better," Arkady said indulgently, and the friends walked away.

"What's her name did you say?" asked Bazarov.

"Fenichka ... Fedosya," Arkady said.

"And her patronymic? One must know that, too."

"Nikolayevna."

"*Bene*. What I like about her is that she is not too bashful. Somebody else might blame her for it, I suppose. That's nonsense! Why should she be? She's a mother— well, she's in the right."

"She's right enough," observed Arkady, "but my father. ..."

"And he's right, too," Bazarov broke in.

"I shouldn't say so."

"I don't suppose you like the idea of there being another heir in the family?"

"You ought to be ashamed of yourself, thinking me capable of such thoughts?" Arkady retorted hotly. "That's not the reason why I consider my father wrong; I believe he should have married her."

"Oho-ho!" Bazarov said calmly. "So that's how magnanimous we are! You still attach importance to marriage; I ought to know better."

The friends walked on a few paces in silence.

"I've looked over your father's place," resumed Bazarov. "The farm cattle are poor, the horses are just nags, the buildings have seen better days, and the hands look like a bunch of downright loafers; as for the steward—he's either a knave or a fool, I can't quite make out which."

"You're pretty censorious today, Yevgeny Vassilich."

"And those goody-goody peasants will cheat your father, as sure as eggs is eggs. You know the saying: 'The Russian muzhik will gobble up God himself.'"

"I begin to agree with my uncle," Arkady said. "You have a downright bad opinion of Russians."

"What's the odds! The one good thing about the Russian is the rotten opinion he has of himself. What really matters is that two and two make four, the rest is nonsense."

"And is nature nonsense too?" Arkady said, gazing thoughtfully into the distance at the variegated fields bathed in the mellow light of the sun, which was now low in the skies.

"Yes, nature is nonsense, too, in the way you understand it. Nature's not a temple but a workshop, and man in it is a workman."

The lingering notes of a violoncello drifted across to them from the house. Somebody was playing feelingly, if inexpertly, Schubert's *Expectations*, and the sweet melody floated silver-toned on the air.

"What's that?" Bazarov said in amazement.

"It's my father."

"Your father plays the 'cello?"

"Yes."

"Why, how old is he?"

"Forty-four."

Bazarov suddenly burst into a laugh.

"What are you laughing at?"

"Upon my word! A man at the age of forty-four, a *pater familias*, living in the country, playing the 'cello!"

Bazarov was still laughing. But Arkady, however much he stood in awe of his mentor, did not even smile this time.

X

About a fortnight passed. Life at Maryino ran its usual course. Arkady led the life of a sybarite, Bazarov worked. Everyone in the house had got used to him, to his casual ways, his terse joky manner of speech. Indeed, Fenichka herself had so far accepted him that she had him wakened one night when Mitya was seized with convulsions; and he had answered the call, sitting up with her for nearly two hours, half-bantering, half-yawning, as was his wont, and had relieved the baby. Pavel Petrovich, however, hated him with all the intensity of his being: he thought him proud, insolent, cynical and plebeian; he suspected that Bazarov did not respect him, as good as despised him—him, Pavel Kirsanov! Nikolai Petrovich was a bit afraid of the young "nihilist" and doubted whether his influence on Arkady was a good one; yet he willingly listened to him and willingly attended his physical and chemical experiments. Bazarov had brought a microscope with him and spent hours over it. The servants, too, grew fond of him, though he liked to chaff them: they felt that he was one of them, not of the gentry. Dunyasha was not averse to giggling with him and would cast sidelong glances full of meaning at him as she tripped by. Pyotr, a very stupid and conceited person with tensely wrinkled brows, whose only merits were courteous manners, an ability to read by syllables and a habit of frequently cleaning his little coat with a clothes brush —even Pyotr would grin and brighten up whenever Bazarov took notice of him; the farm urchins trailed after "the doctor gent" like so many puppies. Old Prokofich was the only one who did not like him; he would serve him at table with a sullen face, called him a "miscreant"

and "rapscallion" and likened him with his whiskers to
a pig in the bush. Prokofich was in his own way an aristocrat, no less so than Pavel Petrovich.

The best time of the year set in—early June. The
weather was exceptionally fine; true, there was a remote
menace of another outbreak of cholera, but the inhabitants of that gubernia were already accustomed to its
visitations. Bazarov usually got up very early and went
out two or three versts, not for a walk—he was no lover
of aimless walks—but to collect herbs and insects. Sometimes he took Arkady with him. On the way back they
would often start an argument, Arkady usually getting
the worst of it, for all that he spoke the most.

One day they were rather late getting back; Nikolai
Petrovich went out into the garden to meet them, and,
drawing level with the arbour, he suddenly caught the
sound of quick footsteps and the voices of the two young
men. They were coming down the other side of the arbour
and could not see him.

"You don't know my father well enough," Arkady was
saying.

Nikolai Petrovich stood stock-still.

"Your father's a good fellow," Bazarov said, "but he's
a back number, his singing days are over."

Nikolai Petrovich strained his ears. . . . Arkady said
nothing.

"The back number" stood for a minute or two without
stirring, then slowly retraced his steps.

"The other day I found him reading Pushkin," Bazarov resumed. "That's the limit, really. You ought to explain things to him. After all, he's not a boy—it's time
he dropped that nonsense. Fancy being romantic in our
times! Give him something worthwhile to read."

"What would you advise?" Arkady asked.

"Well, I should say Büchner's *Stoff und Kraft* for a
start."

"I think so, too," Arkady assented. "*Stoff und Kraft* is
written in a popular style."

*   *   *

"So there you are," Nikolai Petrovich was saying to his brother that day after dinner, sitting in the latter's study. "You and I have become back numbers, our singing days are over. Ah well! Perhaps Bazarov is right; but frankly, there's one thing I'm very sorry for: this was just the time when I hoped that Arkady and I would become close friends, but it seems that I've dropped behind while he has gone ahead, and we can't understand each other."

"What makes you think he has gone ahead? And in what way does he differ so strikingly from us?" Pavel Petrovich said impatiently. "That signior, the nihilist fellow, has knocked all that into his head. I detest that wretched medico: if you ask me, he's just a charlatan; I'm sure that for all his frogs he isn't much up in physics either."

"No, brother, you are wrong—Bazarov is a clever and well-informed man."

"And horribly conceited," Pavel Petrovich interrupted again.

"Yes," Nikolai Petrovich said, "he is conceited. But I suppose that's as it should be; one thing I can't make out though. I seem to be doing everything to keep up with the times: I have settled the peasants and started a farm—the whole gubernia calls me a Red; I read, I study, and in general try to keep an open mind for everything modern—and yet they say my singing days are over. Why, brother, I am really beginning to think they are!"

"How is that?"

"Well, judge for yourself. Today I was sitting reading Pushkin. I remember, it was *The Gypsies*. All of a sudden Arkady comes up to me, and, without saying a word, with a look, you know, of kindly commiseration, gently takes the book away from me as if I were a child, puts another one in front of me, a German one ... smiles, and goes away, carrying Pushkin off with him."

"Dear me! And what was the book he gave you?"

"Here it is."

And Nikolai Petrovich drew out of his tail pocket Büchner's notorious booklet, ninth edition.

Pavel Petrovich turned the booklet over in his hands.

"Humph!" he grunted. "Arkady Nikolaich is solicitous about your education. Well, did you try to read it?"

"I did."

"Well?"

"Either I'm stupid, or it's all twaddle. I suppose I must be stupid."

"You haven't forgotten your German, have you?" asked Pavel Petrovich.

"No, I understand German."

Pavel Petrovich turned the book over in his hands again and threw his brother a glance from under his brows. Neither said anything.

"By the way," Nikolai Petrovich broke the silence, clearly anxious to change the subject. "I have received a letter from Kolyazin."

"Matvei Ilyich?"

"Yes. He's come down to make an official inspection of the gubernia. He's a bigwig now and writes to say that he has a kinsman's desire to see us, and invites the two of us and Arkady to call on him in town."

"Are you going?" asked Pavel Petrovich.

"No. And you?"

"I shan't go either. Dashed if I'm going to drag myself fifty versts for nothing. *Mathieu* wants to show himself off to us in all his glory: the deuce he does! He'll have plenty of local incense without our burning any to him. A great man, indeed—a privy councillor! If I had continued in the service and stayed in that silly harness I'd have been an adjutant general by now. Then, don't forget, you and I are back numbers."

"Yes, brother; it's about time to call in the undertaker and let him take our measure," Nikolai Petrovich said, fetching a sigh.

"You won't catch me giving in so soon," his brother muttered. "I have a feeling that we'll come to grips with that medical fellow yet."

And come to grips they did, that very evening, at tea. Pavel Petrovich came down to the drawing room ready for battle, irritated and determined. He was only waiting for an excuse to hurl himself at the enemy, but an excuse was long in coming. Bazarov was generally not talkative in the presence of the "old Kirsanov boys" (as he called the brothers) and that evening he felt out of sorts and drank cup after cup of tea in silence. Pavel Petrovich chafed with impatience; at last he saw his chance.

The name of a neighbouring landowner cropped up during the conversation. "A rotter, a wretched aristocrat," Bazarov said airily—he had met the man in St. Petersburg.

"Allow me to ask," Pavel Petrovich began, his lips quivering, "according to you the words 'rotter' and 'aristocrat' are synonymous?"

"I said 'wretched aristocrat'," Bazarov retorted, lazily taking a sip of his tea.

"Exactly, I presume you hold the same opinion of 'aristocrats' as you do of 'wretched aristocrats'. I consider it my duty to inform you that I do not share that opinion. I venture to say that everyone knows me for a man of liberal views and a champion of progress; but precisely for that reason I respect aristocrats, the real ones. Remember, my dear sir," (at these words Bazarov raised his eyes to Pavel Petrovich's face) "remember, my dear sir," he repeated vehemently, "the English aristocrats. They will not yield an iota of their rights and that is why they respect the rights of others; they demand that people fulfil their obligations to them and for that very reason they fulfil *their own* obligations to others. The aristocracy has given England her freedom and it upholds that freedom."

"We've heard that tune before," Bazarov said. "But what are you trying to prove?"

"What I'm atrying to prove of, my dear sir, is this" (when angry Pavel Petrovich intentionally lapsed into bad grammar. The whim was a survival of Alexandrian traditions. The bigwigs of the day, on the rare occasions when they used their mother tongue, affected a slovenliness of speech, as much as to say: we are native Russians, but we are also grandees, who are permitted to disregard the rules of grammar). "What I'm atrying to prove of is that unless a person has self-respect, a sense of personal dignity—and those instincts are well-developed in the aristocrat—there can be no secure foundation for the social ... *bien public* ... social structure. Individuality, my

dear sir,—that's the main thing; individuality must stand
as firm as a rock, for it is the foundation which everything is built upon. I am well aware, for instance, that
you find my habits, my dress, even my personal fastidi-
ousness an object of amusement, but I assure you that
these things are a matter of self-respect, a matter of duty,
yes, sir, duty. I live in the country, in the backwoods, but
I will not lose my self-esteem, my sense of personal
dignity."

"By your leave, Pavel Petrovich," Bazarov said. "You
talk about self-respect, yet you sit doing nothing. Just how
does that benefit the *bien public*? You could be doing that
without self-respect."

Pavel Petrovich paled.

"That's quite a different thing. I am not obliged to
explain to you just now why I sit and do nothing, as you
pleased to put it. I merely want to say that aristocratism
is a principle, and only immoral or shallow people can
live nowadays without principles. I told Arkady that the
day after he arrived and I am telling that to you now.
Isn't that so, Nikolai?"

Nikolai Petrovich nodded.

"Aristocratism, liberalism, progress, principles," Bazarov was saying meanwhile, "goodness, how many foreign . . . and useless words! A Russian has no need for
them at any price."

"What does he need then, pray? According to you, we
are outside humanity, outside its laws. Why, the logic of
history demands. . . ."

"Who wants that logic? We get along without it."

"What do you mean?"

"What I say. You, I trust, don't need logic to put a
piece of bread into your mouth when you are hungry. Of
what use are these abstract ideas?"

Pavel Petrovich threw up his hands.

"I don't understand you, after that. You insult the
Russian people. I don't understand how one can
deny principles, maxims! What are you actuated by
then?"

"I've already told you, Uncle, that we don't recognise
authorities," interposed Arkady.

"We are actuated by what we consider useful," Bazarov said. "These days negation is more useful than anything else—so we negate."

"Everything?"

"Yes, everything."

"What? Not only art, poetry, but even ... it's shocking to utter. . . ."

"Everything," Bazarov repeated with unutterable coolness.

Pavel Petrovich stared at him. He had not expected this. Arkady on the other hand flushed with pleasure.

"But, look here," Nikolai Petrovich broke in. "You negate everything or, to be more exact, you destroy everything. But who is going to do the building?"

"That's not our affair. The ground has to be cleared first."

"The present state of the nation demands it," Arkady added importantly. "We must meet these demands, we have no right to indulge our personal egoism."

The last remark was obviously not to Bazarov's taste—it savoured of philosophy, that is to say, romanticism, for Bazarov regarded even philosophy as romanticism; but he did not want to contradict his young disciple.

"No, no!" Pavel Petrovich exclaimed with sudden vehemence. "I am not going to believe that you gentlemen really know the Russian people, that you are representatives of its needs, its aspirations! No, the Russian people is not what you imagine it to be. It has a sacred regard for tradition, it is patriarchal, it cannot live without faith. . . ."

"I'll not dispute that," Bazarov interrupted. "I am prepared even to agree with you there."

"If so, then. . . ."

"It still doesn't prove anything."

"Exactly, it doesn't prove anything," Arkady chimed in with the assurance of an experienced chess player who has anticipated a possible dangerous move on the part of his opponent and is therefore unperturbed.

"What do you mean, it proves nothing?" Pavel Petrovich muttered in astonishment. "Then you are going against your own people?"

"What if we are?" Bazarov cried. "When the people hear the noise of thunder they believe that it's the prophet Elijah taking a ride in his chariot across the skies. What then? Would you have me agree with them? Yes, they're Russians—but am I not a Russian too?"

"No, you are not a Russian, after what you have been saying! I cannot own you as a Russian."

"My grandfather ploughed the land," Bazarov said with arrogant pride. "Ask any of your muzhiks which of us he'd more readily acknowledge as his fellow-countryman, you or I. Why, you don't even know how to talk to him."

"Yet you talk to him and despise him at the same time."

"What if he deserves to be despised! You criticise my outlook, but what makes you think that it is something accidental in me, that it's not an outcome of that national spirit which you so zealously defend?"

"To be sure! Of what use to anyone are nihilists?"

"As to whether they are of any use or not is not for us to decide. I daresay even you consider yourself useful in a way, too."

"Now, gentlemen, don't let us become personal, please," cried Nikolai Petrovich, rising from his seat.

Pavel Petrovich smiled, and placing a hand on his brother's shoulder, pressed him back into his seat.

"You needn't worry," he said, "I shan't forget myself, precisely because of that feeling of self-respect which our friend ... our friend the doctor pokes such cruel fun at. Excuse me," he resumed, turning once more to Bazarov, "do you by any chance believe your doctrines to be new? If so, you are deluding yourself. The materialism you preach has passed current many a time before and has never had a leg to stand on. . . ."

"Another foreign word," Bazarov interjected. He was beginning to lose his temper, and his complexion had assumed a coarse coppery hue. "In the first place we do not preach anything; that is our custom. . . ."

"What *do* you do?"

"I'll tell you. Until quite recently we talked about our officials taking bribes, about the lack of roads, the poor state of commerce and the courts of justice. . . ."

"Ah, yes, of course, you are denunciators—that's what it's called, I believe. I myself agree with many of your accusations, but. . . ."

"Then it dawned on us that just talking about our sores was a waste of breath, that it merely led to banality and doctrinarianism; we saw that those clever fellows of ours, the so-called progressive men and denunciators, were of no earthly use, that we were wasting our time, talking nonsense about art, unconscious creativeness, parliamentarism, the bar and the devil knows what else, when it was simply a question of men's daily bread, when we were suffocating from crass superstitions, when all our stock companies were going smash simply because there's a dearth of honest men, when the very emancipation the government was fussing over would hardly do us any good, because the muzhik would be only too glad to rob himself so as he could get drunk in the pothouses."

"I see," Pavel Petrovich interrupted. "So you have convinced yourself of all this and have made up your mind not to tackle anything seriously?"

"And have made up our mind not to tackle anything," Bazarov echoed back grimly. He suddenly felt annoyed with himself for having loosened his tongue before this aristocrat.

"And do nothing but damn?"

"Do nothing but damn."

"And that's called nihilism?"

"That's called nihilism," Bazarov repeated, this time with pointed insolence.

Pavel Petrovich narrowed his eyes slightly.

"I see!" he said in a singularly calm voice. "Nihilism is to cure all our ills, and you, you are our deliverers and heroes. So. But what makes you take the others to task, the denunciators, for instance? Don't you go about ranting like the rest of them?"

"Whatever our faults, that is not one of them," Bazarov muttered.

"What then? Do you act? Do you intend to act?"

Bazarov did not answer. Pavel Petrovich controlled himself with an effort.

5*

"Hm! To act, to demolish. . ." he went on. "But how set about the business of demolishing without even knowing the why or wherefore?"

"We demolish because we are a force," Arkady remarked.

Pavel Petrovich surveyed his nephew and smiled ironically.

"Yes, a force—an unleashed power," Arkady said, drawing himself up.

"You wretched boy," Pavel Petrovich cried, no longer able to contain himself. "At least *you* might stop to think what it is you are lending support to in Russia with that hackneyed maxim of yours! Really, it's enough to try the patience of an angel! Force! There's force in the savage Kalmuck and the Mongol, too—but who wants it? We cherish civilisation, yes, sir, and the fruits of civilisation. Don't tell me these fruits are paltry: the worst kind of dauber, *un barbouilleur*, a piano-thumper hired for five kopeks a night at dance parties is more useful than you are, because he is a representative of civilisation and not of brute Mongolian force! You fancy yourselves to be progressive men, but all you are good for is to squat in a Kalmuck tent! Force! And don't forget, you strong gentlemen, that there are just four and a half of your fraternity against the millions of others who will not allow you to trample their sacred creeds and who will crush you!"

"If we're crushed, it serves us right," Bazarov said. "But that's easier said than done. We're not so few as you imagine."

"What? Do you seriously think you can stand up against a whole nation?"

"Moscow was burnt by a farthing candle, you know," Bazarov replied.

"I see. First we're as proud as Lucifer, then we start mocking at everything. So that's the latest fad among the young, so that's what captures the imagination of inexperienced youngsters! There, if you please, sits one of them, right beside you—he all but worships you, look at him!" (Arkady turned away with a frown). "And this contagion is already widespread. I have been told that our painters in Rome never set foot inside the Vatican. Raphael is considered almost fool, because, don't you see, he's an authority; and they themselves are disgustingly impotent and barren, with an imagination that does not carry them beyond the *Girl at a Fountain*! And even that is painted execrably. According to you they are the right sort, are they not?"

"According to me," Bazarov answered, "Raphael is not worth a brass farthing, and they're no better either."

"Bravo, bravo! Do you hear that, Arkady ... that's how modern young men should speak! Come to think of it, why shouldn't they follow you? Formerly young men had to study; they didn't want to be thought ignoramuses, so they had to work hard willynilly. But now they merely have to say: 'Everything in the world is nonsense!' and, lo! the trick is done. The young men are delighted. And really, before they were simply fatheads, and now they've suddenly become nihilists."

"Well, there goes your belauded sense of self-respect," Bazarov observed phlegmatically, while Arkady flared up, his eyes flashing. "Our argument has gone a bit too far. I think we had better drop it. And I'll be prepared to agree with you," he added, getting up, "when you can show me a single institution in our national life, whether domestic or social, which does not merit utter and ruthless denunciation."

"I'll show you millions of such institutions," cried Pavel Petrovich, "millions. Take our village community, for example."

Bazarov's lips curled in a sneer.

"As for the village community," he said, "you'd better talk to your brother about that. He now has firsthand knowledge, I believe, of the village community, mutual guarantee, temperance and all that eyewash."

"The family, what about the family as it exists among our peasants?" shouted Pavel Petrovich.

"That's another question I would advise you not to go into too deeply. I daresay you've heard about the practice of adultery with one's daughter-in-law? Take my advice, Pavel Petrovich, give yourself a couple of days— you will hardly find anything in less. Go over all our classes, examine each one closely, and Arkady and I will meanwhile...."

"Go about jeering at everything," Pavel Petrovich interjected.

"No, dissect frogs. Come on, Arkady. Good day, gentlemen!"

The two friends went out. The brothers were left alone, and at first they merely looked at one another in silence.

"Well," Pavel Petrovich began at length, "there you have our young generation! There they are—our successors!"

"Successors," Nikolai Petrovich echoed with a sad sigh. He had been on tenterhooks all through the dispute, now and again stealing pained glances at Arkady. "Do you know what I have been thinking, brother? Once I had a quarrel with our dear mother; she shouted and wouldn't listen to me. At last I told her that she couldn't understand me, that we belonged to different generations. She was terribly offended, and I thought: 'It can't be helped. It's a bitter pill, but it's got to be swallowed.' Well, now it's our turn and our successors can say to us: 'You are not of our generation, swallow the pill.' "

"You're much too benign and modest," Pavel Petrovich said. "I'm convinced, on the contrary, that you and I are much more in the right than those young gentlemen, though we do, perhaps, express ourselves in an old-fashioned way, *vieilli*, and have none of their cocksureness. But how smug the young people of today are! You ask a fellow: 'What wine will you have, red or white?' 'I'm in the habit of taking red,' quoth he in a bass voice, with a face so solemn as if all the world were looking at him at that moment."

"Will you have any more tea?" Fenichka asked, putting her head in at the door. She had not the temerity to come into the drawing room while there were sounds of dispute there.

"No, you can tell them to take the samovar away," replied Nikolai Petrovich, and rose to meet her. Pavel Petrovich wished him a curt *bon soir* and retired to his study.

XI

Half an hour later Nikolai Petrovich went into the garden to his favourite arbour. He fell a prey to sad thoughts. He saw now clearly for the first time that he and his son were drifting apart and that the rift would grow wider as time went on. In vain then, out there in St. Petersburg, had he sat for days on end in the winter, poring over new books; in vain had he lent an eager ear to the talk of the young men; in vain had he felt so elated at being able to slip in a word of his own during their lively discussions. "My brother says that we are right," he thought. "Vanity aside, I really think they are farther from the truth than we are, and yet I feel they have something that we haven't got, they have an advantage over us. Youth? No, it isn't only that. Isn't it because they have less of the grand manner than we have?"

Nikolai Petrovich's head sank on his breast and he passed a hand over his face.

"But to reject poetry?" he mused anew. "To have no feeling for art, nature. . . ."

And he looked round him, as if trying to understand how one could have no feelings for nature. Evening was drawing in; the sun was hidden behind an aspen wood, which stood within half a verst of the garden; its shadow stretched unendingly across the motionless fields. A peasant was riding on a little white horse down a dark-strip of road along the wood; his whole figure was clearly visible, even to a patch on his shoulder, though he rode in the shade; the legs of the trotting horse made a clear pretty picture. The sun beams filtered through the wood, shedding such a warm glow on the aspen trunks that they looked like pines, and their foliage appeared almost blue, while above rose the pale blue of the sky faintly roseate with the flush of sunset. The swallows winged their way high up in the sky; the wind had dropped; belated bees buzzed lazily and drowsily among the lilac blossoms; midges swarmed in a column over a solitary far-stretching bough. "God, how beautiful!" thought Nikolai Petrovich, and his favourite verse came to his lips, but he remembered Arkady and *Stoff und Kraft* and fell silent; and he lingered there, giving himself up to the sad solace of lonely thoughts. He liked daydreaming: country life had developed that trait in him. Not so long ago he had sat thus daydreaming while waiting for his son at the little inn, but a change had since come about, the relations which had then been vague had now taken shape—and definite shape! Once more he recalled his dead wife, but not as he had known her for many years, a house-wifely matron but a young girl with a slender waist, an innocent questioning gaze, and tightly coiled hair over a childlike neck. He recollected their first meeting. He was a student at the time. He had met her on the staircase of his lodgings, and, accidentally brushing against her, had turned round to apologise and only managed to stammer: "Pardon, monsieur"; she had lowered her head and smiled, and, seeming suddenly to take fright, had run away, then, at a bend in the stairs, had thrown him a swift glance, assumed a serious air and blushed. And then the first timid visits, the half-words and half-smiles, the perplexity, the sadness and the yearnings, and finally the breathless rapture. . . . Whither had it all fled? She had become his wife, he had been happy as few men are happy in this world. "But," mused he, "those first sweet moments of bliss—why could they not live on forever?"

He did not try to analyse his thoughts, but he yearned to retain those halcyon days with something stronger than memory, he longed to feel his Maria near him again, to sense the warmth of her, the touch of her breath; he could almost feel her hovering presence. . . .

"Nikolai Petrovich," Fenichka's voice sounded near him, "where are you?"

He started. He felt neither distress nor shame. He never even admitted the possibility of comparison between his wife and Fenichka, but he was sorry that she had sought him out. Her voice immediately brought him back to reality, to his grey hairs, his advancing age.

The dream world which he had been about to enter, which had already risen from the dim waves of the past, shifted and vanished.

"I'm here," he answered, "I'll soon come, you go along."
"There it is, the grand manner," it flashed through his

mind. Fenichka peered in at him without speaking and disappeared; he was astonished to find that night had crept in while he had been dreaming. Everything round him was dark and hushed, and Fenichka's face had swum past looking so pale and small. He half-rose to go home, but his melting heart was too full, and he slowly began to pace the garden, now gazing wistfully at the ground, now looking up at the sky which was already bright with clustering stars. He walked until he was almost exhausted, but the uneasiness within him, a kind of yearning, a vague, saddening anxiety would not be allayed. Oh, how Bazarov would have mocked him had he known what was then passing in his soul! And Arkady too would have disapproved. Tears started to his eyes, unbidden tears— he, a man of forty-four, a farm owner, an employer; this was a hundred times worse than the violoncello.

Nikolai Petrovich continued to pace the garden, and could not bring himself to go into the house, that peaceful, snug abode which smiled at him with all its lighted windows; he could not tear himself away from the darkness, the garden, the caressing touch of the fresh air on his face, the heartache and the yearning. . . .

At a bend in the path he came upon Pavel Petrovich. "What's the matter?" he asked Nikolai Petrovich. "You're as pale as a ghost, you're not well; why don't you lie down?"

Nikolai Petrovich told him in a few words the state of mind he was in and withdrew. Pavel Petrovich walked to the end of the garden and he too became lost in thought, he too raised his eyes skyward. But his fine dark eyes reflected nothing but the light of the stars. He was not born a romanticist, and that fastidious, dry but passionate soul of his, so misanthropically French, was not given to dreaming.

*   *   *

"Do you know what?" Bazarov was saying to Arkady that night. "I've had a brainwave. Your father was talking today about an invitation he had received from that distinguished relative of yours. Your father's not going;

what do you say to taking a run up to town—that gentleman has invited you, too. Look at the weather we're having; let's go and look the town over. We'll knock around
for five or six days and have a good time!"

"Will you come back here?"

"No, I'll have to be going to my father's. He lives
thirty versts from town, you know. I haven't seen him for
ages, and mother, too; must let the old folks have their
bit of fun. They're good souls, especially father—an amusing old boy. I'm the only child, you know."

"Do you intend to stay there long?"

"I don't think so. It will probably be dull."

"Will you drop in here on your way back?"

"I don't know.... I'll see. Well, what do you say?
Let's go!"

"Just as you like," Arkady said without enthusiasm.

Inwardly he was overjoyed at his friend's proposition,
but deemed it his duty not to show him his true feelings.
Was he not a nihilist after all?

The next day he and Bazarov left for town. The young
members of the Maryino household were sorry at their
going; Dunyasha in fact shed a few tears ... but the old
folks felt relieved.

XII

The town whither our friends repaired was under the
jurisdiction of a young governor, who was both a progressive and a despot, as is often the case in this old Russia of ours. During the first year of his administration he
contrived to fall out both with the gubernia Marshal of
the Nobility—a retired cavalry captain of the guards,
owner of a stud farm and a convivial host—and with his
own subordinates. The resultant dissensions reached such
a pitch that the Ministry at St. Petersburg eventually decided to send a commissioner to investigate the matter
on the spot. The choice fell on Matvei Ilyich Kolyazin,
son of the Kolyazin under whose guardianship the Kirsanov brothers had lived in St. Petersburg. He too was of
the "younger school", that is to say, he had recently turned
forty, but he already aimed at becoming a statesman

and wore a star on either side of his breast—one of them, it is true, a foreign decoration, and nothing much to boast of. Like the governor upon whom he had come to pass his verdict, he was considered a progressive, and though he was a bigwig he did not resemble the majority of bigwigs. He had a very exalted opinion of himself; his vanity knew no bounds, but he bore himself simply, looked kindly, listened indulgently, and laughed so good-humouredly that one might have taken him on sight for a "sterling fellow". When occasion demanded, however, he could put on airs, as the saying goes. "What's wanted is energy," he would assert at such times, *"l'énergie est la première qualité d'un homme d'Etat";* nevertheless, he was usually made a fool of, and there was not an official of any experience who could not lead him by the nose. Matvei Ilyich professed a deep regard for Guizot, and tried to impress all and sundry that he himself did not belong to the conservative bureaucrats and the *routiniers,* that not a single manifestation of public life passed him unnoticed. This kind of coinage he was conversant with. He even followed the trend of modern literature, albeit with an air of careless majesty: thus would a grownup, on meeting a procession of small boys in the street, sometimes join it. Actually Matvei Ilyich had not advanced much beyond those officers of state of Alexandrian days, who prepared for an evening reception at Madame Svechina's St. Petersburg salon by perusing a page of Condillac in the morning, save that his methods were different, more up-to-date. He was a smart courtier, a cunning blade, and nothing more; in business matters he was incompetent, in sagacity poor, but he knew how to look after his own affairs: nobody could lead him by the nose there, which, after all, is the main thing.

Matvei Ilyich received Arkady with the geniality of an enlightened dignitary, nay, we would even say, with facetiousness. He was astonished, however, when he heard that his kinsmen to whom he had extended his invitation, had stayed behind in the country. "Your Dad always was a queer fellow," he said, swinging the tassels of his gorgeous velvet dressing gown, then turning suddenly upon a young official looking the last word in respect-

ability in a close-buttoned uniform sharply enquired with
a preoccupied air: "What is it?" The young man, whose
lips had stuck together through prolonged disuse, rose to
his feet and looked at his superior with a puzzled air.
Having thus nonplussed his subordinate, Matvei Ilyich
paid no further attention to him. Our dignitaries generally like to puzzle their subordinates; the methods they use
to attain that end are varied. One device, a very popular one, or, as the English say, "quite a favourite", is
when the high official suddenly ceases to understand the
simplest words and makes out that he is deaf. He will
ask, for example: "What day is it?"

He will be told with the utmost deference:

"It is Friday today, Your Exc ... c ... c ... lency."

"Eh? What? What's that? What did you say?" that
high functionary will ask with a strained look.

"It is Friday, your Exc ... c ... lency."

"How? What? What's Friday? What about Friday?"

"Friday, your Ex ... ccc ... ccc ... lency, a day of the
week."

"The deuce it is, what will you be teaching me next!"

Matvei Ilyich was, after all, a dignitary, even though
he was considered a liberal.

"I advise you, my friend, to make a call on the Governor," he said to Arkady; "you understand, I'm giving you
this advice not because I entertain old-fashioned ideas
about having to kowtow to those in authority, but simply
because the Governor is a decent fellow; besides, you
would probably like to make the acquaintance of the local
society. You're not a bear, I hope? He's giving a grand
ball the day after tomorrow."

"Will you be at the ball?" asked Arkady.

"He's giving it for me," Matvei Ilyich replied almost
in a tone of regret. "Do you dance?"

"I do, but rather poorly."

"That's a pity. There are some pretty girls around
here, and besides it's a shame for a young man not to
be able to dance. Mind you, I have no old-fashioned notions on that score; I don't for a minute believe that a
man's wit should be in his feet; but Byronism is absurd,
il a fait son temps."

"It's not a question of Byronism at all, Uncle."

"I'll introduce you to the ladies here, I'm taking you under my wing," Matvei Ilyich said and laughed self-complacently. "You'll find it warm there, eh?"

A servant came in and announced the President of the Administrative Chamber, a sweet-eyed old man with a puckered mouth who was a great Nature-lover, especially on a summer day, when, he said, "Every little bee takes a little bribe from every little flower...". Arkady withdrew.

He found Bazarov at the inn, where they had put up, and was a long time persuading him to visit the Governor's. "Ah, well," Bazarov gave in at last. "In for a penny, in for a pound. Let's take a look at the landed gentry, that's what we came for anyway!"

The Governor received the young men affably, but did not offer them a seat and did not sit down himself. He was always busy and bustling; the first thing in the morning he would get into a tight-fitting uniform and an exceedingly tight cravat; he missed his meals and went without sleep in the eternal bustle and excitement of issuing orders. He had been nicknamed Bourdaloue in the gubernia, and this was an allusion not to the famous French preacher, but to the Russian word *bourda*—meaning wish-wash. He invited Kirsanov and Bazarov to the ball at his house, and two minutes later reinvited them, taking them to be brothers and calling them Kaisarov.

As they were going home from the Governor's, a man suddenly jumped out of a passing droshky—a short man, wearing a tunic of the Pan-Slavist mode,* who, with a shout of "Yevgeny Vassilich!" darted up to Bazarov.

"Oh! It's you, Herr Sitnikov," Bazarov said continuing to stride along the pavement. "What wind brings you here?"

"Would you believe it, just sheer accident," the latter replied, and turning to the cab he waved his hand half a dozen times and sang out: "Follow us, cabman, follow us! My father has some business here," he went

* A heavily braided jacket of Hungarian origin affected by adherents of Pan-Slavism in Russia in the middle of the nineteenth century.—*Trans.*

on, skipping over the gutter, "and asked me to attend to it. I heard today that you had arrived and looked you up already." (Indeed, on returning to their rooms, the friends found a visiting card with the corners turned down and with the name of Sitnikov inscribed on one side in French and on the other in Slavonic script.) "I hope you're not coming from the Governor's?"

"You can stop hoping, we're coming straight from him."

"Ah! In that case I'll call on him, too. Yevgeny Vassilich, introduce me to your ... to the...."

"Sitnikov, Kirsanov," Bazarov muttered without stopping.

"Very flattered, I'm sure," began Sitnikov, sidling along, smirking and hastily peeling off his much too elegant gloves. "I've heard a lot about.... I'm an old acquaintance of Yevgeny Vassilich's—his disciple, I might say. I'm indebted to him for my conversion...."

Arkady looked at Bazarov's disciple. There was an air of dull anxious tensity about the small but not disagreeable features of his sleek-looking face; his small, deep-sunk eyes had an intent uneasy stare and his laugh, too, was uneasy—a short, wooden laugh.

"Would you believe it," he went on, "when I first heard Yevgeny Vassilich say we shouldn't recognise any authorities, I was simply delighted ... it was like a revelation! Here, I thought, at last I have found a man! By the way, Yevgeny Vassilich, you must meet a certain lady here, who is entirely capable of understanding you and for whom your visit will be a genuine treat; I believe you've heard of her?"

"Who is she?" Bazarov asked without enthusiasm.

"Kukshina, Eudoxie—Yevdoxia Kukshina. A remarkable character, *émancipée* in the true sense of the word, an advanced woman. Do you know what? Let's call on her right now, all of us. She lives nearby. We'll have lunch there. I don't suppose you've had your lunch yet?"

"Not yet."

"Well, that's fine. She is not living with her husband, you know—quite independent."

"Is she pretty?" Bazarov said.

"Well ... I shouldn't say so."

"Then what the devil are you making us go there for?"

"Ha, ha, that's a good one.... She'll stand us a bottle of champagne."

"Go on! You can soon tell the practical man. By the way, what's your old man doing, still tax-farming?"

"Yes," Sitnikov said, hastily, with a squeaky laugh. "Well, let's go along, shall we?"

"I don't know, really."

"You wanted to see people, go along," Arkady said in an undertone.

"What about yourself, Mr. Kirsanov?" put in Sitnikov. "You've got to come, too; it won't do."

"How can we all suddenly descend on her like that?"

"That's all right. You don't know Kukshina, she's a trump!"

"Will there be a bottle of champagne?" Bazarov asked.

"Three bottles!" Sitnikov cried. "I vouch for that!"

"What with?"

"My head."

"Better your father's moneybags. All right, let's go."

XIII

The small mansion in the Moscow style where Avdotya Nikitishna (or *Yevdoxia*) Kukshina resided, stood in a street that had recently been destroyed by fire; our provincial towns, as anyone knows, catch fire once every five years. Over a visiting card nailed askew on the door was a bellpull, and in the hall the visitors were met by a housemaid—or was it a lady's companion?—in a lace cap—unmistakable signs of the mistress' progressive tendencies. Sitnikov enquired whether Avdotya Nikitishna was at home.

"Is that you, *Victor?*" cried a shrill voice from an adjoining room. "Come in."

The woman in the cap vanished.

"I am not alone," Sitnikov said, throwing a jaunty look at Arkady and Bazarov; he adroitly slipped out of his symbolical tunic from which he emerged in a nondescript sleeveless garment of peasant fashion.

"Never mind," replied the voice. "*Entrez.*"

The young men went in. The room in which they found themselves was more like a study than a drawing room. Papers, letters, thick Russian magazines, for the most part uncut, lay scattered about on dusty tables; cigarette-ends were littered all over the place. On a leather sofa reclined a lady, still young, blond, and somewhat dishevelled, in a none too immaculate silk gown, with large bracelets on her stubby arms and a lace kerchief on her head. She got up from the sofa and, carelessly drawing about her shoulders a velvet pelisse lined with yellowed ermine, she murmured languidly, "Good morning, *Victor*," and shook Sitnikov's hand.

"Bazarov, Kirsanov," he said, imitating Bazarov's jerky manner of speech.

"Delighted," said Kukshina, staring at Bazarov with round eyes, 'twixt which was lonesomely perched a pink blob of a turned-up nose, and added: "I've heard of you," and shook hands with him too.

Bazarov made a wry face. There was nothing repulsive about the dowdy little figure of the emancipated woman, but the expression of her face had an unpleasant effect. One almost felt like asking: "What's the matter, are you hungry? Or are you bored? Or are you nervous? What are you acting funny for?" Like Sitnikov she did not seem to be at all happy in her mind. She spoke and moved about in a manner that was at once over-free and awkward; evidently she considered herself a good-natured simple creature, and yet, whatever she did, one always had the impression that she was doing the very thing she did not want to do; she seemed to be doing everything, as children say, on purpose—that is to say, not simply, not naturally.

"Yes, I've heard about you, Bazarov," she repeated. (She had the habit, peculiar to many provincial and Moscow ladies, of addressing men by their surnames from the very first day of their acquaintance.) "Would you like a cigar?"

"Cigars are all right," said Sitnikov, who by this time was lolling in an armchair with one leg perched on his knee, "but let's have some lunch. We're terribly hungry; and what do you say to a bottle of champagne?"

"Sybarite," Yevdoxia said, laughing. (When she laughed she bared her upper gums.) "He is a sybarite, Bazarov, isn't he?"

"I like the comforts of life," Sitnikov declared pompously. "That does not prevent me from being a liberal."

"But it does, it does!" Yevdoxia cried, yet ordered her maid to attend to both the lunch and the champagne. "What do you think about it?" she added, addressing Bazarov. "I'm sure you share my opinion."

"Certainly not," Bazarov retorted. "A piece of meat is better than a piece of bread, even from the chemical standpoint."

"Do you go in for chemistry? I'm crazy about it. I've even invented a mastic of my own."

"A mastic? You?"

"Yes, I. Do you know what for? To make dolls' heads, so's they won't break. I am a practical person too, you know. But it's not ready yet. I must look up Liebig. By the way, have you read Kislyakov's article on female labour in the *Moskovskiye Vedomosti*? You must read it. You're interested in the problem of women's rights, aren't you? And the schools, too? What does your friend do? What's his name?"

Madame Kukshina let fall her questions one after the other with a languid carelessness, and without waiting for a reply; spoiled children speak like that to their nurses.

"My name is Arkady Nikolaich Kirsanov," Arkady said, "and I don't do anything."

Yevdoxia laughed.

"Isn't that charming! Why don't you smoke? Do you know, Victor, I'm cross with you."

"What for?"

"I hear you've been praising George Sand again. An unenlightened woman, that's all she is! You can't compare her to Emerson! She has no ideas about education, or physiology, or anything. I'm sure she never heard of embryology—a pretty thing not to know these days!" (Yevdoxia even threw up her hands.) "Ah, what a splendid article Yelisevich has written on that subject! He's a gentleman of genius!" (Yevdoxia constantly used the word "gentleman" instead of "man".) "Bazarov, sit down on

the sofa next to me. You may not know it, but I'm terribly afraid of you. . . ."

"And why—if I may ask?"

"You are a dangerous gentleman: you're so critical.
Goodness gracious. It's funny, my talking like some coun-
try lady from the backwoods. But I really am a landlady.
I manage the estate myself, and would you believe it, my
steward, Yerofei, is a remarkable type—just like Cooper's
Pathfinder: there's a kind of natural simplicity about him!
I've settled here for good; dreadful town, don't you think
so? But what can you do!"

"It's as good as any other," Bazarov said coolly.

"Such petty interests—that's the worst about it! I used
to spend the winter in Moscow . . . but my spouse, M'sieu'
Kukshin, has now set up house there. Besides, Moscow
nowadays . . . somehow, it's not what it used to be. I was
thinking of going abroad; I very nearly went last year."

"To Paris, of course?" Bazarov said.

"To Paris and Heidelberg."

"Why Heidelberg?"

"Oh, but Bunsen's there!"

Here Bazarov found himself at a loss.

"*Pierre* Sapozhnikov . . . do you know him?"

"No, I don't."

"Oh, I say, *Pierre* Sapozhnikov—he's always at Lydia
Khostatova's."

"I don't know her either."

"Well, he offered to accompany me. Thank God, I'm
independent, I have no children. . . . What's that I said?—
Thank God! On second thought, that doesn't matter."

Yevdoxia rolled a cigarette with tobacco-stained fingers, licked it down, sucked it, and lit up. The maid came
in with a tray.

"Ah, here's lunch! Will you have a snack first? Victor,
uncork the bottle—that's in your line."

"Yes, so it is," Sitnikov mumbled and laughed again
shrilly.

"Are there any pretty women here?" Bazarov asked,
draining his glass.

"Yes," answered Yevdoxia, "but they're all so empty-
headed. Take *mon amie* Odintsova, for instance—she's

not bad looking. It's a pity her reputation is not quite. . . .
But that's not so bad—the thing is she has no breadth of
outlook, no independent views, nothing. Our entire system of education should be changed. I've been thinking of
that: our women are very badly brought up."

"It's a hopeless case," put in Sitnikov. "They deserve
nothing but contempt, and that's what I feel for them—
absolute and utter contempt!" (To be able to feel contempt and to vent that feeling was a pleasure Sitnikov
revelled in; especially did he attack women, never sus-
pecting that a few months hence would find him grovel-
ling before his own wife for no other reason than that she
was née Princess Durdoleosova.) "Not one of them would
be able to understand our conversation; not one of them
is worth the breath we serious men waste on them!"

"But there is no need for them to understand our conversation at all," Bazarov said.

"What are you talking about?" queried Yevdoxia.

"Pretty women."

"What? Then you are of the same opinion as Proud-
hon?"

Bazarov drew himself up haughtily.

"I share no one's opinions. I have my own."

"To hell with authorities!" Sitnikov shouted, glad of
the opportunity to say something brave in the presence
of a man to whom he played the sycophant.

"But even Macaulay. . ." Kukshina began.

"To hell with Macaulay!" Sitnikov yelled. "Are you
defending those petticoats?"

"Not petticoats, but the rights of women, which I have
sworn to defend to the last drop of my blood."

"To hell!—" but here Sitnikov broke off. "I'm not dis-
puting that," he muttered.

"No, I can see you are a Pan-Slavist!"

"No, I'm not a Pan-Slavist, though, of course. . . ."

"No! no! no! You are a Pan-Slavist. You're an advo-
cate of the Domostroy.* All you need is a horsewhip to
lay about you!"

"A horsewhip's not a bad thing," Bazarov interposed,
"but we've come to the last drop. . . ."

* An ancient Russian code of worldly wisdom.—*Trans.*

"Of what?" broke in Yevdoxia.

"Of champagne, my dear Avdotya Nikitishna, of champagne—not of your blood."

"I can't stand it when women are attacked," Yevdoxia went on. "It's terrible, terrible. Instead of attacking them you'd do better to read Michelet's *De l'amour*. It's wonderful! Gentlemen, let's talk about love," Yevdoxia added, letting her arm drop languidly on a rumpled sofa cushion.

A sudden silence fell.

"No, why talk about love," Bazarov said. "You just mentioned Odintsova.... That's what you called her, I believe? Who's that lady?"

"Oh, she's charming! Just sweet!" squealed Sitnikov. "I'll introduce you to her. Very clever girl, awfully rich, and a widow. Unfortunately, she's not quite developed yet: she should become more closely acquainted with our Yevdoxia. Here's to your health, *Eudoxie*! Let's clink! *Et toc, et toc, et tin-tin-tin! Et toc, et toc, et tin-tin-tin!!...*"

"Victor, you're a naughty boy."

The lunch was a protracted affair. The first bottle of champagne was followed by a second, then a third and even a fourth. Yevdoxia chattered away without pause; Sitnikov echoed whatever she said. They talked a good deal about marriage—as to whether it was a prejudice or a crime, and whether people were born alike or not, and what was individuality. Matters eventually reached a point when Yevdoxia, flushed with wine and thumping the keys of a discordant piano with a click of her flat-nailed fingers, started to sing in a raucous voice, first some Gypsy songs and then Seymour-Schiff's romanza: "Granada Slumbers On", while Sitnikov wrapped a scarf round his head and at the words:

> *"Let thy lips, dear, with mine*
> *In fiery kiss be sealed"*

imitated a languishing lover.

Arkady could stand it no longer.

"Gentlemen, this is beginning to look like Bedlam," he remarked aloud.

Bazarov, who had occasionally thrown in an ironical remark—being more engrossed with the champagne than anything else—yawned outright, rose, and, without taking leave of the hostess, left the room followed by Arkady. Sitnikov dashed out after them.

"Well, what do you say, what do you say?" he asked, hopping fawningly from side to side. "Didn't I tell you? A remarkable woman! We could do with more of them like her. She is in a way an example of the highest morality."

"And is that establishment of *thy* father's also a sample of the highest morality?" asked Bazarov, pointing to a pothouse which they happened to be passing.

Sitnikov laughed his squealing laugh again. He was terribly ashamed of his origin, and was not sure whether he should feel flattered or offended at Bazarov's unexpected familiarity.

XIV

Several days later the ball was held at the Governor's house. Kolyazin was the "hero of the day". The Marshal of the Nobility made known to all and sundry that, strictly speaking, he had come only out of respect for him, while the Governor contrived even at the ball and even when he was sitting still to "issue orders". Kolyazin's geniality could only be equalled by his majestic mien. He beamed on everybody, on some with a shade of loathing, on others with a shade of respect; he acted the gallant *"en vrai chevalier français"* with the ladies and laughed all the time a loud, hearty laugh, as behooves a statesman. He patted Arkady on the back and called him "dear nephew" for all to hear, bestowed on Bazarov, who was rigged out in a rather old dress suit, a fleeting, absent, but indulgent glance and a vague but affable grunt, in which one could only make out an "I" and an "ever so"; he extended a finger to Sitnikov and smiled on him, though with his head averted this time; even for Kukshina, who showed up without a crinoline and in soiled gloves, but with a bird of paradise in her hair, he had a murmured *"enchanté"*.

The place was crowded, and there were plenty of gentlemen dancing partners; the civilians were mostly "wallflowers", but the military danced assiduously, particularly one of them who had spent six weeks in Paris where he had picked up some racy ejaculations such as *"Zut"*, *"Ah fichtrre"*, *"pst, pst, mon bibi"*, and so forth. He pronounced them to perfection, with real Parisian *chic*, yet he would say *"si j'aurais"* when he meant *"si j'avais"*, use the word *"absolument"* in the sense of *certainly*, in short, he spoke that Russian corruption of French which so amuses Frenchmen when they are not obliged to assure our fellow-countrymen that we speak their language like angels, *"comme des anges"*.

Arkady, as we know, was a poor dancer, and Bazarov did not dance at all; they both seated themselves in a corner where they were joined by Sitnikov. With a sneer on his face and passing sarcastic remarks he looked insolently round the room, and seemed to be enjoying himself immensely. Suddenly his face changed and, turning to Arkady, he muttered with a guilty look as it were: "Odintsova is here."

Arkady turned and saw a tall woman in a black gown standing in the doorway of the hall. He was struck by the stateliness of her carriage. Her bare arms hung gracefully down the sides of her slender body; a sprig of fuchsia drooped prettily from her gleaming hair on to her sloping shoulders; a pair of limpid eyes looked out intelligently and placidly—yes, placidly not pensively—from under a slightly overhanging clear brow, and her lips were touched by an almost imperceptible smile. Her face seemed to radiate a soft and gentle force.

"Do you know her?" Arkady asked Sitnikov.

"Rather. Would you like to be introduced?"

"I don't mind ... after this quadrille."

Bazarov's attention was also drawn to Odintsova.

"Who's that figure?" he asked. "She looks out of the common run."

After the quadrille was over Sitnikov led Arkady up to Odintsova; obviously, he did not know her so well as he had intimated: his speech was confused and she regarded him in some surprise. But her face assumed an expression of warm interest when Arkady's name was mentioned. She asked whether he was not the son of Nikolai Petrovich.

"Yes, I am."

"I met your father twice and have heard a lot about him," she went on. "I am very glad to meet you."

An adjutant flew up at that instant and invited her to a quadrille. She consented.

"Do you dance?" Arkady asked respectfully.

"Yes. What makes you think I don't? Do I look as old as all that?"

"Oh, no ... but in that case, will you give me the mazurka?"

Odintsova smiled indulgently.

"Very well," she said, looking at Arkady not exactly patronisingly, but as married sisters look upon very young brothers.

Odintsova was not much older than Arkady—she was twenty-nine—but in her presence he felt like a schoolboy, a callow student, as though the difference in their ages was much greater. Matvei Ilyich came up to her with stately mien and honeyed speeches. Arkady fell back but kept his eyes on her all the time, and followed her throughout the quadrille. She spoke with the same ease to her dancing partner as she had to the statesman, gently she nodded her head and turned her eyes and laughed softly once or twice. Her nose was somewhat fleshy, like most Russian noses, and her complexion was not perfectly clear; yet Arkady decided that he had never met a more fascinating woman. The music of her voice kept sounding in his ears; the very folds of her gown hung somehow differently, not as on other women, but more gracefully and flowingly, and her movements were smooth and unaffected.

A feeling of timidity overcame Arkady when, at the first sounds of the mazurka, he took a seat beside the lady, and, striving to make conversation, all he could do was to pat his hair in tongue-tied embarrassment. But his timidity and agitation did not last long; Odintsova's calmness communicated itself to him: in less than a quarter of an hour he was chatting with her easily about his father, about his uncle, about life in St. Petersburg and in the country. Odintsova listened with an air of polite sympathy, slightly opening and closing her fan; his conversation was interrupted when she was invited now and again to dance; Sitnikov, among others, invited her twice. She would come back to her seat again, pick up her fan, without any visible sign of quickened breathing, and Arkady would resume the conversation, filled with a sense of elation at being near her, speaking to her, looking into her eyes, gazing at her beautiful brow and the whole of her sweet, grave and intelligent face. She spoke little herself, but her words showed a knowledge of the world; from some of her remarks Arkady inferred that this young woman had lived through and thought over a good deal.

"Who was that standing with you, when Mr. Sitnikov led you up to me?" she asked him.

"Why, did you notice him?" Arkady asked in his turn. "He has a fine face, hasn't he? His name's Bazarov, he's a friend of mine."

And Arkady began talking about "his friend".

He spoke of him in such detail and with so much enthusiasm, that Odintsova turned round and regarded him closely. Meanwhile the mazurka was drawing to a close. Arkady was sorry to lose his partner: he had spent such a pleasant hour with her! True, during all that time, he had been aware of an undercurrent of condescension on her part, as of something he should be grateful for . . . but the hearts of the young are not oppressed by such sensations.

The music stopped.

"*Merci,*" Odintsova said rising. "You have promised to come and see me—bring your friend along with you. I'm very curious to meet a man who has the courage to believe in nothing."

The Governor came up to Odintsova, announced that supper was ready, and offered her his arm with a preoccupied air. She looked back at Arkady with a parting smile and a nod as she moved away. He made her a low bow, gazed at her retreating figure (how shapely it looked in the clinging black silk with its greyish sheen) and, thinking to himself "she has already forgotten my existence", he experienced a feeling of gentle resignation. . . .

"Well?" Bazarov asked Arkady as soon as the latter had joined him in their corner. "Did you have a good time? A gentleman has just been telling me that this lady is—oh-ho-ho!; he looked like a fool to me, though. What's your opinion—is she really oh-ho-ho?"

"I don't quite understand that definition," Arkady said.

"Don't be such an innocent!"

"Well then, I don't understand that gentleman of yours. Odintsova is very charming, to be sure, but she's so cold and reserved, that. . . ."

"Still waters run deep, you know!" Bazarov threw in. "You say she's cold. That just suits your taste—you are fond of ice cream, aren't you?"

"Perhaps," Arkady muttered. "I'm no judge of that. She wants to meet you and asked me to bring you down to see her."

"I can imagine the colours you painted me in! You did the right thing, though. Take me down. Whatever she is, a provincial lioness, or an *émancipée* of the Kukshina type, she certainly has shoulders the likes of which I haven't set eyes on for a long time."

Bazarov's cynicism jarred on Arkady, but—as often happens—he rebuked his friend for something entirely different to what he actually disliked in him.

"Why don't you want to admit freedom of thought in women?" he said in a low tone.

"Because, my dear chap, as far as I can see, only scarecrows go in for free thought among women."

With that the conversation ended. The two young men left immediately after supper. Kukshina sent them a nervously spiteful though half-timid kind of laugh: her vanity had been deeply wounded by the fact that neither of them had paid her any attention. She was last to leave the ball, and after three in the morning danced a polka-mazurka with Sitnikov in the Parisian style, with which edifying spectacle the Governor's gala ball came to an end.

XV

"Let's see what species of mammals this person belongs to," Bazarov was saying to Arkady the next day as they mounted the stairs of Odintsova's hotel. "My nose tells me there's something wrong here."

"I'm surprised at you!" Arkady cried. "Do you mean to say, that you, Bazarov, are so narrow-minded as to believe. . . ."

"Don't be so funny!" Bazarov broke in carelessly. "It's time you knew that in our idiom 'wrong' means 'right'. It's all grist to the mill. You were telling me yourself today about the odd circumstances of her marriage, though, to my way of thinking, there's nothing odd about marrying a rich old man; on the contrary, it's a sensible thing to do. I don't believe town gossip; but I like to think, as our educated Governor puts it, that there's something in it."

Arkady said nothing and knocked at the door. A young servant in livery showed the two friends into a large room, furnished, like all rooms in Russian hotels, in bad taste, but full of flowers. Presently Odintsova came in, wearing a simple morning dress. She looked even younger in the light of the spring sun. Arkady introduced Bazarov and noted, with secret surprise, that he seemed to feel embarrassed, while Odintsova was perfectly at her ease, just as she had been the night before. Bazarov, conscious of his embarrassment, felt annoyed. "Well, I never—overawed by a petticoat!" he thought, and, lolling in an armchair no whit worse than Sitnikov, he began talking with exaggerated nonchalance, while Odintsova regarded him steadily with her clear eyes.

Anna Sergeyevna Odintsova was born of Sergei Nikolayevich Loktev, a notorious beau, adventurer and gambler, who after keeping it up and cutting a figure for fifteen years in St. Petersburg and Moscow, ended by losing his last kopek and being obliged to retire into the country where, however, he shortly died, leaving a very scant property to his two daughters—Anna, aged twenty, and Katerina, aged twelve. Their mother, who came of an impoverished family of princes, died in St. Peters

burg when her husband was still in his prime. Anna's
plight, on the death of her father, was a difficult one.
The brilliant education which she had received in St.
Petersburg had not equipped her for housekeeping and
estate management and all the cares of life in rustic
obscurity. She knew no one in the whole parish, and
had no one to seek advice from. Her father had shunned
his neighbours, whom he had despised and who had despised him, each in their own way. She did not lose her
head, however, and promptly invited her mother's sister—Princess Avdotya Stepanovna X— to live with them.
The latter was a spiteful, snobbish old lady, who, on
taking up her abode in her niece's house, took for herself all the best rooms, grumbled and complained from
morning till night, and never took a walk in the garden
unattended by her only serf, a sour-faced lackey in a
shabby pea-green livery with sky-blue galloons and a
cocked hat. Anna patiently bore all her aunt's whims, and
leisurely set about her sister's upbringing, seemingly reconciled to the idea of wasting her youth in retirement.
But fate decreed otherwise. She happened to catch the
eye of a certain Odintsov, a very rich man of about six
and forty, an eccentric hypochondriac, stout, heavy and
sour, though neither stupid nor ill-natured; he fell in love
with her and proposed. She consented to become his
wife; he lived with her for about six years, and on his
death bequeathed to her his whole fortune. Anna Sergeyevna stayed on in the country for about a year after
his death, then went abroad with her sister, but visited
only Germany; feeling homesick, she came back to live at
her beloved Nikolskoye, within forty versts of the town
of N—. There she had a fine richly appointed house with
a beautiful garden and greenhouses; the late Odintsov had
never denied himself anything. Anna Sergeyevna rarely
made an appearance in town, going there usually on
business and then only for a short time. She was not popular in the gubernia; her marriage with Odintsov had
created quite a stir, and many cock-and-bull stories were
spun about her; she was said to have abetted her father
in his sharp practices, and had been induced to go abroad, it was insinuated, in order to hush up a scandal,

"Draw your own conclusions!" shocked gossipmongers
would wind up. "She's been through fire and water," it
was said of her; and the provincial wag was known to
have added: "and boiling oil." All this gossip reached
her ears, but she ignored it: hers was an independent and
rather determined character.

Odintsova sat back in her chair with her hands folded,
listening to Bazarov. He was rather unusually talkative
and was patently putting himself out to entertain, which
gave Arkady more cause for wonder. He could not decide whether Bazarov was succeeding in his purpose or
not. Anna Sergeyevna's face betrayed nothing of what
was passing in her mind: she preserved throughout the
same unchanged subtle expression of friendliness; her
lovely eyes were alight with attention but it was a placid
attention. Bazarov's affected manners during the first few
minutes of his visit had struck her unpleasantly, like a
bad odour or a strident sound; but she was quick to perceive that he was feeling embarrassed, a fact which she
even found flattering. Vulgarity alone she shrank from,
and vulgarity was not one of Bazarov's faults. This was
a day of surprise for Arkady. He had expected Bazarov
to talk with such a clever woman as Odintsova about his
convictions and opinions; indeed, she had herself expressed a wish to meet a man "who has the courage to
believe in nothing"; instead of which here was Bazarov
discussing medicine, homeopathy and botany. Odintsova,
it appeared, had not been wasting her time in seclusion:
she had read some good books and her Russian was excellent. She began speaking about music, but finding that
Bazarov rejected art, she gently led the way back to
botany, though Arkady had started talking about the significance of folk melodies. Odintsova still treated him like
a younger brother: it was as though she merely appreciated
in him the kindliness and artlessness of youth, nothing
more. The conversation, unhurried, diverse, and animated,
lasted over three hours.

Our friends at length got up to take their leave. Anna
Sergeyevna regarded them with a friendly look, held out
to both of them her beautiful white hand and, after a
moment's thought, said with a hesitant, but kindly smile:

"If you're not afraid of being bored, gentlemen, come and see me at Nikolskoye."

"Oh, I say, Anna Sergeyevna," Arkady cried, "I'd consider it one of the greatest joys. . . ."

"And you, M'sieu' Bazarov?"

Bazarov merely bowed—and Arkady, as a last surprise, saw that his friend was blushing.

"Well," he said to him out in the street, "do you still believe that she's 'oh-ho-ho'?"

"I don't know what to make of her! She's all frozen up!" retorted Bazarov, adding, after a pause: "Milady, the grand duchess. All she needs is a train behind her and a coronet on her head."

"Our grand duchesses don't speak Russian like that," Arkady said.

"She's been through the mill, my dear chap, she's had a taste of our bread."

"Say what you like, but she's sweet," Arkady said.

"A gorgeous body!" Bazarov continued. "What a study for the dissecting room."

"Stop that, Yevgeny, for God's sake! There's a limit, you know."

"All right, don't get the wind up, mollycoddle. Anyway, she's first rate. Must go down and see her."

"When?"

"What about the day after tomorrow? What's the use of hanging around here? To drink champagne with Kukshina? Or to flap our ears at that Liberal dignitary, the relative of yours? The day after tomorrow then let it be. By the way, my father's bit of a farmstead is not far from there. It's the Nikolskoye on the N— road, isn't it?"

"Yes."

"*Optime*. Don't let's dawdle; only fools dawdle—and wise birds. A gorgeous body, by gad!"

Three days later the two friends were on their way to Nikolskoye. It was a bright day, not too hot, and the sleek little stage horses trotted along at a brisk pace, swinging their plaited tails. Arkady gazed down the road and smiled, he knew not why.

"Congratulate me," Bazarov suddenly exclaimed, "it's the 22nd of June today, my Saint's Day. We'll see what luck he'll bring me. They're waiting for me at home today," he added, dropping his voice. "Never mind, let them wait!"

XVI

The country house in which Anna Sergeyevna lived stood on an open hillside within a stone's throw of a yellow brick church with a green roof, white columns and fresco paintings over the portal representing the Resurrection of Christ in the "Italian" manner. In the foreground was the prone figure of a swarthy helmeted warrior, remarkable for the rotundity of his contours. Beyond the church a long straggling village stretched in two rows with here and there a chimney pot projecting above the thatched roofs. The manor house was built in the same style as the church, a style commonly known with us as Alexandrian; the house, too, was painted yellow and had a green roof, white columns and a frontal with a blazon on it. The provincial architect had designed both buildings with the approval of the late Odintsov, who tolerated no silly and fanciful, as he expressed it, innovations. The house was flanked on both sides by the dark trees of an old garden, while a drive lined by trimmed fir trees led up to the entrance.

Our friends were met in the hallway by two stalwart footmen in livery, one of whom immediately ran off in search of the butler. The butler, a fat man in a black frock coat, promptly answered the call and conducted the guests up a carpeted staircase to their room containing two bedsteads and all the necessary toilet articles. This was apparently a well-regulated house: everything was spick and span, everything discreetly fragrant, like the waiting rooms of a ministry.

"Anna Sergeyevna requests you to join her in half an hour," announced the butler. "Is there anything you wish in the meantime?"

"No, nothing, my dear man," Bazarov answered, "unless you'd be good enough to fetch a glass of vodka."

"Yes, sir," the butler said somewhat surprised, his boots creaking as he withdrew.

"What *grand genre!*" Bazarov said. "I believe that's what it's called in your set? Grand duchess is about right."

"A fine grand duchess," Arkady retorted, "who straightway invites a couple of priceless aristocrats like you and me."

"Especially me, a coming bonesetter, son of a bonesetter and a deacon's grandson. You know that I'm the grandson of a deacon, I suppose?" And added after a brief pause with curling lip: "Like Speransky. She certainly indulges herself, that lady, I must say! Aren't we expected to appear in dress suits?"

Arkady merely shrugged, but he, too, felt a bit uncomfortable.

Half an hour later Bazarov and Arkady went down into the drawing room. This was a spacious, airy room, rather luxuriously, but none too tastefully furnished. The massive expensive furniture was ranged in the conventional prim manner along the walls, which were papered in brown with a gold pattern; the late Odintsov had ordered it in Moscow through a friend and agent of his, a wine merchant. Over the central divan hung a portrait of a fat fairhaired gentleman who seemed to be looking down the visitors with displeasure.

"The old boy, I suppose," Bazarov whispered to Arkady and, wrinkling his nose, added: "Shouldn't we beat a retreat?"

At this moment the hostess entered. She was wearing a light barège dress; her hair, brushed smoothly back from the ears, imparted a girlish look to her clear fresh face.

"Thank you for having kept your word to stay as my guests," she began. "It's not bad here, really. I'll introduce you to my sister; she plays the piano well. That doesn't interest you, M'sieu' Bazarov, but M'sieu' Kirsanov, I believe, is fond of music; besides my sister I have an old aunt living with me, and one of the neighbours sometimes drops in for a game of cards; there you have all our company. And now let us sit down."

Odintsova made this little speech with peculiar distinctness, as though she had learned it by heart; then she turned to Arkady. Her mother, it appeared, had known Arkady's mother and had been her confidante during Nikolai Petrovich's courtship. Arkady began speaking warmly about his mother, while Bazarov proceeded to examine the albums. "What a meek lamb I've become," he said to himself.

A beautiful borzoi in a blue collar ran into the drawing room, its claws pattering on the floor, followed by a girl of about eighteen, dark-haired and warm-skinned, with a somewhat round but attractive face and small dark eyes. She carried a basket filled with flowers.

"Here's my sister, Katya," Odintsova said with a nod in her direction.

Katya curtsied, sat down beside her sister, and began to sort out the flowers. The borzoi, whose name was Fifi, went up to each of the guests in turn, wagging its tail and thrusting its cold muzzle into their hands.

"Did you pick all those yourself?" Odintsova asked.

"Yes," replied Katya.

"Is auntie coming down to tea?"

"Yes, she is."

When Katya spoke she smiled very charmingly, in a shy candid way, and had an amusing stern habit of looking upward. Everything about her was delightfully fresh and unsophisticated—her voice, the tender down on her face, her pink hands with the pale rings on the palms, and the slightly contracted shoulders. She was constantly changing colour and taking breath.

Odintsova turned to Bazarov.

"You're looking at those pictures out of politeness, Yevgeny Vassilich," she began. "It doesn't amuse you. You'd better draw closer to us and let's discuss something."

Bazarov drew his chair closer.

"What would you like to discuss?" he asked.

"Whatever you like. I warn you that I love an argument."

"You?"

"Yes, I. You seem surprised. Why is that?"

"Because, as far as I can judge, you are of a calm, cold disposition, and one has to let himself be carried away in an argument."

"You have got to know me rather quickly, haven't you? For one thing, I am impatient and insistent—ask Katya; secondly, I am easily carried away."

Bazarov looked at her.

"Perhaps, you know best. So you want to argue—all right. I've been looking at the views of Saxonian Switzerland in your album; you said that they couldn't amuse me. You said that because you don't credit me with artistic feeling—it's true, I don't possess any; but those views might interest me geologically, as a study of mountain structure, for instance."

"Excuse me; as a geologist, you'd sooner refer to a book, to some special work on the subject, but not to a drawing."

"A drawing would show me graphically, what a book would tell me on ten pages."

Anna Sergeyevna said nothing for a while.

"Haven't you really any sense of the artistic at all?" she said, her elbows on the table, thereby bringing her face closer to Bazarov's. "How do you manage without?"

"What's the use of it, I'd like to know?"

"Well, if only to study and know people."

Bazarov smiled ironically.

"For one thing, experience can do that for me; and in the second place, let me tell you, the study of personalities is a waste of time. All people are alike, both in body and soul; every one of us has a brain, a spleen, a heart, and lungs similarly arranged; and the so-called cardinal virtues are the same in all of us; slight modifications do not count. One human specimen is sufficient to judge the rest by. People are like trees in a forest; no botanist is going to bother over each individual birch tree."

Katya, who was leisurely selecting flowers for a nosegay, looked up at Bazarov with a perplexed expression, and encountering his swift, careless glance, coloured to the roots of her hair. Anna Sergeyevna shook her head.

"Trees in a forest," she repeated. "In your opinion then, there's no difference between a foolish person and a clever one, between a good and a bad person?"

"Yes, there is: as between a sick person and a healthy one. A consumptive's lungs are not in the condition that yours or mine are, although they are made the same way. We know approximately what causes bodily ailments; moral disease is merely the result of bad education and all the nonsense that people's heads are crammed with from childhood; in short, the outrageous state of society is at the bottom of it all. Improve society, and there will be no disease."

Bazarov said all this with an air as if he were thinking to himself: "Whether you believe me or not, I don't care!" He smoothed his whiskers with a slow movement of his long fingers, while his eyes moved restlessly about the room.

"And you believe," said Anna Sergeyevna, "that when society is improved there will no longer be any foolish or wicked people?"

"In any case, under a sensible arrangement of society it is immaterial whether a person is foolish or clever, wicked or good."

"Yes, I understand; we shall all have the same kind of spleens."

"Exactly, madam."

Odintsova turned to Arkady.

"And what is your opinion, Arkady Nikolayevich?"

"I agree with Yevgeny," he replied.

Katya regarded him from under knitted brows.

"You astonish me, gentlemen," Odintsova said, "but we shall discuss that another time. I hear auntie coming down for tea; we must spare her ears."

Princess X—, Anna Sergeyevna's aunt, a slight, frail woman with a wizened little face and staring malicious eyes under a grey scratch wig, entered the room, and with barely a nod to the guests, lowered herself into a wide velvet-covered armchair which no one else dared sit in. Katya put a stool under her feet; the old lady did not thank her, did not even glance up, her hands merely stirred under the yellow shawl, which almost enveloped her puny body. The princess was fond of yellow; even the ribbons on her cap were a vivid yellow.

"How did you sleep, auntie?" Odintsova said, raising her voice.

"That dog is here again," the old woman grumbled, and seeing Fifi make several uncertain steps in her direction, she exclaimed: "Shoo, shoo!"

Katya called Fifi and opened the door.

Fifi bounded out joyously, anticipating a stroll, but finding herself outside alone began to scratch at the door and whine. The princess scowled, and Katya had half a mind to go out.

"Tea is ready, I should imagine?" Odintsova said. "Let us go, gentlemen; auntie, come and have tea."

The princess rose without a word and was first to leave the room. The rest followed her into the dining room. A liveried servant boy noisily pulled out another sacred and cushioned armchair into which the princess deposited herself; Katya, who was pouring out the tea, gave her hers first, in a teacup decorated with a coat-of-arms. The old lady put some honey in her tea (she considered it wasteful to have sugar with her tea, although she never spent a kopek on anything) and suddenly asked in a hoarse voice:

"And what does *Prince* Ivan write?"

Nobody answered her. Bazarov and Arkady soon perceived that nobody paid any attention to her, though they treated her with respect. "They keep her for swank, because she's princely spawn," Bazarov thought. After tea Anna Sergeyevna suggested a stroll; but it began to drizzle, and the company, with the exception of the princess, returned to the drawing room. The neighbour who was fond of a game of cards dropped in. He was a stout, grey-haired little man by the name of Porfiry Platonich, very polite and easily amused, with short legs, which looked as if they had been carried out for him. Anna Sergeyevna, who was most of the time in conversation with Bazarov, asked him whether he would care to join them in an old-fashioned game of *preference*. Bazarov consented saying it was necessary to prepare himself for the duties of a country practitioner.

7*

"Take care," observed Anna Sergeyevna, "Porfiry Platonich and I will beat you. And you, Katya," she added, "play something for Arkady Nikolayevich; he is fond of music, and we'll listen, too."

Katya reluctantly crossed over to the piano; and Arkady, who was really fond of music, reluctantly followed her: he had a suspicion that Odintsova was dismissing him, and his heart, as every young man's at his age, had been stirring with a vague languorous feeling, like a presentiment of love. Katya opened the piano, and without looking at Arkady asked in a low voice:

"What would you like me to play for you?"

"Whatever you wish," Arkady answered indifferently.

"What kind of music do you like?" Katya asked again, without changing her position.

"Classical," Arkady answered in the same tone.

"Do you like Mozart?"

"Yes."

Katya took out Mozart's Sonata-Fantasia in C Minor. She played very well, though rather primly and unemotionally. With eyes fixed on the music and teeth clenched hard, she sat rigidly erect, and only towards the end of the sonata her face grew flushed and a wisp of hair uncurled over her dark eyebrow.

Arkady was particularly struck by the finale of the sonata, where the delightful vivacity of the carefree melody is suddenly invaded by a surge of such poignant, almost tragic grief. But the thoughts roused in him by the strains of Mozart's music had nothing to do with Katya. Looking at her, he simply thought: "This young lady doesn't play at all badly, and she's not bad-looking either."

Having finished the sonata, Katya asked, her hands still on the keys: "Enough?" Arkady said he did not dare trouble her any more, and started talking to her about Mozart, asking whether she had chosen that sonata herself or whether somebody had recommended it to her. But Katya answered him in monosyllables; she withdrew into herself. Once she had withdrawn into her shell she was generally long in coming out again; her face on such occasions would wear a dogged, almost dull look. She could not exactly be called shy; she was only mistrustful and slightly cowed by her sister's tutelage, a fact which the latter, of course, never suspected. Arkady bridged an awkward pause by calling Fifi, who had come back into the room, and patting her head with a benevolent smile. Katya busied herself again with her flowers.

Meanwhile, Bazarov was piling up forfeits. Anna Sergeyevna played a skilful hand, and Porfiry Platonich was well able to stand up for himself too. Bazarov's loss, insignificant though it was, was not altogether pleasant. Over supper Anna Sergeyevna once more broached the subject of botany.

"Let us go for a walk tomorrow morning," she said to him. "I want you to tell me the Latin names of wild plants and their properties."

"What do you want the Latin names for?" Bazarov asked.

"There must be order in everything," she replied.

*   *   *

"What a wonderful woman Anna Sergeyevna is!" Arkady exclaimed, alone with his friend in their room.

"Yes," Bazarov answered, "she's a brainy woman. She's seen a thing or two, let me tell you."

"In what sense do you say that, Yevgeny Vassilich?"

"In a good sense, my dear fellow, in a good sense, Arkady Nikolaich! I'm sure she manages her estate splendidly, too. But it's not she who is wonderful, it's her sister."

"What? That dark little thing?"

"Yes, that dark little thing. There's where you have all the freshness, and innocence, and timidity, and reticence and everything else. She's worth taking up. You could mould her into anything you want; but the other one knows all the tricks of the trade."

Arkady said nothing, and each went to bed with his own thoughts.

*   *   *

Anna Sergeyevna, too, was thinking of her guests that evening. She liked Bazarov, liked him for his absence of affection and his very bluntness. She found in him something new, something she had never come across before, and she was habitually curious.

Anna Sergeyevna was a rather queer creature. While having no prejudices or even strong beliefs, she never gave ground and never covered any. She saw many things clearly, many things interested her, but nothing satisfied her completely; she scarcely desired complete satisfaction. Her mind was at once inquisitive and apathetic; her doubts were never allayed to the point of forgetfulness and never grew to the point of anxiety. Had she not been rich and independent she might, perhaps, have thrown herself into the fray and known passion. But she lived an easy life, though at times she felt bored, and her days passed in unhurried procession with only an occasional ripple of excitement. Roseate visions sometimes sprang up before her mind's eye, but she relaxed when they had gone and felt no regrets at their passing. Imagination sometimes carried her away beyond the pale which the decrees of conventional morality permit; but even then her blood coursed unquickened through her calm lovely body. Sometimes, on coming out of a fragrant bath, all warm and languorous, she would fall to musing on life's paltriness, its sorrows, its toil and evils. Her heart would suddenly swell with daring impulses, and noble aspirations; but a current of air would blow from the half-opened window and Anna Sergeyevna would shrink and complain and very nearly lose her temper, and all she wanted was to stop that horrid draught from blowing on her.

Like all women cheated of love, she longed for something, she knew not what. Actually she wanted nothing, although it seemed to her she wanted everything. She could barely stand the late Odintsov (it had been a marriage of convenience on her part, though she would not, perhaps, have consented to become his wife unless she had considered him a good man) and had conceived a

secret loathing for all men, whom she always thought of
as a messy, heavy, limp lot of helplessly tiresome creatures. Somewhere abroad she had once met a handsome
chivalrous-looking young Swede with frank blue eyes
beneath an open brow; he had made a powerful impression on her, but this had not prevented her from returning to Russia.

*   *   *

"A queer man, that medico!" she mused, as she lay in
her luxurious bed under a light silk coverlet, her head
resting on lace-covered pillows. Anna Sergeyevna had
inherited some of her father's love of luxury. She had
been very fond of her sinful but kindhearted parent, and
he had adored her, joking with her as an equal and confiding in her without restraint. She hardly remembered
her mother.

"He's a queer fellow!" she repeated to herself. She
stretched, smiled, clasped her hands behind her head,
then ran her eyes over a page or two of a silly French
novel, dropped the book and fell asleep, all fresh and
cool in her fresh fragrant lingeries.

Soon after breakfast the next morning. Anna Sergeyevna went botanising with Bazarov and did not return until dinner time; Arkady did not go anywhere and spent
nearly an hour with Katya. He had not found her company boring, and she herself had proposed repeating yesterday's sonata; but when Odintsova returned at last and
he caught sight of her, his heart felt a momentary pang.
She came down the garden with a rather tired step; her
cheeks were glowing and her eyes under her round straw
hat were shining brighter than usual. She was toying
with the slender stalk of a wild flower; her light mantle
had slipped to her elbows, and the broad grey ribbons
of her bonnet clung on her breast. Bazarov walked behind, self-assured and careless as usual, but Arkady did
not like the expression of his face, cheerful and even
gentle though it was. Muttering "'morning!" through his

teeth, Bazarov went to his room, while Odintsova absently shook Arkady's hand, and passed on her way.

"Good morning," Arkady thought. "As if we hadn't seen each other today."

XVII

Time (we all know) sometimes flies like a bird, sometimes crawls like a snail; but a man is happiest when he does not even notice whether it passes swiftly or slowly. It was in such a state of mind that Arkady and Bazarov spent fifteen days at Odintsova's. This was partly due to the well-ordered run of life Odintsova had introduced in her home. She strictly adhered to this regulated mode of life and made others do the same. Everything in the course of the day was done at its appointed time. In the morning, punctually at eight, the household assembled for breakfast; between breakfast and lunch everybody did as he pleased, while the mistress discussed business with her steward (her estate worked on the quitrent basis), the butler and the housekeeper. Before dinner the company gathered once more for a chat or to do some reading; the evening was devoted to walks, cards and music; at half past ten Anna Sergeyevna retired to her room, issued her orders for the morrow, and went to bed. Bazarov did not like this monotonous and rather solemn regularity of the daily life. "It's like moving on rails," he said; the liveried footmen and dignified butlers offended his democratic tastes. He believed that they might as well go the whole hog and dine in the English manner, in full dress and white tie. He once broached the subject with Anna Sergeyevna. She had such a way with her that no one hesitated to speak his mind plainly before her. She heard him out and said: "From your point of view perhaps you are right—in that respect I suppose I am the grand lady; but if you dared to live an unordered life in the country you'd be bored to death," and she went on doing things her own way. Bazarov grumbled; but both he and Arkady found the life in Odintsova's house so pleasantly easy precisely because things "moved on rails". Indeed, a change had taken place in both young men from

the very first days of their sojourn at Nikolskoye. Bazarov, who was obviously in Anna Sergeyevna's good
graces, though she rarely agreed with him, began to reveal
signs of uneasiness hitherto foreign to him: he was irri-
table, untalkative, sulky, and restless; while Arkady, who
had entirely made up his mind that he was in love with
Odintsova, abandoned himself to a quiet melancholy. This
melancholy, however, did not prevent him from cultivating
Katya's friendship; it even helped him to establish very
pleasant, friendly relations with her. "*She* doesn't appreciate me? Oh, all right! But here's a gentle creature
who doesn't reject me," Arkady thought, and his heart
once more knew the sweetness of generous impulses.
Katya was dimly aware that he sought comfort in her
society and she did not deny either him or herself the innocent pleasure of a half-shy, half-trusting friendship.
When Anna Sergeyevna was present they avoided talking
to each other; Katya always seemed to shrink under her
sister's keen eye, while Arkady, as befits a man in love,
had no attentions for anybody when his beloved was near
at hand; he really felt at home, however, only with Katya. He realised that entertaining Odintsova was a thing
he was not equal to; he was shy and tonguetied when
alone with her, and she did not know what to say to him:
he was too young for her. With Katya, on the contrary,
Arkady was quite at ease; he was indulgent, and gave her
free rein to voice her impressions inspired by music, by
the reading of a book or poetry and similar trifles, himself unaware that these *trifles* attracted him too. Katya
for her part did not interfere with his moping moods.
Arkady enjoyed Katya's company, and Odintsova Bazarov's, and it usually happened that both couples, after
being together for a while would presently drift apart,
especially when out strolling. Katya *adored* nature,
and Arkady loved it too, though he never dared admit
it; Odintsova was indifferent to it, and so was Bazarov.
The fact that our friends were almost constantly separated was not without consequences: their relations underwent a gradual change. Bazarov no longer spoke to
Arkady about Odintsova and even stopped criticising her
"aristocratic airs"; he still spoke highly of Katya, but

advised his friend to restrain her sentimental inclinations; his praise, however, was hurried, his counsels dry,
and altogether he talked much less with Arkady than before. He seemed to be avoiding him, seemed to be
ashamed.

Arkady noticed all this, but kept his opinions to himself.

The actual reason for this "new turn" was the feeling
which Odintsova had inspired in Bazarov, a feeling which
tormented and maddened him, but which he would have
promptly denied with a sneering laugh and cynical remark had anybody even remotely hinted at the possibility
of what was actually happening to him. Bazarov was a
great admirer of women, but love in the ideal or, as he
expressed it, romantic sense, he called tommyrot, unpar-
donable folly; chivalry he looked upon as something in
the nature of a monstrosity or a disease, and on more than
one occasion expressed his surprise that Toggenburg with
all the minnesingers and troubadours had not been put
in a madhouse. "If you like a woman," he said, "try to
get down to brass tacks; if it doesn't come off, never mind,
snap your fingers, there are plenty of others." Odintsova
had caught his fancy; the rumours concerning her, the
freedom and independence of her ideas, her obvious liking for him—all this, one would think, was grist to his
mill; but he soon became aware that he would not be
able to "get down to brass tacks" with her, and as for
snapping his fingers, he found to his dismay that he could
not do it. His pulse quickened at the mere thought of her;
he could easily have come to terms with the pulse, but
something else had happened to him, something he never
would have admitted, something he had always jeered at,
and against which all his pride rose up in arms. When
talking with Anna Sergeyevna he went out of his way to
show his careless scorn for everything romantic, but when
left alone he was shocked to discover the romanticist within himself. He would then go off into the woods, and
stride about there aimlessly, breaking branches as he went
along and cursing both her and himself under his breath;
or else he would creep into the hayloft, and, stubbornly
shutting his eyes, try to force himself to sleep, which, of

course, he did not always succeed in doing. Suddenly he would imagine those chaste arms entwining his neck, those proud lips responding to his kisses, and those profound eyes gazing tenderly—yes, tenderly, into his, and his head would reel, he would forget himself for a moment until indignation would get the better of him. He caught himself at all kinds of "shameful" thoughts, as though the devil were teasing him. At times he thought he noticed a change in Odintsova too, something peculiar in the expression of her face, as if. . . . At this point he would stamp his foot or gnash his teeth and shake his fist in his own face.

As a matter of fact, Bazarov was not wholly mistaken. He had caught Odintsova's fancy; he interested her and she thought of him a great deal. In his absence she was not bored and did not miss him; but she became animated directly he appeared upon the scene; she willingly remained alone with him and willingly talked to him, even when he made her angry or offended her good taste and refined habits. It seemed as if she wanted to test him and herself while she was at it.

One day while walking with her in the garden he suddenly announced gloomily that he intended leaving soon for his father's place in the country. The colour fled from her cheeks, and a pang shot through her heart; so strong a pang that it surprised her and long afterwards she wondered what it could have meant. Bazarov had announced his departure not with the idea of testing her, of seeing what would come of it: he never "made things up". That morning he had seen his father's steward, Timofeich, who had had charge of him when he was a child. This Timofeich, a spry seedy-looking little old man with bleached yellow hair, a red weather-beaten face and tiny drops of moisture in his shrunken eyes, unexpectedly appeared before Bazarov in his short peasant coat of stout grey-blue pilot cloth girdled by a bit of old belt and in tarred high boots.

"Hullo, old bean!" Bazarov had exclaimed.

"Good morning, master Yevgeny Vassilich," the old man had said, and his face suddenly wreathed in wrinkles and lit up with a happy smile.

"What brings you here? You've come for me, I suppose?"

"Goodness gracious, sir, no!" Timofeich mumbled (he bore in mind the strict injunction his master had given him when he set out). "I was going to town on the master's business when I heard about Your Honour being here, so I dropped in on the way—to have a look at your Honour ... but as for bothering you, I'd never think of it!"

"Tell me another one," Bazarov had interrupted him. "Is this on your way to town?"

Timofeich had shifted from one foot to the other and said nothing.

"Is father all right?"

"Yes, sir, thank God."

"And mother?"

"Arina Vlasyevna, too, thank God."

"They're waiting for me, I suppose?"

The little fellow cocked his tiny head.

"Ah Yevgeny Vassilich, how could it be otherwise! As sure as there's a God above, it makes one's heart bleed to look at your parents."

"Well, all right, all right! Don't lay it on. Tell them I'll be coming soon."

"Very good, sir," Timofeich had said with a sigh.

As he left the house he jammed his cap onto his head with the help of both hands, clambered into a ramshackle racing sulky, which he had left standing by the gates, and trotted off, but not in the direction of the town.

＊　＊　＊

That evening Odintsova was sitting in her room with Bazarov, while Arkady paced up and down the drawing room listening to Katya playing. The princess had retired to her room upstairs; she disliked all visitors, and these "wild ones", as she called them, in particular. In the common rooms she merely sulked; but in the privacy of her own chamber, before her maid, she would break out into such violent abuse that the cap on her head together with the wig would start dancing. Odintsova knew this.

"What is this about your going away," she began, "and what about your promise?"

Bazarov started.

"What promise?"

"Have you forgotten? You wanted to give me some lessons in chemistry."

"I'm sorry. My father is expecting me; I can't dally any longer. But you can read Pelouse et Frémy, *Notions générales de climie;* it's a good book and written in simple language. You'll find everything you need there."

"Do your remember telling me that no book was as good as.... I have forgotten how you expressed it, but you know what I mean ... do you remember?"

"I'm sorry!" Bazarov repeated.

"Must you go?" Odintsova said, lowering her voice.

He glanced at her. She had thrown her head back against the armchair with her arms, bared to the elbow, folded on her breast. She looked paler in the light of a solitary lamp screened by a perforated paper shade. The soft folds of her loose white gown enveloped all her form; the tips of her feet, likewise crossed, were barely visible.

"Why should I stay?" Bazarov said.

Odintsova turned her head slightly.

"What do you mean—why? Aren't you enjoying yourself here? Or do you think nobody will be sorry you've gone?"

"I'm sure of it."

Odintsova was silent for a while.

"You are wrong there. Anyway I don't believe you. You couldn't have meant that seriously." Bazarov had not stirred. "Yevgeny Vassilich, why don't you say something?"

"What can I say? I don't think people are worth being sorry about—I all the more."

"Why so?"

"I'm a serious uninteresting man. I'm no good at making conversation."

"You're fishing for compliments, Yevgeny Vassilich."

"It's not my habit. You ought to know that the refinements of life which you cherish so much are beyond me."

Odintsova bit the corner of her handkerchief.

"You may think whatever you like, but I shall find it dull when you go away."

"Arkady will remain," Bazarov said.

Odintsova gave a little shrug.

"I'll find it dull," she repeated.

"Really? At any rate you won't find it dull long."

"What makes you think so?"

"You told me yourself that you are bored only when your routine is upset. You have arranged your life with such impeccable regularity that there can be no room for boredom in it, or yearnings . . . no painful feelings of any kind."

"So you think I'm impeccable . . . I mean, that I have arranged my life so well?"

"Rather! For example: in a few minutes it will strike ten, and I know beforehand that you will drive me away."

"No, I won't, Yevgeny Vassilich. You may remain. Open that window . . . I feel hot."

Bazarov got up and pushed the window. It flew open with a bang. He had not expected it to open so easily; and besides his hands shook. The dark soft night peeped into the room with its almost black sky, its murmuring trees and the fresh smell of the cool sweet air.

"Pull the blind and sit down," Odintsova said. "I want to have a chat with you before you go away. Tell me something about yourself; you never talk about yourself."

"I try to talk to you about useful things, Anna Serge-yevna."

"You are very modest. But I'd like to know something about you and your family, about your father, for whom you are deserting us."

What is she saying all this for? Bazarov thought.

"It's not in the least interesting," he said, "especially for you; we are lowly folk."

"And I am an aristocrat, I suppose?"

Bazarov looked up at her.

"Yes," he said with exaggerated harshness.

She smiled.

"I see you don't know me well enough, though you claim that all people are alike and not worth studying. I

shall tell you my story some day . . . but first tell me about
yourself."

"I don't know you well enough," Bazarov repeated.
"Perhaps you are right; perhaps every person is really a
riddle. Take yourself, for example; you shun society, you
dislike it, yet you invite two students down to stay with
you. Why do you, with your intellect and your beauty,
live in the country?"

"What? What did you say?" Odintsova said quickly.
"With my . . . beauty?"

Bazarov frowned.

"Never mind," he muttered, "I want to say   that I
can't make out why you live in the country?"

"You can't understand it, you say. But you have tried
to explain it to yourself I suppose?"

"Yes . . . I suppose you stay permanently in one place
because you like to pamper yourself, you are fond
of comfort and ease and indifferent to everything
else."

Odintsova smiled again.

"You simply refuse to believe that I am capable of
letting myself go, don't you?"

Bazarov threw her a look from under his brows.

"Out of curiosity, perhaps; nothing else."

"Indeed? Well, now I understand why you and I have
become friends; you're like me, you know."

"You and I have become friends. . ." Bazarov murmured huskily.

"Yes!. . . But I'd forgotten that you wanted to go."

Bazarov rose to his feet. The lamp shone dimly in the
middle of the darkened, fragrant, secluded room; through
the fluttering blind the night poured in its tantalising
freshness and mysterious whisperings. Odintsova did not
stir a limb, but a secret excitement was gradually taking
possession of her. It communicated itself to Bazarov. He
suddenly realised that he was alone with a beautiful
young woman.

"Where are you going?" she said slowly.

He answered nothing and sank back into his chair.

"And so you consider me a cold, pampered, spoiled
thing," she went on in the same tone, without removing

her eyes from the window. "I always thought I was un-happy."

"You unhappy! Why? Surely you don't attach any importance to foul gossip?"

Odintsova frowned. She was annoyed at his having interpreted her in *this* way.

"This gossip does not even amuse me, Yevgeny Vassilich, and I'm too proud to let it annoy me. I'm unhappy because ... I have no desire, no zest for living. You look at me incredulously and are probably thinking: there speaks the 'aristocrat' all dressed up in lace and sitting in a plush armchair. I don't deny that I love what you call comfort and yet I have little zest for life. Try and reconcile those inconsistencies if you can. In any case it's all romanticism to you."

Bazarov shook his head.

"You enjoy good health, independence, wealth; what more do you need? What do you want?"

"What do I want?" Odintsova repeated and sighed. "I am very tired, I am old; it seems as if I have been living for ever so long. Yes, I'm old," she added, gently drawing the ends of her mantle over her bare arms. Her eyes met Bazarov's, and she blushed slightly. "I have so many memories behind me: life in St. Petersburg, wealth, then poverty, then my father's death, my marriage, then a trip abroad, as it should be ... lots of memories, but nothing to remember, and ahead of me a long, long road and no goal.... I don't feel like going on."

"Are you so disillusioned?" asked Bazarov.

"No," Odintsova said slowly, "but I am unsatisfied. I think that if I could form a strong attachment for something...."

"You want to fall in love," Bazarov interrupted her, "but you cannot—that's your misfortune."

Odintsova contemplated the sleeves of her mantle.

"You think I am not capable of falling in love?" she murmured.

"Hardly. Only I shouldn't have called it a misfortune. On the contrary, the person who has had that thing happen to him is the one to be pitied."

"What thing?"

"Falling in love."

"How do you know that?"

"By hearsay," Bazarov said moodily.

You're flirting, he thought; you're bored and so you are teasing me for want of anything better to do, while I. . . . Indeed, his heart contracted with pain.

"And then I suppose you are too demanding," he said, leaning his whole body forward and toying with the fringe of his armchair.

"Perhaps. I believe in everything or nothing. A life for a life. Take mine and give me yours, but there must be no regrets, no drawing back. Otherwise, better not."

"Well," observed Bazarov, "those are fair conditions, and I'm surprised that you haven't yet . . . found what you want."

"Do you think it's so easy to give yourself up utterly?"

"Not if you stop to reflect, and bide your time, and put too high a value upon yourself; but it's quite easy to give yourself up without thinking."

"How do you expect a person not to prize himself? If I am not worth anything, of what use is my devotion to anybody?"

"That's not my concern; let the other person decide whether I'm worth anything or not. The main thing is to be capable of surrender."

Odintsova leaned forward in her chair.

"You speak as though you have been through it yourself," she said.

"I just passed an opinion, Anna Sergeyevna; all this, you know, is not in my line."

"But would you be capable of giving yourself up?"

"I don't know—I shouldn't like to boast."

Odintsova made no reply and Bazarov fell silent. The sounds of the piano floated across to them from the drawing room.

"Katya is playing rather late today," Odintsova observed.

Bazarov got up.

"Yes, it is rather late and time for you to retire."

"Wait a minute, what is the hurry? I have something to tell you."

"What is it?"

"Wait a minute," Odintsova whispered.

Her gaze rested on Bazarov; she seemed to be studying him closely.

He took a turn about the room, then suddenly went up to her, hurriedly said "Good-bye," squeezed her hand so that she nearly cried out, and strode out. She lifted her crushed fingers to her lips and blew on them; obeying a sudden impulse she jumped up from the armchair and ran swiftly to the door, as if to call Bazarov back. A maid came in with a decanter on a silver tray. Odintsova stopped, dismissed her, then returned to her seat and her thoughts. Her plait had come undone and fell snake-like on her shoulder. The lamp burned for a long time in Anna Sergeyevna's room and for a long time she sat motionless, only now and then stroking her arms nipped by the cold air of night.

* * *

Bazarov came into his bedroom, two hours later, dishevelled and gloomy, his boots wet with dew. He found Arkady at the writing table with a book in his hand, his coat buttoned right up.

"Haven't you gone to bed yet?" he said with a shade of annoyance.

"You were sitting with Anna Sergeyevna a long time tonight," said Arkady, ignoring his question.

"Yes, I was with her all the time you and Katya were playing the piano."

"I wasn't playing," Arkady began, then fell silent. He felt the tears welling up to his eyes, and he did not want to cry in front of his sarcastic friend.

XVIII

The next day when Odintsova came down to breakfast, Bazarov sat bent over his cup for a long time, then suddenly looked up at her. She turned to him as though he had nudged her, and he thought her face looked paler. She presently retired to her room and did not come down again till lunch. It had been raining since the morning and it was impossible to go out for a walk. The whole company gathered in the drawing room. Arkady found a recent issue of a magazine and began reading it aloud. The princess, as usual, first looked surprised, as though he were doing something indecorous, then glared at him, but he paid no attention to her.

"Yevgeny Vassilich," said Anna Sergeyevna, "come up to my room. I wanted to ask you. . . . You spoke yesterday about a manual. . . ."

She got up and made for the door. The princess looked round with an expression that seemed to say: "Just look how amazed I am!" then went back to stare at Arkady, but he raised his voice and, exchanging glances with Katya who sat next to him, went on reading.

*   *   *

Odintsova walked swiftly to her study. Bazarov followed her with downcast eyes, and only his ear caught the faint swish and rustle of her silk gown gliding in front of him. Odintsova lowered herself into the same armchair which she had occupied the night before, and Bazarov, too, sat down in his old seat.

"What was the name of that book?" she asked after a slight pause.

"Pelouse et Frémy, *Notions générales. . .*" replied Bazarov. "I'd also recommend Ganot, *Traité élémentaire de physique expérimentale.* The plates in this work are clearer and as a textbook it is. . . ."

Odintsova put out her hand.

"Excuse me, Yevgeny Vassilich, but I didn't call you here to discuss textbooks. I wanted to resume the talk we had yesterday. You went away so suddenly. You won't be bored, will you?"

"I'm at your service, Anna Sergeyevna. But what it we were talking about yesterday?"

Odintsova threw him a sidelong glance.

"We were talking, I believe, about happiness. I was telling you about myself. Speaking of happiness, by the way, why is it that even when we are enjoying, say, some good music, or a lovely evening, or a conversation with people we like—why does it all seem more like a hint of some vast happiness existing elsewhere, rather than real happiness, that is, the kind we ourselves possess? Why is it? Or perhaps you haven't experienced anything of the sort?"

"You know the saying: 'our neighbour's crop seems better than our own'," retorted Bazarov. "You admitted yourself yesterday that you were unsatisfied. Such thoughts really don't enter my mind."

"Perhaps you think them absurd?"

"No. They simply don't enter my mind."

"Really? Do you know, I'd very much like to know what you think about."

"What? I don't follow you."

"Listen. I have long wanted to talk things over with you. You do not have to be told—you know it yourself—that you are not of the common run of men: you are still young—all your life is before you. What do you intend to do? What does the future hold for you? I mean—what goal are you aiming at, where are you going, what is in your mind? In short, who are you, what are you?"

"You astonish me, Anna Sergeyevna. You know that I am studying natural science; as for who I am. . . ."

"Yes, who are you?"

"I've already told you that I'm going to be a country doctor."

Anna Sergeyevna made a gesture of impatience.

"Why do you say that? You don't believe it yourself. That might be all right coming from Arkady, but not from you."

"In what way is Arkady. . . ."

"Stop it! Can you possibly be content with such a modest career, and haven't you always said that you don't believe in medicine? You, with your ambition—a country doctor! You say that just to put me off, because you don't trust me. Do you know, Yevgeny Vassilich, I might be capable of understanding you: I was once poor and ambitious myself, just as you are; perhaps I have gone through the same trials as you have."

"That's all very well, Anna Sergeyevna, but you must excuse me. . . . I am not used to unburdening my mind, and then, you and I are so far apart."

"Why far apart? You'll be telling me again that I'm an aristocrat? Oh, come, Yevgeny Vassilich, haven't I shown you that. . . ."

"And besides," Bazarov interrupted, "what's the use of talking and thinking about the future, which mostly doesn't depend upon us? If an opportunity turns up to do something, all very well and good, if not—then at least you have the satisfaction of knowing that you didn't babble about it beforehand."

"You call a friendly talk babble. . . . Or perhaps you consider me, as a woman, unworthy of your confidence? You despise the lot of us, don't you?"

"You I don't despise, Anna Sergeyevna, and you know it."

"I know nothing . . . but supposing I do understand your reluctance to talk about your future; but what is taking place in you now. . . ."

"Taking place!" Bazarov repeated. "As if I were a state or society! In any case, it isn't interesting; besides, a man can't always express what is 'taking place' in him."

"I don't see why one should not be able to speak one's mind."

"Can *you*?" Bazarov asked.

"I can," Anna Sergeyevna answered after a slight hesitation.

Bazarov bowed his head.

"You are happier than I."

Anna Sergeyevna looked at him questioningly.

"Just as you like," she resumed, "but I have a feeling that we shall be good friends. I'm sure that this—how shall I call it—constraint of yours, this reticence, will finally vanish."

"So you have noticed my reticence, and did you say . . . constraint?"

"Yes."

Bazarov got up and went over to the window.

"And would you like to know the reason for this reticence, would you like to know what is taking place within me?"

"Yes," Odintsova repeated, a nameless fear assailing her.

"You won't be angry?"

"No."

"No?" Bazarov stood with his back to her. "Then know that I love you stupidly, madly.... Now you've had your way."

Odintsova put out both her hands before her, and Bazarov pressed his forehead against the window pane. He breathed with difficulty; he was visibly trembling in every limb. But this was not the tremor of youthful timidity, the sweet dismay of first confession that overcame him: this was passion surging through him in violent, heavy waves, a passion that resembled rage, and mayhap was akin to it. Odintsova was both terrified and sorry for him.

"Yevgeny Vassilich," she murmured, and could not keep a note of tenderness out of her voice.

He spun round, threw her a devouring glance, and seizing both her hands, suddenly drew her into his arms.

She did not immediately free herself from his embrace; a moment later, however, found her standing in a far corner out of which she looked at Bazarov. He lunged towards her....

"You didn't understand me," she whispered in swift panic. Another step on his part, it seemed, and she would scream. Bazarov bit his lip and strode out of the room.

Half an hour later the maid brought Anna Sergeyevna a note from Bazarov; it contained one line: "Must I go today, or may I stay till tomorrow?"—"Must you go? I did not understand you—you did not understand me," Odintsova answered, while she thought: "I did not understand myself."

She did not appear until dinner, and kept pacing up and down her room, her hands behind her back, stopping now and then before the window or the mirror and slowly wiping her neck with a handkerchief as though conscious of a burning stain. She asked herself what had prompted her to incite him to open his heart, and whether she had suspected anything. "It's my fault," she said aloud, "but how was I to foresee it?" She blushed at the memory of Bazarov's almost savage face when he rushed up to her.

"Why not?" she said suddenly stopping and tossing her curls. She saw herself in the mirror; the defiant poise of her head, the mysterious smile of half-closed eyes and parted lips seemed at that moment to tell her something which made her feel embarrassed. . . .

"No," she decided at length. "God knows where it may have led us; this is no joking matter; tranquillity is the only thing in the world after all."

Her tranquillity had not been disturbed; but she grew sad and even wept a little, without knowing why—but not because she felt insulted. If anything, she felt guilty. Prompted by various vague emotions, a sense of departing life, a craving for novelty, she had let herself go to a certain limit, forced herself to glance at what lay beyond it, and saw there not even an abyss, but merely emptiness . . . or ugliness.

XIX

For all her self-possession and freedom from prejudice Odintsova nevertheless felt embarrassed when she came into the dining room for dinner. The dinner, however, passed off quite satisfactorily. Porfiry Platonich dropped in and related several anecdotes; he had just returned from town. One item of news that he imparted was that the Governor had ordered his special commissioners to wear spurs, in case he had to send them somewhere urgently on horseback. Arkady talked in an undertone with Katya and paid diplomatic attention to the princess. Bazarov maintained a sullen dogged silence. Odintsova once or twice looked openly at his grim, angry face with its downcast eyes, every feature of which bore the stamp of disdainful resolution, and thought: "No . . . no . . . no. . . ." After dinner she went out into the garden with the rest of the company, and seeing that Bazarov wanted to speak to her, she stepped aside and stopped. He came up to her, and with his eyes still downcast, said huskily:

"I must apologise to you, Anna Sergeyevna. You must be very angry with me."

"No, I am not angry with you, Yevgeny Vassilich," answered Odintsova, "but I'm distressed."

"All the worse. At any rate I've been punished enough. My position, you will admit, is a ridiculous one. You wrote me: 'Must you go?' I cannot and do not want to stay. I shall be gone tomorrow."

"Yevgeny Vassilich, why. . . ."

"Why am I going?"

"No, I didn't mean that."

"The past cannot be retracted, Anna Sergeyevna . . . sooner or later it was bound to happen. Consequently, I must be going, I know only one condition under which I could stay, but that can never be. You will pardon my impudence—but you don't love me, do you, and never will?"

Bazarov's eyes gleamed for an instant under his dark brows.

Anna Sergeyevna made no reply. "I' am afraid of that man," the thought flashed through her mind.

"Good-bye, madam," Bazarov said, as if reading her mind, and turned towards the house.

Anna Sergeyevna followed slowly in his steps, and calling Katya, she took her arm. She kept her by her side until evening. She refused to play cards, and most of the time she laughed, which was not at all in keeping with her pale and harassed look. Arkady watched her wonderingly, the way young men do, that is, he kept asking himself: "What does it all mean?" Bazarov shut himself up in his room; he came down to tea, however. Anna Sergeyevna wanted to say something kind to him, but she was at a loss how to break the ice.

An unexpected incident helped her out of her difficulty: the butler announced the arrival of Sitnikov.

The young progressive's precipitate entrance into the room defied description. Having, with his usual impertinence, decided to pay a visit in the country on a woman whom he hardly knew and who had never invited him,

but who, from information that he had gleaned, was entertaining such clever acquaintances of his, he was nevertheless extremely nervous, and instead of offering the
apologies and greetings that he had prepared beforehand,
he mumbled some drivel about Yevdoxia Kukshina, having sent him to enquire about Anna Sergeyevna's health
and that Arkady Nikolayevich had also expressed his
highest opinion.... At this point he faltered and was
thrown into such confusion that he sat down on his own
hat. But as nobody turned him out and Anna Sergeyevna
even presented him to her aunt and sister, he quickly
regained his composure and was chattering away for all
he was worth. Vulgarity is often a welcome interlude in
life: it slackens strings that are too highly strung and
sobers self-confident or presumptuous feelings by a reminder of their kinship with it. With the arrival of Sitnikov, everything became, as it were, duller—and simpler;
everybody even ate a heartier supper, and the company
retired to bed half an hour before the usual time.

"I can now repeat," said Arkady from his bed to Bazarov, who had also undressed, "what you told me one day:
Why are you so sad? I suppose you've fulfilled some
sacred duty?"

Between the young friends there had lately arisen a
mock habit of careless badinage which is always a sign
of veiled resentment or unspoken suspicions.

"I'm going down to my father's tomorrow," Bazarov
announced.

Arkady propped himself up on his elbow. He was
surprised and yet somehow glad.

"Ah!" he said. "Is that why you're sad?"

Bazarov yawned.

"Curiosity killed the cat."

"What about Anna Sergeyevna?" Arkady went on.

"What about her?"

"I mean, is she letting you go?"

"I don't have to ask her permission, do I?"

Arkady became thoughtful. Bazarov went to bed and
turned his face to the wall.

Several minutes passed in silence.

"Yevgeny," Arkady suddenly said.

"Well?"

"I'm going tomorrow, too."

Bazarov did not say anything.

"Only I am going home," Arkady went on. "We'll go together as far as the Khokhlov Settlement and there you will get Fedot to give you a team. I'd like to meet your folks, but I'm afraid I'd be in their way and yours. You'll come down to our place again, won't you?"

"I've left my things there," Bazarov said by way of reply, without turning his head.

"Why doesn't he ask me why I'm leaving? And as suddenly as he is?" thought Arkady. "Come to think of it, why am I leaving and why is he?" he pursued his thoughts. He could not find a satisfactory answer to his question and his heart filled with bitterness. He realised that it would be hard for him to give up this life to which he had grown so accustomed; but to remain by himself would be rather awkward. Something has happened between them, he told himself. Why should I hang around after he's gone? I'll only get on her nerves, and lose all. He pictured to himself Anna Sergeyevna; then another image gradually began to take shape through the lovely vision of the young widow.

"I'll miss Katya, too," Arkady whispered into his pillow, on which he had already dropped a silent tear. He suddenly tossed back his hair and said aloud: "Why the hell did that ass Sitnikov have to come here?"

Bazarov stirred in his bed, then said:

"My dear chap, you're still an innocent, I see. The Sitnikovs of this world are necessary to us. I need fatheads like him, don't you see? You can't really expect the gods to bake bricks!"

"Humph," thought Arkady to himself, and in a flash all the abysmal depth of Bazarov's conceit was brought home to him. "So you and I are the gods? Or rather, you're the god and I suppose I'm the fathead?"

"Yes," Bazarov repeated gloomily, "you're still an innocent."

Odintsova evinced no great surprise when Arkady told her the next day that he was leaving together with Bazarov; she looked absent-minded and tired, Katya glanced at him gravely and silently; the princess crossed herself under her shawl in a way that he could not help noticing; as for Sitnikov, he was struck all of a heap. He had just come down to lunch in a spruce new suit, this time not of the Pan-Slavist mode; the night before he had left the servant in attendance gasping at the profusion of finery he had brought with him, and now his comrades were deserting him! He minced a little, then began darting hither and thither like a hunted hare on the fringe of a forest and suddenly, almost frantically, and almost in a shriek, announced that he was going, too. Odintsova did not detain him.

"I have a very comfortable carriage," the wretched young man added, addressing Arkady. "I can give you a lift, and Yevgeny Vassilich can take your tarantass; that'll be a good arrangement."

"But it's altogether out of your way, and it's quite a distance to my place."

"That's all right; I have plenty of time; besides I've got some business to attend to down there."

"Tax-farming, I suppose?" Arkady said in a tone too patently contemptuous.

But Sitnikov was too distraught to react with his customary snigger.

"I assure you the carriage is most comfortable," he muttered, "and there'll be room for everybody."

"Don't upset M'sieu' Sitnikov by refusing," said Anna Sergeyevna.

Arkady looked at her and inclined his head significantly.

The guests departed after lunch. Taking leave of Bazarov, Odintsova gave him her hand, saying:

"We shall be seeing each other again, shan't we?"

"As you please," Bazarov answered.

"In that case, we shall."

Arkady came out on the porch steps first, and got into Sitnikov's carriage. The butler deferentially helped him in; he would have dearly loved to hit him or to start crying.

Bazarov got into the tarantass. On reaching the Khokhlov Settlement Arkady waited till Fedot the innkeeper had harnessed the horses, and then, going up to the tarantass, said to Bazarov with his old smile:

"Take me along with you, Yevgeny; I want to go to your place."

"Get in," Bazarov said through his teeth.

Sitnikov, who had been lounging round his conveyance, whistling gaily to himself, gaped on hearing this bit of news, while Arkady coolly transferred his belongings, took his seat beside Bazarov, and with a polite bow to his late companion, shouted: "Get a move on, coachman!" The tarantass rolled away and was soon lost to view. Sitnikov, completely flabbergasted, stole a look at his coachman, but the latter was trailing the thong of his whip over the outrunner's tail. Whereupon Sitnikov jumped into his carriage and, yelling at two passing peasants: "Put your hats on, you chumps!" dragged himself off to town, where he arrived late in the day and where, on the morrow, he told Kukshina what he thought of "those two darned prigs and boors".

On taking his seat in the tarantass next to Bazarov, Arkady gave his hand a hard squeeze and did not say anything for a long time. Bazarov seemed to have understood and appreciated both the handshake and the silence. He had not slept a wink the previous night, nor had he smoked, and he had practically not eaten anything for several days. His profile looked haggard and gaunt beneath a cap pulled down almost over his eyes.

"Well, my dear chap," he broke the silence at last, "let's have a cigar. Is my tongue yellow, have a look?"

"It is," Arkady said.

"I thought so ... and this cigar is tasteless, too. The machine's run down."

"You have been looking bad these last few days," Arkady said.

"Never mind! We'll pick up. It's a bit tiresome though, my mother's such a tenderhearted soul: unless you grow a big belly and eat ten times a day she gets terribly upset. Father's not a bad sort, though; he's been to places and seen a thing or two. No, no use smoking," he added, throwing the cigar into the dusty road.

"It's twenty-five versts to your estate, isn't it?" Arkady asked.

"Yes. But ask that oracle." He pointed to Fedot's man sitting on the box.

The oracle, however, answered: "Oo knows—the versts round here ain't never been measured," and went on swearing softly at the outrunner for "kickin' 'er noddle", meaning tossing her head.

"Yes," Bazarov resumed, "that will be a lesson to you, my young friend, an instructive lesson. God, how silly it is! Every man hangs by a thread, a chasm may yawn at his feet any minute, and he goes about looking for all kinds of trouble, spoils his own life."

"What are you hinting at?" Arkady asked.

"I'm not hinting at anything, I'm telling you straight that we've both been acting the fool. What's the use of talking! But I noticed at the clinic that the man who gets angry at his pain is sure to conquer it."

"I don't quite follow you," Arkady said. "You don't seem to have anything to complain about."

"Since you don't quite follow me, let me tell you this: in my opinion it's better to break stones in the road than let a woman get hold even of your little finger. That's all. . ." Bazarov very nearly came out with his pet word "romanticism", but checked himself and said: "Nonsense. You won't believe me now, but let me tell you this: you and I have been in feminine society and we've enjoyed it; but giving up that kind of society is like taking a cold shower on a hot day. A man has no time to waste on such trifles; a man must be fierce, says a good old Spanish proverb. Look here," he went on, turning to the muzhik on the box, "you brainy fellow—have you got a wife?"

The peasant turned to our friends a flat face with weak-sighted eyes.

"A wife? Yes. 'Course I has."

"Do you beat her?"

"Beat my wife? All depends. Never beat 'em for nuthin'."

"Splendid. Well, and does she beat you?"

The man jerked the reins.

"Fancy saying a thing like that, sir. Must have yer little joke. . . ." He was evidently offended.

"Hear that, Arkady Nikolayevich! And you and I have been given a hiding ... that's the advantage of being educated men."

Arkady gave a forced laugh, and Bazarov turned away, and did not open his mouth again for the rest of the journey.

The twenty-five versts seemed like a fifty to Arkady. At last, a village came into view on a sloping hillside. Here lived Bazarov's parents. Nearby, in a young birch wood, stood a little manor house under a thatched roof. Two peasants in caps stood bickering at the first hut. "You're a big swine," one was saying to the other, "and behave worse than a little 'un." "And your wife's a witch," the other retorted.

"Judging by their unconstrained behaviour," Bazarov pointed out to Arkady, "and the playful turns of speech, you can tell that my father's peasants are none too downtrodden. Here he is himself, coming out onto the steps of his house. Must have heard the bell tinkling. It's him—I recognise his figure. Tut-tut! but hasn't he gone grey, poor fellow!"

XX

Bazarov leaned out of the tarantass, while Arkady craned his neck from behind his friend's back and saw a tall, spare man with dishevelled hair and a fine aquiline nose, wearing an old military coat unbuttoned; he was standing on the porch steps with his legs wide apart, smoking a long pipe and screwing his eyes up against the sun.

The horses stopped.

"You've come at last," said Bazarov's father, continuing to smoke, though the chibouk fairly danced between his fingers.

"Well, get out, get out, let's kiss."

He embraced his son.

"Yevgeny darling, Yevgeny," came a quavering woman's voice. The door flew open, and there appeared upon the threshold a round little old lady in a white cap and a short brightly coloured jacket. She cried out, swayed, and would probably have fallen had not Bazarov supported her. Her plump little arms instantly went round his neck, her head was pressed to his breast and everything around was hushed. All that could be heard were her broken sobs.

Old Bazarov breathed hard and screwed his eyes up more than ever.

"That'll do, Arisha, that'll do," he said, exchanging a look with Arkady, who was standing motionless by the carriage, while the man on the box even turned his head away. "Come, come. Please stop it."

"Ah, Vassily Ivanych," the old lady stammered. "It's such a long time since I've seen my darling, my dearest boy..." and without unclasping her arms she drew back her tear-stained, puckered, radiant face, surveyed him with a blissful, droll kind of look and fell on his neck again.

"Well, yes, of course, it's all in the nature of things," said Vassily Ivanych, "but let us better go in. Yevgeny has brought a visitor with him, I see. Excuse me," he added, turning to Arkady with a little scrape of the foot; feminine weakness, you know; a mother's heart after all...."

Yet his own lips and brows twitched and his chin quivered. He was visibly striving to master his feelings and feign indifference. Arkady bowed.

"Come along, mother, really," Bazarov said and conducted the old lady, overcome with emotion, into the house. Placing her in a comfortable armchair, he hurriedly embraced his father once more and presented Arkady.

"Heartily glad to make your acquaintance," Vassily Ivanych said. "You're welcome to whatever we have: it's a simple life we lead, on a military footing. Arina Vlasyevna, calm yourself, do: you mustn't be so soft! What will the gentleman think of you?"

"My dear sir," the old lady stammered through her tears, "I haven't the pleasure of knowing your name...."

"Arkady Nikolaich," Vassily Ivanych prompted gravely in an undertone.

"I beg your pardon, it's so silly of me." The old lady
blew her nose, then bending her head to right and left
she carefully wiped one eye after the other. "Please
excuse me. Really, I thought I'd die without seeing my
darling b . . . b . . . boy."

"Well, you have him now, madam," Vassily Ivanych
threw in. "Tania," he said to a barefooted girl of thirteen
in a bright red cotton frock who was peeping timorously
from behind the door, "bring the mistress a glass of
water—on a tray, understand? And you, gentlemen," he
added with old-fashioned facetiousness, "pray come into
a retired veteran's study."

"Let me give you just one more hug, Yevgeny dear,"
murmured Arina Vlasyevna. Bazarov bent over her. "My,
what a handsome fellow you've grown!"

"I don't know about handsome," Vassily Ivanych remarked, "but he's a man *homme fait,* as the saying goes.
And now, Arina Vlasyevna, I hope that your maternal
heart has had its fill, and you will see about filling our
dear guests, for, you know, fair words butter no pars-
nips."

The old lady got up from her armchair. "This very
minute, Vassily Ivanych—the table will be laid; I shall
run into the kitchen myself, and have the samovar got
ready, I'll see to everything. It's three years since I've
set eyes on him and looked after his needs, can you
imagine?"

"There, there, look to it, my little hostess, but mind
you don't put us to shame; and you gentlemen, will you
please follow me. Ah, here's Timofeich come to pay you
his compliments, Yevgeny. I suppose he's overjoyed too,
the old dog. Eh? Aren't you glad, you old dog? Please
come this way."

And Vassily Ivanych bustled along, with a shuffle and
scrape of his worn-down slippers.

*   *   *

His entire house consisted of six tiny rooms. The one
to which he brought his guests was called the study.

A heavy-legged table littered with papers that were
dark and almost sooty with ancient dust, occupied the
whole length of the wall between the two windows; the
walls were hung with Turkish weapons, riding crops, a
sword, two maps, some anatomical charts, a portrait of
Hufeland, a hair-woven monogram in a black frame,
and a framed diploma; a leather sofa with depressions
and rents in it here and there stood between two huge
bookcases of silver birch; the shelves were littered with
books, small boxes, stuffed birds, jars and vials; in one
corner stood a broken electrical machine.

"I warned you, my dear guest," began Vassily Ivanych,
"that we live here, so to speak, as at a bivouac...."

"Do stop it. What are you apologising for?" Bazarov
broke in. "Kirsanov knows very well we're no Croesuses
and that your home is not a palace. Where are we going
to put him up, that's the question."

"Why, Yevgeny, to be sure—I have a splendid little
room in the wing: your friend will be comfortable
there."

"So you've got a new wing, have you?"

"To be sure, sir; where the bathhouse is, sir," Timofeich put in.

"That is, next to the bathhouse," Vassily Ivanych added hastily. "It's summertime now.... I'll just run down
there and have the place fixed up; and you, Timofeich,
bring the gentlemen's things in meanwhile. You'll use my
study, of course, Yevgeny. *Suum cuique.*"

"There you are! A funny old boy, and as kind as they
make them," Bazarov said as soon as Vassily Ivanych
had left the room. "He is as eccentric as your father, but
in a different way. He's much too chatty though."

"And I think your mother is a wonderful woman,"
Arkady remarked.

"Yes, she's an artless soul. You'll see what a dinner
she'll give us."

"We weren't expecting you today, sir, and didn't order
any beef," said Timofeich, who had just brought in Bazarov's suitcase.

"We'll manage without the beef; if you haven't got it you haven't. Poverty is no crime, they say."

"How many serfs does your father own?" Arkady asked suddenly.

"The estate is not his, it's mother's; as far as I remember, fifteen."

"Oh no, there's twenty-two all told," Timofeich said, displeased.

There was a sound of shuffling slippers and Vassily Ivanych reappeared.

"Your room will be ready for you in a few minutes," he announced solemnly—"Arkady ... Nikolaich?—did I get it right? And here's your servant," he added, pointing to a lad with a close-cropped head wearing a blue caftan torn at the elbows and somebody else's boots who had come in with him. "His name's Fedya. Permit me to repeat, though my son won't have it—it's the best we can offer you. He can fill a pipe though. You smoke, don't you?"

"I mostly smoke cigars," Arkady answered.

"And very wisely, too. I prefer cigars myself, but in these secluded parts they're very difficult to get."

"Oh, stop playing Lazarus to the rich man," Bazarov broke in once more. "Better sit down here on the sofa and let's have a look at you again."

Vassily Ivanych chuckled and sat down. He greatly resembled his son, except that his forehead was not so high and broad and his mouth was more generous, and he incessantly fidgeted and shrugged as though his clothes were too tight for him under the armpits, and blinked his eyes, cleared his throat and fiddled with his fingers, whereas his son maintained a careless kind of immobility.

"Playing Lazarus!" Vassily Ivanych repeated. "Don't imagine, Yevgeny, that I want to stir our guest, so to speak, to pity with a sort of—there, what a godforsaken spot we live in. On the contrary, I'm of the opinion that for an active-minded person there is no such thing as a godforsaken spot. At any rate I try my hardest not to become moss-grown, as they say, and keep abreast of the times."

Vassily Ivanych pulled out of his pocket a new lemon-coloured *foulard* that he had picked up on his way to Arkady's room, and went on, flourishing the handkerchief:

"I say nothing of the fact that I have, for instance, with no inconsiderable loss to myself, made my peasants tenant farmers and gone halves with them in my land. I deemed this to be my duty, and the most judicious thing to do, though other landlords don't dream of it; I allude to the interests of science and education."

"Yes; I see you have there *The Friend of Health* for 1855," observed Bazarov.

"A friend of mine sends it me for old times' sake," Vassily Ivanych said hastily. "But we also have some idea, for instance, about phrenology," he added, speaking more for Arkady's benefit, and pointing to a small cast of a head charted with numbered squares which stood on a shelf. "We're not entirely unacquainted with Schenlein, for example, or Rademacher."

"Do they still swear by Rademacher in this gubernia?" Bazarov asked.

Vassily Ivanych coughed.

"Er—this gubernia. . . . Of course, you gentlemen know better, you are way ahead of us. You are our successors, after all. In my time, a Humoralist like Hoffmann, or a man like Brown with his vitalism seemed very funny to us, yet they had once created a stir. Some new man with you has taken the place of Rademacher, and you pay him homage, but in twenty years, perhaps he, too, will look ridiculous."

"Let me tell you in consolation," said Bazarov, "that we now consider medicine ridiculous and pay homage to nothing."

"What do you mean? But you're going to be a doctor, aren't you?"

"I am, but that has nothing to do with it."

Vassily Ivanych tamped down the hot ashes in the bowl of his pipe with his middle finger.

"Well, maybe, maybe—I won't argue. What am I, after all? A retired army surgeon, *voilà tout,* and now I've become a farmer. I served in your grandfather's brigade," he addressed Arkady once more. "Yes, sir, I've seen

9*

a thing or two in my time. Been in all kinds of society and known all manner of people! The man you see before you—yes I, held the pulse of such men as Prince Wittgenstein and the poet Zhukovsky! As for those in the southern army, those mixed up in the events of December the 14th* you know" (at this point Vassily Ivanych pursed his lips significantly)—"I knew every one of them. Of course, I had nothing to do with it. My business was to wield the lancet and nothing more! But your grandfather was a highly respected man, a real soldier."

"Come, admit that he was just a blockhead," Bazarov put in indolently.

"Goodness, Yevgeny, the expressions you use! Of course, General Kirsanov did not belong to. . . ."

"Let's drop him," flung in Bazarov. "Coming up here I was pleased to see how well your birch wood has done."

Vassily Ivanych brightened.

"And you'll see what a fine garden I have now! Planted every tree with my own hands. And there's fruit, and berries and all kinds of medicinal herbs. You young people may be smart, but old Paracelsus spoke the holy truth when he said: *in herbis, verbis et lapidibus*! I've given up my practice, as you know, but once or twice a week I have to dig out the old stuff. People come asking for advice, and you can't very well kick them out. Some poor beggar drops in occasionally and wants to be treated. And there are no doctors at all around here. Would you believe it, one of the neighbours, a retired major, goes in for doctoring too. I once asked somebody whether he had ever studied medicine. No, they said, he hasn't, he does it mostly out of charity. . . . Ha-ha! out of charity! Eh? Isn't that great? Ha-ha! Ha-ha!"

"Fedya, fill me a pipe," Bazarov said sternly.

"There's another doctor here who comes to visit a patient," Vassily Ivanych plunged on in a sort of desperation, "and learns that the patient has already been gathered to his fathers: the servant doesn't even let him

---

* An allusion to the abortive Decembrist uprising of December 14 (Old Style) 1825.—*Trans.*

in, saying there isn't any need now. The doctor was rather taken aback, not having expected it, and asks: 'Tell me, did your master have the hiccups before he died?'—'Yes sir, he did.'—'And did he hiccup much?'— 'Oh, yes.'—'Ah, well, that's good,' and took himself off. Ha-ha-ha!"

The old man laughed alone; Arkady arranged his face into a smile. Bazarov merely puffed at his pipe. The talk went on thus for nearly an hour; Arkady meanwhile had gone to his room, which proved to be the bathhouse ante-room, but was cosy and clean. At length Tania came in and announced that dinner was ready.

Vassily Ivanych got up first.

"Come on, gentlemen! I do hope I haven't bored you. Perhaps the hostess will do better."

*   *   *

The dinner, though hastily prepared, proved to be an excellent one, even a lavish one, except for the wine, which was not up to much, as they say: the almost black sherry which Timofeich had purchased in town from a dealer of his acquaintance had a copperish—or was it resinous, tang to it; and the flies were a nuisance too. Usually a serf boy kept them off with a large green branch; but today Vassily Ivanych had dismissed him for fear of criticism on the part of the younger generation. Arina Vlasyevna had smartened herself up; she put on a high mob-cap with silk strings, and a sky-blue patterned shawl. She cried a little again on seeing her darling Yevgeny, but before her husband could admonish her, she hastily wiped away the tears so as not to wet her shawl. The young men ate alone, as their hosts had long since dined. They were waited on by Fedya, who ob-viously felt encumbered by his out-size boots, assisted by a woman with masculine features and blind of one eye by the name of Anfisushka, who combined the duties of housekeeper, poultrymaid and laundress. Throughout the meal Vassily Ivanych paced up and down the room talk-ing with an almost blissful air about the grave concern which Napoleon's policy and the Italian imbroglio inspired him with; Arkady might not have existed for all the attention which Arina Vlasyevna paid him. With her little fist propping up her round face, to which a pair of puffy cherry-coloured lips and the moles on her cheek and over her eyebrows imparted a very benign expression, she did not tear her eyes away from her son and sighed all the time. She was dying to know how long he was going to stay, but was afraid to ask him. "What if he says—two days," she thought with a sinking heart. After the roast Vassily Ivanych disappeared for a moment and returned with an uncorked half-bottle of champagne. "Here," he exclaimed, "though we do live in the backwoods, we have something to cheer the heart with on a festive occasion." He poured out three goblets and a wineglass, toasted the health "of our inestimable guests", drained his glass at a gulp militarywise and made Arina Vlasyevna drink her wineglass to the last drop. When the turn came for the preserved fruit, Arkady, who had an aversion for sweet things, felt it incumbent on him to assay four freshly cooked varieties, especially since Bazarov had flatly declined them and lighted a cigar. Then tea appeared upon the scene with cream and butter and cakes; after which Vassily Ivanych invited everybody into the garden to admire the beauty of the evening. As they passed a bench, he whispered to Arkady: "On this spot I do a little philosophising as I watch the sunset: a fitting occupation for an anchorite. And there, further on, I have planted a few trees beloved of Horace."

"What trees are they?" asked Bazarov, who had been listening.

"Why, acacias, of course."

Bazarov began to yawn.

"I believe it's time our travellers sought the arms of Morpheus," Vassily Ivanych said.

"In other words, time to turn in!" Bazarov said. "That's a good idea. It really is time."

He kissed his mother on the forehead by way of good night, while she embraced him and blessed him with a furtive triple sign of the cross. Vassily Ivanych saw Arkady to his room and wished him "the blessed slumber

I enjoyed myself when I was your happy age". Indeed, Arkady slept like a top in his bathhouse anteroom: the place smelt of mint, and two crickets chirped drowsily behind the stove. Vassily Ivanych went to his study where he settled himself on the sofa at his son's feet with the intention of having a chat; but Bazarov instantly dismissed him, saying he wanted to go to sleep, although he actually remained awake till daybreak. He stared wrathfully into the darkness with wide-open eyes: childhood's memories had no fascination for him, and besides, he had not yet shaken off his recent painful impressions. Arina Vlasyevna, after praying to her heart's content, had a good long talk with Anfisushka, who, standing before her mistress as if rooted to the spot and staring at her with her single eye, conveyed to her in mysterious whispers all her views and fancies concerning Yevgeny Vassilyevich. What with joy, the wine and the cigar smoke, the old lady's head was reeling; her husband tried to speak with her, but gave it up as hopeless.

Arina Vlasyevna was a true type of Russian gentlewoman of the old days; she should have lived some two hundred years before, in the days of old Muscovy. She was very pious and impressionable, and believed in all kinds of omens, fortunetelling, charms, and dreams: she believed in imbecilic zealots, household sprites, spooks, ill-omened encounters, evil spells, folk medicine, charmed salt for Maundy Thursday, and the imminent end of the world; she believed that if the candles did not blow out at vespers on Easter Sunday buckwheat would yield a good harvest, and that mushrooms would stop growing if seen by the human eye; she believed that the devil haunted watery places and that every Jew had a bloodstain on his chest; she was afraid of mice, grass snakes, frogs, sparrows, leeches, thunder. cold water, draughts, horses, goats, red-headed people and black cats, and considered crickets and dogs unclean animals; she ate neither veal, nor pigeon, nor crab, nor cheese, nor asparagus, nor artichokes, nor hares, nor watermelons, because a cut watermelon reminded her of John the Baptist's head; of oysters she could not speak without a shudder; she was fond of a good meal—and kept Lent rigorously; she slept

ten hours a day and did not go to bed at all if Vassily
Ivanych had a headache; she had never read anything
besides *Alexis, or a Cabin in the Woods,* wrote one, at
most two, letters a year, and knew what was what in
housekeeping, curing, pickling and preserving, though
she never did a thing with her own hands and was generally indisposed to bestir herself. Arina Vlasyevna was
very kind-hearted and not at all foolish, in her own way.
She knew that the world consisted of masters whose
business it was to give orders and of common people who
had to take them, and so she accepted all demonstrations
of servility without a qualm; she was kind and gentle,
however, to those under her, never turned a beggar away
without giving him something, and never censured people, though she liked to gossip at times. She had been
very attractive in her youth, had played the harpsichord
and spoken a little French; but after years of wandering
with her husband, whom she had married against her
will, she had grown fat and forgotten both music and
French. She loved her son and feared him beyond words;
the management of the estate she left to Vassily Ivanych
—and did not trouble her head any more about it: she
would merely moan in distress, and wave him off with
her handkerchief while her brows would go up in alarm
whenever her old man began talking about his plans and
the changes he intended making. She was obsessed by
imaginary fears, was constantly expecting some great
calamity, and would start crying as soon as she thought
of anything sad.... Such women are rare nowadays. God
knows whether we should be glad of it or not!

XXI

On getting out of bed Arkady opened the window—
and the first thing that met his eyes was Vassily Ivanych.
Clad in a Bokhara dressing gown girded with a large
handkerchief, the old man was pottering about in the
garden. Seeing his young guest he cried out, leaning on
his spade:

"Good morning to you, sir! Did you sleep well?"

"Fine," Arkady said.

"Well, and here am I, as you see, working like a Cincinnatus, to clear a patch for my late turnips. Things have now come to such a pass—and thank God for it I say!—when every man must make his living by his own hands; no use relying on others; a man must work himself. And so, Jean Jacques Rousseau was right, it seems. Half an hour ago, my dear sir, you would have found me in quite a different capacity. A peasant woman came, complaining of the collywobbles—as she calls it, we call it dysentery. I gave her—how had I better express it—an opium infusion, and I pulled another woman's tooth out. I offered the latter to etherise her, but she wouldn't have it. I do it all gratis—*en amateur*. It's nothing new to me, though; I'm a plebeian, you know, *homo novus*—I'm not of the blue blood, like my better half. Wouldn't you like to come out here in the shade and take a breath of fresh air before breakfast?"

Arkady joined him outside.

"Welcome, once more," Vassily Ivanych said touching his greasy skull-cap in military salutation. "You're used to luxury and pleasure, I know, but even the great of this world are nothing loath to beguile the time under a cottage roof."

"Good Lord," Arkady protested, "since when do I belong to the great ones of this world? And I'm not used to luxury either."

"Come, come, sir," parried Vassily Ivanych with a polite grimace. "I may be out of the running now, but I have knocked around the world a bit—and I can tell a bird by its song. I'm something of a psychologist, too, in a way, and a physiognomist. If it weren't for this—as I dare to call it—gift, I'd have gone to the dogs long ago; it doesn't take much to push a little fellow like me to the wall. Let me tell you frankly: the friendship I notice between you and my son gives me sincere pleasure. I have just seen him: he got up very early as usual—you are probably aware of that custom of his—and went off to explore the countryside. Excuse my curiosity, but have you known Yevgeny long?"

"Since last winter."

"I see. May I also enquire—but why not take a seat? May I enquire as a father, with all frankness, what is your opinion of my Yevgeny?"

"Your son is one of the most remarkable men I have ever met," Arkady said earnestly.

Vassily Ivanych's eyes suddenly dilated and a faint flush mantled his cheeks. The spade dropped out of his hand.

"And so, you believe . . ." he started to say.

"I am sure," Arkady went on quickly, "that your son has a great future before him, that he will make your name famous. I was convinced of it the moment we first met."

"How . . . how did that come about?" Vassily Ivanych said, breathlessly. His wide mouth spread in a rapturous smile, which stayed there.

"So you want to know how we met?"

"Yes . . . and generally. . . ."

Arkady began talking about Bazarov with still greater warmth and enthusiasm than he had on that memorable evening when he had danced with Odintsova.

Vassily Ivanych sat listening while he blew his nose, rolled his handkerchief between both hands, coughed and rumpled his hair, then, unable to contain himself any longer, he leaned over to Arkady and kissed him on the shoulder.

"I can't tell you how happy you've made me," he said smiling all the time. "I want you to know that I . . . adore my son; I say nothing about my old woman, of course: she's a mother—and there everything is said! But I dare not show my feelings in front of him, he doesn't like it. He has an aversion to every display of affection; many people disapprove of this hardness of his, which they regard as a sign of pride or insensibility; but men like him should not be measured by the ordinary rule, don't you think so? Well, for example: another man in his place would keep squeezing money out of his parents, but believe it or not, he never took a kopek more than he needed as long as he lived, I swear!"

"He's an honest, unselfish man," Arkady said.

"Unselfish is the word. As for me, Arkady Nikolaich, I do not only adore him, I'm proud of him, and my only ambition is to see the following words written in his biography one day: 'The son of a common army surgeon, who, however, early discovered in him great promise and stinted nothing for his education. . . .' "

The old man's voice broke.

Arkady squeezed his hand.

"What do you think," Vassily Ivanych asked after a brief silence, "it's not in the field of medicine that he will win the fame you prophesy for him, is it?"

"Certainly not medicine, though here too he will rank with the foremost scientists."

"What field do you think, Arkady Nikolaich?"

"It's difficult to say now, but he will be famous."

"He will be famous!" echoed the old man and became lost in thought.

"Arina Vlasyevna asks you to come and have breakfast," Anfisushka said as she passed by carrying a huge dish of ripe raspberries.

Vassily Ivanych started.

"Will there be cooled cream with the raspberries?"

"Yes sir."

"See that it's cool though! Don't stand on ceremony, Arkady Nikolaich, help yourself. Where is Yevgeny so long?"

"Here I am," Bazarov spoke up from Arkady's room.

Vassily Ivanych turned round quickly.

"Aha! Thought you'd pay your friend a visit, but you're too late, *amice*,—we've already had a long chat together. Now we must go and have breakfast—mother's calling us. By the way, I want to talk to you."

"What about?"

"There's a muzhik here who is suffering from icterus. . . ."

"That is, jaundice?"

"Yes, a chronic and very refractory case of icterus. I've prescribed centaury and St. John's wort; made him eat carrot, and gave him soda; but these are all palliatives, something more drastic is needed. Although you make fun of medicine I'm sure you could give me some good advice. But we'll talk of that later. Let's go and have breakfast now."

Vassily Ivanych jumped to his feet, burst into a gay bit of song from *Robert le Diable*:

> *"Le vin, le vin, le vin, le jeu, les belles,*
> *Voilà, voilà, voilà mes seuls amours!"*

"Wonderful, how full of vim he is!" Bazarov said, moving away from the window.

＊　＊　＊

It was noon. The sun beat down hotly through a thin veil of unbroken whitish clouds. A stillness hung over everything; only the cocks in the village crowed away in high feather, evoking in everyone who heard them an odd sensation of drowsiness and ennui; and somewhere high up in the treetops the incessant cheep of a baby hawk sounded like a plaint. Arkady and Bazarov were lying in the shadow of a small haystack, having strewn the ground under them with an armful or two of crisp but still green and fragrant hay.

"That aspen," Bazarov began, "reminds me of my childhood; it stands on the edge of a pit where there used to be a brick barn, and I was convinced at the time that the pit and the tree possessed a peculiar spell; I never felt bored near them. I didn't understand then that I wasn't bored simply because I was a child. And now that I've grown up the spell doesn't work."

"How long did you live here altogether?" Arkady asked.

"For two years running; then we used to come back from time to time; ours was a rambling sort of life, mostly knocking around from town to town."

"And has the house been up long?"

"Yes, a long time. It was built in granddad's time—my mother's father."

"Who was your grandfather?"

"The devil knows. A second major or something. Served under Suvorov and was full of yarns about the march across the Alps. Fibs, no doubt."

"That accounts for the portrait of Suvorov hanging in the parlour. But I like little houses like yours, old and snug, with a peculiar smell all their own."

"Smells of lamp oil and melilot," Bazarov said with a yawn. "And as for the flies in these dear little houses. . . . Ugh!"

"I say," Arkady went on after a little pause, "were you kept down in childhood?"

"You see the kind of parents I have. Can't call them strict, can you?"

"Do you love them, Yevgeny?"

"I do, Arkady!"

"They love you so much!"

Bazarov was silent.

"Do you know what I'm thinking?" he said presently, clasping his hands behind his head.

"No, what is it?"

"I was thinking that my people are having a good time in this world! My father at sixty potters around, talks of 'palliative' remedies, treats sick people, is generous to the peasants, and generally has the time of his life; mother, too, is happy: her day is crammed with so many occupations, and so many oh's and ah's that she hasn't time to stop and think; while I. . . ."

"What about you?"

"I'm thinking: here am I lying under a haystack. The narrow place I occupy is so small compared to the rest of space where I am not and where nobody cares a rap about me; and the little span of my life is such a speck in eternity, where I haven't been and never will be. . . . Yet in that atom, in that mathematical point, the blood circulates, the brain works, desires are kindled. How monstrous! How preposterous!"

"Let me tell you that what you say applies in equal measures to all people."

"You're right," Bazarov said. "What I meant is that they—my parents, that is—are occupied and don't worry about their own insignificance—it doesn't rankle with them ... whereas I ... I am disgusted and furious."

"Furious? But why furious?"

"Why? You ask why? Have you forgotten?"

"I haven't forgotten anything, but still I don't think you have any right to be angry. You're unhappy, I agree, but...."

"Oh, I see, Arkady Nikolaich, your idea of love is like that of all modern young men: chuck-chuck-chuck little hen, and the moment she comes near you take to your heels. I'm not that kind. But enough of that. What can't be helped can't be mended by talk." He turned over on his side. "Aha! Here's a sturdy little ant hauling a half-dead fly. Haul away, little fellow, haul away! Never mind her kicking, make the best of your right as an animal to disregard any feelings of compassion, not like us self-broken fellows!"

"You should be the last to talk about that, Yevgeny! Since when have you been broken?"

Bazarov raised his head.

"That's the only thing I'm proud of. I've not broken myself, and nothing in petticoats will ever break me. Amen! That's over and done with! You won't hear another word from me about it."

The two lay for some time in silence.

"Yes," Bazarov began, "man is a queer animal. When you look on from outside at the secluded lives our 'fathers' lead here, you wonder—what could be better? Eat, drink and know that everything you do is right and sensible. But no, you get bored to death. You want to grapple with people, if only to scold them."

"Life ought to be arranged in such a way that every moment of it should be significant," Arkady remarked thoughtfully.

"That's just it! The significant, though it may some-times be false, is sweet, and one could even put up with the insignificant ... but it's the petty strife, that gets you down, the petty strife."

"Petty strife needn't exist for a man if he doesn't want to recognise it."

"Hm ... what you've said is a *platitude reversed*."

"Eh? What do you mean by that term?"

"Just this: to say, for example, that education is useful, is a platitude; but to say that education is harmful, is a platitude reversed. It looks smarter, but it really amounts to the same thing."

"But where is the truth?"

"Where? I'll answer you like an echo: where?"

"You're in a melancholy mood today, Yevgeny."

"Am I? Probably it's the sun, and then it's bad to eat too many raspberries."

"In that case what about taking a nap?" Arkady said.

"All right; but don't look at me—a man usually looks foolish when he's asleep."

"Do you care what people think of you?"

"I don't know what to say. A real man shouldn't care; a real man is one you don't think about, you must either obey him or hate him."

"Strange! I don't hate anyone," Arkady said after a moment's reflection.

"And I do, a lot. You're a softhearted, sloppy fellow, you couldn't hate anybody! You're too timid, you haven't enough self-confidence."

"And you are self-confident, I suppose?" Arkady interrupted him. "You have a high opinion of yourself, haven't you?"

Bazarov did not answer at once.

"When I meet a man who can hold his own against me," he said slowly, "I'll change my opinion about myself. Hate! Why, today, for example, when we were passing the hut of our *starosta* Philip—it's such a pretty white hut—you said Russia will be a perfect country when the lowliest peasant will have a dwelling like that to live in, and that everyone of us should help to bring that about. But I have come to hate that lowliest peasant, that Philip and Sidor and the rest of them, for whom I am expected to lay myself out, and who won't even say thank you—not that I need his thanks. All right, what if he does live in a white hut, while I'll be feeding the worms— what then?"

"Oh come, Yevgeny. Listening to you today one is inclined to agree with the people who accuse us of lack of principles."

"You speak like your uncle. Generally there aren't any principles—you don't seem to have grasped that yet!—

there are only sensations. Everything depends on them."

"How do you make that out?"

"Quite simple. Take me, for example: my attitude is one of negation—as a matter of sensation! I like negation, my brain is built that way—that's all! Why do I like chemistry? Why do you like apples? It's all a matter of sensation. It's all the same thing. Deeper than that people will never go. Not everybody will tell you that, and I won't be caught telling you that again."

"Well, and is honesty a sensation too?"

"Rather!"

"Yevgeny!" Arkady began in a sad voice.

"Eh? What? Don't like it?" Bazarov interrupted him. "No sir! If you're going to mow everything down then go the whole hog. But that'll do philosophising. 'Nature evokes the silence of sleep,' said Pushkin."

"He never said anything of the kind," Arkady protested.

"Well, if he didn't he might have and should have said it, being a poet. By the way, he must have served in the army."

"Pushkin was never a military man."

"But, my dear fellow, on almost every page he has 'To battle, to battle! For Russia's honour!' "

"You're just making up nonsense! It's nothing short of slander, really."

"Slander! Pooh! You won't frighten me with words like that! However much you slander a person, he really deserves twenty times as much."

"Let's better go to sleep!" Arkady said, annoyed.

"With the greatest pleasure," Bazarov retorted.

But neither of them could sleep. A feeling almost akin to animosity stole into the hearts of the two young men. Five minutes later they opened their eyes and looked at each other in silence.

"Look," said Arkady suddenly, "a dry maple leaf has broken off and fallen to the ground; its movements are exactly like the flight of a butterfly. Isn't it curious? A thing so utterly sad and dead resembles a thing so utterly alive and joyous."

"Oh, my friend, Arkady Nikolaich!" Bazarov exclaimed, "one thing I ask of you—don't speak pretty."

"I speak as best I can. It's downright despotism, if you want to know. If an idea occurred to me, why shouldn't I express it?"

"Very well; but why shouldn't I express mine. I believe that to speak pretty is indecent."

"What is decent then? To swear?"

"Ah! I see you've definitely made up your mind to follow in your uncle's footsteps. How delighted that idiot would be to hear you!"

"What did you call Pavel Petrovich?"

"I called him the right thing—an idiot."

"But that's intolerable!" Arkady exclaimed.

"Aha! The call of the blood," Bazarov said coolly. "I've noticed that it's very strong in people. A man is prepared to renounce everything, and give up all prejudices, but to admit, for example, that his brother who steals other people's handkerchiefs is a thief—that is beyond him. Indeed: *my* brother, *mine*—and not a genius? How can that be?"

"It was a simple sense of justice that made me speak up and not kindred feeling at all," Arkady retorted testily. "But as you don't understand that, as you haven't got the *sensation*—you can't judge it."

"In other words: Arkady Kirsanov is too exalted of mind for me to understand—I bend the knee and say no more."

"Leave off, Yevgeny; we'll finish up by quarrelling."

"I say, Arkady, let's have a good quarrel for once—let's go at it tooth and nail, to utter annihilation."

"We might end up by...."

"By coming to blows?" Bazarov said eagerly. "What of it? Here, in the hay, in these idyllic surroundings, far from the world and the eyes of men—not a bad idea. But you'd be no match for me. I'd grab you by the throat...."

Bazarov spread his long wiry fingers. Arkady turned round and assumed an attitude of defence, jokingly, as it were. But his friend's face looked so sinister, his sneering lips and gleaming eyes held such an ugly threat in them that Arkady quailed.

"Ah! So that's where you've hidden!" came the voice of Vassily Ivanych, and the old army surgeon appeared before the young men clad in a homespun linen jacket and a straw hat, likewise homemade. "I've been looking for you all over. You've chosen a splendid place, however, and an excellent occupation. To lie on the 'earth' and gaze at the 'sky'.... Do you know, there's something significant in that!"

"I only gaze at the sky when I'm about to sneeze," Bazarov growled, and turning to Arkady, added in an undertone: "What a pity he interrupted us."

"Get along with you," Arkady whispered and surreptitiously squeezed his friend's hand. But no friendship will long withstand such clashes.

"When I look at you two young friends," Vassily Ivanych went on, shaking his head and resting his crossed hands on a cunningly twisted stick of his own handiwork with a knob in the shape of a Turk's head, "it does my heart good. What lustihood, what abilities, talents!—brimming youth! Simply ... Castor and Pollux!"

"Just listen to that—spouting mythology!" Bazarov said. "One can soon tell you were a strong Latinist in your time! I believe you were awarded a silver medal for composition, weren't you?"

"Dioscuri, Dioscuri!" Vassily Ivanych repeated.

"Come on, father,—enough of this cooing."

"Once in a blue moon doesn't matter," mumbled the old man. "But I've been looking for you, gentlemen, not to pay you compliments, but to inform you, in the first place, that we shall soon be having dinner; and, secondly, I wanted to warn you, Yevgeny.... You're a clever man, you understand people, and women too, and consequently should adopt a tolerant attitude.... Your mother wanted to have a service read on the occasion of your homecoming. Don't imagine that I'm asking you to attend the service— It's all over now, but Father Alexei...."

"The priest chap?"

"Er, yes, the clergyman; he's ... going to have dinner with us. I didn't know it, as a matter of fact I was even against it ... but, somehow, it happened that way ... he didn't understand me.... Well, and Arina Vlasyevna, too.... He's a very good and sensible man, though."

"He won't eat my portion at dinner, will he?" Bazarov asked.

"Good heavens, no!" Vassily Ivanych laughed.

"Then that's good enough for me. I'll sit down to table with any man."

Vassily Ivanych adjusted his hat.

"I knew beforehand that you were above all prejudice. Look at me, I'm an old man, getting on for sixty-two now, and I haven't any prejudices either." (Vassily Ivanych did not have the courage to admit that he had wanted the service read himself. He was no less pious than his wife.) "And Father Alexei is very anxious to make your acquaintance. You'll like him, you'll see. He's not averse to a game of cards and ... between you and me ... he even smokes a pipe."

"All right. We'll sit down to a game of *yeralash* after dinner, and I'll beat him."

"He-he-he, we'll see about that! Don't be so sure of yourself."

"Why? Going to recall the old days?" Bazarov said with peculiar emphasis.

Vassily Ivanych's bronzed cheeks flushed faintly.

"For shame, Yevgeny. Don't rake up the past. But I don't mind confessing to this gentleman that I did have that passion in my youth—and paid for it too! But isn't it hot. Let me sit down next to you. I'm not in your way, am I?"

"Not at all," Arkady said.

Vassily Ivanych lowered himself with a grunt onto the hay.

"This couch of yours, gentlemen," he began, "reminds me of my army, bivouac days, with the dressing stations rigged up near a haystack like this—that is, if we were lucky enough." He sighed. "Yes, I've been through a lot in my time. There is that curious episode during the plague epidemic in Bessarabia, for example, if you would like to hear it."

"The one you got the St. Vladimir for?" Bazarov said. "We've heard it. By the way, why don't you wear it?"

"I've told you I have no prejudices," Vassily Ivanych muttered—only the day before he had ordered the red

10*

ribbon to be ripped off his coat—and proceeded to nar-
rate the plague episode. "He's fallen asleep," he suddenly
said to Arkady in a whisper, pointing at Bazarov with
a humourous wink. "Yevgeny! Get up!" he added aloud.
"Let's go in to dinner."

Father Alexei, a portly handsome man with thick carefully brushed hair and an embroidered girdle over a
purple silk cassock, proved to be a very shrewd and
quick-witted person. He hastened first to shake hands
with Arkady and Bazarov, as though aware beforehand
that they had no need of his blessing, and generally he
bore himself with ease. He made himself companionable
without being offensive; he laughed at seminary Latin
and stood up for his bishop; he drank two glasses of wine
but declined a third; accepted a cigar from Arkady, but
did not smoke it, saying he would take it home. The only
disagreeable thing about him was a habit he had of slowly
and warily raising his hand to catch flies that settled on
his face, and sometimes he squashed them. He sat down
at the card-table with moderately expressed pleasure and
ended by winning two rubles fifty kopeks from Bazarov
in paper money; nobody in Arina Vlasyevna's house had
any idea about counting silver coinage. The lady sat as
usual next to her son (she did not play cards), her face
propped up by her fist, and got up only to order some
new dish to be served. She was afraid to caress Bazarov
and he did not encourage her; besides, Vassily Ivanych
had admonished her against "bothering" him too much.
"Young men don't like it," he had urged. (the dinner
given that day need hardly be described; Timofeich in
person had galloped off at break of day for a particular
brand of Circassian beef; the *starosta* had gone in the
opposite direction for burbots, gremilles and crawfish;
for mushrooms alone the peasant women had received as
much as forty-two kopeks in copper coins); but Arina Vlasyevna's gaze, bent steadfastly on Bazarov, expressed not
only devotion and tenderness—there was a tinge of sadness in her eyes mingled with curiosity and fear, a sort of
meek reproach.

Bazarov had other things to think of, than to bother
his head about the expression of his mother's eyes; he

rarely addressed her, and when he did it was with a curt question. Once he asked her to give him her hand "for luck"; she slipped her soft little hand into his hard, broad palm.

"Well," she asked after a while, "did it help?"

"Worse than ever," he said with a careless smile.

"He plays a risky game," Father Alexei said rather ruefully, stroking his handsome beard.

"Napoleon's rule, Father," put in Vassily Ivanych, leading with an ace.

"Which brought him to St. Helena," murmured Father Alexei, trumping the ace.

"Would you like some currant juice, darling?" asked Arina Vlasyevna.

Bazarov merely shrugged.

※　※　※

"No!" he said to Arkady the next day. "I'll clear out tomorrow. It's tedious; I want to work, and I can't do it here. I'll go to your place again—I've left all my preparations there. At your place I can at least shut myself up. Here father keeps on telling me: 'My study's at your disposal—nobody will be in your way,' but he doesn't leave my side for a minute. I can't very well shut him out. And mother, too. I hear her sighing behind the wall, but if I go out to her I can't find anything to say to her."

"She'll be very upset," Arkady said, "and so will he."

"I'll be coming back to them."

"When?"

"Before going to St. Petersburg."

"I feel especially sorry for your mother."

"How's that? Has she won you over with her berries?"

Arkady lowered his eyes.

"You don't know your mother, Yevgeny. She's not only a fine woman, she's very clever, really. This morning she talked to me for half an hour, and she was so sensible and interesting."

"Enlarging about me most of the time, I suppose?"

"We talked of other things, too."

"Perhaps; these things are clearer to an outsider. If a woman can sustain a conversation for half an hour it's a good sign. But I'm going all the same."

"You won't find it easy to break the news to them. They're talking all the time about what we'll be doing two weeks from now."

"No, it won't be easy. I had to go and tease my father, dash it! He had ordered one of his tenant serfs to be flogged the other day—and quite right, too; yes, quite right, don't look at me in such horror—because the fellow's an unspeakable thief and drunkard; only father never expected the thing would reach my ears. He was greatly put out, and now I'll have to upset him on top of it. Never mind! He'll get over it."

Bazarov had said: "never mind!" but it took him the whole day to pluck up courage to tell Vassily Ivanych of his intentions. At last, when bidding him good night in his study, he said with a simulated yawn:

"Yes ... nearly forgot to tell you.... Will you please send a relay of horses down to Fedot's tomorrow?"

Vassily Ivanych was astonished.

"Is Mr. Kirsanov leaving us?"

"Yes; and I'm going with him."

Vassily Ivanych spun round on the spot.

"You are going away?"

"Yes.... I have to. See about the horses, please."

"Very well...." the old man faltered, "a relay ... very well ... but ... but.... What's the matter?"

"I must go down to his place for a short time. I'll be back again."

"Yes! For a short time.... All right." Vassily Ivanych took out his handkerchief and bending over almost to the ground blew his nose. "Ah, well! I thought you'd stay ... a little longer. Three days.... That's after three years—not much, not much, Yevgeny!"

"But I'm telling you I'll be back soon. I have to go."

"You have to.... Ah, well! Duty first, of course.... So you want the horses sent out? All right. We hadn't expected this, of course. Arina has asked the neighbour for flowers—wanted to decorate your room." (Vassily Ivanych said nothing about how, every day at peep of dawn, standing with slippers on his bare feet, he conferred with Timofeich, and, drawing out one tattered banknote after another with trembling fingers, he gave him orders for the day's shopping, laying particular stress on eatables and red wine, which the young men appeared to be fond of.) "Freedom above all—that's my rule. . . . Mustn't stand in the way . . . mustn't. . . ."

He suddenly fell silent and made for the door.

"We'll be seeing each other again soon, Father, really."

But Vassily Ivanych, without turning his head, waved his hand wearily and left the room. Coming into his bedroom he found his wife in bed, and began to say his prayers in a whisper, so as not to waken her. She awoke, however.

"Is that you, Vassily Ivanych?" she asked.

"Yes, Mother!"

"You've come from Yevgeny? Do you know, I'm afraid he's not comfortable on the sofa. I told Anfisushka to give him your camp mattress and some new pillows; I'd give him our feather bed, but he doesn't like a soft bed, if I remember."

"Never mind, Mother, don't worry. He's comfortable. Lord have mercy on us poor sinners," he went on in an undertone, finishing his prayer. Vassily Ivanych pitied his old wife and did not want to tell her before morning what sorrow awaited her.

Bazarov and Arkady left the next day. A gloom was cast upon the whole household from early in the morning; the dishes kept slipping out of Anfisushka's hands; even Fedya was baffled and ended by taking off his boots. Vassily Ivanych was fussier than ever: he was obviously putting on a bold front; he talked loudly and stamped about, but his face had grown haggard and his eyes avoided his son's face. Arina Vlasyevna cried softly; she would have broken down completely had not her husband spent over two persuasive hours with her in the morning. When Bazarov, after repeated promises to return not later than in a month, had finally torn himself from the clinging embraces and taken his seat in the tarantass, when the horses had started and the bell had begun to jingle and the wheels to turn, when there was nothing

more down the road for straining eyes to see and the
dust had settled, and Timofeich, bent almost double, had
staggered back to his tiny room; when the old couple
were left alone in a house which, like them, seemed to
have suddenly shrunk and aged—Vassily Ivanych, who
a minute before had been bravely waving his handkerchief on the porch steps, sank into a chair and dropped
his head on his chest. "He has left us, left us!" he murmured. "Found it too dull here. All alone now, all alone!"
he repeated several times, gazing dully before him and
stretching his hand out appealingly. Then Arina Vlasyevna went up to him, and laying her grey head to his,
said: "It can't be helped, Vasya! A son is like a severed
branch. He's like the eagle that comes when it wants and
goes when it wants; and you and I are like mushrooms
on a tree stump—we sit side by side without budging.
Only I will remain the same to you always, and you to
me."

Vassily Ivanych drew his hands away from his face
and embraced his wife, his friend, as he had never embraced her in his youth; she had comforted him in his
grief.

XXII

All the way to Fedot's our friends rode in silence,
merely exchanging a word now and then. Bazarov was
none too pleased with himself. Arkady was not pleased
with him either. Moreover his heart was weighed down
with that unaccountable feeling of sadness which is familiar only to very young men. The coachman rehitched the
horses and, climbing to his seat, asked: "Left or right,
sir?"

Arkady started. The road to the right led to town, and
thence home; the road to the left led to Odintsova's.

He glanced at Bazarov.

"Shall we go to the left, Yevgeny?" he asked.

Bazarov turned his head away.

"Don't be silly!" he muttered.

"I know it's silly," Arkady said. "But what's the harm?
It isn't the first time."

Bazarov pulled his cap down.

"Just as you like," he said at length.

"To the left, coachman!" Arkady cried.

The tarantass bowled off in the direction of Nikol-skoye. Having decided to be "silly", the friends were more silent than ever, and even seemed to be angry.

*   *   *

By the way the butler received them on the porch steps of Odintsova's house, our friends might have guessed how injudiciously they had acted in giving way to their sudden fancy. Obviously they were not expected. They sheepishly cooled their heels for a rather long time in the drawing room. At last Odintsova came in. She greeted them with her usual affability, but was surprised they had come back so soon, and, judging by her slow speech and movements, was not exactly delighted. They hastened to announce that they had dropped in on their way to town and would be moving on in about four hours. She merely uttered a deprecatory little sound, asked Arkady to convey her regards to his father, and sent for her aunt. The princess came in looking sleepy, and this made her shrivelled old face look fiercer than ever. Katya was feeling indisposed and did not leave her room. It suddenly dawned on Arkady that he had been wanting to see Katya almost as badly as Anna Sergeyevna. The four hours passed in desultory talk on this, that and the other; Anna Sergeyevna listened and spoke with an unsmiling face. Only at leave-taking did something of her former friendliness appear.

"I'm in the doldrums just now," she declared, "but you mustn't take any notice and—I say this to both of you— call again in a little while."

Both Bazarov and Arkady responded with a silent bow, got into their carriage and drove straight home to Ma-ryino, where they arrived safe and sound the next evening. Throughout the journey neither had so much as mentioned Odinstova's name; Bazarov in particular had hardly opened his mouth and kept staring away from the road with a kind of fierce tensity.

At Maryino everybody was delighted to see them. Nikolai Petrovich had been getting worried over his son's long absence: he uttered a cry of joy, kicked his feet and jumped up and down on the sofa when Fenichka came running in with shining eyes to announce the arrival of the "young masters"; even Pavel Petrovich experienced a mild thrill and smiled indulgently as he shook hands with the returned wanderers. There followed accounts and questions; Arkady did most of the talking, especially at supper, which lasted until long after midnight. Nikolai Petrovich ordered several bottles of porter, recently delivered from Moscow, to be brought up, and applied himself to it so assiduously that his cheeks became crimson, and he laughed all the time with a kind of childish, nervous laugh. The general excitement spread to the servants' hall. Dunyasha dashed in and out like one possessed, slamming doors, while Pyotr, at three in the morning, was still attempting a *Valse-Cossack* on the guitar. The strings made a pleasant plaintive sound in the still air, but the educated valet got no further than an opening ornamental passage: nature had denied him musical gifts, as she had all others.

*   *   *

Things had been going none too smoothly at Maryino and poor Nikolai Petrovich was having a hard time. The farm was giving increasing trouble—and cheerless, futile trouble it was. The hired labourers were becoming insufferable. Some demanded to be paid off or given a rise, others quitted, taking the advance with them; the horses sickened; the wear and tear of the harness was dreadful; work was done in a slapdash manner; the threshing machine that had been delivered from Moscow proved too cumbersome for practical purposes; a winnowing machine was damaged beyond repair at the first trial; half the cattle sheds were destroyed by fire because a blind old menial had gone to fumigate her cow with a firebrand on a windy night, although the culprit herself had laid all the blame on her master's fad for newfangled kinds of cheeses and dairy farming. The manager suddenly became lazy and even began to grow fat, like every Russian who eats "free bread". On catching sight of Nikolai Petrovich from afar he would make a show of zeal by throwing a bit of wood at a passing pig or shaking his fist at a half-naked urchin, but most of the time he slept. The peasants were in arrears with their rent and stole the master's timber; barely a night passed without the keepers impounding stray peasant horses found grazing on the farm meadows; Nikolai Petrovich had introduced a fine for damage caused by cattle, but the matter usually ended by the horses being returned to their owners after spending a day or two on the master's fodder. To crown all, the peasants began to quarrel among themselves; brothers demanded a division of property; their wives fell out with each other; things would come to a head in a sudden brawl, everybody would come flocking to the office, burst in on the master, often with battered visages and in a drunken state, demanding justice and retribution; a hubbub and a clamour would arise, the wails and whimpering squeals of the women mingling with the curses of the men. One had to arbitrate between the warring parties and shout oneself hoarse, knowing only too well that no proper decision could be reached. There was a shortage of hands for harvesting: a neighbouring farmer of most seemly aspect had contracted to supply reapers at the rate of two rubles per dessiatin, but had cheated Nikolai Petrovich shamelessly; the local peasant women demanded an exorbitant price, and meanwhile the grain was spilling, the mowing still had to be done, and the Guardian Council was threatening and demanding prompt and full payment of interest on the mortgage.

"I'm at the end of my tether!" Nikolai Petrovich had often cried in despair. "I can't very well fight them, and my principles don't allow me to call in the police officer, yet you can't do anything without the fear of punishment!"

"*Du calme, du calme,*" Pavel Petrovich would soothe him, while he wrinkled his forehead, pulled at his moustache and purred.

Bazarov kept aloof from these squabbles: besides, as a guest, all this was none of his business. The day after

he arrived at Maryino he set to work on his frogs, infusoria and chemicals, and was busy with them all the
time. Arkady, on the other hand, deemed it his duty, if
not to help his father, at least to show that he was ready
to help. He heard his father out patiently, and once offered
some advice, not for the sake of its being taken, but to
show his sympathy. The idea of running a farm was not
repugnant to him: if anything, he looked forward to taking up agricultural pursuits, but at the moment his head
was filled with other things. Arkady was amazed to find
himself constantly thinking about Nikolskoye; formerly he
would have merely shrugged his shoulders had anybody
suggested the possibility of his being bored in Bazarov's
company, and under his parental roof, too; but he really
was bored and ached to get away. He took to making
long fatiguing tramps, but that was no help. Once, during
a conversation with his father, Arkady learned that his
father had some letters, and rather interesting ones, from
Odintsova's mother to his late wife, and Arkady worried
his father until he had got those letters from him, Nikolai
Petrovich having had to ransack a score of drawers and
trunks to find them. On coming into possession of these
half-mouldered papers Arkady seemed to calm down, as
though he had seen a goal in front of him which he had
to make. "I say this to both of you," he whispered to
himself over and over again. "She said that herself. Dash
it all, I'll go down, yes I will!" Then he recollected the
last visit, the cool reception, and his old sense of embarrassment and timidity returned. The adventurous
spirit of youth, however, a secret desire to try his luck, to
test his strength under his own auspices, finally overcame
his scruples. Ten days after his return to Maryino found
him once more on his way to town on the pretext of
studying the organisation of Sunday schools, and thence
to Nikolskoye. Eagerly urging on the coachman, he rushed
on to his destination like a young officer into battle: he was
gripped by fear and joy, bursting with impatience. "The
main thing is not to think about it," he kept saying to
himself. The coachman, as luck would have it, proved to
be a game fellow; he stopped at every public house on
the road, saying: "Wet the whistle—or not?" but having

wet the whistle he did not spare the horses. The tall roof
of the familiar house came in sight at length. "What am
I doing?" it suddenly flashed through Arkady's mind.
"Too late now to turn back!" The troika raced down the
road with the coachman whooping and whistling. Now
they had rushed with a clatter of hoofs and a rumble of
wheels over the little wooden bridge, and now the drive
lined by trimmed fir trees swept towards them. There was
the flutter of a pink dress amid the dark greenery, and a
young face peeped out from under the light fringe of a
parasol. He recognised Katya, and she recognised him.
Arkady told the coachman to stop the galloping horses,
jumped out of the carriage, and went up to her. "It's
you!" she murmured, a slow flush mounting to her cheeks.
"Let's join my sister, she's here in the garden; she will
be glad to see you."

Katya led Arkady into the garden. His meeting her
struck him as a peculiarly happy omen; his joy at seeing
her could not have been greater had she been someone
near and dear to him. Things could not have turned out
better—no butler, no announcement. At a bend in the
path he saw Anna Sergeyevna. She was standing with
her back to him. Hearing footsteps, she turned round
slowly.

Arkady felt embarrassed again, but her very first words
immediately set him at his ease. "Hullo, you runaway!"
she said in her kind steady way, and went forward to
meet him, smiling and screwing up her eyes against the
sun and wind. "Where did you find him, Katya?"

"I have brought you something, Anna Sergeyevna,"
he began, "something you least of all expect...."

"You have brought yourself; that's best of all."

XXIII

Having seen Arkady off with mock regret and given
him to understand that he was under no delusion as to the
true object of his journey, Bazarov withdrew into complete seclusion; he was seized by a fever of activity. He
no longer argued with Pavel Petrovich, particularly since

the latter had assumed a more aristocratic air than ever in his presence, and expressed his opinions by sounds rather than words. Only once did Pavel Petrovich venture a bout with the *nihilist* on the then fashionable topic of the rights of the Baltic nobles, but abruptly checked himself, saying with frigid suavity: "But we cannot understand one another, at least, I'm sorry to say I do not understand you."

"To be sure!" Bazarov exclaimed. "A man is capable of understanding everything—how the air flows and what takes place on the sun; but how another man can blow his nose otherwise than he does—that he cannot understand."

"Is that supposed to be witty," Pavel Petrovich said interrogatively and moved away.

True, he sometimes asked to be allowed to witness Bazarov's experiments, and once even brought his perfumed face, laved in some excellent lotion, close to the microscope to examine some transparent infusoria in the process of swallowing a green speck and hastily masticating it with the aid of very nimble cilia situated in the gullet. Nikolai Petrovich visited Bazarov much more often than his brother; he would have come every day "to learn" as he expressed it, had he not been so busy with the farm. He was not in the way of the young naturalist, and usually sat in a corner, watching attentively and only occasionally permitting himself a discreet question. During meals he strove to turn the conversation on physics, geology or chemistry, since all other topics, including farming, not to mention politics, were fraught with the risk of mutual annoyance, if not clashes. Nikolai Petrovich sensed that his brother's hatred of Bazarov had not abated in the least. A trivial incident, among many others, confirmed his suspicions. Cases of cholera had appeared in the neighbourhood and even claimed two victims at Maryino. One night Pavel Petrovich was seized by a rather severe attack. He suffered till morning, but did not resort to Bazarov's skill; when the latter met him the next morning and asked why he had not sent for him, he replied, still pale, but carefully groomed and shaved: "If I remember aright you said yourself that you do not believe in medicine." And so the days passed. Bazarov worked doggedly and gloomily—yet there was one creature in Nikolai Petrovich's house he gladly talked to. That creature was Fenichka.

He usually met her early in the morning in the garden or in the yard; he never went to her room, and she had gone up to his door only on one occasion to ask whether or not she could bathe Mitya. She not only trusted him and was not afraid of him—she felt more at her ease with him than with Nikolai Petrovich. Why that was so it was difficult to say; perhaps it was because she was intuitively aware that Bazarov lacked those attributes of the grand gentleman, that higher something which at once fascinated and awed her. To her he was just an excellent doctor and a simple man. She tended her child in his presence without constraint, and once, when she suddenly felt dizzy and her head began to ache, she took a spoonful of medicine from his hands. In Nikolai Petrovich's presence she seemed to shun Bazarov: she did so not out of guile, but through a sense of propriety. Pavel Petrovich she feared more than ever; he had begun to watch her lately, and would crop up suddenly behind her back in his immaculate suit with a set wary look and his hands in his pockets. "He just freezes you up," Fenichka complained to Dunyasha, who would sigh by way of reply, while thinking of another "unfeeling" man. Bazarov had unsuspectingly become the *cruel tyrant* of her heart.

Fenichka liked Bazarov; and he liked her, too. Even his face would change when he talked to her: it assumed a serene, almost gentle expression, and his customary nonchalance was tinged with a playful regard. Fenichka grew prettier every day. There is a time in a young woman's life when she suddenly begins to bloom and blossom forth like a summer rose; this time had come to Fenichka. Everything favoured it—even the sultry July heat. Clad in a light white dress, she looked whiter and lighter herself: she did not take sunburn, and the heat which she tried in vain to avoid imparted a tender bloom to her cheeks and ears, and pouring a soft lassitude through all her body, was mirrored by a dreamy languor in her pretty eyes. She could hardly do anything; her hands were for ever slipping listlessly to her lap. She could barely walk about, and uttered amusing little exclamations of helplessness.

"You should bathe more often," Nikolai Petrovich used to tell her.

He had fixed up a bathing tent at one of the ponds that had not yet dried up.

"Oh, Nikolai Petrovich! By the time you get to the pond you're almost dead, and by the time you get back it kills you. There isn't a bit of shade in the garden."

"That's true, there isn't any shade," Nikolai Petrovich would say, stroking his eyebrows.

*   *   *

One morning, at a little past six, Bazarov, returning from his walk, came across Fenichka in the lilac arbour, which was long past blossomtime but was still thick and green. She was sitting on a bench with a white kerchief thrown over her head as usual; next to her lay a pile of red and white roses still wet with dew. He wished her good morning.

"Ah! Yevgeny Vassilich!" she said, raising a corner of the kerchief to take a look at him, her arm baring to the elbow as she did so.

"What are you doing here?" Bazarov said, sitting down beside her. "Making a bouquet?"

"Yes, for the breakfast table. Nikolai Petrovich likes it."

"But breakfast's a long way off yet. My, what a mass of flowers!"

"I've picked them now because it will be hot later on and I daren't go out of doors. This is the only time I can breathe freely. This heat makes me awfully weak. I wonder if I'm well?"

"What an idea! Let's feel your pulse." Bazarov took her hand, found the steadily throbbing vein and did not even bother to count the beats. "You'll live to be a hundred," he said, releasing her hand.

"Oh, God forbid!" she exclaimed.

"Why? Wouldn't you like to live long?"

"But a hundred years! Grandma lived to eighty-five—but what a martyr she was! Black and deaf and bent and coughing all the time; simply a burden to herself. What's the use of such a life!"

"Better to be young then?"

"Why, of course!"

"In what way is it better? Tell me!"

"What a question! Well, I'm young now, I can do anything, I can come and go and carry things and I don't have to ask anyone to do them for me. What could be better?"

"To me it's all the same whether I'm young or old."

"How can you say that? What a thing to say!"

"But judge for yourself, Fedosya Nikolayevna—what need have I for my youth? I live all alone, a poor lonely man. . . ."

"That only depends on you."

"That's just the trouble—it doesn't! If only somebody would take pity on me."

Fenichka gave him a sidelong glance, but said nothing. "What's that book you have?" she asked presently.

"This one? It's a learned book, difficult stuff."

"And you are learning all the time! Don't you find it dull? You must know everything there is to know, I should imagine."

"Evidently not. Try and read some of it."

"But I won't understand a thing. Is it in Russian?" said Fenichka taking the heavily bound volume in both hands. "What a thick book!"

"Yes, it's in Russian."

"All the same, I won't understand it."

"I didn't mean you to understand it. I want to look at you while you are reading. The tip of your nose wriggles very prettily when you read."

Fenichka, who had begun to spell out an article "On Creosote", burst out laughing and dropped the book . . . it slipped down from the bench to the ground.

"I like to see you laugh, too," Bazarov said.

"Oh, stop it!"

"I like when you speak. It's like the babbling of a brook."

Fenichka turned her head away. "Oh, how can you!" she murmured, toying with the flowers. "What do you find in my talk? You have spoken to such clever ladies."

"Ah, Fedosya Nikolayevna! Believe me, all the clever ladies in the world are not worth your little finger."

"Oh, what a thing to say!" Fenichka whispered.

Bazarov picked the book up from the ground. "This is a doctor's book, you shouldn't throw it about!"

"A doctor's book?" Fenichka echoed and turned round to him. "Do you know what? Since you gave me those drops—do you remember?—Mitya's been sleeping wonderfully! I don't know how to thank you; you're so kind, really."

"Doctors should really be paid," Bazarov said with a smile. "Doctors, you know, are a selfish lot."

Fenichka looked up at Bazarov with eyes that seemed darker from the pale gleam that set off the upper part of her face. She did not know whether he was joking or in earnest.

"If you wish, we shall be only too pleased. . . . I'll talk it over with Nikolai Petrovich."

"You think it's money I want?" Bazarov broke in. "No, I don't want any money from you."

"What then?" Fenichka said.

"What?" repeated Bazarov. "Guess."

"I'm no good at guessing!"

"Then I'll tell you; I want . . . one of those roses."

Fenichka laughed again and even flung up her hands, so amusing did Bazarov's request seem to her. Although she laughed, she felt flattered. Bazarov looked at her intently.

"Why, certainly," she said at length, and bending over the bench she began to turn the flowers over. "Which would you like, a red one or a white one?"

"A red one, and not too big."

She straightened up.

"Here you are" she said, but instantly snatched her hand back and, biting her lip, glanced at the entrance to the arbour, then listened.

"What is it?" Bazarov said. "Nikolai Petrovich?"

"No. He's gone out to the fields. . . . I'm not afraid of him. But Pavel Petrovich . . . I thought for a moment. . . ."

"What?"

"I thought he was walking around. No . . . it's nobody. Here, take it." Fenichka gave Bazarov the rose.

"What makes you afraid of Pavel Petrovich?"

"He scares me all the time. He doesn't say a word, just looks at me in a queer sort of way. But you don't like him either. Do you remember how you used to argue with him all the time? I don't know what it's all about, but I can see how you turn him this way and that. . . ."

Fenichka showed with her hands how, in her opinion, Bazarov turned Pavel Petrovich about.

Bazarov smiled.

"What if he got the better of me?" he said. "Would you take my part?"

"How could I take your part? And besides, nobody will ever get the better of you."

"You think so? But I know a hand that could knock me over with one finger if it wanted to."

"What hand is that?"

"Don't pretend you don't know. How nice the rose you gave me smells. Just smell it."

Fenichka craned her slim neck and put her face to the flower. The kerchief slipped down to her shoulders, uncovering a soft mass of black, lustrous hair, slightly ruffled.

"Wait, I want to smell it with you," Bazarov murmured, and bending down he kissed her on her parted lips.

She started and pressed both hands against his chest, but pressed feebly, and he was able to renew and prolong the kiss.

A dry cough sounded behind the lilac bushes. Fenichka instantly moved to the far end of the bench. Pavel Petrovich passed the entrance, made a slight bow, and letting fall with a kind of savage gloom "You're here!" walked away. Fenichka hastily picked up her roses and left the arbour. "For shame, Yevgeny Vassilich," she whispered as she went out. There was genuine reproach in her voice.

Bazarov recalled another recent scene, and was struck with a sense of guilt and contemptuous irritation. But he shook his head, ironically congratulated himself on his initiation into the ranks of chartered Celadons and went to his room.

And Pavel Petrovich left the garden and walked slowly to the woods. He remained there a fairly long time, and when he came in to breakfast Nikolai Petrovich solicitously enquired whether he was well—so dark had his countenance grown.

"You know I sometimes suffer from bilious attacks," Pavel Petrovich calmly replied.

XXIV

Some two hours later he knocked at Bazarov's door. "I must apologise for interrupting your scientific studies," he began, settling himself in a chair by the window with both hands resting on a handsome cane with an ivory knob (he usually went about without a cane) "but I must ask you to spare me five minutes of your time—no more."

"All my time is at your disposal," replied Bazarov, over whose face a shadow had flitted as soon as Pavel Petrovich crossed the threshold.

"Five minutes will be enough for me. I have come to put just one question to you!"

"A question? What is it about?"

"Well, then, please listen. At the beginning of your sojourn in my brother's house, when I had not yet denied myself the pleasure of conversing with you, I had occasion to hear your views on many subjects; but, as far as I remember, neither between us nor in my presence was there any talk of duels. May I enquire what your views are on this score?"

Bazarov, who had risen on Pavel Petrovich's entrance, sat down on the edge of the table and crossed his arms.

"My view is this," he said. "From the theoretical standpoint a duel is absurd, but from the practical—that's another matter."

"That is to say, if I understand you rightly, whatever your theoretical opinion of a duel may be, you would not in practice let yourself be insulted without demanding satisfaction?"

"You have guessed my mind exactly."

"Very good, sir. I am very pleased to hear you say so. Your statement relieves me of my uncertainty. . . ."

"Indecision, you wanted to say."

"It's all the same; I express myself so as to be understood; I am not a seminary rat. Your statement relieves me of a regrettable necessity. I have decided to fight a duel with you."

Bazarov stared.

"With me?"

"Yes, sir, with you."

"Good heavens, what for?"

"I could explain the reason to you," Pavel Petrovich began, "but I prefer not to. You are one too many here to my taste; I detest you, loathe you, and if that is not enough. . . ."

Pavel Petrovich's eyes flashed. There was a gleam in Bazarov's too.

"Very well, sir," he said. "Further explanations are unnecessary. You have taken it into your head to try your chivalry out on me. I could deny you that pleasure, but never mind."

"I am greatly obliged to you," Pavel Petrovich answered. "I can now hope that you will accept my challenge without compelling me to resort to violence."

"In other words, speaking without allegory—to that cane?" Bazarov said coolly. "Quite right. You don't have to insult me. It would not be wholly safe either. You can remain a gentleman. I accept your challenge as a gentleman too."

"Splendid," Pavel Petrovich said, and put his cane in a corner. "A few words now as to the conditions of our duel; but first I would like to know whether you consider it necessary to resort to the formality of a trivial quarrel, as a pretext for my challenge?"

"No, let us do without formalities."

"I think so too. I do not think it worthwhile to go

into the real reasons for our difference either. We cannot stand each other. What more need be said?"

"What more, indeed?" Bazarov repeated ironically.

"As regards the conditions of the duel—since we shall not have any seconds—where can we get them—?"

"Precisely, where can we get them?"

"So I have the honour to propose the following: the duel is to take place tomorrow morning, say at six o'clock by the copse, with pistols; the barrier at ten paces. . . ."

"Ten paces? Very well; we hate each other at that distance."

"We can make it eight," observed Pavel Petrovich.

"Certainly, why not!"

"We shall have two shots each; just in case, each of us will put a letter in his pocket blaming himself for his own death."

"Now, that I don't quite agree with," Bazarov said. "It smacks a bit of the French novel and doesn't sound plausible."

"Perhaps. But you will concede that it will not be very pleasant to be suspected of murder?"

"I agree. But there is a way of avoiding that sad contingency. We have no seconds, but we can have a witness."

"Who exactly, may I ask?"

"Why, Pyotr."

"What Pyotr?"

"Your brother's valet. He's a man who enjoys the advantages of a modern education and will play his part with all due *comme il faut*."

"I believe you are jesting, my dear sir."

"Not at all. If you consider my suggestion you will find it sensible and simple. Murder will out, but I undertake to prepare Pyotr for the occasion and bring him to the field of battle."

"You still persist in jesting," Pavel Petrovich said, getting up from his chair. "But after the kind willingness you have shown I have no right to complain. And so, everything is arranged. By the way, have you pistols?"

"How come I to have pistols, Pavel Petrovich? I'm not a soldier."

"In that case I offer you mine. You can rest assured that I haven't used them for five years."

"That's very comforting news."

Pavel Petrovich picked up his cane.

"And so, my dear sir, it remains for me to thank you and leave you to your studies. Your humble servant, sir."

"Till our pleasant meeting tomorrow, my dear sir," Bazarov said, seeing his visitor out.

Pavel Petrovich took his departure, while Bazarov stood before the closed door after Pavel Petrovich had gone, then suddenly exclaimed, "Well, I never! How very fine and how stupid! What a farce we've played! Like a couple of trained dogs dancing on their hind legs. But I couldn't very well refuse him; he might have hit me, and then. . . ." (Bazarov paled at the very thought; all his pride rose up in arms.) "I'd have had to throttle him then like a kitten." He went back to his microscope, but his heart had been stirred and the calm that was necessary for observations had vanished. "He saw us today," he thought. "But could he have got himself so worked up on his brother's account? What a fuss to make over a kiss. There's something else behind it. Pah! Why, I believe he's in love with her himself! Of course he is; it's as clear as daylight. What a holy mess! A bad case," he decided at length, "whichever way you look at it. In the first place I run a risk, and in any case I'll have to leave; and there's Arkady . . . and that lamb Nikolai Petrovich. A bad case!"

The day passed somehow in a peculiarly quiet and listless fashion. Fenichka might have been non-existent; she sat in her room like a mouse in its hole. Nikolai Petrovich looked worried; it had been reported to him that his wheat had developed brand and he had been counting particularly on that crop. Pavel Petrovich oppressed everybody, even Prokofich, with his icy courtesy. Bazarov began a letter to his father, then tore it up and threw it under the table. "If I die," he thought, "they'll hear about it; but I'm not going to die. I'll have a long innings." He told Pyotr to come and see him the next morning at daybreak on important business; Pyotr thought that he wanted to take him to St. Petersburg. Bazarov went to bed late, and was tortured all night by troubled dreams. Odintsova visited his dreams, she was his mother too, and a kitten with black whiskers followerd her about, and that kitten was Fenichka; Pavel Petrovich appeared in the shape of a big forest, with which he had to fight a duel. Pyotr woke him at four o'clock; he dressed quickly and went out with him.

*   *   *

The morning was bright and fresh; fleecy cloudlets stood in the pale azure of the sky; dew lay on the leaves and grasses and gleamed like silver on the spiders' webs; the dark, moist earth still seemed to retain the rosy traces of sunrise; the song of the larks poured down from the skies. Bazarov reached the copse, and sat down in the shade on the fringe of the woods, and only then did he disclose to Pyotr the service that was required of him. The educated valet was frightened out of his wits; but Bazarov set his fears at rest by assuring him that all he had to do was to stand at a distance and watch, and that he bore no responsibility whatsoever. "Just think," he added, "what an important part you're destined to play!" Pyotr spread his hands, stared down at his feet and leaned against a birch tree, his face sickly green.

The road from Maryino skirted the woods; a light dust lay upon it, untouched by wheel or foot since yesterday. Bazarov looked down the road, despite himself, plucked and nibbled blades of grass, and kept on saying to himself: "What folly!" The chill morning air made him shiver once or twice. Pyotr glanced at him mournfully, but Bazarov merely smiled—he was not scared.

There was a sound of hooves on the road. A peasant appeared from behind the trees. He was driving two hobbled horses before him, and in passing Bazarov, he looked at him rather oddly without taking off his cap, which struck Pyotr as an ill omen. "This fellow is up early too," Bazarov thought, "but at least for a purpose; whereas we?"

"I think he's coming," Pyotr whispered.

Bazarov looked up and saw Pavel Petrovich. Attired in a light checked jacket and snow-white trousers, he was striding swiftly down the road, carrying under his arm a case wrapped up in a green cloth.

"Excuse me, I am afraid I have kept you waiting," he said, bowing first to Bazarov, then to Pyotr, giving him his due as something in the nature of a second. "I did not want to wake my valet."

"That's all right," Bazarov answered. "We've only just arrived ourselves."

"Ah! All the better!" Pavel Petrovich looked round. "Nobody in sight, nobody will interfere. Shall we begin?"

"Let's begin."

"I presume you require no further explanations?"

"No."

"Would you like to load?" Pavel Petrovich asked, drawing the pistols from the case.

"No, load them yourself, and I'll measure off the distance. My legs are longer," Bazarov added with a humorous smile. "One, two, three...."

"Yevgeny Vassilich!" Pyotr barely managed to stammer (he shook like an aspen leaf). "Do what you like, but I'll step aside."

"Four, five.... Step aside, old chap; you can even stand behind a tree and stop your ears up, but don't shut your eyes; if anybody drops, run and pick him up.... Six, seven, eight...." Bazarov stopped. "Will that do," he asked, turning to Pavel Petrovich, "or shall I throw in another couple of paces?"

"As you wish," the other retorted, pushing home a second bullet.

"Well, let's throw in another two paces," Bazarov traced a line on the ground with the toe of his boot. "Here's the barrier. By the way, how many paces do we have to take from the barrier? That's an important point too. We didn't discuss it yesterday."

"Ten paces I should say," replied Pavel Petrovich, offering Bazarov the pistols. "Will you be so good as to choose?"

"I will. Come, Pavel Petrovich, don't you agree that our duel is singular to the point of absurdity? Just take a look at our second's face."

"You still wish to treat the matter as a joke," Pavel Petrovich replied. "I do not deny that our duel is peculiar, but I consider it my duty to warn you that I intend to fight in earnest. *A bon entendeur, salut!*"

"Oh, I haven't the slightest doubt we are determined to annihilate each other; but why not have a laugh and combine *utile dulci*? So there we are: my Latin to your French."

"I'm going to fight in earnest," Pavel Petrovich repeated and took up his position. Bazarov in turn counted off ten paces from the barrier and stopped.

"Are you ready?" Pavel Petrovich asked.

"Quite."

"We can close in."

Bazarov moved forward slowly, and Pavel Petrovich advanced on him, his left hand thrust into his pocket and his right steadily raising the muzzle of his pistol. "He's aiming straight at my nose," thought Bazarov, "and how carefully he's squinting, the bounder! This is an unpleasant sensation though. I'll keep my eye on his watch chain." Something whizzed sharply close to Bazarov's ear, followed by an instantaneous report. "I've heard it, so I suppose I'm all right," the thought flashed through his mind. He took another step and pulled the trigger without taking aim.

Pavel Petrovich gave a slight start and clutched his thigh. Blood trickled down his white trousers.

Bazarov threw his pistol down and approached his adversary.

"Are you wounded?" he asked.

"You had the right to call me to the barrier," said Pavel Petrovich. "It's nothing. According to the conditions each of us has another shot."

"Sorry, we'll have to leave that for another time," Bazarov said, supporting Pavel Petrovich, who had begun to grow pale. "Now I am no longer a dueller, but a doctor, and I must examine your wound. Pyotr! Come here! Where are you hiding?"

"It's nothing. . . . I don't need any help," Pavel Petrovich said slowly, "and . . . we must . . . again. . . ." He wanted to tug at his moustache, but his hand dropped nervelessly, his eyes rolled up and he lost consciousness.

"Good Lord! A fainting fit! Fancy that!" exclaimed Bazarov, lowering Pavel Petrovich onto the grass. "Let's see what it's all about!" He pulled out a handkerchief, wiped away the blood, and felt around the wound. "The bone is intact," he muttered, "superficial flesh wound, bullet's gone clean through, one muscle *vastus externus* slightly affected. Fit to dance a jig in three weeks! Fancy fainting! Dear me, these nervous types! Look, what a tender skin."

"Is he killed, sir?" Pyotr spluttered behind him, his voice trembling.

Bazarov turned round.

"Go and fetch some water quickly, old chap—he'll outlive both of us."

But the model servant did not seem to understand what had been said to him, for he did not budge. Pavel Petrovich slowly opened his eyes. "He's gonna die!" Pyotr quavered and began crossing himself.

"You're right. . . . What a stupid face!" the wounded gentleman murmured with a wan smile.

"Go and fetch the confounded water!" Bazarov shouted.

"There's no need to. It was a momentary *vertige*. Help me up. That's better. . . . This scratch merely wants binding up and I'll be able to walk home, or the carriage could be sent out for me. The duel, if you like, will not be resumed. You have acted nobly . . . today, today, mind you."

"There's no need to rake up the past," Bazarov answered. "As for the future, there's no need to worry about that either, because I intend to slip away at once. Now let me tie your leg up; your wound is not dangerous, but still it's advisable to steam the blood. But first let us restore this mortal to his senses."

Bazarov shook Pyotr by the collar and sent him to fetch the carriage.

"Mind you don't scare my brother," Pavel Petrovich admonished him. "Don't you dare tell him anything."

Pyotr ran off; while he was gone for the carriage the adversaries sat on the ground in silence. Pavel Petrovich tried to avoid looking at Bazarov; he had no wish to make up with him; he was ashamed of his arrogance and his failure, ashamed of the whole business he had stirred up, though he realised that it could not have ended more satisfactorily. "At any rate he won't be hanging around here any more," he comforted himself, "that's one good thing." The silence was becoming oppressive and awkward. Both felt ill at ease. Each realised that the other understood him perfectly. Between friends that is a pleasant awareness, but between foes an extremely unpleasant one, particularly when there is no way to clear things up or to part company.

"I didn't tie your leg up too tight, did I?" Bazarov asked at length.

"No, it's all right, it's splendid," replied Pyotr Petrovich, adding after a little pause: "My brother won't be deceived, he'll have to be told that we fell out on politics."

"Very good," Bazarov said. "You can say I scoffed at all the Anglomaniacs."

"Splendid. What do you suppose that man thinks of us?" resumed Pavel Petrovich, pointing to the peasant who had driven the hobbled horses past Bazarov a few minutes before the duel, and who now, coming back the road, pulled himself together and doffed his cap at the sight of the "gentlefolk".

"Who knows!" Bazarov said. "Probably he doesn't think anything. The Russian peasant is the mysterious stranger Mrs. Radcliffe used to talk so much about. You can't make him out. He can't make himself out."

"So that's what you think!" Pavel Petrovich began, then suddenly exclaimed: "Look what that idiot of yours, Pyotr, has gone and done! There's my brother tearing down!"

Bazarov turned and saw a pale-faced Nikolai Petrovich sitting in the carriage. He jumped out before the vehicle stopped and rushed up to his brother.

"What does it all mean?" he cried in an agitated voice. "Yevgeny Vassilich, what is the matter?"

"It's all right," Pavel Petrovich answered. "They shouldn't have bothered you. Mr. Bazarov and I have had a little quarrel, and I've come off a bit the worse for it."

"What is it all about, for God's sake?"

"Well, if you want to know, Mr. Bazarov passed some disparaging remarks on Sir Robert Peel. I hasten to add that it was all my fault, and Mr. Bazarov behaved splendidly. I challenged him."

"But, goodness me, you're bleeding!"

"Did you think I had water in my veins? But this bloodletting is good for me. Isn't that so, doctor? Help me get into the carriage, brother, and don't look so glum. I'll be all right tomorrow. There; that's fine. Go on, coachman."

Nikolai Petrovich followed behind the carriage; Bazarov drew up the rear.

"I must ask you to attend my brother, until another doctor is brought down from town," Nikolai Petrovich said to him.

Bazarov inclined his head.

An hour later Pavel Petrovich was lying in bed with a skilfully dressed leg. The whole house was in an uproar; Fenichka swooned; Nikolai Petrovich furtively wrung his hands, while Pavel Petrovich laughed and joked, especially with Bazarov; he put on a fine cambric shirt, a spruce morning jacket and a fez, would not allow the blinds to be lowered and complained in a droll manner at the necessity of abstaining from food.

During the night, however, his temperature rose, and his head ached. A doctor arrived from town. (Nikolai Petrovich had disregarded his brother's protests, and Bazarov himself had insisted on it; he sat in his room all day long, yellow and grim, and dropped in to see the patient for very brief visits; once or twice he had encountered Fenichka, who recoiled from him in horror.) The new doctor recommended cool drinks, and confirmed Bazarov's assurances that there was absolutely no danger. Nikolai Petrovich told him that his brother had accidentally wounded himself, to which the doctor had replied: "Hm!" but receiving there and then twenty-five rubles in silver, had added: "Surprising, these things do happen, you know!"

Nobody in the house undressed or went to bed. Every now and again Nikolai Petrovich tiptoed into his brother's room and tiptoed out again; the patient dropped into a heavy slumber, groaned a little, said to him in French *"couchez-vous"* and asked for a drink. Nikolai Petrovich once made Fenichka take him a glass of lemonade; Pavel Petrovich gazed at her fixedly and drained the glass. Towards morning the fever rose somewhat and the patient became slightly delirious. At first Pavel Petrovich uttered incoherent words; then he suddenly opened his eyes, and seeing his brother bending solicitously over him, he murmured:

"Don't you think, Nikolai, that Fenichka looks a bit like Nelly?"

"What Nelly, Pavel?"

"Fancy asking. The Princess R—. Especially the upper part of her face. *C'est de la même famille.*"

Nikolai Petrovich said nothing, but he wondered at the tenacity with which old feelings clung to a man.

"That's when they crop up," he thought.

"Oh, how I love that empty creature!" Pavel Petrovich moaned, clasping his hands behind his head in anguish. "No insolent fellow will dare touch her, not while I. . ." he babbled a minute later.

Nikolai Petrovich merely sighed; he never suspected whom those words applied to.

The next day, at about eight in the morning, Bazarov came in to see him. He had packed his luggage and released all his frogs, insects and birds.

"You have come to say good-bye?" Nikolai Petrovich said, rising to meet him.

"Yes, sir."

"I understand you, and entirely approve of you. My poor brother was to blame of course—and he's been punished for it. He told me himself he had placed you in a position that gave you no other option. I do believe that you weren't able to avoid this duel which . . . which to a certain extent was due merely to the constant antagonism of your mutual views." (Nikolai Petrovich got mixed up in his speech.) "My brother is a man of the old stock, quick-tempered and stubborn.... Thank God it ended the way it did. I have taken all the necessary precautions to hush the matter up."

"I'll leave you my address, in case there's any trouble," Bazarov said casually.

"I hope there won't be, Yevgeny Vassilich. I'm very sorry that your sojourn in my house has ... has ended the way it has. I'm all the more grieved since Arkady...."

"I'll probably be seeing him," interposed Bazarov, who always chaffed at every kind of "explanation" and "demonstration". "If not, please give him my regards and please accept my regrets."

"And please accept mine..." Nikolai Petrovich began with a bow. Bazarov, however, had left without waiting for the end of his little speech.

On learning that Bazarov was going away Pavel Petrovich expressed a wish to see him, and shook hands with him. But Bazarov remained as cold as ice; he realised that Pavel Petrovich was trying to be magnanimous. He did not manage to take leave of Fenichka: he only exchanged a look with her through the window. He thought she looked sad. "She'll go under, I'm afraid," he said to himself. "Well, let's hope she'll pull through somehow!" Pyotr broke down entirely and wept on his shoulder, until Bazarov sobered him with a remark about "closing the floodgates", while Dunyasha fled to the wood to hide her agitation. The cause of all this misery climbed into the cart, lit a cigar, and when at a bend in the road three versts down, the Kirsanov farmstead with its new house unfolded for the last time before his gaze, he merely spat, and muttering: "Damned squirarchy!" drew his coat closer about him.

* * *

Pavel Petrovich soon felt better; but he was kept in bed for about a week. He endured what he called his *captivity* patiently, but fussed a good deal over his toilet and demanded frequent perfumings of the room. Nikolai

Petrovich read him magazines, Fenichka waited upon him
as before, bringing him his broth, lemonade, soft-boiled
eggs and tea; but she was seized by a secret terror every
time she entered his room. Pavel Petrovich's unexpected
conduct had frightened the whole household, and her
more than anyone else; Prokofich alone was undisturbed
and talked about gentlemen in his day having plugged
each other too, but then it had been between real gentlemen, and as for such miscreants as these, they would
simply have ordered them to be flogged in the stables
for their impudence.

Fenichka hardly had any pricks of conscience, but
sometimes the thought as to the real cause of the quarrel
worried her; then Pavel Petrovich looked at her so queer-
ly ... she could feel his gaze upon her even when she
had her back to him. She grew thin from constant anxiety,
and, as could be expected, even more charming.

One day—it was in the morning—Pavel Petrovich was
feeling well and moved from his bed to the sofa, and
Nikolai Petrovich, having enquired about his health, went
to visit the threshing floor. Fenichka brought in a cup of
tea, and, setting it down on the table, was about to leave.
Pavel Petrovich detained her.

"Why are you in such a hurry, Fedosya Nikolayevna?"
he began. "Have you anything to do?"

"No, sir. . . . But I must pour the tea."

"Dunyasha will do that without you; keep a sick man
company a little. I want to speak to you by the way."

Fenichka sat down on the edge of an armchair.

"Look here," Pavel Petrovich said, pulling at his
moustache, "I have long wanted to ask you: you seem to
be afraid of me?"

"I, sir?"

"Yes, you. You never look at me, one would think
your conscience was not clear."

Fenichka reddened, but turned her eyes on Pavel Petrovich. Her heart fluttered under his odd regard.

"Your conscience is clear, isn't it?" he demanded.

"Why shouldn't it be?" she whispered.

"Who knows! Whom could you have wronged, I wonder? Me? That's improbable. Somebody else in the house?

That, too, is unlikely. My brother perhaps? But you love him, don't you?"

"I do."

"With all your heart and soul?"

"I love Nikolai Petrovich dearly."

"Do you? Look at me, Fenichka." (He used that name for the first time.) "You know, it's a great sin to lie!"

"I'm not lying, Pavel Petrovich. How could I not love Nikolai Petrovich—I wouldn't care to live after that!"

"And you would not give him up for anybody?"

"For whom could I give him up?"

"One never knows! Why, for that gentleman, say, who has just left."

Fenichka stood up: "My God, why do you torment me, Pavel Petrovich? What have I done to you? How can you say a thing like that?"

"Fenichka," Pavel Petrovich said in a melancholy voice, "I saw it, you know. . . ."

"Saw what, sir?"

"Out there . . . in the arbour."

Fenichka crimsoned to the roots of her hair.

"But it wasn't my fault!" she said with an effort.

Pavel Petrovich sat up.

"Not your fault? Not in the least?"

"Nikolai Petrovich is the only man in the world I love, and I'll love him as long as I live," Fenichka brought out with sudden vehemence, while the sobs rose in her throat. "As for what you say, I'll swear on the Day of Judgment that it was not my fault, and it would be better for me to die now than to be suspected of such a thing, such a sin towards my benefactor, Nikolai Petrovich."

Here her voice broke, and the same instant she became aware that Pavel Petrovich had seized her hand and was squeezing it. She looked at him dumbfounded. His face had turned still paler, his eyes glistened, and, what was most astonishing, a heavy solitary tear rolled down his cheek.

"Fenichka," he said in a strange whisper, "love my brother, love him! He's such a kind, good man! Don't betray him for anybody in the world, don't listen to

anybody! Just think, what can be more terrible than to
love and not be loved! Don't ever forsake my poor Nikolai!"

Fenichka's eyes had dried up and her fear had passed
—so great was her astonishment. But what happened to
her when Pavel Petrovich, yes Pavel Petrovich himself,
pressed her hand to his lips, and clung to it without kissing it, merely sighing fitfully from time to time. . . .

"Goodness gracious!" she thought. "I wonder if it isn't
a fit coming on?"

At that moment all the memories of a ruined life
had flooded upon him.

The staircase creaked under a quick step. . . . He pushed
her away and fell back on his pillow. The door opened—
and in came Nikolai Petrovich, looking gay, fresh and
pink. Mitya, as fresh and pink as his father, clad in a
single undershirt, leaped and wriggled on his chest, his
bare little toes catching in the big buttons of the country-
made coat.

Fenichka ran to him impulsively, and, flinging her
arms around him and her son, nestled her head against
his shoulder. Nikolai Petrovich marvelled: his coy bashful
Fenichka had never shown him signs of affection in the
presence of a third person.

"What is the matter with you?" he said, and glancing
at his brother, transferred Mitya to her arms. "You are
not feeling worse, are you?" he asked, coming up to Pavel
Petrovich.

The latter buried his face in a cambric handkerchief.
"No . . . nothing . . . I'm all right. . . . On the contrary, I
feel much better."

"You shouldn't have been in such a hurry to move to
the sofa. Where are you going," Nikolai Petrovich added,
turning to Fenichka, but she had already closed the door
behind her. "I wanted to show you the little fellow; he
misses his uncle. What made her carry him off? What is
the matter with you, though? Has anything happened
here between you?"

"Brother!" Pavel Petrovich said solemnly.

Nikolai Petrovich started. He was awestruck, he could
not explain why.

"Brother," Pavel Petrovich repeated, "give me your word that you will carry out my request."

"What request? What do you want to say?"

"It's very important; all the happiness of your life, I believe, depends upon it. I have been thinking a good deal lately about what I am going to tell you. . . . Brother, fulfil your obligation, the obligation of an honest and upright man, put a stop to temptation and the bad example you are setting—you, the best of men!"

"What do you mean, Pavel?"

"Marry Fenichka. . . . She loves you; she is the mother of your child."

Nikolai Petrovich stepped back and flung up his arms.

"And you say that, Pavel? You, whom I always considered a determined opponent of such marriages! You say that! Why, don't you know that it was only out of respect for you that I did not do what you rightly call my duty!"

"You were wrong to have respected me in that case," Pavel Petrovich said with a dejected smile. "I'm beginning to think Bazarov was right when he accused me of being an aristocrat. No, dear brother, it's time we stopped putting on airs and thinking about society: we are old and humble folk; it's time we discarded the worldly vanities. Aye, let us start doing our duty, as you say; and I shouldn't wonder if it brought us happiness too."

Nikolai Petrovich embraced his brother.

"You have opened my eyes completely!" he cried. "Haven't I always said that you were the kindest and cleverest man in the world; and now I see you are as sensible as you are generous."

"Easy, easy," Pavel Petrovich interrupted him, "don't jar the leg of your sensible brother who, at the age of nearly fifty, fought a duel like a junior ensign. And so, this matter is settled: Fenichka will be my . . . sister-in-law."

"Dear Pavel! But what will Arkady say?"

"Arkady? Why, he'll be jubilant! Marriage is not one of his principles, but then his sense of equality will be flattered. No, really, what's this idea of caste *au dix-neuvième siècle*?"

12*

"Ah, Pavel, Pavel! Let me kiss you again. Don't be afraid, I'll be careful."

The brothers embraced.

"What about announcing your decision to her now?" Pavel Petrovich said.

"What's the hurry?" Nikolai Petrovich answered. "Why, did you discuss it with her?"

"Discuss it with her? *Quelle idée!*"

"Well, that's fine. First of all get well—this won't run away from us. This wants thinking over carefully...."

"But you have decided, haven't you?"

"Of course I have, and I thank you from the bottom of my heart. I'll leave you now; you must have a rest; this excitement is no good for you.... But we'll talk it over again. Go to sleep, my dear, and God grant you good health!"

"What is he thanking me for?" Pavel Petrovich thought, when he was left by himself. "As if it didn't depend upon him! As for me, as soon as he marries I'll go off somewhere far away, to Dresden or Florence, and live there till I give up the ghost."

Pavel Petrovich dabbed his forehead with Eau de Cologne and shut his eyes. In the bright light of day his handsome emaciated head lay on the white pillow like the head of a corpse.... He was indeed a living corpse.

XXV

In the garden at Nikolskoye Katya and Arkady were sitting on a grassy bank in the shade of a tall ash; at their feet lay Fifi, her long body gracefully curved in what sportsmen call "the hare stance". Both Katya and Arkady were silent; he was holding a half-opened book in his hands while she was picking the remaining crumbs of white bread from a basket and throwing them to a small family of sparrows which, with the timorous audacity of their kind, were hopping and chirruping at her feet. A gentle breeze stirred among the ash leaves, throwing shifting patches of pale-gold sunshine on the shaded path and Fifi's tawny back; Arkady and Katya were enclosed in deep shadow; now and then a strip of brilliance would blaze up in her hair. Neither spoke; but their very silence, the way they sat side by side, breathed a trustful intimacy; each seemed to be unaware of his neighbour, yet secretly glad of his nearness. Their faces, too, had changed since we last saw them: Arkady looked calmer, Katya more animated, bolder.

"Don't you think that the Russian word for ash tree is very apt," Arkady said. "No other tree stands out in the air so lightly and clearly."*

Katya looked up and murmured "yes," and Arkady thought: "She does not rebuke me for talking *pretty*."

"I don't like Heine," Katya said, indicating the book in Arkady's hands with her eyes, "either when he laughs or when he cries: I like him when he is wistful."

"And I like him when he laughs," Arkady observed.

"There speak the old traces of your satiric trend. . . ." ("Old traces!" thought Arkady. "If only Bazarov heard it.") "You wait, we shall convert you."

"Who will convert me? You?"

"Who? My sister; Porfiry Platonich, with whom you no longer quarrel; auntie, whom you accompanied to church the other day."

"I couldn't very well refuse, could I? As to Anna Sergeyevna, she agreed with Yevgeny on many points, you remember."

"My sister was under his influence then, as you were."

"As I was! Why, have you noticed that I've escaped his influence?"

Katya was silent.

"I know, you never did like him," Arkady resumed.

"I am in no position to judge him."

"Do you know what, Katerina Sergeyevna? Every time I hear you say that I don't believe it. There isn't a person any one of us could not judge! It's just an excuse."

"Well then, if you want to know—I wouldn't exactly say that I don't like him, but I feel that he's a stranger to me and I am a stranger to him . . . and so are you."

---

* The Russian for ash tree is *yassen,* which also means *clear, bright.—Trans.*

"How is that?"

"How shall I put it. . . . He's predatory, while we are tame."

"And am I tame too?"

Katya nodded.

Arkady scratched his ear.

"I say, Katerina Sergeyevna, isn't that rather offensive?"

"Why, would you like to be predatory?"

"Predatory—no; but strong, energetic."

"It's not a thing you can want. . . . Now your friend— he doesn't want it, but he has it."

"Hm! So you think he had a big influence over Anna Sergeyevna?"

"Yes. But nobody can have the better of her for long," Katya added in a low voice.

"What makes you think so?"

"She's very proud . . . no, not that . . . she puts great store by her independence."

"Who doesn't?" Arkady said, and in the same instant it flashed upon him: "Of what use is it?"—"Of what use is it?"—also passed through Katya's mind. Young people who see each other often on a friendly footing constantly think the same thoughts.

Arkady smiled and, moving slightly closer to Katya, said in a whisper:

"Confess that you are a little afraid of her."

"Of whom?"

"Of *her*," Arkady repeated meaningly.

"What about you?" Katya countered.

"I too. Notice, I said: I *too*."

Katya wagged a forefinger at him.

"That surprises me," she went on. "You were never so much in my sister's good graces as you are now— ever so much more than during your first visit."

"Is that so?"

"Didn't you notice it? Aren't you glad?"

Arkady pondered.

"In what way could I have won Anna Sergeyevna's disposition? It's not really because of your mother's letters I brought her, is it?"

"It's that, and other reasons as well, which I won't tell you."

"Why not?"

"I won't!"

"Oh, I know—you're very obstinate."

"I am."

"And observant."

Katya threw him a sidelong glance.

"Does that make you angry? What are you thinking of?"

"I was thinking, where did you get such keen powers of observation. You are so timid, so mistrustful, you shun everybody...."

"I have lived by myself a good deal; but do I shun everybody?"

Arkady threw her a grateful glance.

"That's all very well," he went on, "but people in your position, I mean with your wealth, rarely possess that gift; truth doesn't reach them any more easily than it does kings."

"But I am not rich."

Arkady was taken aback and did not at once grasp her meaning. "Indeed, the estate's her sister's!" it dawned on him; the thought was not an unpleasant one.

"How nicely you said that!" he murmured.

"Why?"

"You said it nicely; simply, without shame or affectation. By the way, I should imagine that the feelings of a person who knows and admits that he is poor have a peculiar touch of vanity about them."

"I never experienced anything of the kind, thanks to my sister; I just mentioned my position because it happened to come up."

"Just so. But confess that you have in you a little of that vanity I've just been speaking about."

"For example?"

"For example, you wouldn't—pardon the question—you wouldn't marry a rich man, would you?"

"If I loved him very much.... No, even then, I don't think I would."

"Ah! You see!" exclaimed Arkady, adding after a pause: "Why wouldn't you marry him?"

"Because there's a song about the lowly bride. . . ."

"Perhaps it's because you want to dominate, or. . . ."

"Oh, no! What for? On the contrary, I am ready to submit, it's only inequality that is unbearable. I can understand a person submitting and yet retaining her self-respect; that's happiness; but a life of subordination. . . . No, I've had enough of that."

"Had enough of that," Arkady echoed. "Yes, yes," he went on, "you have your sister's blood in your veins; you're just as independent as she is; only you are more reticent. You would never, I'm sure, declare your feelings first, no matter how strong and sacred they were. . . ."

"How could it be otherwise?" Katya said.

"You are equally clever; you have as much character as she has, if not more."

"Don't compare me to my sister, please," Katya broke in hastily. "You place me at too great a disadvantage. You seem to have forgotten that my sister is beautiful and clever and . . . you of all people, Arkady Nikolaich, should not be saying such things, and with a serious face too."

"What do you mean by: 'you of all people,' and what makes you think I'm joking?"

"Of course you're joking."

"Do you think so? What if I'm convinced of what I'm saying? What if I believe that I haven't expressed myself forcefully enough?"

"I don't understand you."

"Really? Well, now I see that I've been praising your powers of observation too highly."

"What do you mean?"

Arkady made no reply and turned away, while Katya hunted for some more crumbs in the basket and threw them to the sparrows; but the sweep of her hand was too vigorous, and they flew away without having had a peck.

"Katerina Sergeyevna," Arkady suddenly spoke up, "I suppose it's all the same to you; but I want you to know that I wouldn't prefer your sister or anybody else in the world to you."

He got up and walked quickly away, as though frightened by his own outburst.

Katya dropped both her hands, together with the basket, on her lap and, with head bent, looked long after Arkady's retreating figure. A blush slowly kindled in her cheeks; her lips, however, were unsmiling, and her dark eyes expressed bewilderment and a feeling of something else—something she could not yet give a name to.

"You're alone?" Anna Sergeyevna's voice sounded nearby. "I thought you went into the garden with Arkady?"

Katya's eyes travelled slowly to her sister (elegantly, even exquisitely dressed, she stood in the pathway and tickled Fifi's ears with the tip of her open parasol) and she answered as slowly:

"Yes, I'm alone."

"So I see," the former retorted with a little laugh. "He's gone to his room, I suppose?"

"Yes."

"Have you been reading together?"

"Yes."

Anna Sergeyevna took Katya by the chin and raised her head.

"You haven't quarrelled, I hope?"

"No," Katya said, and gently removed her sister's hand.

"How solemn you sound! I thought I'd find him here and offer him to take a walk with me. He's been after me all the time about it. They've brought a pair of shoes for you from town, go and try them on: I noticed yesterday that yours were quite worn out. Generally you don't pay enough attention to yourself, and you have such charming little feet! Your hands are lovely too . . . a bit too large though; you should make the most of your feet then. But there, you have no coquetry in you at all."

Anna Sergeyevna proceeded down the path with a faint swish of her beautiful gown; Katya rose to her feet and, taking Heine with her, went away too—but not to try in the shoes.

"Charming little feet," she was thinking as she slowly and lightly ascended the sun-baked stone steps of the veranda, "charming little feet, you say.... Well, he'll be at them."

She immediately felt abashed, and took the rest of the steps at a run.

Arkady walked down the passage to his room; the butler overtook him and announced that Mr. Bazarov was waiting for him in his room.

"Yevgeny!" Arkady muttered with something akin to dismay. "Has he been here long?"

"Just arrived, sir, and asked not to be announced to Anna Sergeyevna, but to be led straight up to your room."

"I wonder if anything is amiss at home?" Arkady thought and racing up the stairs he pulled open the door. Bazarov's appearance instantly reassured him, though a more practised eye would have perceived in the still energetic but thinner figure of the unexpected visitor signs of an inner perturbation. With a dusty coat flung over his shoulders and a cap on his head, he was seated on the window sill; he did not get up even when Arkady flung himself on his neck with noisy exclamations.

"This is a surprise! What brings you here?" he repeated over and over again, bustling about with the air of a man who believes himself pleased and wants to show it. "Everything is all right at home, I hope, everybody is well?"

"Everything's all right, but not everybody is well," Bazarov said. "Stop chattering, send for a drink of kvass, sit down and listen to what I'm going to tell you in a few, but, I hope, pithy words."

Arkady became subdued, and Bazarov told him about his duel with Pavel Petrovich; Arkady was startled and even distressed; but he deemed it wiser not to show it; he merely asked whether his uncle's wound was not really dangerous, and being told that it was quite an interesting one—but not from the medical standpoint—he smiled wryly, while his heart was filled with a nameless fear and shame. Bazarov seemed to understand what was passing in his mind.

"Yes, my dear fellow," he said, "that's what comes of living with feudal lords. You'll become a feudal lord yourself, before you know it, and take part in knightly

tournaments. Well, so I decided to wing my way home,"
Bazarov wound up his story—"and on the way dropped
in here to ... tell you all about it, I should say, if I
didn't think it silly to tell a useless lie. No, I dropped in
here—damned if I know why! You see, it's a good thing
for a man now and then to seize himself by his topknot
and pull himself out like a radish out of its bed; that's
what I did recently.... But I wanted to have another
look at what I had parted with—the bed I grew in."

"I hope these words don't apply to me," Arkady said
agitatedly. "I hope you don't think of parting with *me*."

Bazarov gave him a close, almost piercing look.

"Will that distress you so much? I think *you* have
already parted with me. You're so clean, fresh as a
daisy ... you must be getting along splendidly with Anna
Sergeyevna."

"What do you mean—getting along?"

"Why, didn't you come down from town for her sake,
little duckling? By the way, how are the Sunday schools
faring? Aren't you in love with her? Or have things come
to a point when you can put on a modest front?"

"Yevgeny, you know I've always been frank with you;
I assure you, I swear to God, that you are mistaken."

"Hm! A new word," Bazarov observed in an undertone. "There's no need to get excited, it doesn't matter to
me in the least. A romanticist would say: I feel that we
have reached the parting of the ways, but I merely say
that we are fed up with each other."

"Yevgeny...."

"My dear chap, there's no harm in that; think of the
things people get fed up with in this world. And now,
what about saying good-bye? Since I've been here I have
a nasty kind of feeling, as though I've been wading
through Gogol's letters to the Governor's lady of Kaluga.
By the way, I ordered the horses not to be unharnessed."

"Oh come, you can't do that!"

"Why not?"

"I say nothing about myself, but it will be extremely
impolite to Anna Sergeyevna, who will certainly be
wanting to see you."

"That's where you're mistaken."

"On the contrary, I believe I'm right," Arkady retorted. "What's the use of pretending? If it comes to that, didn't you come down here because of her?"

"That may be so, but still you're mistaken."

Arkady, however, was right. Anna Sergeyevna wanted to see Bazarov and sent him an invitation through the butler. Bazarov changed before going to her; it appeared that he had packed his new suit so that it could easily be got at.

Odintsova received him not in the room where he had so suddenly made love to her, but in the drawing room. She graciously proffered him her finger tips, but her face wore a tense look.

"Anna Sergeyevna," Bazarov hastened to say, "first of all I want to reassure you. You now see a mortal who has long since come to his senses and hopes that his folly has been forgotten. I am going away for long, and you will agree, though I am not a soft creature, it would not be a pleasant thing to carry away with me the thought that you will remember me with loathing."

Anna Sergeyevna drew a deep breath like a person who has climbed a high hill, and her face broke into a smile. She extended her hand again to Bazarov and responded to the pressure of his own.

"Let bygones be bygones," she said, "all the more that, honestly speaking, I sinned too, if not by coquetry, then in some other way. There—let's be friends as of old. That was a dream, wasn't it? And who remembers dreams?"

"Who indeed? And then love . . . love is nothing but an affectation."

"Really? I'm awfully glad to hear it."

Thus did Anna Sergeyevna express herself, and thus did Bazarov express himself; both thought they were speaking the truth. But was there the truth, the whole truth, in what they said? They did not know themselves, least of all does the author. But they fell to conversing as though they fully believed each other.

Among other things Anna Sergeyevna asked Bazarov how he had spent his time at the Kirsanovs'. He was on the point of telling her about his duel with Pavel Petrovich, but was checked by the thought that she might believe he was posing, and he answered that he had been working all the time.

"And I was in the doldrums at first," Anna Sergeyevna said. "God knows why—I even thought of going abroad, can you imagine! Then it passed; your friend Arkady Nikolaich arrived, and I fell into the old rut again, into my real role."

"What role is that, may I ask?"

"The role of aunt, chaperone, mother—call it what you will. By the way, formerly I couldn't quite understand your close friendship with Arkady Nikolaich, you know. I used to think him rather insignificant. But I've come to know him better now, and find that he's clever. . . . The main thing, he's young, young . . . not like you and me, Yevgeny Vassilich."

"Is he still shy of you?" Bazarov asked.

"Why, was he. . ." Anna Sergeyevna broke off, then added, after a moment's reflection, "he's become more trustful now, he talks to me. He used to avoid me. True, I never sought his company. Katya and he are great friends."

Bazarov felt annoyed. "Everlasting woman's wiles!" he thought.

"You say he avoided you," he said with cold sneer, "but it was probably no secret to you that he was in love with you?"

"What? He too—?" Anna Sergeyevna let fall unguardedly.

"He too," Bazarov repeated with a humble bow. "Do you mean to say you didn't know it and that this is news to you?"

Anna Sergeyevna dropped her eyes.

"You are mistaken, Yevgeny Vassilich."

"I don't think so. But perhaps I should not have mentioned it."—"That will teach you to be artful," he added to himself.

"Why not? But I think here again you attach too much importance to a momentary impression. I am beginning to think that you are prone to exaggeration."

"Let's not discuss this, Anna Sergeyevna."

"Why not," she retorted, and forthwith changed the subject. She felt ill at ease with Bazarov after all, although she had told him and persuaded herself that everything was forgotten. While chatting with him in the most casual way and even joking with him, she yet felt vaguely nervous. Thus do passengers at sea chat and laugh unconcernedly, for all the world as if they were on *terra firma*, yet at the slightest hitch or the slightest sign of anything untoward happening their faces instantly betray a peculiar alarm, testifying to a constant sense of constant danger.

Anna Sergeyevna's talk with Bazarov did not last long. She became lost in thought, replied absent-mindedly and finally suggested going into the sitting room, where they found the princess and Katya. "And where's Arkady Nikolaich?" the hostess asked, and on learning that he had not shown up for more than an hour, she sent for him. It took some time to find him: he had taken himself off to the depths of the garden and with chin propped on his clasped hands was sitting sunk in thought. They were profound and grave, were those thoughts of his, but not despondent. He knew that Anna Sergeyevna was sitting alone with Bazarov, yet he felt no pangs of jealousy as he used to; on the contrary, his face had a soft light upon it; a look of wonder, of gladness, and resolve.

XXVI

The late Odintsov had disliked innovations, but tolerated "some play of refined taste", a consequence of which was the erection in his garden, between the hothouse and the pond, of a structure resembling a Greek portico, built of Russian bricks. The rear blank wall of this portico, or gallery, contained six niches for statues which Odintsov had intended bringing over from abroad. These statues were to represent: Solitude, Silence, Meditation, Melancholy, Modesty and Sentiment. One of these, the Goddess of Silence, with a finger on her lips, had been delivered and set in its place; but the same day the household urchins had broken the nose off, and though a local plasterer had undertaken to fix up a new nose "twice as good as the old one" Odintsov had had the statue removed, a place being found for it in a corner of the threshing shed, and there it had stood for many years striking superstitious terror into the hearts of the women-folk. The front part of the portico had long been over-grown with brushwood: only the capitals of the column were visible above the dense foliage. Inside the portico it was cool, even at noon. Anna Sergeyevna shunned the place ever since she had seen a grass snake there; but Katya often came there to sit on a large stone seat built in one of the niches. Here, in the cool shade, she would sit and read, work or give herself up to that sensation of utter peace which is no doubt familiar to everyone, and the charm of which consists in a barely conscious, mute awareness of the sweeping wave of life surging cease-lessly both around and within us.

The day after Bazarov's arrival, Katya was sitting on her favourite seat, with Arkady once more beside her. He had persuaded her to come with him to "the portico".

It was about an hour before lunchtime; the dewy morn-ing had turned to sultry day. Arkady's face had preserved the expression of the day before; Katya looked worried. Her sister had called her to her study soon after break-fast, and after having stroked and caressed her—a thing that always scared Katya somewhat—had advised her to be more discreet with Arkady and, in particular, to avoid secluded talks with him, which, she let it be known, had been noticed by her aunt and the whole household. Besides, the evening before Anna Sergeyevna had been out of sorts; and Katya herself had felt uneasy, as though conscious of some guilt. While yielding to Arkady's re-quest, she promised herself that this would be the last time.

"Katerina Sergeyevna," he began with a sort of bashful sangfroid, "ever since I've had the happiness of living with you under one roof, I've discussed many things with you, but there is one—er ... matter of great impor-tance to me I haven't yet touched on. You passed a re-mark yesterday about my having been converted here," he went on, seeking and at the same time avoiding Katya's questioning gaze. "As a matter of fact I have changed a good deal, and you know that better than anybody— you, to whom I really owe this change."

"I? Me?" Katya said.

"I am no longer the bumptious boy who first came here," Arkady went on. "After all, I'm getting on for twenty-four; I still want to be useful, I want to devote all my efforts in the service of truth; but I no longer seek my ideals where I sought them before. I find that . . . they are much nearer. Till now I did not know myself, I set myself tasks that were beyond my strength. My eyes have recently been opened, owing to a certain feeling. . . . I'm not expressing myself quite clearly, but I hope you'll understand me."

Katya did not say anything, but she no longer looked at Arkady.

"I believe," he resumed in a more agitated voice, while a chaffinch in the birch tree overhead blithely sang its song, "I believe it's the duty of every honest man to be entirely frank with those . . . with those people who . . . in short, with those who are near to him, and therefore I . . . I intend. . . ."

Here Arkady's eloquence failed him; he faltered, floundered and was obliged to make a pause. Katya kept her eyes cast down. She did not seem to understand what he was driving at and appeared to be waiting for something.

"I suppose that I will surprise you," Arkady began, nerving himself once more to the task, "all the more since this feeling applies to a certain extent . . . to a certain extent, mind you,—to you. Yesterday, you remember, you reproached me for not being serious enough," Arkady went on with the air of a man who has stumbled into a quagmire, feels that he is sinking deeper at every step, yet presses on in the hope of quickly getting clear. "That reproach is frequently pointed . . . falls on . . . young men, even when they have ceased to deserve it; did I possess more self-assurance. . . ." ("Why don't you help me out, for God's sake!" Arkady was thinking frantically, but Katya still did not turn her head.) "If only I dared to hope. . . ."

"If only I could be sure of what you say," fell the clear voice of Anna Sergeyevna.

The words died on Arkady's lips, and Katya turned pale. Close to the bushes screening the portico ran a path. Anna Sergeyevna was walking along that path accompanied by Bazarov. Katya and Arkady could not see them, but they heard every word, the rustling of a gown, their very breathing. They took several steps and came to a standstill, as though deliberately, right in front of the portico.

"There, you see," Anna Sergeyevna went on, "we're both wrong; neither of us is in the first flush of youth, especially I; we have seen something of life, we are tired; we are both—why beat about the bush?—clever: at first we became interested in one another; curiosity was stirred ... and then. ..."

"And then I fizzled out," Bazarov threw in.

"You know that was not the cause of our drifting apart. But be that as it may, we did not need each other, that's the point; we had too much—how shall I put it—too much in common. We did not grasp it immediately. Arkady, on the other hand. ..."

"Do you need him?" Bazarov asked.

"Oh come, Yevgeny Vassilich. You say he has taken a fancy to me, and I've always had the feeling that he likes me. I know I'm old enough to be his aunt, but I won't conceal from you that he is beginning to occupy my thoughts. There's a peculiar charm in this young, fresh feeling. ..."

"The word *fascination* is more commonly used in such cases," Bazarov interrupted her; his voice, though calm, had a note of suppressed bitterness in it. "Arkady was as close as wax with me yesterday and said nothing about you or your sister. ... That's an important symptom."

"He's like a brother to Katya," Anna Sergeyevna said, "and that's what I like in him, though perhaps I ought not to allow such intimacy between them."

"Is that the voice of ... a sister?" Bazarov drawled.

"Of course ... but why are we standing? Let's walk on. What an odd conversation ours is, don't you think so? I would never have thought I would be speaking to you in this way. You know I am afraid of you ... and yet I trust you, because you are really very kind."

"To begin with, I'm not at all kind; and secondly I don't mean anything to you any more, and you tell me that I am kind. . . . It's like placing a wreath of flowers on a dead man's head."

"Yevgeny Vassilich, we have no power. . ." she had begun, but a gust of wind, rustling amid the leaves, carried her words away.

"But then you are free," Bazarov said after a pause. The rest was indistinguishable; the footsteps retreated . . . silence fell.

Arkady turned to Katya. She had not changed her position, only her head was bent lower.

"Katerina Sergeyevna," his voice shook and he clenched his hands, "I love you forever and for good. I love nobody but you. That is what I have been wanting to tell you, to know your mind, and ask you for your hand, because I am not rich and feel I'm prepared to sacrifice everything. . . . You don't answer? You don't believe me? You think I am speaking lightly? But recall the last few days! Couldn't you have seen that everything else—I assure you—everything else, all that, has long vanished without a trace? Look at me, say something. . . . I love . . . I love you. . . . Believe me!"

Katya looked at him with moist shining eyes and after long hesitation murmured, with the shadow of a smile: "Yes."

Arkady leapt from his seat. "Yes! You said 'Yes', Katerina Sergeyevna! What does it mean? Does it mean that I love you, or that you believe me. . . . Or . . . or . . . I dare not utter it. . . ."

"Yes," Katya repeated, and this time he understood her. He seized her large beautiful hands, and, breathless with rapture, pressed them to his heart. He could scarcely stand on his feet and kept on repeating: "Katya, Katya. . ." while she began to cry in an ingenuous little way, laughing softly at her own tears. He who has not seen such tears in the eyes of his beloved, who has never thrilled to the gratitude and shame of it, has never known how happy mortal man can be on this earth.

*   *   *

Early next morning, Anna Sergeyevna sent for Bazarov and with a forced laugh handed him a folded sheet
of notepaper. It was a letter from Arkady, in which he
asked for her sister's hand.

Bazarov ran his eye over the letter and checked an
impulse to betray the feeling of malicious glee that suddenly welled in him.

"So that's it," he uttered, "and you, no earlier than
yesterday, I believe, thought that he entertained a broth-
erly love for Katerina Sergeyevna. What do you intend
to do now?"

"What would *you* advise?" Anna Sergeyevna asked,
still laughing.

"Well," replied Bazarov, also with a laugh, although
he no more felt like laughing than she did, "I think you
should give the young folks your blessing. The match is
a good one in all respects: Kirsanov is fairly well off,
he's the only son, and his father's a decent fellow, he
won't oppose it."

Odintsova took a turn about the room. Her face changed
from red to white.

"You think so?" she said. "Ah well! I see no objec-
tions.... I'm glad for Katya's sake ... and for Arkady
Nikolaich's, too. Of course, I'll wait for his father's answer. I'll send him down to him. It turns out after all that
I was right yesterday when I told you that we were both
getting old. How is it I didn't notice anything? That's
what surprises me!"

Anna Sergeyevna laughed again and instantly turned
away.

"Young people today are too clever by half," Bazarov
remarked, laughing too. "Good-bye," he went on after
a slight pause. "I hope you'll see the matter through to
a happy ending; I'll look on from a distance and rejoice."

Odintsova turned to him quickly.

"Why, are you going? Why shouldn't you stay *now*?
Do stay.... It's thrilling to talk to you ... like walking
on the brink of a precipice. At first it's a bit terrifying,
then somehow you pluck up courage. Do stay."

"Thanks for the invitation, Anna Sergeyevna, and for your flattering opinion of my conversational gifts. But I've been moving too long as it is in alien spheres. Flying fish can keep in the air for a certain time, but back into the water they must soon flop; please allow me to flop back into my element."

Odintsova studied him. His pale face twitched with a bitter smile. "That man loved me!" she thought, and suddenly felt sorry for him. She stretched out her hand to him in sympathy.

But he understood her.

"No!" he said, falling back a step. "I'm a poor man, but have never accepted alms. Good-bye, madam, and keep well."

"I'm sure that this is not the last we're seeing of each other," Anna Sergeyevna said with an involuntary gesture.

"I shouldn't wonder. This world is full of surprises," Bazarov answered, and went out.

*   *   *

"So you've decided to build a nest?" he was saying to Arkady the same day, squatting in front of the suitcase he was packing. "Well, not a bad idea. But why were you so sly about it? I expected you to sail on an entirely different tack. Or perhaps you were taken unawares yourself?"

"As a matter of fact I didn't expect it at the time I left you," replied Arkady. "But why are you fencing yourself, saying 'it's a good idea'; don't I know your views on marriage?"

"Ah, my dear friend!" Bazarov said. "The way you talk! Do you see what I'm doing: there's an empty space in my suitcase and I'm filling it up with hay; it's the same with the suitcase of life: fill it up with whatever you like so long as there is no void. Don't take offence, please; you probably remember the opinion I always had of Katerina Sergeyevna. Some girls pass as clever only because they sigh cleverly, but yours will hold her own, and gain a hold on you too, I vow—but that's as it should be." He slammed the lid down and stood up. "And now I repeat to you at parting—it's no use fooling ourselves —we are parting for good, and you realise that yourself. You have acted wisely; you are not made for our bitter, crabbed, lonely life; you haven't the daring or the fury, you have only the audacity, the ardour of youth; that's no good for our job. You gentlemen of the nobility can't work up more than a noble humility or a noble indignation, and that's not worth a rap. You don't fight, for instance—yet you think you are heroes—whereas we hanker for a fight. Why, our dust would eat your eyes out, our dirt would besmirch you; besides, you do not come up to us, you admire yourself, you like to wallow in self-reproach; we're tired of all that, we want something new! We have others to break! You're a decent chap, but you're after all a softy, a chip of a liberal gentleman's block— *et voilà tout*, as my parent would say."

"You're saying good-bye to me for good, Yevgeny," Arkady said sadly, "and have you no other words to say to me?"

Bazarov scratched the back of his head.

"I have, Arkady, I have other words too, but I shan't use them, because that would mean being romantic, mushy. You go on and get married, feather your little nest, and multiply, the more kiddies the better. They'll be fine fellows if only because they'll come into the world at the right time, not like you and me. Aha, I see the horses are ready! Time to go! I've taken leave of everybody.... Well? Let's embrace, what do you say?"

Arkady flung himself on the neck of his former preceptor and friend, tears gushing from his eyes.

"Ah, youth, youth!" Bazarov said calmly. "But I rely on Katerina Sergeyevna. You'll see how soon she'll console you!"

* * *

"Good-bye, old chap!" he said to Arkady, after having climbed into the cart, and pointing to a pair of jackdaws perched side by side on the stable roof, he added: "There's an object lesson for you!"

"What does that mean?" asked Arkady.

"What? Are you that bad in natural history or have you forgotten that the jackdaw is the most respectable of domestic birds? Follow the example! Good-bye, signior!"

The cart creaked and rolled away.

*   *   *

Bazarov had spoken the truth. Talking that evening to Katya, Arkady completely forgot his preceptor. He was already beginning to fall under her sway; Katya felt it and was not surprised. He was to go to Maryino the next day to talk the matter over with Nikolai Petrovich. Anna Sergeyevna did not want to put any restraint on the young people, and if she did not leave them alone together for too long it was merely for the sake of propriety. She magnanimously kept the princess out of their way—the news of the forthcoming marriage had reduced that lady to a tearful frenzy. At first Anna Sergeyevna had feared that the sight of their happiness would be rather painful to her, but it turned out the other way: the sight not only did not distress her, she found it entertaining, even touching. It both pleased and saddened her. "It seems Bazarov was right," she mused. "Curiosity, nothing but curiosity, and a love of ease, and selfishness. . . ."

"Children!" she said aloud, "is love an affectation?"

But neither Katya nor Arkady understood her. They were shy of her; the conversation they had involuntarily overheard stuck fast in their minds. Anna Sergeyevna, however, soon set them at ease; she had no difficulty in doing so, for her own mind was at ease too.

XXVII

The old Bazarov couple were the more delighted at their son's sudden return that they had least been expecting him. Arina Vlasyevna ran about the house in such a flutter of excitement that Vassily Ivanych likened her to a "grouse hen": indeed, her bobtailed little jacket gave her a birdlike appearance. As for himself, all he did was to grunt and nibble the amber tip of his pipe, and gripping his neck with his hands, kept twisting his head as though testing to see whether it was properly screwed on, then he would suddenly open his mouth wide and laugh soundlessly.

"I've come to stay for six whole weeks, old chap," Bazarov told him, "and I want to do some work, so please don't disturb me."

"You'll forget what I look like, that's how much I'll disturb you!" retorted Vassily Ivanych.

And he was as good as his word. Having reinstalled his son in his study he all but hid himself from him and restrained his wife from too exuberant a display of affection. "My dear," he said to her, "the last time Yevgeny was here we annoyed him a little with our attentions: we'll have to be wiser now." Arina Vlasyevna agreed with her husband, but gained little by it, for she saw her son only at mealtimes now and was afraid to talk to him at all. "Yevgeny dear!" she would say, and before he could look round she was fumbling with her reticule strings and stammering: "Nothing, nothing, I was just..." and then she would go to Vassily Ivanych, and, propping her cheek up in her hand, would say: "How could we find out, dear, what Yevgeny would like for dinner today—cabbage soup or borsch?"—"But why didn't you ask him yourself?"—"I didn't want to bother him!" Bazarov, however, soon stopped shutting himself up. His burst of activity petered out, to be followed by a dreary boredom and a vague restlessness. There was a strange lassitude in all his movements, and even his gait, usually firm and impetuously confident, underwent a change. He no longer took his solitary walks and began to seek company: he took his tea in the parlour, prowled about the garden with Vassily Ivanych and had a "mum" smoke with him; once he asked after Father Alexei. The change gladdened Vassily Ivanych at first, but his joy was shortlived. "Yevgeny worries me," he complained in private to his wife: "It's not as if he was displeased or angry—that wouldn't

be so bad; he's distressed, he's miserable—that's the worst
of it. Doesn't say a word all the time, I'd rather he
scolded us; he is getting thinner and I don't like his complexion at all."—"God above us!" whispered the old
lady; "I'd put a holy amulet on his neck, but I don't suppose he'd let me." Vassily Ivanych very tactfully tried to
sound him out once or twice about his work, his health
and Arkady. But Bazarov answered him in a reluctant,
offhand way, and noticing one day that his father was
trying to worm something out of him, he said with annoyance: "Why do you walk around me on tiptoe? It's
worse than before."—"There, there, I didn't mean anything!" poor Vassily Ivanych put in hastily. His political
hints were no more successful. He once broached the
subject of progress and the imminent emancipation of the
peasantry in the hope of rousing his son's interest; but
the latter remarked indifferently: "I was passing down
the fence yesterday and heard the peasant boys yelling
a current ditty: *I'm sick with love for you sweetheart,*
instead of one of the good old songs—there's progress for
you."

Sometimes Bazarov would take a walk through the village and, in his usual bantering way, enter into conversation with one of the peasants. "Well," he would say to
him, "trot out your views on life, old chap; you're said
to have in you all the power and future of Russia, you're
to start a new era in history—you're going to give us a
real language and real laws!" The fellow would either
say nothing or come out with something like this: "Aye,
that we can ... now, ye see, the point is.... Our position's like this."

"You just explain to me what this *mir* of yours is?"*
Bazarov interrupted. "Isn't it the *mir* that rests on three
fishes?"

"It's the earth, sir, that be standing on three fishes," the
man explained in a benign, patriarchal singsong voice;
"Our *mir,* to be sure, is under the masters' will, seeing

---

* The Russian word *mir* has a double meaning: *Village Commun-*
ity and the *World.—Trans.*

that you're our fathers, in a manner o' speaking. An' the stricter the master the better the muzhik likes it."

After listening to an oration of this kind Bazarov once contemptuously shrugged his shoulders and turned away, leaving the peasant to shuffle off.

"What 'ave ye been talking about?" a dour-faced middle-aged peasant asked his fellow villager from the doorstep of his hut. "About tax arrears?"

"Tax arrears, no!" replied the first peasant, with no longer a trace of the patriarchal singsong in his voice, which now sounded disdainfully grim. "Chap just wanted to jabber, that's all. He's a gent, what does he understand?"

"Aye, what does he understand!" the other muzhik echoed, and wagging their heads and adjusting their girdles they fell to discussing their own affairs. Alack! Bazarov of the contemptuously shrugging shoulders, Bazarov who knew how to speak to the peasants (so he had boasted in a dispute with Pavel Petrovich)—this self-assured Bazarov never suspected that to them he was something in the nature of a tomfool.

However, he found an occupation for himself at last. Once in his presence Vassily Ivanych was dressing a peasant's injured foot, but the old man's hands shook and he could not manage the bandages; his son helped him, and henceforth began to take a hand in his practice, though he continued to poke fun both at the remedies he himself advised and at his father, who promptly made use of them. Bazarov's jibes, however, did not put Vassily Ivanych out in the least; they even amused him. Holding his greasy dressing gown together across his stomach with two fingers and puffing at his pipe, he turned a delighted ear to his son's disparaging comments, and the more malicious they were the more heartily did the happy father laugh, revealing every one of his blackened teeth. He even repeated these sometimes inane or senseless extravagances, and for several days, for instance, went about reiterating without rhyme or reason: "Oh, worse than useless," simply because his son had used that expression on learning that he attended matins. "Thank God, he's cheered up a bit!" he whispered to his wife. "He made,

short work of me today, it was simply great!" The thought
that he had such an assistant delighted him and filled
him with pride. "Yes, my dear," he would say to a peasant woman clad in a man's drab overcoat and a Russian
peasant headdress, while he handed her a bottle of Gou-
lard's extract or a jar of henbane ointment, "you ought
to thank your lucky star, my good woman, that my son
happens to be staying with me: you're being treated by
the latest scientific methods, do you realise that? The
Emperor of the French, Napoleon, hasn't a better doctor."
And the woman, who had come complaining of "having
the racks" (the meaning of which words, by the way, she
didn't know herself), would merely bow and fish the
doctor's fee out from her bosom in the shape of four eggs
wrapped up in the corner of a towel.

Once Bazarov even extracted a tooth for a passing
haberdashery pedlar, and though it was just an ordinary
tooth as teeth go, Vassily Ivanych kept it as a curiosity
and showed it to Father Alexei, repeating ceaselessly:

"You just look at those roots! The strength Yevgeny
has! That pedlar fellow was simply hoisted out of his
seat. Why, I don't think an oak could have stood it!"

"Remarkable!" Father Alexei would observe at length,
not knowing what to say and how to shake off the ecstatic
old man.

*   *   *

One day a peasant from a nearby village brought his
brother, who was ill with typhus, to Vassily Ivanych. The
poor fellow lay dying, face downwards, on a bundle of
hay; his body was covered with dark blotches and he had
been unconscious for some time. Vassily Ivanych expressed
his regret that it had not occurred to anybody to seek
medical aid before, and declared that there was no hope.
Indeed, by the time the peasant reached home his brother
had died in the cart.

Three days later Bazarov came into his father's room
and asked whether he had some lunar caustic.

"I have; what do you want it for?"

"I need it . . . to cauterise a cut."

"Who for?"

"For myself."

"Yourself? What for? What cut? Where is it?"

"Here, on my finger. I went to the village today, you know, the one they brought that typhus peasant from. They decided to make a post-mortem for some reason or other, and I hadn't had any practice of that kind for some time."

"Well?"

"Well, so I asked the local doctor to let me do it; well, I cut my finger."

Vassily Ivanych suddenly turned pale, and without uttering a word, rushed into his study and reappeared immediately with a stick of lunar caustic in his hand. Bazarov was about to take it and go.

"For God's sake, let me do it myself," Vassily Ivanych muttered.

Bazarov smiled ironically.

"You're a greedy one for a bit of practice!"

"Don't joke, please. Show me your finger. It's not much of a cut. Does it hurt?"

"Press harder, don't be afraid."

Vassily Ivanych stopped.

"Don't you think, we'd better sear it with an iron, Yevgeny?"

"That should have been done before; as a matter of fact, even the lunar caustic is useless now. If I've been infected, it's too late already."

"Too late. . . ." Vassily Ivanych could barely utter the words.

"I should think so! More than four hours have passed."

Vassily Ivanych cauterised the cut again.

"Didn't the district doctor have any lunar caustic?"

"No."

"How could that be, my God! A doctor—and not to have such an essential thing!"

"You should have seen what his lancets looked like," Bazarov said and walked out.

All that evening and the next day Vassily Ivanych invented all possible excuses for going into his son's room, and though he did not mention a word about his cut and

even tried to talk about everything else under the sun,
he peered so intently into his eyes and watched him so
anxiously that Bazarov lost his patience and threatened
to go away. Vassily Ivanych promised that he would stop
fretting, the more so that Arina Vlasyevna, from whom
he had of course concealed everything, had also begun
to worry him as to why he did not sleep and what had
come over him. He kept this up for two whole days,
though he did not at all like the look of his son, whom
he stealthily watched. On the third day, however, at dinner, he could contain himself no longer. Bazarov sat with
his eyes downcast and did not touch his food.

"Why don't you eat, Yevgeny?" he said, looking as
unconcerned as he could. "The food's very tasty, I think."

"I don't eat because I don't want to."

"Have you lost your appetite? How's your head?" he
added timidly. "Does it ache?"

"It does. Why shouldn't it?"

Arina Vlasyevna sat up, all ears.

"Don't be angry, Yevgeny, please," Vassily Ivanych
went on, "but won't you let me feel your pulse?"

Bazarov got up.

"I can tell you without feeling my pulse that I have a
high temperature."

"Have you been shivery too?"

"Yes. I'll go and lie down; send me some lime-flower
tea. Probably caught a cold."

"No wonder I heard you coughing last night," Arina
Vlasyevna said.

"Caught a cold," Bazarov repeated and left the room.

Arina Vlasyevna busied herself brewing lime tea, and
Vassily Ivanych went into the next room and clutched
his hair in speechless anguish.

Bazarov remained in bed that day, and spent the night
in a heavy half-waking slumber. At one o'clock in the
morning he opened his eyes with an effort, and seeing
the pale face of his father, illuminated by the dim light
of the icon lamp, bending over him, he told him to go
away; the old man obeyed, but returned immediately on
tiptoe and standing half-hidden behind the bookcase
door watched his son with an unshifting gaze. Arina Vla-

syevna was up too, and would peep through the half-
open door to see "how darling Yevgeny was breathing",
and take a look at Vassily Ivanych. All she could see,
however, was his bent, motionless back, but even that
made her feel easier. In the morning Bazarov attempted
to get up; he became dizzy and his nose began to bleed;
he went back to bed. Vassily Ivanych tended him silently;
Arina Vlasyevna came in and asked how he was feeling.
He answered: "Better," and turned his face to the wall.
Vassily Ivanych waved both his hands at his wife; she
bit her lip so as not to cry, and went out. Everything in
the house suddenly seemed to go dark; everybody wore
long faces, a strange hush descended upon everything; a
noisy cock in the farmyard was carried off to the village,
wondering at this summary treatment. Bazarov continued
to lie with his face to the wall. Vassily Ivanych tried
putting various questions to him, but they tired Bazarov,
and the old man sat in his armchair without stirring,
cracking his fingers now and then. He went out into the
garden for a few moments, stood there like a stone image,
as if petrified with unutterable amazement (his face these
days generally wore a look of permanent amazement) and
returned again to his son, trying to avoid his wife's anxious questioning. At last she clutched his arm and whispered in a convulsed, almost menacing voice: "What's
the matter with him?" At that he would pull himself together and force himself to smile by way of reply; but
to his horror, he began to laugh instead. He had sent for
a doctor in the morning. He thought it necessary to tell
his son about it, for fear of making him angry.

Bazarov suddenly turned over on the sofa, stared dully
at his father and asked for a drink.

Vassily Ivanych gave him some water and took the
opportunity to touch his forehead, He was in a high fever.

"I'm booked, old chap," Bazarov began in a slow
hoarse voice, "I'm infected, and in a few days you'll be
burying me."

Vassily Ivanych staggered as if someone had hit him
in the legs.

"Yevgeny!" he stammered. "What are you talking
about? God bless you! You've caught a chill. . . ."

"Come, come," Bazarov broke in unhurriedly. "Fancy a doctor saying that. All the symptoms of blood poisoning, you know it yourself."

"Where are symptoms ... of blood poisoning, Yevgeny?... You do say things!"

"And what's this?" Bazarov said, and turning back his shirt sleeve he showed his father sinister red patches that had broken out on his body.

Vassily Ivanych started and went cold with horror.

"What of it," he brought out at last, "what if ... even if it is anything...."

"*Pyaemia,*" his son prompted.

"Er, yes ... anything epidemic...."

"*Pyaemia,*" Bazarov repeated grimly and distinctly. "Have you forgotten your exercise books?"

"Yes, yes, all right, have it your way.... We'll pull you through all the same!"

"Not likely. But, that's not the point. I didn't expect to die so soon; that's a stroke of bad luck. You and mother should now make the best of your strong religious feeling; here you have an opportunity of putting it to the test." He drank some more water. "And I want to ask you to do one thing for me ... while my head is still my own. Tomorrow or the day after my brain will hand in its resignation, you know. I'm not sure even now whether I'm talking sense. While I was lying here I seemed to see red hounds chasing around me, and you came to a point over me, as though I were a woodcock. I feel kind of drunk. Can you follow me?"

"Why, you're speaking quite normally, Yevgeny."

"All the better; you told me you've sent for a doctor.... That's your bit of fun ... now, do me a favour too: send a messenger...."

"To Arkady Nikolaich?" the old man broke in.

"Who's Arkady Nikolaich?" Bazarov murmured half-musingly. "Oh, that fledgling! No, don't bother him, he's become a jackdaw now. Don't be surprised, it's not delirium yet. Send a messenger to Odintsova, Anna Sergeyevna, she has an estate in these parts.... Do you know her?"—Vassily Ivanych nodded.—"Tell her that Yevgeny, that is Ba-

zarov, sends his regards and asks her to be told that he is
dying. Will you do that?"

"I will. . . . But you are not going to die, Yevgeny, it's
impossible. . . . Now, think for yourself. . . . Would it be
fair?"

"I don't know about that but see that you send a messenger."

"I'll send a man straight away and write her a note
myself."

"No, what for? Just tell her that I send my regards,
nothing else. Now I'll go back to my hounds. Funny! I try
to bring my thoughts round to the idea of death, but nothing comes of it. All I see is a smudge . . . and nothing
more."

He turned heavily to the wall once more; and Vassily
Ivanych left the study, and dragging himself to his wife's
bedroom, he dropped down on his knees before the holy
images.

"Pray, Arina, pray!" he moaned. "Our son is dying."

❈   ❈   ❈

The doctor arrived—the same practitioner who had
failed Bazarov with the lunar caustic—and after examining
the patient, advised the wait-and-see method of treatment,
with several added words about the possibility of recovery.

"Have you ever seen people in my condition who don't
go off to Elysium?" Bazarov asked, and suddenly gripping
the leg of a heavy table standing near the sofa, he shook
it and shifted it from its place.

"All the strength is still there," he said, "yet I must
die!. . . An old man, at least, has had time to grow out of
the habit of living, but I. . . . Try to negate death after that.
He negates you and that's all there is to it! Who is crying?"
he added after a while. "Mother? Poor mother! Whom will
she now feed her marvellous borsch to? And you, too,
Vassily Ivanych, have turned on the waterworks, I see?
Well, if Christianity doesn't help, be a philosopher,
or a stoic! You boasted of being a philosopher, didn't
you?"

"What philosopher am I!" wailed Vassily Ivanych, the tears streaming down his cheeks.

*   *   *

Bazarov grew worse hour by hour; the disease was progressing rapidly, as is frequently the case in surgical blood poisoning. He had not yet lost consciousness and understood what was being said; he was still fighting. "I don't want to rave," he whispered, clenching his fists, "what nonsense!" Then he would say: "Come on, subtract ten from eight, what is the result?" Vassily Ivanych went about like one insane, suggesting one remedy after another, and kept covering his son's feet. "Cold wrappings. . . an emetic . . . mustard poultices to the stomach . . . bloodletting," he muttered over and over again. The doctor, whom he implored to stay, nodded assent to everything he said, and gave the sick man lemonade, while for himself he would request now a pipe, now "a warming stimulant", by which he meant vodka. Arina Vlasyevna sat on a low seat by the door and only went out now and again to pray; some days ago a hand-mirror had slipped out of her fingers and broken, and she always held that to be a bad omen; Anfisushka could not find words to comfort her. Timofeich rode off to Odintsova.

Bazarov had a bad night. He ran a high fever. Towards morning he felt slightly better. He asked Arina Vlasyevna to comb his hair, kissed her hand, and took one or two sips of tea. Vassily Ivanych brightened up a little.

"Thank God!" he kept on saying. "The crisis has come . . . the crisis has passed."

"Nonsense!" Bazarov said. "What's in a word! You hit on a word, say 'crisis' and you're comforted. Surprising how people still believe in words. Tell a man, for example, that he's a fool without beating him and he'll be miserable; call him a clever fellow without giving him any money and he'll be tickled."

This little speech of Bazarov's, which was reminiscent of his old "quips", delighted Vassily Ivanych.

"Bravo! Well said!" he cried, making as though he were clapping his hands.

Bazarov smiled sadly.

"Well then, what do you think," he said, "has the crisis come or passed?"

"All I see is that you're better, that's the main thing," said Vassily Ivanych.

"Very well, rejoice—that's always a good thing. Did you send to her?"

"Yes, of course."

* * *

The change for the better did not last long. The patient suffered a relapse. Vassily Ivanych sat by Bazarov's bedside. Something more than ordinary anguish seemed to be preying on the old man's mind. He tried several times to speak but could not.

"Yevgeny!" he brought out at last. "My son, my dear, darling boy!"

The unusual appeal had its effect on Bazarov. He turned his head slightly, and with an obvious effort to shake off his torpor, he said: "What is it, my dear father?"

"Yevgeny," Vassily Ivanych went on and dropped on his knees before Bazarov, though the latter had not opened his eyes and could not see him. "Yevgeny, you're better now; please God you'll get well now; but take this opportunity, for your mother's sake and mine—do your Christian duty! It's terrible that I have to tell you this; but it would be more terrible . . . it's forever, Yevgeny . . . just think what it means. . . ."

The old man's voice broke, and queer look crept into his son's face, though he still lay with his eyes shut.

"I don't object, if that can comfort you," he murmured at last. "But I don't think you need hurry yet. You say yourself I'm better."

"You are, Yevgeny, you are; but who knows, it's all God's will, and if you'd perform this duty. . . ."

"No, I'll wait," Bazarov interrupted. "I agree with you that the crisis has set in. If we're mistaken, well!— even an unconscious man can receive the last sacrament."

"But, Yevgeny dear. . . ."

"I'll wait. And now I want to sleep. Don't disturb me."
And he laid his head back in its former position.

The old man got up, sat down in the armchair, and taking hold of his chin, began biting his fingers. . . .

*   *   *

The sound of a spring carriage, a sound which is so noticeable in the quiet of the country, suddenly struck his ear. Ever nearer and nearer rumbled the light wheels; one could now hear the snorting of the horses. . . . Vassily Ivanych darted to the window. A two-seater drawn by a team of four horses swept into his yard. Without stopping to think what this might mean, he rushed out onto the porch on a sudden impulse of unreasoning joy. A liveried footman opened the carriage door and a lady in a black veil and a black mantle stepped out.

"I am Odintsova," she said. "Is Yevgeny Vassilich still alive? Are you his father? I have brought a doctor with me."

"My good angel!" Vassily Ivanych cried, and seizing her hand he pressed it convulsively to his lips, while the doctor accompanying her, a bespectacled little man with a German face, was descending leisurely from the carriage. "He's alive, my Yevgeny's still alive, and now he'll be saved! Wife! Wife! An angel from heaven has come to us. . . ."

"What is that, good God!" stammered the old lady, running out from the parlour, and in a state of utter bewilderment, threw herself at Anna Sergeyevna's feet and began frantically kissing the hem of her gown.

"Oh, please, what are you doing!" Anna Sergeyevna kept saying, but Arina Vlasyevna was deaf to her protests, and Vassily Ivanych kept repeating: "Angel! Angel!"

"*Wo ist der Kranke*? Ver iss der patient?" the doctor said not without some indignation.

Vassily Ivanych caught himself.

"Here, this way please, *wertester Herr Kollege*," he added, remembering old times.

"Ah!" the German uttered with a sour grin.

Vassily Ivanych led him into the study.

"A doctor from Anna Sergeyevna Odintsova," he said, bending down to his son's ear. "And she's here too."

Bazarov instantly opened his eyes. "What did you say?"

"I said, Anna Sergeyevna Odintsova is here and has brought you a doctor, this gentleman here."

Bazarov's eyes travelled round the room.

"She's here . . . I want to see her."

"You'll see her, Yevgeny; let us first have a talk with the doctor. I'll tell him your case history since Sidor Sidorych" (that was the name of the district practitioner) "is gone, and we'll hold a little consultation."

Bazarov glanced at the German. "Well, do it quickly, but don't speak Latin, I know what *jam moritur* means."

"Der Herr scheint des Deutschen mächtig zu sein," said the new disciple of Aesculapius, turning to Vassily Ivanych.

"Ich . . . habe. . . . Better speak Russian," the old man said.

"Ach! So, so, verr goot. . . ."

And the consultation began.

*   *   *

Half an hour later Anna Sergeyevna, accompanied by Vassily Ivanych, entered the sickroom. The doctor had already told her in a whisper that there was no hope for the patient's recovery.

She glanced at Bazarov . . . and stopped dead in the doorway, struck by the at once flushed and ashy face with its dull eyes fixed upon her. She was frightened with a chill, harrowing sense of fear; the thought that she would have felt differently had she loved him, flashed through her mind.

"Thanks," he said with an effort. "I didn't expect it. That's kind of you. So we meet again, as you promised."

"Anna Sergeyevna was so good. . ." Vassily Ivanych began.

"Father, leave us alone. Anna Sergeyevna, do you mind? I believe that now. . . ."

14*

He indicated his prostrate helpless body with a motion of his head.

Vassily Ivanych left the room.

"There, thanks," Bazarov repeated. "That's a royal favour. They say royalty too visit the dying."

"Yevgeny Vassilich, I hope. . . ."

"Heigh-ho! Anna Sergeyevna, let's speak the truth. It's all up with me. I've been caught in the wheel. So there was no sense in thinking about the future. Death is an old story, yet always a new one to somebody. I've managed to keep my courage up so far . . . and then the coma will set in, and then phewt!" He made a feeble gesture. "Well, what shall I tell you. . . . That I loved you? There was no sense in that before, still less now. Love is a form and my own form is decomposing. Let me tell you rather how lovely you are! There you stand, so beautiful. . . ."

Anna Sergeyevna shuddered involuntarily.

"Never mind, don't worry . . . sit down there. . . . Don't come near me—my disease is contagious, you know."

Anna Sergeyevna swiftly crossed the room and sat down in an armchair near the sofa on which Bazarov lay.

"How kind!" he whispered. "Ah, how near, and how young, fresh and pure . . . in this hideous room! Well, farewell! Live long, that's best of all, make the most of things while there is time. Just look, what a revolting sight: a half-crushed worm, but still showing off. Yet I used to think: I'll kick up a lot of dust yet, who said die? There's plenty to be done, why, I feel like a giant! Now the giant's chief anxiety is how to die decently, though nobody cares a straw. . . . All the same, I won't wag my tail."

Bazarov fell silent and began fumbling for the glass. Anna Sergeyevna gave him a drink without taking off her glove, hardly daring to breathe.

"You will forget me," he resumed, "the dead are no company for the living. My father will tell you, no doubt, what a man Russia is losing. . . . That's nonsense; but don't disillusion the old man. We all live in a fool's paradise, you know. And be kind to Mother. You won't find

such people if you search your world high and low. . . .
Russia needs me. . . . No, apparently she doesn't.
Who is needed? The cobbler is needed; the tailor
is, the butcher . . . he sells meat . . . . the butcher. . . .
Look here, I'm getting mixed up. . . . There's a forest
here. . . ."

Bazarov put his hand to his forehead.

Anna Sergeyevna leaned over towards him.

"Yevgeny Vassilich, I'm here. . . ."

He instantly took his hand away and raised himself
on his elbow.

"Farewell," he said with sudden force and his eyes lit
up with a last gleam. "Farewell. . . . Listen. . . . I didn't
kiss you that time, you know. . . . Breathe on the dying
lamp, let it go out. . . ."

Anna Sergeyevna put her lips to his brow.

"That's all!" he murmured and sank back on his pillow.
"Now . . . darkness. . . ."

Anna Sergeyevna quietly left the room.

"Well?" Vassily Ivanych asked her in a whisper.

"He's fallen asleep," she replied in a voice that was
barely audible.

Bazarov was to wake no more. In the evening he fell
into a coma and the next day he died. Father Alexei per-
formed the religious rites over him. During the ceremony
of Extreme unction, when the consecrated oil was applied
to his chest, one eye opened and it seemed as though, at
the sight of the priest in his vestments, the fumes of incense rising from the censer and the candles in front of
the icons, something akin to a shudder of horror flitted
across the livid face of the dying man. When at length
he breathed his last, and the whole house resounded
with cries of lamentation, Vassily Ivanych was seized
with a sudden frenzy. "I said I would murmur at it," he
shouted hoarsely, his face distorted and aflame, shaking
his fist in the air as though defying somebody, "and I
will murmur, I will!" But Arina Vlasyevna, all in tears,
clung to his neck, and both dropped to their knees on
the floor. "And there they knelt," Anfisushka afterwards
related in the servants' hall, "side by side, with drooping
heads, like two poor lambs at noontide. . . ."

But the heat of noon passes, then comes evening and night, bringing a return to the peaceful haven where sweetly sleep the tired and weary....

XXVIII

Six months had passed. White winter had come with the hush of its bitter cloudless frosts, its heavy blanket of crunching snow, the warm-tinted rime on the trees, pale emerald skies, wreaths of smoke over the chimneys, clouds of steam eddying from quickly opened doors, fresh frost-nipped faces and the hurried trot of chilled horses. A January day was drawing to a close; the cold breath of evening gripped the still air in an icy clutch and the blood-red glow of sunset swiftly faded. The lights went up in the Maryino home; Prokofich, in black frock coat and white gloves was, with unusual solemnity, setting the table for seven. A week ago, in the little parish church, a double wedding had taken place unostentatiously and almost without witnesses: that of Arkady and Katya, and of Nikolai Petrovich and Fenichka; and on this day Nikolai Petrovich was giving a farewell dinner in honour of his brother, who was leaving for Moscow on business; Anna Sergeyevna had gone to Moscow, too, immediately after the wedding, after having generously endowed the young newlyweds.

Exactly at three o'clock everyone sat down to the table. Mitya was given a place there too; he now had a nurse in a brocaded cap. Pavel Petrovich was seated between Katya and Fenichka; the "husbands" sat next to their wives. Our friends had changed of late: they all seemed to be better-looking and more grown up; Pavel Petrovich alone had grown thinner, but this gave an added touch of elegance and the grand seigneur manner to his expressive features. Fenichka too had altered. In a fresh silk gown, with a broad velvet headdress and a gold chain round her neck, she sat respectfully immobile, respectful to both herself and everything around her, and smiling with an air that seemed to say: "Please excuse me, it's not my fault." Everybody else was smiling too and looking apologetic about it too; all felt a bit awkward and a bit sad, but really very happy. Everybody waited on everybody else with amusing courtesy, as though all had agreed to play an innocent comedy. Katya was the calmest of all: she looked trustingly about her, and one could tell that she had become as dear to Nikolai Petrovich as the apple of his eye. Towards the end of the dinner he got up, and lifting his glass turned to Pavel Petrovich.

"You are leaving us ... you are leaving us, dear brother," he began, "but, of course, not for long; still, I want to tell you that I ... that we ... how I ... how we.... That's the trouble, speechmaking is not in my line! Arkady, say something."

"No, Dad, not offhand."

"And do you think I can! Oh, well, brother, let me just embrace you and wish you all the very best, and come back to us quickly!"

Pavel Petrovich kissed everybody, including, naturally, Mitya; and in addition he kissed Fenichka's hand, which she had not yet learnt to proffer properly, and quaffing his replenished glass, uttered with a deep sigh: "Good luck to you, my friends! *Farewell*!" This English tailpiece passed unnoticed; but everybody was touched.

"To the memory of Bazarov," Katya whispered into her husband's ear, and clinked glasses with him. Arkady responded by squeezing her hand; he did not venture, however, to propose this toast aloud.

*   *   *

This would seem to be the end? But perhaps some reader is curious to know what the other characters of our story are doing at the present time, at this particular moment. We are ready to gratify him.

Anna Sergeyevna recently married, not for love but by conviction, one of Russia's future public men, a very clever lawyer of sound common sense, firm will and remarkable rhetoric—a man still young, good-natured and cold as ice. They get on extremely well together, and may eventually come to know happiness, perhaps love—

who can tell? The Princess X— died, unremembered on the very day of her death. The Kirsanovs, father and son, have settled down at Maryino. Things are beginning to look up with them. Arkady has become a keen husband-man and the farm is yielding a fairly large income. Nikolai Petrovich has become a *mirovoy posrednik** and works with might and main; he is constantly touring his district and making long speeches (he nurtures a belief that the muzhiks should be "made to listen to reason", meaning to reduce them to a state of stupefaction by constantly drumming into them one and the same thing) though, frankly speaking, he does not quite satisfy either the educated nobility who hold forth turgidly or mourn-fully, as the case may be, on *emancipation* (with a nasal pronunciation) or the uneducated nobility who baldly curse "that damned *'muncipation*". He is too mild for either. Katerina Sergeyevna has given birth to a son Nikolai, and Mitya is already spry of foot and active of tongue. Fenichka—Fedosya Nikolayevna, adores nobody so much, after her husband and Mitya, as her daughter-in-law, and when the latter sits down to play the piano, she could listen to her all day long. In passing, a word about Pyotr. He has become utterly benumbed with stu-pidity and self-importance, has refined his pronunciation to the point of unintelligibility, but has married, too, and taken an appreciable dowry with his bride, the daughter of an urban market gardener who had turned down two good suitors because they possessed no watches, whereas Pyotr had a watch and a pair of patent shoes besides.

On the Brühl Terrace in Dresden, between two and four in the afternoon, the fashionable promenade hour, you may meet a man of about fifty, quite grey and to all appearances suffering from gout, but still handsome, ele-gantly dressed, and with that peculiar grace that is ac-quired only through long contact with the higher circles of society. This is Pavel Petrovich. He left Moscow to go abroad for the sake of his health and took up his abode

---

*Arbiter of the peace, or Arbitrator, a post introduced in Russia after the emancipation of the peasantry for settling differences be-tween peasants and landlords.—*Trans.*

in Dresden, where he associates for the most part with
Englishmen and Russian visitors. With the Englishmen
he bears himself simply, almost modestly, but with a sense
of dignity; they find him somewhat boring, but respect in
him the *perfect gentleman*. With the Russians he is more
casual, gives rein to his spleen, cracks jokes at his own
expense and theirs; but it is all done with a charming
manner of inoffensive insouciance. He holds Pan-Slavist
views, which, as everyone knows, are considered *très
distingué* in high society. He reads nothing Russian, but
he has on his desk a silver ash tray in the shape of a
muzhik's bast sandal. He is run after very much by our
tourists. Matvei Ilyich Kolyazin, who is *in the temporary
opposition,* paid a majestic call on him on his way to the
Bohemian waters; the natives for their part, of whom he
sees very little, stand in almost reverent awe of him.
Nobody can book a ticket for the court choir or the theatre
as easily and quickly as *der Herr Baron von Kirsanoff*.
He still tries, to the best of his ability, to do good; he
still makes a slight stir—wasn't he once a society lion?—
but life to him is a burden—a heavier burden than he
himself suspects. One need only glance at him in the Russian church, where he stands apart, leaning against the
wall, lost long in thought without stirring, in tight-lipped
bitter silence, and then suddenly collects himself and
begins to cross himself with an almost imperceptible motion of his hand.

Kukshina, too, is living abroad. She is now in Heidelberg, and is no longer studying natural sciences, but
architecture, in which she claims to have discovered new
laws. She still hobnobs with the students, especially with
young Russian physicists and chemists, of whom Heidelberg is full and who astonish the naïve German profes-
sors first by their very sober view of things and then by
their utter inertness and sheer laziness. With two or three
such chemists who are unable to distinguish oxygen from
nitrogen, but are chock-full of negation and self-respect,
and with the great Yelisevich, Sitnikov, also aspiring to
greatness, whiles away the tedious hours in St. Petersburg,
where, he assures us, he is carrying on Bazarov's "cause".
Rumour has it that he recently received a thrashing, but

he got his own back: in a mean little paragraph squeezed into a mean little journal he insinuated that his assailant was a coward. He calls that irony. His father bullies him as of old, and his wife considers him a ninny ... and a man of letters.

There is a small country graveyard in a remote corner of Russia. Like nearly all our graveyards, it presents a sorry sight: the ditches around it are covered with a rank overgrowth; the drab wooden crosses have pitched forward and are rotting under their once painted roofs; the tombstones have all shifted, as though someone were pushing them from below; two or three starveling trees hardly afford a meagre shade; sheep wander freely over the graves. But there is one grave that no man touches and no beast tramples: only birds alight thereon and sing there at dawn. It is surrounded by an iron railing, and two fir trees have been planted at each end: in this grave lies Yevgeny Bazarov. Here, from the nearby village, often comes a now decrepit old couple—husband and wife. Supporting each other, they plod on with weary footsteps; they come to the enclosure, fall down upon their knees and cry long and bitterly, and long do they gaze at the mute tombstone under which lies their son; they exchange a brief word, dust the stone and set straight a branch of the fir tree, then pray once more and are unable to tear themselves away from this spot, where they seem to be nearer to their son and to the memories of him. ... Can it be that their prayers, their tears are fruitless? Can it be that love, sacred devoted love, is not all-powerful? Nay! However passionate, however sinning and rebellious the heart that lies buried in the grave, the flowers that grow thereon gaze at you serenely with their innocent eyes; it is not of eternal peace alone they speak to us, of that great peace of "impassive" nature; they speak to us, too, of eternal reconcilement and of the life eternal. ...

THE END

A NEST OF THE GENTRY

1

A fair spring day was drawing to a close. Little rosy
clouds hung high in the clear sky, seeming to melt in the
azure depths as they floated slowly past.

Before the open window of a handsome house in the
suburbs of the gubernia town of O— (it was in the year
1842) sat two women; one was about fifty years of age,
the other an old lady of seventy.

The name of the former was Marya Dmitriyevna Kalitina. Her husband, ex-public prosecutor of the gubernia,
noted in his day as a man of business, an active, resource-
ful man of stubborn and choleric temper, had been dead
for ten years. He had received a good education and
graduated the university; but having been born among
the humbler orders he realised early in life the necessity
of making his way in the world and lining his pocket. It
had been a love match on Marya Dmitriyevna's side, for
he had been a good-looking man, clever, and amiable
when he chose. Marya Dmitriyevna (*née* Pestova) had
lost her parents in childhood. She spent some years in
Moscow in a ladies' institute and on her return lived on
the family estate in the village of Pokrovskoye, about
fifty versts from O— with her aunt and an elder brother.
This brother shortly moved to St. Petersburg, where he
held a government post, and treated his sister and aunt
high-handedly till sudden death cut short his career.
Marya Dmitriyevna inherited Pokrovskoye, but she did
not live there long: a year after her marriage to Kalitin,
who had conquered her heart in the space of a few days,
Pokrovskoye was exchanged for a more lucrative estate
which, however, was unattractive and had no homestead.
At the same time Kalitin took a house in the town of O—

in which he and his wife took up their permanent abode. The house stood in a large garden which on one side overlooked the open country. "And so," decided Kalitin, who was no lover of rural amenities, "there'll be no going off to the country." At bottom Marya Dmitriyevna more than once rued the loss of her pretty Pokrovskoye with its smiling brook, its broad meadows and green groves; but she never in any way opposed her husband, of whose wisdom and knowledge of the world she stood in profoundest awe. However, when after fifteen years of married life, he died leaving her with a son and two daughters, Marya Dmitriyevna had grown so accustomed to her house and town life that she had no wish to leave O—.

In her youth Marya Dmitriyevna had had the reputation of being a pretty blonde; even at fifty her features had not lost all their charm, though they were rather puffy and had lost their delicacy. She was sentimental rather than kindhearted, and retained her school-day mannerisms even at a mature age; she coddled herself, was easily irritated and would even grow tearful if her habits were interfered with; but she could also be very gracious and kind when humoured and nobody gainsaid her. Her house was one of the most agreeable in the town. She had a pretty fortune, not so much from her own legacy as through her husband's thrift. Both daughters lived with her; her son was attending one of the best colleges in St. Petersburg.

The old lady sitting with Marya Dmitriyevna at the window was that same aunt, her father's sister, with whom she had once spent several years in the seclusion of Pokrovskoye. Her name was Marfa Timofeyevna Pestova. She was by repute an eccentric old lady of independent character, told everyone the truth to his face, and was able to keep up a show of opulence even on the most scanty means. She had had a strong aversion to Kalitin, and directly her niece married him she returned to her little village, where for ten whole years she lived in the ramshackle hut of a muzhik. Marya Dmitriyevna was a little afraid of her. A little sharp-nosed woman, black-haired and keen-eyed even in her old age, Marfa

Timofeyevna walked with a sprightly step, held herself erect and spoke rapidly and distinctly in a high-pitched resonant voice. She was always to be seen in a white lace cap and white dressing jacket.

"What's the matter?" she asked Marya Dmitriyevna suddenly. "What are you sighing about, my dear?"

"Oh, nothing," answered the other. "What lovely clouds!"

"Do you feel so sorry for them?"

Marya Dmitriyevna made no reply.

"I wonder why Gedeonovsky doesn't come?" observed Marfa Timofeyevna, nimbly plying her knitting needles. (She was knitting a big woollen scarf.) "He would help you sigh—or tell you some fibs."

"How hard you always are on him! Sergei Petrovich is a worthy man."

"Worthy!" echoed the old lady deprecatingly.

"And how devoted he was to my poor husband!" said Marya Dmitriyevna. "To this day he cannot speak of him without emotion."

"I should think he would! Didn't your husband pick him up out of the gutter?" muttered Marfa Timofeyevna, and her knitting needles moved faster.

"Mind you, he's such a meek person to look at," she began again, "with his head all grey, but no sooner does he open his mouth than out comes a lie or a bit of scandal. And he a civil servant too, in the rank of councillor! Ah, but then he's only the son of a village priest."

"Every one has his faults, auntie; that's his weak side, to be sure. Sergei Petrovich has had no education. I admit—he doesn't speak French; but he is a very agreeable person, say what you like."

"Of course, he is always kissing your hands. What if he doesn't speak French! For that matter, I don't shine myself in French tattle. It were better he didn't speak at all in any language—he wouldn't be telling lies. But here he comes—talk of the devil," added Marfa Timofeyevna glancing into the street. "Here's your agreeable person, stalking along. As lean and lanky as a stork he is!"

Marya Dmitriyevna tidied her curls. Marfa Timofeyevna eyed her ironically.

"What's that, my dear, not a grey hair, surely? That
Palashka of yours should be told off. Really, where does
she think her eyes are?"

"Really, auntie, you always..." murmured Marya
Dmitriyevna in a grieved tone, drumming her fingers on
the arm of her chair.

"Sergei Petrovich Gedeonovsky"—piped a rosy-cheeked
servant boy, popping his head in at the door.

II

A tall man entered, dressed in a neat frock coat,
shortish trousers, grey suede gloves and double cravat—
a black one on top and a white one underneath. His
whole aspect breathed of decorum and respectability,
from his well-favoured countenance and smoothly brushed
temples to his flat-heeled, soft-padded topboots. He
bowed first to the lady of the house, then to Marfa
Timofeyevna, and slowly drawing off his gloves, stooped
over Marya Dmitriyevna's hand. Having kissed it rever-
ently, in fact twice, he seated himself with deliberation
in an armchair, and rubbing his fingertips, observed with
a smile:

"And is Elizaveta Mikhailovna quite well?"

"Yes," replied Marya Dmitriyevna, "she's in the garden."

"And Elena Mikhailovna?"

"Lenochka's in the garden, too. Is there anything new?"

"I should say there is," replied the visitor, blinking
slowly and pursing his lips. "Hm! ... there certainly
is some news, and very astonishing news at that. Lavretsky, Fyodor Ivanych, is here."

"Fedya!" cried Marfa Timofeyevna. "Come, good
man, you are not making it up, are you?"

"Why, of course not, I saw him myself."

"That doesn't prove anything."

"He looks extremely well," continued Gedeonovsky,
affecting not to have heard Marfa Timofeyevna's re-

mark. "He is broader in the shoulders and has a fine
colour."

"Looks extremely well," repeated Marya Dmitriyevna
slowly. "One would not think he has any reason to be
looking well."

"Yes, indeed," took up Gedeonovsky, "another man
in his position would have thought twice before appear-
ing in society."

"How's that?" interposed Marfa Timofeyevna.
"That's sheer nonsense! The man has come back home—
where would you have him go? Now, I understand if
he were in any way to blame!"

"The husband is always to blame, madam, you can
take it from me, when his wife misbehaves."

"You say that, my good sir, because you have never
been married." Gedeonovsky listened with a constrained
smile.

"If I may be so inquisitive," he enquired after a short
silence, "who is that pretty scarf for?"

Marfa Timofeyevna threw him a swift glance.

"It's for a man who never gossips, who is not a humbug and doesn't tell lies, if there is such a man in the
world. I know Fedya well; his only fault is that he
pampered his wife. Then, of course, he married for love,
and they've never done any good, these love matches,"
threw in the old lady, giving Marya Dmitriyevna a look
out of the corner of her eye and getting up. "And now,
my dear sir, you can pull to pieces whomsoever
you please, even me for all I care; I'm going, I won't
be in your way." And Marfa Timofeyevna walked
out.

"That's how she always is," said Marya Dmitriyevna,
following her aunt with her eyes. "Always!"

"Your aunt's getting on in years, you know. . . . It
can't be helped!" remarked Gedeonovsky. "She said
something about being a humbug. But who is not that
nowadays? Life's like that today. A friend of mine, a
very worthy man and of no mean rank, let me tell you,
used to say that nowadays even a hen can't pick up a
grain without shamming—she will always go for it
sideways. But when I look at you, dear lady, I see the

soul of an angel; ah, permit me to kiss your snow-white little hand."

Marya Dmitriyevna smiled faintly and held out her dimpled hand with the little finger thrust out. He pressed his lips to it. Drawing her chair closer to him, she bent slightly forward and asked him in an undertone:

"So you have seen him? Is he really—all right—er, quite well and cheerful?"

"Yes, quite cheerful," said Gedeonovsky *sotto voce.*

"Haven't you heard where his wife is?"

"She was lately in Paris; now there is talk of her having gone off to Italy."

"It is really dreadful—Fedya's position; I wonder how he bears up under it. Misfortune, of course, can be anybody's lot; but he, one might say, has become the talk of Europe."

Gedeonovsky sighed.

"Yes, yes, indeed. You know, they say she has been associating with artists and pianists—society lions, I believe they call them—and all sorts of strange creatures. She's utterly shameless."

"I'm ever so sorry," said Marya Dmitriyevna. "He's one of the family, after all—he's a distant cousin of mine, you know, Sergei Petrovich."

"Why, of course. Don't I know everything that concerns your family. I should say I do."

"Will he come to see us, do you think?"

"I should imagine so; though I hear he intends to go to his country place."

Marya Dmitriyevna lifted up her eyes.

"Ah, Sergei Petrovich, Sergei Petrovich, when I come to think of it,—how discreet we women must be!"

"Not all women are alike, Marya Dmitriyevna. There are unfortunately some women—flighty, you know ... and the age, too, has something to do with it; and then they are not brought up properly in childhood." (Sergei Petrovich drew a blue checked handkerchief out of his pocket and began to unfold it.) "There are such women, aye, there are." (Sergei Petrovich dabbed each eye in turn with a corner of his handkerchief.) "But, generally speaking, if one may be allowed to say so, that is.... The dust in town is awful," he concluded.

"*Maman, Maman,*" cried a winsome little girl of eleven, darting into the room, "Vladimir Nikolaich is coming on horseback!"

Marya Dmitriyevna got up; Sergei Petrovich got up too and made a bow. "Elena Mikhailovna, my compliments," he said, and turning aside into a corner for the sake of decorum, he started to blow his long straight nose.

"What a fine horse he has!" continued the little girl. "He was at the wicket just now and told Liza and me he would come round to the porch." There came a sound of approaching hoofs, and a graceful young man astride a beautiful bay horse came into view in the street and stopped before the open window.

III

"How do you do, Marya Dmitriyevna!" cried the rider in a resonant pleasant voice. "How do you like my new purchase?"

Marya Dmitriyevna stepped to the window.

"How do you do, Woldemar. Oh, what a splendid horse! Where did you buy it?"

"I bought it from the army contractor.... He made me pay a pretty penny, the rogue."

"What is its name?"

"Orlando.... It's a silly name. I want to change it.... *Eh bien, eh bien, mon garçon* ... what a restive beast he is!"

The horse snorted, pranced and tossed its foam-flaked muzzle.

"Lenochka, pat him. Don't be afraid."

The little girl put her hand out of the window, but Orlando suddenly reared and shied.

The rider with perfect sangfroid gave it a flick of his whip across the neck, and digging his legs into its sides brought it, despite its resistance, back to the window.

15*

"*Prenez garde, prenez garde,*" Marya Dmitriyevna kept on reiterating.

"Lenochka, pat him," said the young man. "I won't let him have things his own way."

The girl put her hand out again and timidly patted the quivering nostrils of the champing, restive horse.

"Bravo!" cried Marya Dmitriyevna. "But now get off and come inside."

The rider adroitly veered his horse's head, gave him a touch of the spur, and riding at a brisk gallop down the street, entered the courtyard. Presently he ran into the drawing room through the hall door swinging his riding whip; simultaneously there appeared in another doorway a tall, slender, dark-haired girl of nineteen, Marya Dmitriyevna's eldest daughter, Liza.

IV

The young man whom we have just introduced to our reader was Vladimir Nikolaich Panshin. He was a civil servant in St. Petersburg, acting on special commissions in the Ministry of the Interior. He had come to the town of O— on a temporary official commission and was in attendance on the governor, General Zonnenberg, to whom he was distantly related. Panshin's father, a retired cavalry captain and notorious gambler, a man with honeyed eyes, a creased face and a nervous twitch about the mouth, had spent all his life rubbing shoulders with nobility; he haunted the English clubs of both capitals and had the reputation of being an adroit, though not very trustworthy man of the hail-fellow kind. Despite his adroitness he was nearly always on the brink of penury, and left his only son a meagre and heavily mortgaged property. He did, however, in a way, provide for his son's education. Vladimir Nikolaich spoke French excellently, English well and German badly. That was how it should be: respectable folk considered it bad form to speak German well; but to employ a German phrase on a suitable occasion—preferably facetiously—was

quite the thing, *c'est même très chic,* as the Petersburg
Parisians say. At fifteen Vladimir Nikolaich could enter
a drawing room without embarrassment, dawdle pleasantly therein and depart at the proper time. Panshin's
father procured his son numerous connections. When
shuffling cards between two rubbers or after a successful "grand slam" he would never miss an opportunity of
putting in a word for his "Volodka" to any personage
of importance who liked a game of skill. For his part,
Vladimir Nikolaich, during his stay at the university,
which he graduated with a degree of bachelor, made the
acquaintance of several young men of quality and was
received into the best houses. He was welcome everywhere; he was very good-looking, nonchalant, amusing,
always in good health and sociable; deferential when
he should be, audacious when he dared to be; an excellent fellow, *un charmant garçon.* Life smiled on him.
Panshin quickly learnt the secrets of high society; he
could yield a genuine respect for its decrees; he could
dally with trifles with an air of flippant gravity and
make pretence of regarding grave matters as trifles; he
danced admirably and dressed in the English mode. In
a short time he won the reputation of being one of the
most amiable and accomplished young men in St. Petersburg. Panshin was indeed exceedingly adroit, more so
than his father; but then he was endowed with no mean
talents. He could turn his hand to anything: he sang
charmingly, sketched dexterously, wrote verses and was
not at all bad at theatricals. He was only in his twenty-
eighth year and was already a *Kammerjunker* and held
a very good position. Panshin had complete confidence
in himself, in his intelligence and sagacity; he made his
way boldly and blithely; his life was smooth sailing.
He was used to being a general favourite with old and
young alike and fancied he knew people, especially
women: he certainly knew their common foibles. Having
a penchant for the arts, he was conscious of an innate
ardour, an imaginative zeal and even rapture, and consequently permitted himself certain deviations from the
rule: he sowed some wild oats, associated with people
who were beyond the pale of good society and, in gener-

al, carried himself with a free and easy air; at heart, however, he was cold and crafty, and during the most boisterous revelry his shrewd brown eye was always alert and watchful of what was going on; this bold, independent young man could never give himself up entirely to a ruling passion. To do him justice, he never boasted of his conquests. He found his way into Marya Dmitriyevna's house directly he arrived in O— and he soon made himself quite at home there. Marya Dmitriyevna simply doted on him.

Panshin bowed courteously to everybody in the room, shook hands with Marya Dmitriyevna and Elizaveta Mikhailovna, patted Gedeonovsky lightly on the shoulder, and swinging round, he took hold of Lenochka's head and imprinted a kiss on her forehead.

"Aren't you afraid to ride such a vicious horse?" Marya Dmitriyevna asked him.

"He's very docile, really; but I'll tell you what I really am afraid of: I'm afraid to play whist with Sergei Petrovich; yesterday at the Belenitsyns' he beat me clean."

Gedeonovsky gave a little simper of a laugh; he strove to ingratiate himself with this brilliant young official from St. Petersburg—the Governor's favourite. In his conversation with Marya Dmitriyevna he frequently alluded to Panshin's remarkable accomplishments. "Indeed, how could one help praising him," he used to say. "The young man is succeeding in the highest spheres, he's an exemplary official and not a bit uppish." As a matter of fact, in St. Petersburg, too, Panshin was looked upon as a competent official: his capacity for work was remarkable; he spoke of it lightly, as behoves a man of the world who does not attach much importance to his labours, but he was an "efficient executive". Principals like such subordinates; he himself had no doubt that he would rise to ministerial eminence in time if he chose.

"You say, sir, that I beat you clean," said Gedeonovsky, "but who was it won twelve rubles of me the other day? And then again. . . ."

"Oh, you wicked man," Panshin interjected in a tone

of kindly though contemptuous nonchalance and, turning his back on him, he went up to Liza.

"I couldn't get the Oberon overture here," he began. "Belenitsyna merely boasted when she said she had all the classical music—she really has nothing but polkas and waltzes; but I've written to Moscow and within a week you will have the overture. By the way," he went on, "I wrote a new song yesterday, the words are mine too. Would you care to hear it? I don't know what it's like. Belenitsyna thought it a pretty piece, but her opinion's not worth much. I should like to know what you think of it. But, never mind, it can wait. . . ."

"Why wait?" interposed Marya Dmitriyevna. "Why not now?"

"As you please," replied Panshin with a sweetly radiant smile that disappeared from his face as suddenly as it had appeared. Pushing up the stool with his knee, he sat down to the piano, and striking a few chords, began to sing, clearly enunciating his words:

> *The moon doth soar o'er vales of weeping willows,*
> *Through clouds she gleams,*
> *And from on high she rules the briny billows*
> *With majic beams.*
>
> *Thou art, O love, the moon that stirs my soul's tide—*
> *Its boundless sea—*
> *Which ebbs and flows with grief and joy*
> *where shoals bide,*
> *In tune with thee.*
>
> *For thee my soul doth yearn, to thee complaining:*
> *With love I swoon,*
> *But thou serene and calm I see remaining*
> *Like yon fair moon.*

The second verse Panshin brought out with special force and feeling; the turbulent accompaniment was reminiscent of the sound of waves. After the words "with love I swoon" he sighed softly, lowered his eyes and dropped his voice, *morendo*. When he had finished, Liza praised the tune, Marya Dmitriyevna said it was "charming!" and Gedeonovsky even burst out with "delightful! Both the music and the words are simply delightful!" Lenochka gazed in childish awe at the singer. In short, the company was very pleased with the young dilettante's composition; but in the hallway stood an old man who had apparently just arrived, and whom, to judge by the look of his downcast face and the gesture he made with his shoulders, Panshin's song, pretty though it was, afforded anything but pleasure. Pausing to flick the dust off his boots with a coarse handkerchief, the man suddenly narrowed his eyes, sullenly tightened his mouth, bent his already stooping figure and slowly entered the drawing room.

"Ah! Christopher Fyodorych, good evening!" exclaimed Panshin, anticipating the rest of the company and jumping up from his seat. "I had no idea you were here—I would never have had the nerve to sing my song before you. I know you don't approve of light music."

"I hear it not," rejoined the newcomer in very bad Russian, and bowing to everyone present, he stopped awkwardly in the middle of the room.

"I suppose, Monsieur Lemm," said Marya Dmitriyevna, "you've come to give Liza her music lesson?"

"No, not Elizaveta Mikhailovna, but Elena Mikhailovna."

"Ah! Very well. Lenochka, go upstairs with M. Lemm."

The old man was on the point of following the little girl out, but Panshin intercepted him.

"Don't go away after the lesson, Christopher Fyodorych," he said. "Elizaveta Mikhailovna and I are going to play a Beethoven sonata."

The old man growled something under his breath, and Panshin went on in German, mispronouncing the words:

"Elizaveta Mikhailovna showed me the religious cantata you dedicated to her—a beautiful thing! Please, do not think me incapable of appreciating serious music; on the contrary. It is tedious sometimes, but so very wholesome."

The old man reddened to the roots of his hair, and with a sidelong glance at Liza he hurriedly left the room.

Marya Dmitriyevna asked Panshin to sing his song again; but he demurred that he did not wish to offend the ears of the learned German and offered Liza instead to tackle the Beethoven sonata. Thereupon Marya Dmitriyevna sighed and for her part suggested to Gedeonovsky that he should take a walk with her in the garden. "I should like," she said, "to continue our talk and ask your advice about our poor Fedya." Gedeonovsky smirked, bowed, picked up with two fingers his hat, on the brim of which he had laid his carefully folded gloves, and followed Marya Dmitriyevna out of the room. Panshin and Liza remained alone in the room; she got out the sonata and opened it; they sat down to the piano in silence. From above came the faint sound of scales, practised by the halting fingers of little Lenochka.

V

Christopher Theodore Gottlieb Lemm was born in the year 1786 in the Kingdom of Saxony, in the town of Chemnitz, of poor musicians. His father played the French horn, his mother the harp. When only five he was practising on three different instruments. At eight years of age he was left an orphan and at ten was earning his livelihood by his art. For a long time he led an itinerant life, playing wherever he could—at inns, fairs, peasants' weddings and balls; eventually he got into an orchestra where, rising by degrees, he finally became conductor. As a performer he was pretty poor, but he had a thorough knowledge of music. At twenty-eight he migrated to Russia. He was invited by a grand gentleman who detested music himself but kept an orchestra for the sake of ostentation. Lemm stayed with him for seven years in the capacity of musical director and parted company with him with nothing to show. That gentleman went bankrupt, he had wanted to give Lemm a promissory note, but subsequently thought better of it —in short, he did not pay him a farthing. Lemm was advised to leave the country, but he did not want to return home a beggar from Russia, that great Russia, the

El Dorado of the artist; he decided to remain and try
his luck. The poor German had been trying his luck for
twenty years: he had stayed with various of the gentry,
had tried both Moscow and provincial towns, had
suffered and endured much, tasted poverty and buffeted
the waves; but the thought of returning to his native
land never deserted him amid all his tribulations; that
thought alone bore him up. Fate, however, did not vouch-
safe him this last and first bliss: at fifty, ill and prema-
turely infirm, he became stranded in the town of O—
and there he stayed for good, giving up all hope of leaving Russia, which he abhorred. He contrived to eke out
a precarious existence by giving lessons. Lemm's appearance was not lovely to behold. He was short of stature
and bent, with crooked shoulders and indrawn stomach,
large flat feet and bluish-white nails on the stiff, horny
fingers of his blue-veined red hands; he had a puckered
face, hollow cheeks and tightened lips which he was for
ever twisting and gnawing at and which, added to his
habitual taciturnity, produced an almost gruesome effect.
His grey hair strayed in tufts over a low brow, his little
immobile eyes smouldered like dying embers; he moved
in a lumbering gait, swinging his unwieldy bulk forward
at each step. Some of his gestures reminded one of the
uncouth preening of a caged owl when it feels it is being
observed and can but peer helplessly about with its
enormous, timorously blinking and somnolent yellow
eyes. A deep gnawing grief had laid its ineffaceable seal
on the poor musician; it had marred and maimed his by
no means engaging aspect; but to those who were not
prone to be influenced by first impressions there was
something good, and honest, something uncommon in
this ravaged creature. An admirer of Bach and Handel,
a master of his craft, endowed with a vivid imagination
and that strength of mind which is a feature of the German race, Lemm might in time—who knows?—have
ranked with the great composers of his country, had the
tide of life favoured him; but not under a lucky star
was he born! He had written a great deal in his time,
but was not to see a single one of his compositions
published: he could not handle things the right way,

curry favour in the right place, bestir himself at the right time. Once, a long time ago, an admirer and friend of his, also a German and also poor, published two of his sonatas at his own expense, but the whole edition remained on the shelves of the music shops; they were swallowed up in oblivion, as though someone had cast them into the river overnight. Lemm finally resigned himself to his fate; and his years were telling too; his mind, like his hands, had become callous and benumbed. He lived alone in a little house not far from the Kalitins, with an old cook he had taken out of the almshouse (he had never married). He took long walks, read the Bible, a volume of Protestant hymns, or Shakespeare in Schlegel's translation. He had not written any music for a long time; but apparently Liza, who was his best pupil, had been able to rouse him from his lethargy; he had composed for her the cantata which Panshin had mentioned. The words for this cantata he had borrowed from his Psalm Book, to which he had added some verses of his own. It was intended for two choruses—a chorus of the happy and a chorus of the unhappy, which merged together at the end and sang in unison, "Merciful God, forgive thy sinners and deliver us from evil thoughts and earthly hopes." On the title page, painstakingly inscribed and even embellished, was the legend: "Only the righteous are just. A Religious Cantata. Composed and dedicated to my dear pupil, Miss Elizaveta Kalitina, by her teacher, C.T.G. Lemm." The words, "Only the righteous are just" and "Elizaveta Kalitina" stood in a circle of rays. Underneath was added: "For you alone, *für Sie allein.*" This was why Lemm had reddened and looked reproachfully at Liza; he was deeply pained when Panshin spoke of his cantata before him.

VI

Panshin loudly and resolutely struck the first chords of the sonata (he was playing the second part), but Liza did not begin. He stopped and looked at her. Liza's eyes, which were fixed on him, expressed displeasure; her lips were unsmiling, and her countenance was stern, almost sad.

"What's the matter?" he asked.

"Why didn't you keep your word?" she said. "I showed you Christopher Fyodorych's cantata on the understanding that you would say nothing to him about it."

"I'm sorry, Elizaveta Mikhailovna, the words slipped out."

"You've upset him, and me too. Now he won't trust me either."

"I couldn't help it, Elizaveta Mikhailovna. Ever since I was a youngster I could never bide the sight of a German; I've always had an itch to tease him."

"How can you say such a thing, Vladimir Nikolaich! This German is a poor, lonely, broken man—don't you feel sorry for him? Can you wish to tease him?"

Panshin looked abashed.

"You are right, Elizaveta Mikhailovna," he said. "It's that eternal imprudence of mine. No, don't remonstrate; I know myself. My indiscretion has caused me a lot of harm. Thanks to that I am considered an egoist."

Panshin paused. On whatever subject he began a conversation he invariably ended up by talking about himself, and he did this with a disarming grace, unaffectedly and genially—unconsciously, as it were.

"Take your own house, for instance," he went on, "your mother, of course, is well disposed towards me, she is so kind; you ... well, I don't know what you think of me; as for your aunt, she simply can't bear me. I've probably offended her too by some imprudent, silly speech. She doesn't like me, now does she?"

"No," admitted Liza after a moment's hesitation, "she doesn't."

Panshin ran his fingers over the keys; a faintly ironical smile played about his lips.

"What about you?" he said. "Do you consider me an egoist too?"

"I know you so little," replied Liza, "but I don't consider you an egoist; on the contrary, I ought to be grateful to you. . . ."

"I know, I know what you are going to say," Panshin broke in, running his fingers once more over the keys, "for the music, for the books I let you have, for the bad sketches I adorn your album with *et cetera, et cetera.* I could do that and still be an egoist. I dare to hope you do not find my company boring or believe me a bad fellow, but still you probably think that I wouldn't even —now how does that saying run—spare neither friend nor father for the sake of a joke."

"You are inattentive and forgetful, like all society people," observed Liza, "that is all."

Panshin frowned slightly.

"Come," he said, "don't let us talk about me any more; let us go on with the sonata. There's one thing I want to ask you though," he added, smoothing out the leaves of the music-book on the stand, "please think me what you like, call me an egoist even—so be it! But don't call me a society man; that appellation's hateful.... *Anch'io sono pittore.* I'm an artist too, maybe a poor one, and that—the fact that I'm a poor artist—I'm going to prove to you here and now. Let us begin."

"Yes, let us begin," said Liza.

The first *adagio* went off fairly well, though Panshin frequently blundered. His own things and music that he had practised he could play nicely, but he was bad at reading music at sight. The second part of the sonata— a fairly quick *allegro*—was altogether sad work; at the twentieth bar Panshin, who was two bars behind, gave it up and pushed his chair back with a laugh.

"It's no use!" he exclaimed. "I can't play today; thank goodness Lemm didn't hear us; he would have had a fit."

Liza got up, shut the piano and turned to Panshin.

"What shall we do then?" she asked.

"How like you that question is! You can never sit idle for a moment. Well, if you like, let's do some sketching while it's still light. Maybe the other Muse—the Muse of Painting—what d'ye call her? can't remember ... will be more disposed towards me. Where is your album? If I remember aright, that landscape of mine is not finished."

Liza went out into the next room to fetch the album, and Panshin, left to himself, drew out of his pocket a cambric handkerchief, rubbed his nails, and, squinting a little, contemplated his hands. They were white and exquisite; on the thumb of his left hand he wore a gold spiral ring. Liza came back; Panshin took a seat near the window and opened the album.

"Ah!" said he. "So you've begun to copy my landscape—fine. Very good indeed! Only just here—pass me a pencil—the shadows are not quite heavy enough. Look here."

And Panshin dashed off several long strokes. He was for ever drawing the same landscapes: large straggling trees in the foreground, a bit of meadow in the background and jagged mountains on the skyline. Liza watched him over his shoulder.

"In drawing, as in life generally," observed Panshin, inclining his head first to the right then to the left, "the main thing is—lightness and daring."

Just then Lemm entered the room, and, bowing stiffly, was about to retire; but Panshin, flinging aside album and pencils, barred his way.

"Where are you going, my dear Christopher Fyodorych? Aren't you staying for tea?"

"I go home," said Lemm gruffly, "my head aches."

"Oh, come now—do stay. We'll discuss Shakespeare."

"My head aches," repeated the old man.

"We started on the Beethoven sonata here without you," went on Panshin, putting an arm around him affectionately and smiling sweetly, "but we couldn't get on at all. Would you believe it, I couldn't play two consecutive notes rightly."

"You'd better haf sung dat song of yours again," retorted Lemm, removing Panshin's hands, and withdrew.

Liza ran after him. She overtook him on the porch.

"Christopher Fyodorych, listen," she said in German, walking down with him to the gate across the green sward of the courtyard, "I have offended you—please forgive me."

Lemm made no reply.

"I showed Vladimir Nikolaich your cantata; I was sure he would appreciate it—and he really does like it very much."

Lemm stopped.

"That's all right," he said in Russian and then added in his native tongue: "but he can't understand anything; don't you see that? He's a dilettante—and nothing more!"

"You are unfair to him," urged Liza; "he understands everything and can do almost everything himself."

"Yes, but it's all second-rate, light stuff, cheap work. People like it and like him, and he is pleased—so everything is fine. I am not angry; that cantata and I—we are both old fools; I'm a little bit ashamed, but that doesn't matter."

"Forgive me, Christopher Fyodorych," murmured Liza again.

"All right," he repeated once more in Russian. "You are a good girl ... but here is somebody coming. Goodbye. You are a very good girl."

And Lemm bent a hurried step towards the gate, through which there passed a stranger—a gentleman in a grey coat and broad-brimmed straw hat. Greeting him with a polite bow (he always greeted strangers; from acquaintances he would turn away on meeting them in the street—such was his rule), Lemm went past and disappeared behind the fence. The stranger gazed at his retreating figure in surprise, and glancing attentively at Liza, walked straight up to her.

VII

"You don't recognise me," he said, doffing his hat, "but I recognised you, although it's eight years since I saw you last. You were a child then. I am Lavretsky. Is your mother at home? May I see her?"

"My mother will be very glad to see you," said Liza, "she has heard of your arrival."

"Your name, I believe, is Elizaveta?" said Lavretsky, mounting the steps of the porch.

"Yes."

"I remember you well; even then you had a face one does not easily forget; I used to bring you sweets."

Liza blushed and thought to herself: what an odd man! Lavretsky stopped for a moment in the hall. Liza went into the drawing room whence came the sounds of Panshin's voice and laughter; he was communicating a piece of town gossip to Marya Dmitriyevna and Gedeonovsky who had already returned from their walk in the garden, and laughed loudly at his own story. On hearing Lavretsky's name, Marya Dmitriyevna was thrown into a flutter, went pale and came forward to meet him.

"How do you do, my dear cousin!" she cried in a languid, almost tearful voice. "I am awfully glad to see you!"

"How are you, my good cousin," said Lavretsky, giving her hand a friendly squeeze. "How has Providence been treating you?"

"Sit down, sit down, my dear Fyodor Ivanych. Oh, how glad I am. First of all let me introduce to you my daughter, Liza. . . ."

"I've already introduced myself to Elizaveta Mikhailovna," broke in Lavretsky.

"Monsieur Panshin. . . . Sergei Petrovich Gedeonovsky. . . . Sit down, do! So here you are; I can't believe my eyes really! How are you?"

"As you see, I'm doing well. And you too, cousin, touch wood! Don't look any the worse after these eight years."

"When you come to think of it, it's a long time since we've seen each other," said Marya Dmitriyevna pensively. "Where have you come from? Where did you leave . . . that is, I wanted to say," she caught herself up, "I mean, have you come for long?"

"I've just arrived from Berlin," answered Lavretsky, "and tomorrow I am leaving for the country—probably for long."

"You will live at Lavriky, of course?"

"No, not at Lavriky; there's a little village of mine about twenty-five versts from here; I intend to go there."

"Is that the place you inherited from Glafira Petrovna?"

"The very same."

"But Fyodor Ivanych! You have such a lovely house at Lavriky!"

Lavretsky frowned slightly.

"Yes ... but there's a small house in that village. For the time being I will be quite content with it. I don't need anything more for the present."

Marya Dmitriyevna was so confounded that she stiffened in her chair and made a gesture of despair. Panshin came to her aid and engaged Lavretsky in conversation. Marya Dmitriyevna recovered her composure, sank back into her armchair, and occasionally inserted a word, gazing meanwhile with such commiseration at her visitor, sighing so expressively and nodding so lugubriously that the latter finally lost patience and enquired rather sharply whether she was quite well.

"Thank God, I am," replied Marya Dmitriyevna, "why do you ask?"

"Just so. For a moment I thought you were not quite yourself."

Marya Dmitriyevna assumed a look of injured dignity. "Oh, if that's how it is," she thought, "I certainly shan't worry: it seems, my fine fellow, that with you it's like water off a duck's back; anyone else in your stead would have wasted to a shadow, whereas you're bursting with health." Marya Dmitriyevna did not bandy words with herself; aloud she expressed herself more elegantly.

Lavretsky certainly did not look like a victim of fate. His ruddy-complexioned, typical Russian face, with its large white brow, somewhat fleshy nose and wide clean-cut mouth seemed to breathe the vitality and pristine vigour of his native steppes. He had a strapping well-knit figure, and his fair hair grew in curls like a boy's. His eyes alone, which were blue and prominent and somewhat immobile, betrayed a pensiveness—or was it weariness?—and his voice sounded a little too level.

Panshin in the meantime kept up the flagging conversation. He turned the talk on the merits of sugar refin-

ing about which he had recently read two French book-
lets, and proceeded to expound their contents with serene modesty, without, however, mentioning a word
about them.

"Why, if that is not Fedya!" the voice of Marfa Timofeyevna was suddenly heard through the half-open
door leading into the next room: "Fedya, to be sure!"
And the old lady came briskly into the room. Before
Lavretsky could rise to his feet she was already embrac-
ing him. "Let's have a look at you," she exclaimed,
stepping back a pace. "Eh, what a bonny fellow you are.
A little bit older, but none the worse for that, I vow!
Now, don't kiss my hands—come kiss me, man, if you
don't mind my creased cheeks. I don't suppose you
asked after me—now, is auntie still alive? Why, you
were born in my hands, you rogue! Well, never mind
that; how could you be expected to think of me! But it's
splendid of you to have come. Here, my dear," she
added, turning to Marya Dmitriyevna, "haven't you
offered him anything?"

"I don't want anything," Lavretsky hastened to declare.

"But have a cup of tea, at least, my dear. Goodness
gracious! He has come from God knows where and is
not even offered a cup of tea! Liza, go and see to it,
quickly! I remember when he was a little fellow he was
a terrible glutton, and I shouldn't be surprised if he
were fond of eating now too."

"My respects, Marfa Timofeyevna," said Panshin,
sidling up to the flustered old lady with a low bow.

"Excuse me, sir," replied Marfa Timofeyevna. "I
didn't notice you what with all this excitement. You look
more than ever like your dear mother," she resumed,
turning to Lavretsky, "except your nose, your father's
it was and your father's it has remained. Well, and have
you come for long?"

"I am leaving tomorrow, auntie."

"Where are you going?"

"To my place at Vassilyevskoye."

"Tomorrow?"

"Tomorrow."

"Well, if it's tomorrow, tomorrow be it. God be with you, you know best. But see you come and say good-bye before you go!" The old lady patted his cheek. "I never thought to see you again; not that I am going to die; oh no, I think I'll last another ten years at least: we Pestovs are a tenacious lot; your grandfather used to say we had double lives; but Lord only knows how long you'd have gone on loitering abroad. Aye, but it really is a treat to see you; can you still lift ten poods with one hand, as you used to do? Your father, absurd person though he was—excuse me for saying so—did a good thing when he engaged that Swiss fellow for your education; do you remember the fist fights you had to-gether; gymnastics, I believe they call it? Dear me, here am I cackling away, and only interfering with Mr. Pan-shín's discussion" (she would never call him Pánshin, which was the right stress). "Let us have tea though; come and have it out on the terrace, my dear; we have delicious cream, not the kind of stuff you get in those Londons and Parises of yours. Come on, come on, and you, Fedya dear, give me your arm. My goodness, how hefty it is! No fear of coming a cropper with you."

The company rose and went out onto the terrace, ex-cept Gedeonovsky who had quietly slipped out. Through-out Lavretsky's conversation with the lady of the house, with Panshin and Marfa Timofeyevna, he had sat in a corner, blinking attentively and gaping in childish curiosity; now he was hurrying away to spread news of the new arrival through the town.

That same day, at eleven o'clock in the evening, this is what took place in Madame Kalitina's house. Down-stairs, on the threshold of the drawing room, Vladimir Nikolaich, seizing an opportune moment, was taking his leave of Liza, and saying, with her hand in his: "You know what makes me come here; you know why I am constantly paying visits to your house; why speak of it, when everything is so clear?" Liza made no reply, she did not smile, but with slightly lifted eyebrow was gazing at the floor and blushing, and did not withdraw

16*

her hand; while upstairs in Marfa Timofeyevna's room,
by the dim light of an oil lamp hanging in front of
the tarnished old icons, Lavretsky was sitting in an
armchair, his elbows propped on his knees and his face
buried in his hands; the old lady, standing in front of
him, silently stroked his hair. Over an hour had he been
with her, after having bidden the hostess good night; he
had hardly spoken with his kind old friend, and she
had not questioned him.... Indeed, what was there to
talk about, where the need for questions? She understood
everything, and she gave him all the tender sympathy
his brimful heart could ever need.

VIII

Fyodor Ivanovich Lavretsky (we must beg the
reader's indulgence to break off the thread of our story
for a time) was of old noble stock. The first of the
Lavretskys came over from Prussia in the reign of Vas-
sili Tyomny* and received an investiture of two hundred
chetverts of land in Byezhetsk-Verkh. Many of his des-
cendants held various offices and served under princes
and noblemen in distant provinces; none of them,
however, attained greater eminence than the rank of
dapifer or considerable opulence. Richer and more remarkable than all the Lavretskys was Fyodor Ivanych's
greatgrandfather Andrei—a cruel, insolent, astute and
crafty man. To this day lives the fame of his tyranny,
his turbulent disposition, preposterous munificence and
unquenchable cupidity. He was very corpulent and tall,
swarthy-complexioned and beardless, spoke with a burr
and looked somnolent; but the softer his tone, the more
those about him quaked. The wife he took unto himself
was his compeer. Goggle-eyed, with an aquiline nose,
and a round sallow visage, a Gipsy by birth, shrewish
and vindicative, she never yielded to her husband, who
was nearly the death of her, but whose death she nevertheless did not survive, despite the cat-and-dog life she

* Basil the Blind (1415-1462).—*Trans.*

led him. Andrei's son, Pyotr—Fyodor's grandfather—
bore no resemblance to his father: he was a simple
landowner of the steppes, rather giddy-headed, vociferous
and torpid, coarse but not ill-natured, hospitable
and fond of the hunt with hounds. He was over thirty
when he succeeded to an estate with two thousand serfs
in perfect condition; but he soon turned them all adrift,
sold part of his estate and spoiled his menials. All sorts
of lowly folk, frequenters and strangers alike, swarmed
like cockroaches to his roomy, warm and ill-kept mansion; all this brotherhood ate its fill of whatever it
could, drank itself drunk, and helped itself to whatever
it could lay hands on, extolling and blessing the gracious
host; and their host, when he was in the doldrums, would
call his guests toadeaters and rascals, but would find life
dull without them. Pyotr Andreich's wife was a mild
and gentle thing, whom he had taken from a neighbouring family at his father's behest and choice; her name
was Anna Pavlovna. She never meddled in anything,
was a cheerful hostess, and gladly made calls herself,
although to be powdered, she would aver, was a plague.
"They would put," she used to relate in her old age,
"a felt hood on your head, comb all your hair up, smear
grease over it, cover it with flour and stick iron pins
all over the place—you couldn't wash it off for no
money; but you daren't pay visits without being
powdered—people would take it as an affront; ah, but
what a torture it was!" She was fond of taking a ride
behind spirited race horses, was ready to play cards
from morning till night and would always cover up her
score of farthing forfeits when her husband came up
to the card table; yet her entire dowry, all her money,
she had given up entirely into his keeping. She bore
him two children: a son, Ivan, Fyodor's father, and a
daughter, Glafira. Ivan was not brought up at home, but
lived with a rich old aunt, the Princess Kubenskaya; she
had made him her heir (his father would not have let
him go otherwise). She dressed him up like a doll,
engaged all sorts of teachers for him and placed him
in charge of a tutor, a Frenchman and former abbé—a
disciple of Jean Jacques Rousseau, by the name of

Courtin de Vaucelles—a subtle, scheming man, the very,
as she expressed it, *fine fleur* of emigration, and ended
by marrying this *"fine fleur"* almost at the prime age
of seventy years; she transferred all her possessions to
his name and shortly afterwards, all painted up and
perfumed with scent *à la Richelieu*, surrounded by Negro
page boys, lap dogs and noisy parrots, she died on a
crooked silken Louis XV divan with a Petitot enamelled
snuffbox in her hand, died forsaken by her husband—
the smooth-tongued M. Courtin had deemed it wise to
make off to Paris with her money. Ivan was in his
twentieth year when this unexpected disaster (we mean
the princess' marriage, not her death) overtook him; he
was loath to remain in his aunt's home where, from a
wealthy heir, he had suddenly found himself in the
position of a sponger; in St. Petersburg the society in
which he had grown up was closed to him; the hard
work and obscurity of a petty post in the civil service
was repugnant to him (this was early in the reign of
the Emperor Alexander); he was obliged to return to
the country and his father's home. His old home seemed
dirty, poor and ugly; the dreariness and squalor of
these backwoods shocked him at every step; he was bored
to death; on the other hand, everybody in the house,
except his mother, looked askance at him. His father
disliked his city ways, his frock coats, ruffles, books, his
flute, his fastidious habits, which betrayed an obvious
disgust; he frequently complained and grumbled at his
son. "He turns up his nose," he used to say, "at everything here; he is finicky with his food, won't eat, is
squeamish about the smell of humanity, or the stuffiness
of a room, the sight of drunkenness gets on his nerves,
and you daren't punish a serf in his presence; he won't
enter the civil service—his health is poor, if you please;
pah, the mollycoddle! And only because his head's full
of that Voltaire." The old man had conceived a special
grudge against Voltaire and that "infidel" Diderot,
although he had never read a word of their writings:
reading was not his forte. Pyotr Andreich was not
mistaken: Diderot and Voltaire, and, for that matter,
Rousseau and Raynal and Helvetius and many other

similar writers, too, were crammed in his son's head; but they were in his head alone. Ivan Petrovich's former preceptor, the retired abbé and encyclopedist had done no more than fill his pupil's head with the whole of eighteenth-century wisdom, lock, stock and barrel, and he went about with his head chock-full of it; there it was in him, but without filtrating into his blood, or entering his innermost being or manifesting itself in firm convictions.... And could one really demand convictions in a young man of fifty years ago, when we have not grown up to them even today? His father's guests, too, felt uncomfortable in the presence of Ivan Petrovich: he shunned them and they were afraid of him; as to his sister Glafira, who was twelve years his senior, he could not get on with her at all. This Glafira was a queer creature: ugly, hunchbacked and gaunt, with grim, dilated eyes and thin, tight-lipped mouth, she in appearance, voice and quick angular gestures resembled her grandmother, the Gipsy, Andrei's wife. Headstrong and ambitious, she would not hear of matrimony. The coming home of Ivan Petrovich was not to her liking; as long as the Princess Kubenskaya had charge of him she had hoped to get at least half her father's estate; she took after her grandmother in miserliness too. Furthermore, Glafira was envious of her brother; he was so well educated, spoke French so well with a Parisian accent, whereas she could barely say "*bon jour*" or "*comment vous portez-vous*". True, her parents were entirely ignorant of French, but she felt none the better for it. Time hung heavily on Ivan Petrovich's hands, he was bored to distraction. He had spent no more than a year in the country, but that year seemed to him like ten. To his mother alone he would unburden his heart, sitting for hours in her low-ceilinged chambers, listening to the good woman's artless chatter and gorging himself with jam. Among Anna Pavlovna's maids there happened to be a very pretty girl with clear gentle eyes and delicate features called Malanya, a clever demure lass. She caught his fancy at once and he fell in love with her: he loved her timid mien, her bashful answers, her gentle voice and gentle smile; his love for her grew

stronger every day. And she too became attached to Ivan
Petrovich with all the strength of her soul, she loved him
as only Russian girls can love—and she yielded to his
love. No secret can be kept long in the household of a
country squire: soon everyone knew of the young master's
liaison with Malanya; the news of it eventually reached
the ears of Pyotr Andreich. At any other time he would
probably have overlooked such a trivial matter; but he
had long harboured a grudge against his son and he
snatched at the opportunity to humiliate this Petersburg
wiseacre and dandy.

A hubbub and clamour broke loose; Malanya was
locked up in the lumber room; Ivan Petrovich was sum-
moned to his father. Anna Pavlovna too came running
out at the tumult. She made an attempt to pacify her
husband, but Pyotr Andreich would no longer listen to
reason. He pounced upon his son, heaped reproaches on
him for looseness of morals, irreligion, and duplicity;
incidentally he vented on him all his pent-up resentment
against the Princess Kubenskaya, and rained insults
upon him. At first Ivan Petrovich said nothing and held
himself in check, but when his father took it into his
head to threaten him with disgraceful punishment he
could contain himself no longer. "So," he said to himself,
"the infidel Diderot is dragged out again—well then, I'll
let you have him; you wait, I'll make you sit up." Whereupon, in a calm and steady voice, though with an inner
tremor, Ivan Petrovich informed his father that his reproach of immorality was unmerited; that although he
did not intend to justify his guilt, he was prepared to
atone for it, the more so that he felt himself to be above
all prejudices,—in fact—was prepared to marry
Malanya. In uttering these words Ivan Petrovich in-
dubitably gained his end; Pyotr Andreich was so
astonished that he stared at his son dumbfounded for a
moment; but the next instant he recovered, and just as
he was, clad in his squirrel-lined jacket and with slippers
on his bare feet, he flung himself on Ivan Petrovich with
his fists; his son, as luck would have it, had that day
dressed his hair *à la Titus*, and donned a new English
frock coat, high boots with little tassels and tight-fitting

spruce buckskin breeches. Anna Pavlovna shrieked at the top of her voice and hid her face in her hands, while her son dashed through the house, ran out into the courtyard, darted through the kitchen garden, across the park and out onto the road and kept running for all he was worth till he no longer heard the heavy tramp of his father's pursuit and his gasping ejaculations. . . . "Stop!" he fulminated. "Stop, you scoundrel, or I'll bring a curse down on you!" Ivan Petrovich found refuge with a neighbouring squire, while Pyotr Andreich dragged himself home spent and perspiring. Still panting for breath, he forthwith announced that he disinherited his son and withdrew his benediction, ordered all his ridiculous books to be burned and the girl Malanya to be instantly dispatched to a distant village. Some good people sought out Ivan Petrovich and told him all about it. Humiliated and enraged, he swore vengeance on his father, and that same night he waylaid the peasant's cart which was conveying Malanya to her exile, abducted her, galloped away with her to the nearest town and wedded her. He was supplied with money by the neighbour, a warmhearted retired sea dog who was never out of his cups, but who took a keen delight in every kind of "romantic adventure", as he termed it. The next day Ivan Petrovich wrote Pyotr Andreich a scathingly cold and polite letter and set out for the village where his second cousin, Dmitri Pestov, lived with his sister, Marfa Timofeyevna, whom the reader already knows. He gave them an account of what had happened, declared his intention of going to St. Petersburg to look for a situation, and entreated them, at least for a time, to take care of his wife. At the word "wife" he wept bitterly and despite his city education and philosophy, he humbly went down on his knees, like a lowly Russian suppliant, and even knocked his forehead against the floor. The Pestovs, being the tenderhearted compassionate folk they were, willingly acceded to his request; he spent three weeks with them, secretly hoping that his father would respond; but there was no response, nor could there be. On hearing of his son's marriage Pyotr Andreich took to his bed and forbade the very mention of his son's name; but his mother furtively borrowed from the archdeacon and sent him five hundred rubles together with a little icon for his wife; she dare not write but sent a message by word of mouth to Ivan Petrovich through a wiry little muzhik who could walk as much as sixty versts a day, that he was not to distress himself too much, that, please God, everything would turn out all right and his father would forgive him; that she too would have preferred a different daughter-in-law, but as this was apparently the will of God, she sent Malanya Sergeyevna her maternal blessings. The wiry little muzhik got a ruble for his pains, asked to be allowed to see the new mistress, whose god-father he happened to be, kissed her hand and trotted off.

Ivan Petrovich, meanwhile, had left for St. Petersburg with a light heart. The future was obscure; poverty, perhaps, awaited him, but he had done with the detestable country life, and, above all, he had not betrayed his pre-ceptors, he had actually "brought into play" and vindicated Rousseau, Diderot and *la Déclaration des droits de l'homme.* A sense of duty done, a feeling of elation and pride swelled his heart. Separation from his wife did not greatly distress him; indeed, the need of constantly living with her under the same roof would have disturbed him more. That thing was done; now other things had to be attended to. In St. Petersburg, in spite of his assumptions, he met with luck: the Princess Kubenskaya, already deserted by Monsieur Courtin, but still alive, by way of making amends to her nephew, commended him to all her friends and made him a present of 5,000 rubles—practically all that was left of her money—together with a Lepique watch with his monogram engraved in a festoon of cupids. Three months had barely elapsed before he obtained a position in the Russian mission in London and sailed overseas on the first English vessel leaving port (steamships were not even thought of then). Several months later he received a letter from Pestov. The good fellow congratulated Ivan Petrovich on the birth of a son, who had come into the world in the village of Pokrovskoye on the 20th of August, 1807 and had been christened Fyodor in honour of his namesake, the Holy Martyr. Feeling very poorly,

Malanya Sergeyevna had added only a few lines; but even these few lines astonished Ivan Petrovich—he was not aware that Marfa Timofeyevna had taught his wife to read and write. Ivan Petrovich, however, did not long give himself up to the tender feeling of paternal pride; he was paying court to one of the then celebrated Phrynes or Laises (classical names were still in the fashion); the Peace of Tilsit had just been concluded, and the world, caught up in a dizzy whirl, went pleasure-mad; his head, too, was turned by the black eyes of a saucy belle. He had little money, but he played a lucky game of cards; he struck up numerous acquaintances, joined in every kind of entertainment—in a word, he sailed along in full trim.

IX

Resentment over his son's marriage rankled in old Lavretsky's heart a long time; had Ivan Petrovich returned six months later with a penitent heart and thrown himself on his father's mercy, he would probably have forgiven him, first having given him a scolding and a rap or two with his gnarled stick by way of intimidation; but Ivan Petrovich lived abroad and did not seem to give the matter a thought. "Have done! Don't you dare!" Pyotr Andreich would admonish his wife every time she attempted to soften his heart, "the whelp, he should thank his lucky stars that I did not bring my curse on him; my fahter would have strangled the rascal with his own hands, and it would have been the right thing to do, too." At these awful speeches Anna Pavlovna could only cross herself furtively. As for his son's wife, Pyotr Andreich at the beginning washed his hands of her, and in response to a letter from Pestov in which the good man mentioned his daughter-in-law, he sent him word that he refused to hear about any daughter-in-law, and considered it his duty to warn him that it was against the law to shelter fugitive serfs; but, later on, when news of the birth of a grandson reached him, he was mollified, ordered secret enquiries to be made as to how the young

mother was faring after childbirth and sent her some
money without letting her know it was from him. Fedya
was not quite a year old when Anna Pavlovna fell
mortally ill. A few days before she died, bed-ridden,
with timid tears suffusing her dimming eyes, she told her
husband in the presence of the confessor, that she wished
to see and bid farewell to her daughter-in-law and give
her grandchild her blessing. The distressed old man set
her mind at rest, and immediately dispatched his own
carriage for his daughter-in-law, calling her for the first
time Malanya Sergeyevna. She came with her son and
Marfa Timofeyevna, who would not hear of her going
alone and was determined to take her part if need be.
More dead than alive from fright, Malanya Sergeyevna
entered Pyotr Andreich's study. A nurse followed carrying Fedya. Pyotr Andreich eyed her in silence; she went
up to kiss his hand; her quivering lips could barely shape
themselves into a soundless kiss.

"Well, my unleavened gentlewoman," he broke the
silence at length, "how are you? Let's go to the mistress."

He rose and bent over Fedya; the baby smiled and
stretched its pale little hands out to him. This went
straight to the old man's heart.

"Ah," he murmured, "poor little bird! Pleading for
your daddy? I shall not forsake you, little one."

Malanya Sergeyevna, directly she stepped into Anna
Pavlovna's bedroom, dropped on her knees by the door.
Anna Pavlovna motioned her to approach the bedside,
embraced her and blessed her son; then, turning to her
husband a face ravaged by cruel pain, she tried to
speak. . . .

"I know, I know what you want to say," murmured
Pyotr Andreich. "Don't fret; she will stay with us, and
for her sake I will forgive Vanka."

With an effort Anna Pavlovna clutched her husband's
hand and raised it to her lips. That evening she was no
more.

Pyotr Andreich was true to his word. He notified his
son that for the sake of his mother's dying wish and the
baby Fyodor he restored to him his blessing and was giving Malanya Sergeyevna a home in his house. She was

given two rooms in the mezzanine; he presented her to his most honoured guests, the one-eyed brigadier Skurekhin and his wife; made her a gift of two serving wenches and an errand boy; Marfa Timofeyevna took her leave of her; she had conceived a strong dislike for Glafira with whom she had thrice quarrelled in the course of a day.

The poor woman's position was at first difficult and embarrassing; but in time she got used to it and to her father-in-law. He, too, grew accustomed to her and even fond of her, though he hardly ever spoke to her and his very kindness bore a trace of unconscious disdain. Malanya Sergeyevna's heaviest cross was Glafira, her sister-in-law. Glafira had contrived already during her mother's lifetime to gradually gain control over the whole household; everybody, including her father, was at her beck and call; not a piece of sugar was issued without her license; she would rather die than yield an inch of her authority to another mistress—and what a mistress! She had taken her brother's marriage more to heart than had Pyotr Andreich; she determined to get even with the upstart, and Malanya Sergeyevna became her slave from the very first hour. Indeed, how was she to pit herself against the wayward, haughty Glafira, she who was so docile, lost and bewildered, timorous and sickly? A day did not pass without Glafira reminding her of her former status and commending her for knowing her proper place. Malanya Sergeyevna would have readily put up with these reminders and commendations, however unpalatable they were ... but she was deprived of Fedya—there was the misery. On the pretext that she was incapable of devoting herself to his upbringing, she was scarcely allowed to see him; Glafira saw to that herself; the child was placed under her complete control. Malanya Sergeyevna in her grief entreated Ivan Petrovich in her letters to come home quickly; Pyotr Andreich too wanted to see his son; but the latter merely wrote back excuses, thanked his father for his wife's comfort and for the money sent him, promised to return soon—but did not come. The year 1812 finally brought him home. When they first met after six

years' separation, father and son embraced without
mentioning a word of old grievances; indeed this was
not the time for it; all Russia was up in arms against the
foe, and both felt that Russian blood was flowing in their
veins. Pyotr Andreich accoutred a whole regiment of
the national militia at his own expense. But the war
came to an end, the danger passed; Ivan Petrovich was
once more bored, the lure of distant places was on him,
he was drawn to the world to which he had grown accustomed and where he felt at home. Malanya Sergeyevna
could not hold him; she meant too little to him. Even
her fond hopes were dashed—her husband, too, thought
it more befitting to entrust Fedya's upbringing to Glafira.
Ivan Petrovich's poor wife could not survive this blow,
she could not get over another separation; in the space of
a few days, she uncomplainingly resigned her being.
Throughout her life she had never been able to set her
face against anything, and now too she did not show
any fight against her illness. No longer able to speak,
with the shadows of death creeping over her face, her
features still wore their former look of patient bewilderment and gentle meekness; she gazed at Glafira with the
same dumb resignation, and like Anna Pavlovna, who on
her deathbed had kissed her husband's hand, so did she
too kiss Glafira's hand, entrusting to her, Glafira, her
only son. Thus ended her earthly career this kind and
gentle creature, plucked, God only knows why, like an
uprooted sapling from its native soil to be tossed aside
with its roots in the sun; she had drooped and faded into
oblivion and no one mourned her. Malanya Sergeyevna's
maids and Pyotr Andreich were the only souls sorry for
her. The old man missed her kind face, her mute presence. "Fare thee well, meek child," he murmured softly
as he bowed before her for the last time in church. He
wept as he threw a handful of earth into her grave.
    He did not survive her long; not more than five years.
In the winter of 1819 he passed away quietly in Moscow,
whither he had moved with Glafira and his grandson. He
had asked to be buried beside Anna Pavlovna and
"Malasha". Ivan Petrovich was in Paris at the time,
enjoying himself; he had resigned his post soon after

1815. On hearing of his father's death he made up his mind to return to Russia. Arrangements had to be made for the superintendence of the estate, and judging by Glafira's letter, Fedya was now getting on for thirteen, and it was time to give serious attention to his education.

X

Ivan Petrovich returned to Russia an Anglomaniac. His short-cropped hair, starched front, long-skirted pea-green frock coat with its numerous capes, the dour expression of his face, a manner at once brusque and indifferent, his way of speaking through his teeth, his sudden wooden laugh, his unsmiling countenance, his one invariable topic of conversation—politics or political economy—his passion for underdone roastbeef and port wine—everything about him breathed of Great Britain. But, strange as it may seem, while having become such an Anglomaniac, Ivan Petrovich had also become a patriot—at least he called himself one, though he was ill-acquainted with Russia, had not preserved a single Russian habit and spoke Russian in a very odd way: in ordinary conversation his speech was clumsy and listless and teemed with Gallicisms; but no sooner did the conversation turn on important topics than Ivan Petrovich would come out with expressions such as: "afford new tests of self-assiduity", "it does not conform with the very nature of things", and so forth. Ivan Petrovich had imported several plans in manuscript dealing with the organisation and betterment of the state; he was very displeased with everything he saw; the lack of system particularly provoked his spleen. On meeting his sister, the first thing he did was to announce his determination to introduce radical reforms, warning her that henceforth, everything would be run on a new system. Glafira Petrovna said nothing; she only clenched her teeth and thought—"what's to become of me?" But when she got back to the country with her brother and nephew her fears were soon allayed. Certain changes were indeed made in the house: spongers and toadeaters were

summarily banished from the house, among them two old
women, one of whom was blind, the other stricken with
palsy, and a major of Ochakov days in his dotage who,
on account of his really ravenous appetite, was fed on
nothing but rye bread and lentils. An order was also
promulgated not to receive former guests—they were all
superseded by a distant neighbour, a blond scrofulous
baron, a very genteel and very stupid gentleman. New
furniture arrived from Moscow; spittoons, bells and
washing stands were introduced; breakfast was served
in a new way; foreign wines replaced vodka and homemade liqueurs; new liveries were made for the servants;
a new motto was added to the family arms: *"in recto
virtus...."* Actually Glafira's authority in no wise
diminished: all the shopping and dispensing was still
under her control; the Alsatian valet, brought over
from foreign parts, had tried to challenge her authority
and lost his place, although he enjoyed his master's
patronage. As for husbandry and management of the
estates—Glafira Petrovna had a say in these matters too
—everything remained as before, despite Ivan Petrovich's oft expressed intention of breathing new life
into this chaos—everything, that is, except a raising of
quitrents here and there, a tightening up of the corvée
and an edict forbidding the peasants to apply directly
to Ivan Petrovich. The patriot, it transpired, had a great
contempt for his fellow countrymen. Ivan Petrovich's
system was applied in full force only on Fedya: his education really underwent "a radical transformation"; his
father applied himself to the task to the exclusion of
everything else.

XI

During Ivan Petrovich's absence abroad, Fedya, as we
have already stated, was on Glafira's hands. He was not
eight years old when his mother died; he saw her occasionally and loved her passionately; the memory of
her, of her gentle, pallid face, her melancholy gaze and
timid caresses, was engraved indelibly in his heart; he
but dimly realised the position she occupied in the house;

he was aware of a barrier which stood between them and
which she neither dared nor was capable of destroying.
He shunned his father, and the latter, it must be said,
never caressed him; his grandfather had now and then
stroked his head and allowed him to kiss his hand, but
he had called him an unlicked cub and thought him
stupid. After Malanya Sergeyevna's death he fell entirely
into his aunt's clutches. Fedya was afraid of her, afraid
of her bright piercing eyes and sharp voice; he dare not
utter a sound in her presence; if he so much as stirred
in his chair she would hiss at him: "What now? Sit still!"
On Sundays, after Mass, he was allowed to play, that is,
he was given a fat book, a mysterious book, the work of
a certain Maximovich-Ambodik entitled "Symbols and
Emblems". This book contained about a thousand, for
the most part very enigmatical, pictures with as many
cryptic interpretations of them in five languages. A
plump and naked cupid played a prominent part in these
illustrations. To one of them, under the title "The Saffron
and the Rainbow" was appended the explanation "The
influence hereof is vast"; another, depicting "A Heron
Flying with a Violet in Its Beak" bore the inscription
"All are known to thee". "Cupid and the Bear Licking
Her Cub" signified "little by little". Fedya studied these
pictures, they were all familiar to him to the smallest
detail; some of them, invariably the same, set him
pondering and loosed his imagination; other amusements
he knew not. When it was time for him to learn languages
and music Glafira Petrovna engaged for a mere song an
old maid, a hare-eyed Swede, who had a smattering of
French and German, could play the piano at a pinch
and, to crown all, pickled cucumbers famously. In the
society of this governess, his aunt and the old servant
maid, Vassilyevna, Fedya spent the best of four years.
He would often be found sitting in the corner with his
"Emblems"; many a long day had he sat there; the low-
ceilinged room exuded a scent of geranium, a solitary
tallow candle flickered dimly, the cricket chirped
drowsily, wearily; the little clock ticked hurriedly on the
wall, somewhere behind the wainscot a mouse furtively
scratched and gnawed, and the three old women sat like

the Fates, swiftly and silently plying their needles, the shadows from their hands casting weird quivering shapes in the gloom—and as weird and gloomy were the thoughts that gathered in the child's head. Fedya could certainly not be called an interesting child; he was rather pale, but fat, unwieldy and awkward—a veritable muzhik, as Glafira Petrovna used to say; the colour would have come quickly into his cheeks had he been let out oftener in the fresh air. He studied quite well, though he was often lazy; he never cried, but at times a fit of sullen obstinacy would come over him, and then nobody could manage him. Fedya loved no one of those around him.... Woe betide the heart that has not loved in youth!

Thus Ivan Petrovich found him, and proceeded without loss of time to enforce his system. "I want, first and foremost, to make a man of him, *un homme*," he said to Glafira Petrovna, "and not only a man, but a Spartan." Ivan Petrovich inaugurated his plans by first rigging his son out in a Scotch kilt; the twelve-year-old fellow began to strut about barekneed with a feathered bonnet on his head; the Swedish lady gave way to a young Swiss tutor, an accomplished master of gymnastics; music, as an unmanly pursuit, was discarded entirely; the natural sciences, international law, mathematics, carpentry, after the precept of Jean Jacques Rousseau, and heraldry as a means of promoting chivalrous feelings—these were to be the occupations of the future "man"; he was roused at four o'clock in the morning, forthwith doused with cold water and made to run on a string round a high pole; he ate one meal a day, consisting of a single dish, rode on horseback, and practised shooting from an arbalest; on every suitable occasion he was exercised in strength of will, after the model of his parent, and every evening he set down in a special book an account of the day and his impressions. Ivan Petrovich, for his part, wrote him words of counsel in French, in which he called him *mon fils* and addressed him as *vous*. In Russian Fedya addressed his father as "thou", but dare not sit down in his presence. The "system" left the boy bewildered, sowed confusion in his head and cramped his mind; the new mode of living, however, had

a beneficial effect on his health: at first he went down
with a fever, but soon recovered and grew into a sturdy
youngster. His father was proud of him and called him,
in his peculiar dialect, "a son of nature, my handiwork".
When Fedya had attained the age of sixteen Ivan Petrovich saw fit, in good season, to breed in him a contempt
for the opposite sex—and our young Spartan, with
shyness in his soul and the first down shading his lip,
brimful of manhood, virility and young blood, tried to
feign indifference, aloofness and rudeness.

Time was meanwhile passing. Ivan Petrovich spent
most of the year in Lavriky (that was the name of his
principal patrimony) but in the winter he would go to
Moscow alone, where he put up at an inn, sedulously
frequented his club, holding forth and expounding his
plans in drawing rooms, and bore himself more than ever
like an Anglomaniac, a malcontent, a public man. Then
came the year 1825, bringing sorrow and misery in its
train. Intimate friends and acquaintances of Ivan Petrovich drained the bitter cup. Ivan Petrovich promptly
withdrew to the seclusion of his country house and shut
himself off from the world. Another year passed, and
Ivan Petrovich's health suddenly began to decline; he
became infirm and ill. The freethinker started going to
church and bespoke public prayers; the European began
to use the Russian steam bathhouse, dine at two o'clock,
go to bed at nine and fall asleep to the old butler's
chatter; the public man burnt all his schemes and all
his correspondence, quaked before the governor and
cringed before the police inspector; the man of hardened
will winced and whimpered when he had a boil or when
the soup was cold. Glafira Petrovna once more assumed
control over the whole house; once more stewards,
bailiffs and all manner of common folk could be seen
coming to the back entrance to speak to "the old
skinflint", as the menials called her. The change in Ivan
Petrovich had a staggering effect on his son; he was now
getting on for nineteen and had begun to reflect and dis-
engage himself from the oppressive hand of his parent.
He had previously noticed the discrepancy between his
father's words and actions, between his ample pronounce-

17*

ments in favour of liberalism and sordid tyranny; but he had not expected such a violent change. The inveterate egoist now revealed himself in his true colours. Young Lavretsky was on the eve of going to Moscow to prepare for the university, when suddenly another affliction came down on the head of Ivan Petrovich: he became blind, hopelessly blind, in a single day.

Not trusting the skill of Russian doctors he applied for permission to go abroad. It was refused. He then took his son with him and for three whole years travelled all over Russia, from one doctor to another, wandering ceaselessly from town to town and driving his physicians, his son and servants to despair with his pusillanimity and fretfulness. He returned to Lavriky an abject creature, a snivelling querulous child. Bitter days set in for everybody in the household. Ivan Petrovich was quiet only at mealtime; never before had he eaten so much and so greedily; the rest of the time he gave himself and others no peace. He prayed, grumbled at fate, cursed himself, politics, his system, held up to execration everything he had vaunted and taken pride in, everything he had once taught his son to look up to; he averred that he did not believe in anything, then resumed his prayers; he could not endure a moment's solitude and demanded that his household keep him company day and night and entertain him with stories, which he interrupted from time to time with exclamations of "you're a confounded liar—what twaddle!"

Glafira Petrovna bore the brunt of it all; he simply could not do without her—and she carried out to the last every whim of the sick man, though sometimes she dare not answer him immediately lest her voice betray the rage that choked her. Thus he dragged on for another two years and died early in May after having been carried out on the balcony in the sunlight. "Glasha, Glashka! Where's my broth, you old foo..." he stammered with faltering tongue, and ere he had finished, was silent evermore. Glafira Petrovna, who had snatched the cup of broth out of the butler's hands, stood still, looked her brother in the face, slowly, sweepingly crossed herself and silently withdrew; and his son, who was

present, said nothing too; he leaned on the balustrade
of the balcony and stood gazing a long time into the
garden, all fragrant and green and resplendent in the
golden rays of the spring sunshine. He was twenty-three
years old; how terribly, how cruelly swift those twenty-
three years had flown! ... Life was opening before him.

XII

After burying his father and handing over the household affairs and superintendence of his bailiffs to the
invariable Glafira Petrovna, young Lavretsky went to
Moscow, whither he felt drawn by an obscure but irresistible force. He realised the defects of his education and
formed a resolution to make up as far as possible for
lost time. He had read a great deal in the last five years
and seen a few things; many were the ideas that had
fermented in his head; a professor might well have envied
some of his accomplishments, yet he was ignorant of many
things that every schoolboy knew. Lavretsky realised
that he was not free; he was secretly conscious of the
fact that he cut an odd figure. The Anglomaniac had
played a cruel trick on his son; his freakish education
had borne fruit. For long years he had implicitly obeyed
his father's will; when, finally, he began to see through
him, the evil was already done, his habits had become
second nature. He could not get on with people: at the age
of twenty-three, with an inextinguishable desire for love
in his shy heart, he had never yet had the temerity to
look a woman in the face. With his clear, though somewhat heavy intellect, and common sense, his tendency to
obstinacy, contemplation and indolence he should have
been thrown early into the whirlpool of life, instead of
which he had been kept in artificial seclusion. ... And
now the spell was broken, but he continued to stand on
the same spot, reticent and locked up within himself. It
was ludicrous at his age to put on a student's uniform; but
he was not afraid of ridicule—his Spartan training had
at least the effect of rendering him impervious to the
opinion of others—and he donned, without embarrass-

ment, the student's uniform. He entered the department
of physics and mathematics. Stalwart and ruddy-faced,
tongue-tied, with a full-grown beard, he produced an
odd impression on his fellow students; how could they
guess that this grim-looking man, who punctually attended the lectures, driving up in a spacious country
sleigh drawn by two horses, was almost a child. They
thought him a queer fish of a pedant, they did not seek
his company and did not need it, and he held himself
aloof. During his first two years in the university he
became intimate with only one student from whom he
took lessons in Latin. This student, whose name was
Mikhalevich, was an enthusiast and a poet; he became
sincerely attached to Lavretsky and was the innocent
cause of an important change in his destiny.

One day at the theatre (Mochalov was then at the
zenith of his fame and Lavretsky did not miss a single
performance) he saw a girl in a box in the dress circle,
and though no woman ever passed his sombre figure
without setting his heart beating, it had never throbbed
so violently before. With elbows propped on the velvet
of the box the girl sat without stirring: the warm vivacity
of youth quivered in every feature of her dark, rounded,
attractive face; an elegant mind was mirrored in the
lovely eyes gazing with a soft regard from under delicate eyebrows, in the swift smile of her expressive lips,
in the very poise of her head, her arms, her neck; she
was exquisitely dressed. Beside her sat a wizened sallow
woman of about forty-five in a low-necked dress and
black toque, with a toothless smile on an anxiously rapt
and vacuous face, while in the inner recesses of the box
could be seen an elderly man in a loose-fitting frock
coat and high cravat, with an expression of stolid
solemnity and something akin to unctuous suspiciousness
in his beady eyes, with dyed moustache and side whiskers, a ponderous insignificant-looking forehead and
creased cheeks—by every sign a retired general. Lavretsky
did not take his eyes off the lovely vision; suddenly the
door of the box opened and Mikhalevich entered. The
appearance of this man, his almost sole acquaintance in
Moscow, in the society of the one girl who was absorb-

ing his whole attention, struck Lavretsky as odd and significant. Continuing to gaze into the box he noticed that all its occupants treated Mikhalevich as an old friend. The performance on the stage ceased to interest Lavretsky; even Mochalov, though he was that evening "in form", did not make the usual impression on him. At one very pathetic moment on the stage Lavretsky involuntarily glanced up at the beauty; she was straining forward, her cheeks aglow; under his insistent regard her eyes, which had been glued on the stage, slowly turned and rested on him. . . . All night those eyes haunted him. The artificially built dam broke down at last: he was all aquiver and in fever of excitement. The very next day he went to see Mikhalevich. From him he learnt that the lovely creature's name was Varvara Pavlovna Korobyina, that the old couple with her in the box were her father and mother and that he, Mikhalevich, had made their acquaintance the year before during his stay at Count N—'s place near Moscow where he had been "coaching". The enthusiast lauded Varvara Pavlovna to the skies. "My dear fellow," he exclaimed in his mellow voice, "that girl, I say, is a wonder, a genius, an artist in the true sense of the word, and awfully kind, too." Noting from Lavretsky's enquiries the impression Varvara Pavlovna had made on him, he volunteered to present him to her, adding that he was considered one of the family, that the general was not a bit uppish and the mother was so stupid she thought the moon was made of green cheese. Lavretsky coloured, mumbled something unintelligible and made off. He fought his timidity for five whole days; on the sixth the young Spartan got into a new uniform and placed himself at Mikhalevich's disposal; the latter, being one of the family, merely combed his hair, and both repaired to the Korobyins.

XIII

Varvara Pavlovna's father, Pavel Petrovich Korobyin, a retired major-general, had spent all his life in the service in St. Petersburg, had the reputation in his youth of

being a good dancer and smart soldier, had served, because of reduced circumstances, as adjutant to two or
three mediocre generals and married the daughter of one
of them with a dowry of twenty-five thousand rubles; had
mastered to a nicety the art of military parade and army
drill, and so plodded on, until, after twenty years of
service, he received the rank of general and the command of a regiment. At this juncture he might have
relaxed his efforts and devoted himself leisurely to
feathering his nest; indeed, this was what he intended
doing, but for a slight miscarriage in his plans: he had
devised a new method of negotiating public funds—the
method seemed an excellent one in itself, but he was
chary where he should not have been and got himself
reported; there was a disagreeable affair, nay, a nasty
affair. The general managed somehow to extricate himself, but his career was ruined and he was advised to
retire. He knocked about for another two years in
St. Petersburg hoping to run into something in the nature
of a sinecure, but nothing came his way; his daughter
meanwhile had graduated a girls' college and expenses
were increasing every day. ... Much against his will he
decided to remove to Moscow where they could live on
the cheap, rented a low tiny house in Staro-Konyushenni
Street with a huge blazon on the frontal and settled down
to the Moscow life of a retired general, on an income
of 2,750 rubles a year. Moscow is a hospitable city, ready
to welcome all the world and his wife, not to mention a
general. And so the thickset, still soldierly-looking figure
of Pavel Petrovich soon began to make its appearance in
the best drawing rooms of Moscow. His nape with its
straggling wisps of dyed hair and the soiled ribbon of the
Order of St. Anne which he wore across his raven-black
cravat became a familiar sight to all the pallid and
languid young men loitering dejectedly about the card
tables during the dancing. Pavel Petrovich knew how to
claim his due in society; he spoke little and, by force of
habit, in a nasal voice—of course, he dropped that tone
when speaking to persons above him; played a discreet
game of cards, ate abstemiously at home and enough for
six at receptions. Of his wife nothing more can be said

than that her name was Kalliopa Karlovna; there was a
drop of moisture in her left eye by virtue of which
Kalliopa Karlovna (she was of German extraction, by
the way) considered herself a woman of sentiment; she
was constantly in a flutter of anxiety, as though she were
underfed, and wore tight-fitting velvet dresses, a toque
and tarnished hollow bracelets. The only daughter of
Pavel Petrovich and Kalliopa Karlovna, Varvara Pavlovna, had only turned seventeen when she graduated
college, where she was considered to be, if not the pret-
tiest, at least the cleverest pupil and the best musician,
and where she had received her cipher;* she was not
yet nineteen when Lavretsky first set eyes on her.

XIV

The Spartan shook in his shoes when Mikhalevich led
him into the rather untidy drawing room of the Korobyins
and introduced him. But his nervousness soon vanished:
in the general the geniality inherent in all Russians was
heightened by that curious affability peculiar to all people
with a somewhat sullied reputation; the general's lady
very soon effaced herself; as for Varvara Pavlovna, she
was so composed and serenely gracious that one was immediately set at ease in her presence: indeed all her
exquisite form, her smiling eyes, the ingenuous slope of
her shoulders and rosy-tinged arms, her light yet languid
tread, even the sound of her voice, so lingeringly sweet,
breathed a seductive charm, elusive like a faint perfume,
a soft and tender, yet still bashful, langour, something
which words cannot describe but which stirred and
excited—certainly not a feeling of timidity. Lavretsky
turned the conversation on the theatre, on the performance
of the previous day; she forthwith started to speak about
Mochalov and did not merely sigh and exclaim but passed
some pertinent remarks, femininely discerning, on his
acting. Mikhalevich mentioned music; she sat down to the

---

* A mark of distinction in the shape of a gold monogram with
the royal cipher.—*Trans.*

piano without the least constraint and played with precision some of Chopin's mazurkas, which were just becoming the fashion. When dinnertime came Lavretsky
would have taken his leave, but was induced to stay; at
dinner the general regaled him with excellent Lafitte for
which the general's valet had been dispatched post haste
to Depré's wine vault in a hired cab. Lavretsky returned
home late in the evening and sat for a long time without
undressing, his eyes screened by his hand, spellbound.
He seemed to be realising for the first time what it was
that made life worth living; all his assumptions and re-
solutions, all that stuff and nonsense had vanished
instantaneously into thin air; his whole soul merged into
a single feeling, a single desire—the desire of happiness,
possession, love, the sweet love of a woman. From that
day he became a frequent visitor at the Korobyins. Six
months later he declared his love to Varvara Pavlovna
and asked her to become his wife. His proposal was accepted; the general had long ago, almost on the eve of
Lavretsky's first visit, sounded Mikhalevich as to how
many serfs Lavretsky owned; Varvara Pavlovna, who
throughout the young man's courtship and even when
he was proposing to her had preserved her usual
equanimity and sereneness of mind—Varvara Pavlovna,
too, was quite aware that her suitor was a rich man; as
for Kalliopa Karlovna, she thought, *"Meine Tochter
macht eine schöne Partie,"* and bought herself a new
toque.

XV

And so his proposal was accepted, but with certain
stipulations. In the first place, Lavretsky was to leave the
university at once; what girl marries a student, and what
a queer idea for a landowner, a rich man, to be taking
lessons at twenty-six like a schoolboy? Secondly, Varvara
Pavlovna took upon herself the ordering and buying of
her trousseau and even the choosing of the bridegroom's
wedding presents. She possessed a large fund of practical
sense and good taste and a very great love of comfort,

with an equal capacity for procuring it. Lavretsky was particularly struck by this capacity of hers when, immediately after the wedding, they set out together for Lavriky in the comfortable carriage she had purchased. What forethought, care and preparation on Varvara Pavlovna's part were manifest in everything around him! What charming dressing cases appeared in various snug corners, what exquisite toilet sets and coffeepots, and how prettily Varvara Pavlovna herself prepared the coffee in the morning!

Lavretsky was not in a frame of mind to be observant at the time: he was beatifically happy, drunk with joy; he gave himself up to it like a child. . . . He was indeed as innocent as a child, this young Alcides. And was not his adorable young wife a vision of delight; did she not hold forth a secret promise of voluptuous, unutterable joys? She fulfilled more than the promise. Arriving at Lavriky in the height of the summer, she found the house gloomy and dirty, the servants old-fashioned and ludicrous, but she deemed wise not to give a hint of this to her husband. Had she intended settling down in Lavriky, she would have changed everything there, beginning, of course, with the house itself; but the idea of remaining in those godforsaken steppes never entered her mind for a moment; she lived there as in a bivouac, meekly enduring all the inconveniences and whimsically making fun at them. Marfa Timofeyevna came to see her former charge; Varvara Pavlovna liked her very much, but she did not like Varvara Pavlovna. The new mistress did not get on with Glafira Petrovna either; she would have left her in peace, had not old Korobyin been desirous of getting his hands into his son-in-law's affairs; to superintend the estate of such a near relative, he said, was not beneath the dignity even of a general. It is conceivable that Pavel Petrovich would even have condescended to manage the property of a total stranger. Varvara Pavlovna led the attack very skilfully; without showing herself to the fore, apparently completely absorbed in her honeymoon bliss, in the halcyon joys of country life, in her music and reading, she worked Glafira up by degrees to a pitch when the latter rushed

fuming one morning into Lavretsky's study and, flinging
a bunch of keys on the table, declared that she could not
go on managing the house and refused to stay. Lavretsky,
who had been duly prepared for the contingency, at once
consented to her departure. This Glafira Petrovna had not
anticipated. "Very well," she said, her eyes darkening,
"it looks as if I'm one too many here; I know who's driving me from here, from my home. Only mark my word,
nephew,—you too will never find a home anywhere, and
it's an eternal wanderer you'll be. That's all I want to
say to you." That day she left for her own little country
place, and a week later General Korobyin arrived, and
with a pleasant melancholy of mien and gesture took
over the management of the whole estate into his
hands.

In September Varvara Pavlovna took her husband
away with her to St. Petersburg. She spent two winters
in St. Petersburg (for the summer they went to ·stay at
Tsarskoye Selo) in a beautiful, airy, elegantly furnished
flat; they contracted many acquaintances among the
middle and even higher circles of society, paid visits
and entertained a good deal, and held the most charming musical soirées and dance parties. Varvara Pavlovna
attracted guests as a flame does moths. This kind of
hectic life was not quite to Fyodor Ivanych's taste. His
wife advised him to take a post in the government
service; in consideration of his father's memory and his
own inclinations he was loath to enter the government
service, but stayed on in St. Petersburg for Varvara
Pavlovna's sake. It was soon borne in on him, however,
that no one hindered him from seeking seclusion; indeed,
did he not have the quietest and most comfortable study
in St. Petersburg, was not his solicitous wife even ready
to help him in this? And henceforth everything went
well. He applied himself once more to what he considered
his unfinished education, he began to read again and even
took up the study of the English language. It was curious
to see his strapping broad-shouldered figure for ever
bent over his writing table, his full, bearded, ruddy face
half hidden behind the pages of a dictionary or note-
book. He devoted his mornings to studies, then he had

a capital dinner (Varvara Pavlovna was an excellent housekeeper) and in the evenings he stepped into a charmed, perfumed, dazzling world, peopled by gay young faces—and the centre of this world was the same sedulous hostess, his wife. She gladdened him with the birth of a son, but the poor boy was short-lived; he died in the spring; and in the summer, following the doctor's advice, Lavretsky took his wife abroad to a watering place. She was in need of distraction after such a misfortune, and her health too could do with a warm climate. They spent the summer and autumn in Germany and Switzerland, and for the winter, as one could be led to expect, they moved to Paris. In Paris Varvara Pavlovna blossomed forth like a rose, and contrived a little nest for herself as quickly and ingeniously as she had done in St. Petersburg. She found very pretty apartments in a quiet but fashionable neighbourhood; made her husband a dressing gown the like of which he had never worn before; engaged a spruce-looking maid, an excellent cook and a smart footman; purchased a charming turnout and an exquisite piano. Within a week she was crossing the street, wearing her shawl, opening her parasol and putting on her gloves like a trueborn Parisienne. And she soon formed a circle of acquaintances. At first only Russians visited her, then Frenchmen appeared, very affable, courteous bachelors, with excellent manners and euphonious names; they all spoke volubly, bowed with easy grace and screwed up their eyes in an agreeable manner; white teeth flashed from under rosy lips, and as for smiling, they were inimitable! Each brought his friends and soon *la belle madame de Lavretzki* became known from Chaussée d'Antin to Rue de Lille. In those days (it was in the year 1836) the breed of journalists and reporters who now swarm all over the place like ants in a scattered anthill had not hatched out yet, but even then there was a certain M. Jules who used to turn up in Varvara Pavlovna's salon, a gentleman of ill-favoured countenance and scandalous repute, insolent and despicable, like all duellers and men who have taken punishment. Varvara Pavlovna found this M. Jules very repellent, but she received him because he did some writing for various newspapers and continually brought up her name, now calling her *Madame de L. . .tzki*, then *Madame de***, cette grande dame russe si distinguée, qui demeure rue de P. . .*; told the world at large, or rather some hundreds of subscribers who were not in the least interested in *Madame de L. . .tzki*, what a charming and gracious lady she was, how she possessed the wit of a Frenchwoman (*une vraie française par l'esprit*)—Frenchmen have no higher praise than that—what a remarkable gift she had for music and how delightfully she waltzed (Varvara Pavlovna indeed waltzed in a way that lured all hearts to the hem of her flying skirts) . . . in a word, he spread her fame abroad, and that, surely, is a pleasant thing. Mademoiselle Mars had by that time quitted the stage, and Mademoiselle Rachelle had not yet made her appearance; in spite of that Varvara Pavlovna was a *habitué* of the theatre. She was enraptured with Italian music and laughed at the wreck of Odry, yawned decorously at the Comédie Française and was moved to tears by the acting of Madame Dorval in ultra-romantic melodrama; and above all—Liszt himself had played twice in her salon, and he had been so nice, so simple— it was just thrilling! In such agreeable sensations passed the winter, at the close of which Varvara Pavlovna was even presented at court. As for Fyodor Ivanych, he was not bored, though life sometimes weighed heavily on his shoulders—it was so empty. He read the papers, attended lectures at the Sorbonne and Collège de France, followed the debates in the Chambers, and started to translate a well-known scientific treatise on irrigation. "I am not suffering the grass to grow under my feet," he reflected, "it will all come in handy; but next winter I must get back to Russia at all costs, and buckle down to the job." It is difficult to say whether he had any clear-formed idea of exactly what this job was to consist in, and the Lord only knows whether he would have succeeded in getting back to Russia in the winter—meanwhile he was leaving with his wife for Baden-Baden. . . . An unexpected event upset all his plans.

XVI

Chancing one day to enter Varvara Pavlovna's boudoir in her absence, Lavretsky saw a carefully folded slip of paper lying on the floor. He mechanically picked it up, mechanically unfolded it and read the following, which was written in French:

"My darling angel Betsy! (I can't get myself to call you Barbe or Varvara.) I waited for you in vain at the corner of the boulevard; come to our little apartment at half past one tomorrow. Your amiable fat husband (*ton gros bonhomme de mari*) is usually busy with his books at that time; we will sing again that song of your poet *Pouskine (de votre poète Pouskine)* you taught me: 'Old husband, cruel husband!' A thousand kisses on your little hands and feet. I await you.

Ernest."

The import of what he had read did not sink at once into Lavretsky's mind; he read it a second time—and his head began to swim, the floor swayed beneath him like the deck of a lurching ship. He emitted a cry, gasped and wept all at once.

He lost his head entirely. He had so blindly trusted his wife; the possibility of deception, faithlessness, had never entered his mind. This Ernest, his wife's lover, was a blond pert-looking boy of 23 with a little snub nose and a natty moustache, the most insignificant of all her acquaintances. A few minutes passed, half an hour went by; Lavretsky still stood crushing the fateful note in his hand and staring blankly at the floor; pallid faces seemed to loom at him through a maze of whirling darkness; his heart contracted painfully; he seemed to be falling, falling into a bottomless abyss. The familiar rustle of silk brought him out of his torpor; Varvara Pavlovna, in hat and shawl, had just returned from her walk. Lavretsky quivered from head to foot and rushed out of the room: he felt capable at that moment of tearing her limb from limb, beating her to death, peasant-wise, strangling her with his own hands. Varvara Pavlovna was amazed, she tried to stop him; all he could do was to whisper "Betsy" and rush out of the house.

Lavretsky took a cab and told the driver to take him out of town. The rest of that day and all night long he prowled about, stopping incessantly and throwing up his hands in a gesture of despair; at one moment he carried on like a madman, at another things struck him suddenly as funny, he even felt gay. In the morning, feeling chilled, he went into a wretched tavern on the outskirts of the city, asked for a private room, and sat down on a chair before the window. He was seized with a fit of yawning. He could scarcely stand on his feet, he was physically spent and distraught—but he did not feel fatigue; fatigue, however, was taking toll of him: he sat and stared into space, comprehending nothing; he could not understand what had happened to him, why he was alone, with his limbs stiff and numb, with a taste of bitterness in his mouth and a stone on his heart, in a strange empty room; he could not understand what had made her, Varya, give herself to this Frenchman, and how she, knowing that she was unfaithful, could go on being just as composed, affectionate and trustful to him as before! "I can't make it out!" his parched lips whispered. "Who can vouch now that in St. Petersburg too she didn't...." He left the question unfinished, and yawned again, shivering and shaking from head to foot. Bright and gloomy memories stung him with equal anguish; it suddenly crossed his mind that she had several days ago sat down to the piano in his and Ernest's presence and sung "Old husband, cruel husband". He recalled the expression of her face, the queer sparkle in her eyes and the flush on her cheeks—and he jumped up; he wanted to go to them and say: "You shouldn't have played jokes on me; my greatgrandfather used to hang the muzhiks up by their ribs, and my grandfather was a muzhik himself"—and then to kill them both. Then it seemed to him that it was all a dream, nay, not even a dream, but some kind of tomfoolery—all he had to do was to shake himself and look round.... He looked round, and like a hawk that sinks its claws into its prey, anguish sunk deeper and deeper into his soul. To crown all, Lavretsky

was expecting to become a father in a few months' time. . . . The past, the future, his whole life was poisoned. Finally, he returned to Paris, took a room in a hotel and sent M. Ernest's note to Varvara Pavlovna with the following letter:

"The enclosed slip of paper will tell you all. I must say, by the way, that it was not like you, who are always so careful, to be dropping such important papers." (Poor Lavretsky had pondered and cherished this phrase for hours.) "I cannot see you any more; I presume you will not insist on meeting me either. I am fixing you an annual allowance of fifteen thousand francs—I cannot give more. Send your address to the country office. Do whatever you please; live wherever you please. I wish you happiness. No reply is needed."

Lavretsky wrote that he needed no reply ... but he looked forward to, he hungered for a reply, for an explanation of this inexplicable, inconceivable affair. Varvara Pavlovna wrote him by return a long letter in French. This was the crowning stroke; his last doubts vanished—and he felt ashamed for having entertained any. Varvara Pavlovna did not defend herself: all she wanted was to see him; she begged him not to pass his irrevocable verdict. The letter was cold and constrained, though here and there were traces of tears. Lavretsky smiled grimly and bade the messenger say that everything was all right. Three days later he was no longer in Paris: but he went to Italy and not to Russia. He did not know himself why he chose Italy; it did not really matter where he went—so long as it was not home. He wrote to his steward about his wife's allowance and ordered him at the same time to take over the affairs of the estate at once from General Korobyin, without waiting for him to draw up an account, and arrange for His Excellency's departure from Lavriky; he pictured to himself vividly the discomfiture and air of baffled dignity of the evicted general, and in the midst of his grief, felt a sort of malicious satisfaction. He wrote simultaneously to Glafira Petrovna asking her to return to Lavriky and sent her a power of attorney drawn up in her name; Glafira Petrovna, however, did not return to Lavriky and inserted a notice in the papers that the letter of attorney was null and void, which was quite unnecessary on her part. From his concealment in a small Italian town Lavretsky was tempted for a long time to follow the movements of his wife. He gleaned from the newspapers that she had gone from Paris to Baden-Baden, as she had planned; her name shortly appeared in a paragraph signed by our friend M. Jules. Through the author's customary flippancy of style one could discern a note of friendly condolence; a sense of deep revulsion overwhelmed Fyodor Ivanych when he read that paragraph. Afterwards he learned that a daughter had been born to him; two months later he was notified by his steward that Varvara Pavlovna had drawn her first quarter's allowance. Then the rumours went from bad to worse and culminated in a tragic-comic story which was blazed abroad through all the newspapers and in which his wife played an unenviable role. It was all over now: Varvara Pavlovna had become a "notoriety".

Lavretsky no longer followed her movements; but he could not pull himself together for a long while. At times he was overcome by such a longing for his wife that he felt like giving everything up, perhaps even ... forgiving her, just for the sake of hearing once more her caressing voice, feeling the touch of her hand in his. Time, however, was taking its own. It was not written for him to be a martyr of suffering; his robust nature reasserted itself. His eyes had been opened: even the blow that he had sustained did not seem so unexpected; he understood his wife—we can only truly understand those who are near to us when we part with them. He could resume once more his studies and take up his work, though with nothing like his former zeal; scepticism, brought on by life's trials and his early training, had crept into his heart for good. He became indifferent to everything around him. Four years passed, and he at last felt he had the strength to return home, and meet his own people. Stopping neither at St. Petersburg nor Moscow he came to the town of O— where we parted from him, and whither we will now ask the gentle reader to return with us.

XVII

At about ten o'clock on the following morning Lavretsky was seen ascending the porch steps of the Kalitins, house. He was met by Liza coming out in her hat and gloves.

"Where are you off to?" he asked.

"To Mass. It's Sunday today."

"Do you go to church?"

Liza looked at him in an astonished silence.

"I beg your pardon," said Lavretsky. "I ... I didn't mean that. I've come to say good-bye to you. I am leaving for the country in an hour's time."

"It's not far from here, is it?" asked Liza.

"About twenty-five versts."

Lenochka came out attended by a maid.

"Well, don't forget us," said Liza, descending the steps.

"Don't forget me either. Oh, by the way," he added, "since you are going to church—perhaps you'll pray for me too."

Liza stopped and turned round to face him.

"If you wish," she answered, looking at him squarely. "I'll pray for you too. Come along, Lenochka."

In the drawing room Lavretsky found Marya Dmitriyevna alone. She smelled of Eau-de-Cologne and mint. She complained of a headache and of having had a bad night. She received him with her usual languid affability and gradually dropped into conversation.

"Vladimir Nikolaich is an agreeable young man—don't you think so?" she asked him.

"What Vladimir Nikolaich is that?"

"Why, Panshin, the one who was here yesterday. You've made quite an impression on him; let me tell you confidentially, *mon cher cousin*, he is simply head over heels in love with my Liza. Well, he's of a good family, he has a promising career, he's clever, and a *Kammerjunker* too, and if it's the Lord's will ... all I can say, as a mother, is that I will be very glad. It's a great responsibility, of course; the happiness of the children certainly does depend on the parents, you can't get away from it, you know; here I've been all this time quite alone, doing

18*

everything myself and all that; who brought up the children, who taught them, if not I? Even now, if you please, I have engaged a French governess."

Marya Dmitriyevna plunged into a description of her cares and worries and maternal feelings. Lavretsky listened in silence, twisting his hat in his hands. His frigid heavy gaze disconcerted the garrulous lady.

"And how do you like Liza?" she asked.

"Elizaveta Mikhailovna is a very nice girl," rejoined Lavretsky. He got up, took his leave with a bow and went in to see Marfa Timofeyevna. Marya Dmitriyevna cast a look of displeasure at his retreating figure and thought: "What a boor of a fellow he is, a real muzhik. Now I can understand why his wife couldn't stay faithful."

Marfa Timofeyevna sat in her room surrounded by her domestic staff. This consisted of five creatures, almost all equally dear to her heart: a cropful canny bullfinch, of which she became fond since he had stopped whistling and filching water, a timorous, shrinking little dog named Roska, an ill-tempered cat Matross, a swarthy fidgety little girl of nine with great eyes and a sharp little nose called Shurochka, and an elderly woman of about fifty-five in a white cap and short brown jacket worn over a dark dress, by the name of Nastasya Karpovna Ogarkova. Shurochka was a child of the humbler classes, and an orphan. Marfa Timofeyevna had taken her out of pity, like Roska; she had found both the child and the dog in the street; both were thin and hungry; both were wet with the autumn rain; nobody missed Roska, while Shurochka was gladly relinquished by her uncle, a drunken shoemaker, who did not have enough to eat himself and used to hit his niece over the head with his last instead of feeding her. Nastasya Karpovna's acquaintance Marfa Timofeyevna had made during a visit to a monastery; she had accosted her in church (Marfa Timofeyevna alleged she had taken a fancy to her for the succulent zest with which she said her prayers), had chatted with her and invited her to a cup of tea. She had not parted with her since. Nastasya Karpovna was a very cheerful and mild-tempered woman, a childless widow, and poor gentlewoman; she had a round head of grey hair, soft

white hands, a soft face with large kindly features and a
rather droll turned-up nose; she had a profound reverence
for Marfa Timofeyevna, who was very fond of her for
all that she used to poke fun at her soft heart: she had a
weak spot for young men and would blush like a girl at
the most innocent joke. Her capital consisted of 1,200
rubles all told; she lived at Marfa Timofeyevna's expense,
but on an equal footing with her—Marfa Timofeyevna
would not suffer any kind of servility.

"Ah! Fedya!" she cried, as soon as she saw him. "You
didn't see my family last night—here we are, all gathered for tea; it's our second holiday tea. You can pet
them all; only Shurochka won't let you, and the cat'll
scratch. Are you going away today?"

"Yes," Lavretsky seated himself on a low stool. "I've
already said good-bye to Marya Dmitriyevna. I've seen
Elizaveta Mikhailovna too."

"Call her Liza, my dear fellow; since when is she
Mikhailovna to you! Now don't fidget, or you'll break
Shurochka's stool."

"She was going to church," went on Lavretsky. "I
didn't know she was so pious."

"Yes, Fedya, she is very devout: more than you or
I, Fedya."

"Aren't you devout then?" put in Nastasya Karpovna
with a lisping voice. "You haven't been to early service
today, but you are going to attend the evening one."

"No, my dear; you'll go alone—I've grown lazy,"
replied Marfa Timofeyevna. "I've been letting myself go
with the tea." She used *thou* when speaking to Nastasya
Karpovna, though she treated her as an equal—she was
a Pestov after all: three Pestovs had been in the diptych
of Ivan the Terrible; Marfa Timofeyevna would not
forget that.

"I wanted to ask," resumed Lavretsky, "Marya Dmitriyevna's just been telling me about this ... what's his
name?—Panshin. What kind of gentleman is he?"

"Lord, what a chatterbox that woman is!" muttered
Marfa Timofeyevna. "I suppose she's been telling you
confidentially what a fine suitor she has baited. Why
doesn't she hugger-mugger with that priest's son of hers,

and leave other people alone. There's nothing in the
wind yet, thank God! Yet she must go gossiping about it."

"Why thank God?" asked Lavretsky.

"Because that fine fellow is not to my liking; and what
is there to be glad about, anyway?"

"You don't like him?"

"No, I don't. He can't captivate everyone. Enough that
Nastasya Karpovna here's in love with him."

The poor widow was filled with dismay.

"Oh, how can you, Marfa Timofeyevna, haven't you
the fear of God!" she exclaimed, her face and neck
flushing scarlet.

"And he knows, the rogue," broke in Marfa Timofeyevna, "he knows the way to a woman's heart: he's
made her a present of a snuffbox, you know. Ask her for
a pinch of snuff, Fedya, you'll see what a handsome thing
it is, there is a picture of a hussar on horseback on the
lid. Now, don't you try to defend yourself, my dear."

Nastasya Karpovna could only raise her hands in a
gesture of despair.

"What about Liza?" asked Lavretsky. "Does she like
him?"

"I believe she likes him—but there, God knows! A
strange heart, you know, is like a dark forest, the more
so a girl's. Take Shurochka's heart, for instance,—try
and make it out! Why has she hidden herself since you've
come, instead of going out?"

Shurochka smothered a giggle and dashed out of the
room. Lavretsky got up from his seat.

"Yes," he said slowly, "a girl's heart is a riddle."

He began to take his leave.

"Well, shall we be seeing you again soon?" asked
Marfa Timofeyevna.

"Very likely, auntie; it's not far from here, you know."

"Oh, of course, you are going to Vassilyevskoye. You
don't want to live in Lavriky; well, that's your business;
only mind you pay a visit to your mother's grave, and
your grandmother's too while you are at it. You've probably picked up a lot of clever ideas in foreign parts, and
who knows, maybe they will feel in their graves that you
have come to them. And, Fedya, don't forget to have a

service sung for Glafira Petrovna; here take this ruble coin for it. Come, come, take it. It's me who wants to have that office done. I wasn't too fond of her when she was alive, but there's no denying she had an independent character, that maid. She was a shrewd piece, she was, and didn't ill-treat you. Well, God bless you, or I'll be boring you."

And Marfa Timofeyevna embraced her nephew.

"And Liza will not be marrying Panshin, don't you worry; she's worth a better husband than that."

"I'm not worrying in the least," answered Lavretsky, and withdrew.

XVIII

Four hours later he was on his way home. His tarantass rolled swiftly along the soft country road. There had been no rain for a fortnight; a fine mist hung milkily in the air and screened the distant woods, from which came an odour of burning. A multitude of shadowy faintly-edged clouds crept across the pale blue sky; a fairly stiff breeze blew in a steady dry gust, without tempering the heat. Resting his head on the cushion and with his arms folded across his chest, Lavretsky watched the flitting fields spreading out like a fan before him, the willow bushes as they slowly drifted past, the silly ravens and rooks looking dully askance at the passing vehicle, the long strips of the field bounds overgrown with wormwood, mugwort and mountain ash; and as he looked at this fresh and teeming nudity of steppe wilderness, the verdure, the long slopes, the gullies with their oak thickets, the grey little villages, the scraggy birch trees, the whole of this long-unvisited Russian landscape, he was stirred by emotions at once sweet and sorrowful that tugged softly at the heartstrings. Slowly his thoughts began to rove; they were as dim and hazy as the shapes of the clouds which also seemed to be roving overhead. He recalled his childhood, his mother, he recalled the scene of her dying hour, how he was brought to her, how she clasped his head to her bosom, started feebly to wail over him, then looked at Glafira Petrovna and checked herself. He recalled his father, at first buoyant, eternally discontented, sonorous-voiced, then blind, pathetic, with unkempt grey beard; he recalled how one day, after having had a drop too much at dinner and spilling the gravy over his napkin, he had suddenly laughed and begun relating his conquests, blinking his sightless eyes and growing red in the face; he recalled Varvara Pavlovna and winced involuntarily, like a man does who suffers a sudden twinge of pain, and shook his head. Then his thoughts dwelt on Liza.

"Here," he thought, "is a new creature just entering on life. A fine girl. I wonder what will become of her? She is attractive too. A pale, fresh face, and such a grave mouth and eyes, and straightforward innocent look. Pity she seems to be a bit too zealous. She's nicely built, moves so lightly and her voice is soft. I particularly like the way she suddenly stops, listens attentively unsmilingly, then becomes thoughtful and tosses back her hair. I don't think either that Panshin is worthy of her. What's wrong with him, though? Besides, what am I daydreaming about? She will go the way all go. I'd better take a nap." And Lavretsky closed his eyes.

He could not fall asleep, but sank into a nodding drowsiness. Memories of the past continued to rise up slowly and take possession of his heart, mingling and mixing with other recollections. For some inexplicable reason Lavretsky switched his thoughts to Robert Peel ... French history ... to how he would win a battle if he were a general—he even seemed to hear the sounds of firing, alarms and excursions. ... His head slipped down, he opened his eyes. ... The same fields, the same steppe scenes; the run-down shoes of the outrunners glinted alternately through the curling dust; the coachman's yellow smock with red gussets billowed out with the wind. ... "A nice homecoming, my dear fellow!" Lavretsky was struck with the thought. He shouted out "Gee up, there!", wrapped his cloak around him, snuggled closer to the cushion. The carriage gave a jolt: Lavretsky sat up and opened his eyes wide. On the hillock before him nestled a little village; a little to the

right could be seen a small decrepit-looking manor house
with closed shutters and an awry little porch; the wide
courtyard, from the very gates, was covered with an
undergrowth of nettles, green and thick as hemp; a barn,
built of oak and still sturdy, stood here too. This was
Vassilyevskoye.

The coachman drew up at the gates; Lavretsky's valet
stood up on the box, and making as though he were
about to jump down, cried out "Hey!" There was a
hoarse, muffled barking, but nothing, not even a dog
came in sight; the valet took another stand for a jump
and shouted "Hey!" again. The feeble barking was re-
newed, and a moment later a man sprang up apparently
from nowhere and came running into the courtyard, clad
in a nankeen caftan, with a head as white as snow; he
stared at the carriage, with his hand cupped to his eyes,
suddenly clapped both hands to his thighs, began to dart
hither and thither, then ran to open the gates. The
tarantass drove into the yard with a crunching sound as
its wheels passed over the nettles and came to a stop
before the porch. The silver-haired man, apparently
very nimble of foot, was already standing at the bottom
of the steps, his legs crookedly straddled; he unfastened
the front, jerked back the hood and helped his master to
alight, then kissed his hand.

"How do you do, my good fellow!" said Lavretsky.
"Your name's Anton, I believe? So you are still alive?"

The old man bowed in silence and shambled off to
fetch the keys. While he was gone the coachman sat
immobile with arms akimbo, gaping at the closed door;
Lavretsky's valet, having jumped down from his perch,
stood as if rooted to the spot in a picturesque pose with
one hand thrown over the box. The old man brought
the keys and twisting his body in needless contortions
like a snake, with jutting elbows, he unlocked the door,
stepped aside and made another low bow.

"So here I am at home, here am I back again," thought
Lavretsky, entering the tiny hall, while the shutters were
flung open one after another with a creak and bang,
and daylight streamed into the deserted rooms.

XIX

The little house to which Lavretsky had come and
where Glafira Petrovna had died two years ago, was
built in the preceding century out of solid pine wood;
it only looked decrepit, but would stand for another
fifty years or more. Lavretsky made a round of all the
rooms, and to the great discomfiture of the torpid dust-
covered old flies sitting motionlessly under the lintels,
he had the windows opened everywhere: nobody had
opened them since the death of Glafira Petrovna. Everything in the house had remained untouched: the little
slim-legged divans in the drawing room, upholstered in
glossy grey damask, frayed and sagging, were a vivid
reminder of the days of Catherine the Great; here in the
drawing room stood the mistress' favourite armchair,
with its high straight back, against which she had never
leaned even in her old age. On the main wall there
hung an old portrait of Fyodor's greatgrandfather
Andrei Lavretsky; the sombre splenetic face scarcely stood
out from the dark warped background; the small
scowling eyes looked grimly from under heavy drooping
eyelids; his black unpowdered hair bristled above a
ponderous rugged brow. From a corner of the frame
hung a dusty wreath of immortelles. "Glafira Petrovna
made that wreath herself," announced Anton. In the
bedroom towered a narrow bedstead under a striped
canopy of some goodly old-time material; a pile of
faded pillows and a threadbare counterpane lay on the
bed, at the head of which hung a holy image depicting
the Presentation of the Blessed Virgin, that same image
which the old maid on her lonely deathbed had pressed
for the last time to her chilling lips. A small dressing
table of inlaid wood with brass fittings and a distorted
mirror in a blackened gilt frame stood by the window.
Adjoining the bedroom was the icon room, a small
chamber with bare walls and a massive image case in
the corner; on the floor lay a threadbare wax-begrimed
rug; on this Glafira Petrovna used to kneel in worship.
Anton went out with Lavretsky's valet to unlock the
stable and the coach house; in his stead there appeared

an ancient little woman of about the same age, with a kerchief tied low down over her eyebrows; her head shook and her eyes gazed vacuously but with an expression of eagerness—the habit of years of unquestioning service—and at the same time with a kind of reverent regret. She pressed her lips to Lavretsky's hand and stood silently in the doorway, awaiting his commands. He could not for the life of him remember her name or recollect ever having seen her; her name, it appears, was Apraxia; forty years ago Glafira Petrovna had expelled her from the house into the poultry yard; she spoke little, however—as though she had lost her senses—and could only stare at him with that cringing look of hers. Besides these two old creatures and three pot-bellied children in long smocks—Anton's greatgrandchildren, there dwelt on the estate a one-armed little peasant who was exempted from servitude; he went about muttering like a woodcock and was no good at anything; no more useful was the decrepit hound that had greeted Lavretsky's homecoming with its bark; it had lived for ten years on a heavy chain, purchased on Glafira Petrovna's orders, and was barely able to move about and drag its burden. After going over the house Lavretsky went into the garden, the sight of which pleased him. It was all overgrown with weeds and burdock and gooseberry and raspberry bushes, but there was a fair amount of shade supplied by numerous old limes which were remarkable both for size and the singular arrangement of their boughs; they had been planted too close together, and at some time or other—perhaps a hundred years ago—had been trimmed. At the end of the garden was a small clear pond fringed with slender brown rushes. Traces of human life fade away quickly; Glafira Petrovna's homestead had not yet grown desolate, but seemed sunk in that quiet slumber in which everything reposes on earth where the taint of the madding crowd has not touched it. Fyodor Ivanych also took a walk through the village; the peasant women regarded him from the doorsteps of their huts, cupping their cheeks in their hands; the men touched their forelocks from a distance, the children scampered away, the dogs barked indifferently. He began to feel hungry, but his servants and the cook were not expected until evening; the waggons with provisions from Lavriky had not yet arrived—and he was obliged to fall back on Anton. The latter dispatched himself with haste to execute his master's wishes: he caught, killed and plucked an old hen; Apraxia scoured and cleaned it and rinsed it like a piece of washing before putting it into the saucepan; when it was finally done, Anton spread the cloth and set the table, laying out a knife and fork, a tarnished three-legged saltcellar and a cut-glass narrow-necked decanter with a round glass stopper; then he informed his master in a singsong voice that dinner was served, and stood behind his chair, swathing his right fist in a napkin and diffusing a pungent, ancient sort of odour, like the smell of a cypress tree. Lavretsky ate some soup and reached for the hen; its skin was all covered with large pimples; a tough tendon ran up each leg, the meat gave off a flavour of wood and lye. When he had finished his meal Lavretsky said he would not mind a cup of tea, if.... "I will bring it right away," the old man interjected, and kept his word. A pinch of tea was hunted up wrapped in a piece of red paper; a small but very mettlesome and noisy samovar was unearthed and sugar too in small soggy-looking fragments. Lavretsky drank tea out of a big cup; he remembered this cup from childhood; playing cards were depicted on the outside, and it had been used only for visitors—and now he was drinking out of it like a visitor. The servants arrived in the evening; Lavretsky did not want to sleep in his aunt's bed; he had a bed put up in the dining room. After snuffing out the candle he sat looking about him for a long while, thinking sad thoughts; he experienced the feeling familiar to any person who has had occasion to spend the night in a long untenanted place; the darkness which closed in on him from all sides seemed to resent the new tenant, the very walls of the house seemed startled. Finally he sighed, drew up the blanket and fell asleep. Anton was up after the rest of the household had retired; he talked in whispers for a long while with Apraxia, groaned in an undertone and crossed himself once or twice; neither had expected their master to settle at Vassilyevskoye, when he had such a fine estate and well-appointed manor so near at hand; it could not occur to them that that place was hateful to him—it was too full of distressful memories. Having done whispering, Anton took a stick and struck the night watchman's board which had hung so long unsounded by the barn, and there in the courtyard settled himself down to sleep, his white head uncovered. The May night was soft and gentle, and the old man slumbered sweetly.

XX

The next day Lavretsky rose early, interviewed the bailiff, visited the threshing floor, ordered the chain to be taken off the house dog, who had merely given a desultory bark but did not detach himself from his kennel, and returning home, became immersed in a sort of peaceful torpor in which he remained all day. "Here is where I've struck bottom," he said to himself more than once. He sat at the window without stirring, listening, as it were, to the current of peaceful life flowing around him, to the rare sounds of country quietude. From somewhere under the nettles came a faint high note; a gnat took up the tune. The note died away, but the gnat went on humming; through the measured, persistent and plaintive buzzing of the flies came the loud drone of a fat bumblebee hitting its head incessantly against the ceiling; outside the cock crowed, hanging hoarsely on the last note; a cart lumbered by; a gate creaked somewhere in the village. "What d'yer say?" sounded the raucous voice of a peasant woman. "Well, dearie," said Anton to a little two-year-old girl he was dandling in his arms. "Fetch the kvass," repeated the woman's voice—and suddenly a dead silence ensued; not a rattle was heard, not a sound; not a leaf stirred in the wind; the swallows wheeled noiselessly one after another over the ground, and their silent flight saddened the heart. "Here is where I've struck bottom," reflected Lavretsky again. "And here life is always, invariably placid and unhurried," he ruminated. "Whoever comes within its circle must resign himself to its power; here cares are banished, and nothing preys on the mind;

here things will go well only with him who makes the
steady tenor of his way like the ploughman behind the
furrows of his plough. And what power, what vigour lie
hidden in this sequestered stillness. Here under the window the sturdy burdock shoots up out of the thick grasses;
above it the lovage throws out its succulent stems, and
still higher the Virgin's bower trails its pink tendrils;
and yonder in the fields gleams the ripe rye, and the oats
are already in ear, and every leaf on every tree and
every blade of grass on its stalk is growing and opening
out to its utmost extent. My best years have been
spent in loving a woman," Lavretsky resumed his reflections, "let the boredom of solitude sober me, let it
soothe and prepare me for leisurely taking up my task."
And once more he listened to the silence, without hope-
fulness—and yet constantly in suspense as though hoping
for something; the silence engulfed him from all sides;
the sun moved slowly across the tranquil blue heavens
and the clouds drifted gently overhead; it seemed as if
they knew whither and why they were drifting. At this
same time life elsewhere was seething, hurrying and
clashing on its way; here it slipped by noiselessly, like
water over marshy grass; and till late in the evening
Lavretsky could not tear himself away from the contemplation of this receding life that glided imperceptibly
by; sorrow for the days that have gone melted in his
heart like the snow of early spring—and, strange as it
may seem, never had love for his native land sat so deep
and strong within him.

XXI

Within a couple of weeks Fyodor Ivanych brought
Glafira Petrovna's little house into order, cleared the
courtyard and the garden; comfortable furniture was
brought from Lavriky, wine, books and journals from
town; horses made their appearance in the stables; in short,
Fyodor Ivanych provided himself for all his needs and
settled down to the life, one could not say whether of a
country landowner or a hermit. His days passed unvarie-
dly, but he was not bored, although he saw nobody; he

devoted himself sedulously to the affairs of the estate, explored the countryside on horseback, and did some reading. He read little, however; he preferred listening to old Anton's narrations. Lavretsky would usually sit down by the window with his pipe and a cup of cold tea; Anton would stand by the door with his hands clasped behind his back and begin his rambling stories of old times, those fabulous days of yore, when oats and rye were not sold by the measure but in great sacks, at two or three kopecks a sack; when impenetrable forests and virgin steppes stretched away on all sides, fast by the town. "And now," complained the old man, who was already on the right side of eighty, "they've done so much felling and ploughing there's hardly room anywhere for a carriage to pass." Anton would relate many stories about his mistress, Glafira Petrovna, too; how prudent and thrifty she was; how a certain gentleman, a young neighbour, had tried to curry favour in this quarter and ridden over often to see her, and how my lady had even deigned to put on her holiday cap with dark crimson ribbons and her yellow gown of tru-tru-levantine for him; but how she had later been in high dudgeon over an indiscreet enquiry on that gentleman's part as to the extent of her means and had forbidden him the house, and how she had summarily commanded that when she died everything to the last little scrap was to go to Fyodor Ivanych. And, indeed, Lavretsky found all his aunt's household goods intact, including the holiday cap with crimson ribbons and the yellow gown of tru-tru-levantine. Of old papers and interesting documents, which Lavretsky hoped to find, there were none, except an old book, in which his grandfather, Pyotr Andreich, had inscribed, in one place: "Celebration in the city of Saint Petersburg of the peace made with the Empire of Turkey by His Excellency Prince Alexander Alexandrovich Prozorovsky"; in another, a recipe for a pectoral with the remark: "These directions were given to the General's lady Praskovya Fyodorovna Saltykova by the chief priest of the Church of the Holy Trinity Fyodor Avksentyevich"; elsewhere a piece of political news: "There seems to be no more talk of the French tigers", and beside it the following entry:

"The *Moskovskiye Vedomosti* announces the death of Senior Major Mikhail Petrovich Kolychev. Would this be the son of Pyotr Vassilyevich Kolychev?" Lavretsky also discovered some old calendars and dreambooks and the mysterious work of M. Ambodik; many were the memories these long-forgotten but familiar "Symbols and Emblems" awakened in him. In Glafira Petrovna's dressing table Lavretsky found a small packet tied with black ribbon, sealed with black sealing wax and thrust into the innermost recesses of the drawer. In the packet there lay, face to face, a pastel portrait of his father in his youth, with soft hair hanging in ringlets about his brow, and almond-shaped languid eyes and parted lips, and an almost obliterated portrait of a pale woman in a white dress with a white rose in her hand—his mother. Glafira Petrovna had never consented to having a portrait of herself made. "I myself, dear master, Fyodor Ivanych," Anton used to relate to Lavretsky, "though I weren't living at the time in the house, still remember your great-grandfather, Andrei Afanasyich; to be sure, I was only getting on for eighteen when he died. Once he came across of me in the garden, and I shook in my shoes, I can tell you; but there, he didn't do nothing, just asked me my name and sent me to his room to fetch a pocket handkerchief. He was a grand gentleman, indeed,—aye, and he would be second to none. And all because he had a wonderful amulet, did your greatgrandfather; a monk from Mount Athos gave it him as a present, this amulet. And he tells him, this monk did, 'I give thee this gift, my lord, for thy kind hospitality; wear it and thou mayest fear no judgment.' You know, dear master, what them times were like: the master could do whatever he wanted; sometimes one of the gentlefolk would take it into his head to gainsay him, but he would just look at him and say: 'You poor fish'—that was his pet saying. And he lived, your greatgrandfather, God bless him, in a little wooden house; and as for the goods he left behind him, silver plate and what not, why all the cellars was packed full of 'em! He was a thrifty one, he was. That decanter you said you like, now that was his too: he used to drink vodka out of it. Now take your grand-

father, Pyotr Andreich—he built himself a stone house
but he never made good; everything went topsy-turvy
and he was worse off than his father, never got any pleasure out of life, squandered all his money, and didn't
leave a thing to remember him by; not even a silver
spoon's come down from him—whatever's left is thanks
to Glafira Petrovna's thrift and care."

"Is it true," Lavretsky broke in, "that they used to call
her old skinflint?"

"Aye, but who used to call her that!" protested Anton
in a tone of displeasure.

Once the old man made bold to ask: "How is it, dear
master, with the mistress, where would she be staying?"

"I have divorced my wife," said Lavretsky with an
effort, "please don't ask about her."

"Yes, sir," replied the old man sadly.

After a lapse of three weeks Lavretsky rode down to
O— on horseback to visit the Kalitins, and spent the
evening with them. Lemm was there; Lavretsky took a
great liking to him. Although, thanks to his father, he
did not play on any instrument, he was passionately fond
of music, real, classical music. Panshin was not at the
Kalitins' that evening. The governor-general had dispatched him on some business out of town. Liza played by
herself and with great precision; Lemm became animated,
and waxing lively, rolled up a piece of paper into a tube
and began using it as a baton. Marya Dmitriyevna at first
laughed at the sight, then went off to bed; Beethoven,
she averred, was too exciting for her nerves. At midnight
Lavretsky saw Lemm off to his lodgings and stopped
there with him till three o'clock in the morning. Lemm
talked a lot; his stooping figure straightened up, his eyes
grew wide and bright; even his hair stood erect above his
brow. It was so long since anyone had taken an interest
in him, and Lavretsky was obviously interested in him,
plying him solicitously and sympathetically with questions. This touched the old man; he ended by showing his
visitor his music, playing and even singing in a lifeless
voice some fragments from his own compositions, including the whole of Schiller's ballad, *Fridolin,* set by him
to music. Lavretsky complimented him, made him repeat

some of the music and, before leaving, invited him to come and stay a few days with him. Lemm, who saw him out of the house, readily consented and gave him a hearty handshake; but, left alone in the fresh, moist air, in the first rays of daybreak, he looked round him, screwed up his eyes, shivered, and crept back to his room with a guilty air: *"Ich bin wohl nicht klug"* (I must be out of my senses), he muttered, getting into his hard short bed. He tried to feign indisposition when, a few days later, Lavretsky had ordered a piano to be brought up from town Ivanych went up to his room and persuaded him into going. What impressed Lemm most of all, was that Lavretsky had ordered a piano to be brough up from town specially for him. They both went to the Kalitins and spent the evening there, but not so agreeably as on the previous occasion. Panshin was there, he talked a great deal about his recent journey, and very amusingly mimicked and copied the country gentry he had met; Lavretsky laughed, but Lemm kept in his corner, where he sat scowling in silence, his huddled-up body making spiderlike stirrings, and he brightened up only when Lavretsky rose to take his leave. Even in the carriage the old man was still reticent and shrinking; but the soft, warm air, the balmy breeze, the faint shadows, the smell of grass and birch buds, the placid radiance of the starlit moonless night, the measured sound of hoofbeats and snorting of the horses, the whole spell of the roadside, the enchantment of the spring and the night sank into the poor German's soul, and he was first to break the silence.

XXII

He began talking about music, about Liza and then once more about music. He seemed to utter his words more slowly when he spoke of Liza. Lavretsky turned the conversation on his compositions, and, half in jest, offered to write him a libretto.

"Hm, a libretto!" rejoined Lemm. "No, that's beyond me; I no longer have the vivid touch, the flight of imagination that is necessary for an opera; my powers are on the wane. . . . But if I were still able to do anything—I would be contented with a romanza; of course, I should want the words to be fitting. . . ."

He fell silent, and sat motionless a long while with his eyes lifted to the heavens.

"For instance," he said presently, "something of this sort—'Ye stars. O ye pure stars! . . .' "

Lavretsky turned slightly towards him and looked at him.

" 'Ye stars, ye pure stars,' " repeated Lemm. " 'Ye gaze down upon both the just and the unjust . . . but only the innocent heart,'—or something like that—'can understand'—no, not that—'can love you.' But I am no poet—not likely! Something of that kind, though, something lofty."

Lemm tilted his hat on the back of his head; in the dim twilight of the clear night his face looked paler and younger.

" 'And ye too,' " he continued, his voice gradually sinking to a murmur, " 'Ye know who loveth, who can love, because ye are pure, ye alone can bring solace. . . .' No, that's not it! I'm no poet," he said, "anyway, something in that style. . . ."

"I'm sorry I am not a poet," observed Lavretsky.

"Vain dreams!" said Lemm, and buried himself in the corner of the carriage. He closed his eyes, as though he were composing himself for sleep.

Some moments passed. . . . Lavretsky listened. . . . "Stars, pure stars, love," whispered the old man.

"Love," Lavretsky repeated to himself. He became lost in thought, and his heart grew heavy.

"That is beautiful music you have set to Fridolin, Christopher Fyodorych," he said aloud. "What do you think—this Fridolin, after the Count presented him to his wife—that's when he became her lover, eh?"

"That's what you think," replied Lemm, "because you probably have experienced. . . ." He stopped suddenly and turned away in confusion. Lavretsky gave a forced laugh, turned away too and looked out at the road.

The stars had grown dimmer and the sky was greying when the carriage drove up to the little porch in Vassi-

lyevskoye. Lavretsky showed his guest to his room, returned to his study and sat down at the window. Out in
the garden the nightingale was singing its last carol before the break of dawn. Lavretsky was reminded of the
nightingale that had sung in the garden at the Kalitins';
he recalled, too, the gentle movement of Liza's eyes when
she turned to the dark window at its first notes. He began
to think about her and his heart was eased again. "Pure
maid," he murmured half-aloud; "pure stars," he added
with a smile and crept away to bed.

But Lemm sat for a long time on his bed, a music book
on his knees. He was haunted by a sweet and wonderful
melody; he was stirred and kindled, he could feel the
languor and sweetness of its hovering presence ... but
he could not grasp it.

"Neither poet nor musician," he muttered at length. . . .
And his weary head sank heavily on the pillow.

XXIII

The next day the host and his guest drank tea in the
garden under an old lime tree.

"Maestro!" said Lavretsky by the way, "you'll have
to write a triumphal cantata soon."

"What is the occasion?"

"The nuptials of Mr. Panshin and Liza. Did you notice
yesterday the attentions he paid her? It looks as though
things are in a fair way there."

"That will never be!" cried Lemm.

"Why not?"

"Because it's impossible. Though," he added after a
pause, "everything's possible in this world. Especially
with you people, here in Russia."

"Let us leave Russia out of it for the time being; what's
wrong with this marriage?"

"It's wrong, all wrong. Elizaveta Mikhailovna is a
frank, serious girl with noble feelings, and he ... he's
a di-let-tan-te, in short."

"But she loves him, doesn't she?"

Lemm rose to his feet.

"No, she doesn't love him, I mean she is innocent of heart and doesn't know herself what love is. Madame von Kalitina tells her that he is a fine young man, and she obeys Madame von Kalitina because she's still a mere child, though she's nineteen: she prays in the morning, prays in the evening—that's all very well; but she does not love him. She can only love what is beautiful, and he's not beautiful, that is, his soul isn't."

Lemm made this little speech fluently and with fervour, pacing to and fro with little steps before the tea table and running his eyes over the ground.

"My dear Maestro!" exclaimed Lavretsky suddenly. "I do believe you're in love with my cousin yourself."

Lemm stopped short.

"Please," he began in a shaky voice, "don't make fun of me like that. I'm not crazy—I'm looking into the dark beyond, and not into the rosy future."

Lavretsky was filled with remorse; he asked the old man's forgiveness. After tea Lemm played him his cantata, and during dinner, at Lavretsky's own lead, began to talk again about Liza. Lavretsky listened with attention and curiosity.

"What do you say, Christopher Fyodorych," he pronounced at length, "everything seems to be in order here now, the garden is in full bloom,—what about inviting her down here for the day with her mother and my old aunt, eh? Would you like it?"

Lemm bent his head over his plate.

"All right," he said in a scarcely audible murmur.

"And we can do without Panshin?"

"We can," rejoined the old man with an almost child-like smile.

Two days later Fyodor Ivanych rode to town to see the Kalitins.

XXIV

He found them all at home, but did not open his mind at once; he wanted to discuss the matter first with Liza. An opportunity presented itself: they were left alone in the drawing room. They fell into conversation; she had already grown accustomed to him,—indeed, she was not shy, as a rule, with anyone. He listened to her, studied her face and mentally went over Lemm's words and endorsed them. It sometimes happens that two acquaintances who are not on intimate terms are suddenly and momentarily drawn together, and the realisation of this intimacy immediately finds expression in mutual glances, quiet friendly smiles and even gestures. This is exactly what happened with Lavretsky and Liza. "So he is like that," was her thought, as she looked at him kindly. "So that is what you are like," he too was thinking. He was not greatly surprised, therefore, when she told him, not without a slight hesitancy, that she had long wanted to ease her mind, but was afraid to offend him.

"Don't be afraid, tell me," he replied, and stopped in front of her.

Liza raised her limpid eyes to him.

"You are so good," she began, and the thought ran through her mind: "he is certainly good." "You will excuse me, I should not really dare speak of it to you ... but how could you ... why did you part with your wife?"

Lavretsky winced, looked at Liza and sat down near her.

"My child," he began, "please do not touch that wound; your hands are tender, but it will hurt all the same."

"I know," Liza went on as though she had not heard him, "she has wronged you, I do not want to justify her; but how can one put asunder what God has joined?"

"Our views on that point are too wide apart, Elizaveta Mikhailovna," retorted Lavretsky somewhat sharply. "We shall not be able to understand each other."

Liza's face paled; her frame quivered slightly, but she did not remain silent.

"You must forgive," she murmured gently, "if you wish to be forgiven."

"Forgive!" broke in Lavretsky. "You should first know the person on whose behalf you are speaking! Forgive that woman, take her back into my home, that empty, soulless creature! And who told you she wants to come back? Why, she is perfectly contented with her lot...

Oh, what's the use of talking about it? Her name ought never to pass your lips. You are too pure, you cannot even know what sort of creature that is."

"Must you abuse her?" said Liza with an effort. Her hands now visibly trembled. "You left her yourself, Fyodor Ivanych."

"But I am telling you," broke out Lavretsky impatiently, "you don't know what that creature is!"

"Then why did you marry her?" whispered Liza, dropping her eyes.

Lavretsky rose quickly to his feet.

"Why did I marry? I was young and inexperienced; I was taken in, infatuated by a beautiful exterior. I didn't know women, I didn't know anything. God grant you a luckier marriage! But, believe me, you can never be sure."

"I might be unfortunate, too," said Liza (her voice had a catch in it); "but then you must resign yourself to your fate; I don't know how to say it, but unless we resign ourselves. . . ."

Lavretsky clenched his hands and brought his foot down.

"Please don't be angry, forgive me," put in Liza hastily.

At that instant Marya Dmitriyevna entered the room. Liza got up to leave the room.

"One moment," Lavretsky suddenly ejaculated. "I have a boon to ask of your mother and you—won't you pay me a visit, make up a housewarming party? You know, I've procured a piano; Lemm is staying with me; the lilac is just now in blossom; you will take a breath of country air and go back the same day—do you agree?"

Liza looked at her mother, and Marya Dmitriyevna assumed a look of distress; but Lavretsky gave her no time to open her mouth and kissed both her hands there and then; Marya Dmitriyevna, always susceptible to touching demonstrations and least expecting such courtesy from "the boor", unbent and gave her consent. While she was considering what day to fix, Lavretsky went up to Liza and, still greatly moved, said to her in a whisper: "Thanks, you're a good girl; I'm sorry. . . ." And her pale face flushed with a happy, shy smile; her eyes smiled too—she had been afraid that she had given him offence.

"Can Vladimir Nikolaich come with us?" enquired
Marya Dmitriyevna.

"Of course," replied Lavretsky, "but wouldn't it be
better if it were just a family party?"

"But I thought. . ." Marya Dmitriyevna started to
say. . . "well, just as you like," she added.

It was decided to take Lenochka and Shurochka.
Marfa Timofeyevna declined to go.

"I'm sorry, my dear," she protested, "it would be too
hard on my old bones; and I don't suppose there is
anywhere to sleep at your place; and I can't sleep in a
strange bed anyhow. Let the young ones romp it."

Lavretsky found no more opportunity of being alone
with Liza; but he looked at her in a way that made her
feel good, and a little shamefaced, and sorry for him.
He gripped her hand at parting; left by herself, she became thougtful.

XXV

When Lavretsky got home he was met on the threshold
of the drawing room by a tall spare man, in a bedraggled
blue coat, with a wrinkled but animated face, dishevelled
grey whiskers, a long straight nose and small inflamed
eyes. This was Mikhalevich, his old university chum.
Lavretsky did not recognise him at first, but embraced
him warmly directly he learned his name. They had not
seen each other since Moscow days. A rain of questions
and exclamations followed; long-buried recollections were
dragged out. Hurriedly smoking pipe after pipe, sipping
occasionally his tea and gesticulating with his long hands,
Mikhalevich related his adventures to Lavretsky; there
was nothing particularly exhilarating in them, he could
not boast of any success in his undertakings—but he
laughed incessantly with a husky nervous laugh. A month
ago he had got a situation in the counting-house of a
rich tax farmer about three hundred versts from the town
of O—, and hearing of Lavretsky's return from abroad,
he had come out of his way to see his old friend. Mikha-

levich talked as impetuously as he did in his youth, with
the same old vehemence and ardour. Lavretsky started
to mention his own circumstances, but Mikhalevich interrupted him, muttering hastily: "I have heard, old chap,
I have heard,—who could have imagined it?" and forthwith switched the talk onto general topics.

"I must be moving on tomorrow, my dear fellow," he
said, "today, however, with your permission, we will stay
up late. I am keen to know how you have turned out,
what your opinions are, your convictions, what you have
become, what life has taught you?" (Mikhalevich still
used the phraseology of the thirties.) "As for me, I have
changed a good bit, old chap: the waves of life have
swept over my breast—who was it said that?—though in
essentials I haven't changed at all; I still believe in the
good and the true; but I do not merely believe—I have
the faith, aye, the faith. Listen, you know I dabble in
poetry; my verses are not poetic, but they're true. I'll
read you my last poem; I've expressed therein my heart-
felt convictions. Listen." Mikhalevich started to read his
poem; it was fairly long and ended with the following
lines:

My heart to new feelings is wholly yielded,
Like a child at heart have I grown:
And all that I worshipped I have burnt,
And all I have burnt I now worship.

Mikhalevich was almost on the verge of tears as he
uttered the two last lines; a slight twitch—a sign of deep
emotion—crossed his wide mouth, his plain face lit up.
Lavretsky sat listening and listening—and a spirit of defiance stirred within him: he was exasperated by this
cut-and-dried ever simmering enthusiasm of the
Moscow student. A quarter of an hour had not elapsed
before an argument sprang up between them, one of those
interminable arguments of which only Russian people are
capable. Straightway, after many years' absence spent in
two different worlds, with a vague understanding of
their own, let alone other people's ideas, splitting hairs
and bandying words, they fell into an argument on the
most abstract subjects, and argued as though it were a

matter of life and death to them both; they shouted and vociferated with such fervour that everybody in the house was startled, and poor Lemm, who since Mikhalevich's arrival had locked himself up in his room, was bewildered and began even to feel vaguely alarmed.

"Then what are you after that? Disillusioned?" shouted Mikhalevich past midnight.

"Do I look like a disillusioned man?" retorted Lavretsky. "They are always pale and sickly—would you like me to lift you up with one hand?"

"Well, if you are not a disillusioned man, you are a *scepteek*, which is worse" (Mikhalevich's accent savoured of his native Ukraine). "What do you mean by being a sceptic? Luck has gone against you—admitted; you're not to blame—you were born with a passionate, loving soul and you were forcibly estranged from women; naturally the first woman you came across fooled you."

"She fooled you too," observed Lavretsky moodily.

"Granted, granted; I happened to be the instrument of fate—dash it, that's twaddle—there's no fate here; an old habit of loose definition. But what does it prove?"

"It proves that I have been crippled in childhood."

"Well, get yourself straight!—you're a man, aren't you? Surely, you don't need to go borrowing stamina! However it is, you can't reduce a particular case, so to speak, to a general law, an immutable rule."

"What's rule got to do with it?" broke in Lavretsky. "I don't admit. . . ."

"No, it's your rule, your rule. . . ." threw in Mikhalevich in his turn.

"You're an egoist, that's what you are!" he was bawling an hour later. "You were after self-pleasure, you sought happiness in life, you wanted to live for yourself. . . ."

"What the dickens is self-pleasure?"

"And you've been let down all round; everything has come toppling down."

"What is self-pleasure, I ask you?"

"And it had to topple down. Because you sought a foothold where there wasn't any; because you built your house on shifting sands. . . ."

"Make yourself clear, don't speak in similes, *because* I can't understand you."

"Because—all right, laugh if you like—because you have no faith, no warmness of heart; you're nothing but mind, just paltry mind ... you're simply an abject, anti-quated Voltairean—that's what you are."

"What, I—a Voltairean?"

"Yes, like your father was, and you don't even suspect it."

"All I can say then is that you're a fanatic!" cried Lavretsky.

"Alas!" replied Mikhalevich ruefully, "I have not yet, unfortunately, earned that lofty designation...."

"I know now what to call you," shouted Mikhalevich at past two in the morning, "you're neither sceptic, nor disillusioned, nor a Voltairean—you're a sluggard, yes, that's what you are—a downright sluggard, a sophisticat-ed sluggard. Unsophisticated sluggards kick their heels for nothing to do, because they're not capable of doing anything; they can't even think, but you're a thinking person—and you let the grass grow under your feet; you could be up and about—but you aren't; you just lie around with a full belly and say: that's how it should be, because whatever men do is all stuff and nonsense, leading nowhere."

"Where did you get the idea that I'm lying about?" protested Lavretsky, "What makes you think I have such ideas?"

"Besides, all you fellows, the whole of your tribe," went on Mikhalevich, nothing daunted, "are just well-read sluggards. You know the German's weak spot; you know what ails the English and the French,—and that pitiful learning of yours is used as a mainstay to justify your shameful sloth, your vile indolence. Some of you even exult in the fact that they lie around, like wise fellows, doing nothing, while others, the fools, are kick-ing up a dust. Yes, sir! There are some fine gentlemen among us—I'm not hinting at you, mind you—who spend all their lives sunk in a stupor of boredom, get used to it, stick in it like ... like a mushroom in white sauce," blurted out Mikhalevich, laughing at his own simile. "Oh,

that stupor of boredom—it will be the death of us Russians! The odious sluggard is for ever making up his
mind to get to work. . . ."

"What are you scolding for?"—it was Lavretsky's turn
to yell. "It's all very well to rant about working . . . doing
things. . . . Tell me better what to do instead of scolding,
Demosthenes of Poltava!"

"Is that all you want? I can't tell you that, sir; every
man must know that himself," retorted Demosthenes
sarcastically. "A landowner! A nobleman, if you please!
And he doesn't know what to do! You have no faith, or
else you would know; where there's no faith there's no
revelation."

"Give me at least time to rest, confound it; let me look
around," pleaded Lavretsky.

"Not a minute's rest, not a second!" retorted Mikhalevich with an imperious gesture. "Not a single second!
Death waits for no man, and life should not wait."

"And what a time, what a place for men to be taking
it into their heads to become sluggards!" he cried at
four in the morning in a voice now slightly hoarse from
shouting. "Here! Now! In Russia! When every individual
has a duty to perform, a grave responsibility to carry in
the face of God, the nation and his own self! We are
sleeping while time is slipping by; we are sleeping. . . ."

"Let me tell you," observed Lavretsky, "that we are
certainly not sleeping now, but rather preventing others
from sleeping. We're screeching like a couple of cocks.
Hark, can that be a third one crowing?"

This sally brought a chuckle from Mikhalevich and
quietened him down. "Well, till tomorrow," he said with
a smile and put his pipe away.

"Till tomorrow," repeated Lavretsky. But the friends
chatted on for more than an hour. . . . However, their
voices were no longer raised, their talk was subdued and
sad and its burden was tender.

Mikhalevich went away the next day, despite all
Lavretsky's efforts to detain him. Fyodor Ivanych could
not persuade him to remain, but they had talked to their
heart's content. Mikhalevich, it appeared, had not a
penny to bless himself with. Lavretsky had noticed with

regret the previous evening the obvious signs and habits
of long-standing poverty; his boots were down at heel,
a button was missing off the back of his coat, his hands
were unused to gloves, there was fluff in his hair; on his
arrival it had not even occurred to him to ask whether
he might have a wash, and at supper he ate voraciously,
tearing the meat with his hands and crunching the bones
with his strong black teeth. It transpired also that the civil
service had not brought him anything, that all his hopes
were now centred on his present employer who had taken
him merely to have "an educated man" about the office.
Notwithstanding, Mikhalevich was not disconcerted and
lived the cynic, idealist and poet that he was, sincerely
solicitous and anxious over the destinies of man and his
own vocation, and giving very little thought to keeping
his own head above water. Mikhalevich was not married,
but had fallen in love times beyond number and had
written poems to all the objects of his passion; one particularly inspired rhapsody was dedicated to a mysterious
"Polish Lady" with dark tresses. . . . True, there were
rumours that this Polish lady was a common Jewess,
familiar to a good many cavalry officers . . . but, come
to think of it, even that does not count.

Mikhalevich did not get on with Lemm: his turbulent
talk and brusque manners alarmed the German, who was
not used to such ways. . . . One poor beggar is quick to
espy another from a distance, but in old age they seldom
become friends—and that is hardly surprising: they have
nothing to share in common, not even hopes.

Before leaving, Mikhalevich had another long chat
with Lavretsky, prophesied his ruin unless he came to
his senses, begged him to turn his serious attention to
the welfare of his peasants, set himself up as an example,
claiming that he had purged himself in the inferno of
suffering, and in the same breath repeated several times
that he was a happy man, and compared himself to the
birds of the air and the lily of the valley. . . .

"A black lily, anyway," observed Lavretsky.

"Come, my dear fellow, don't be a snob," retorted
Mikhalevich, "you'd better thank God that you too have
honest plebeian blood flowing in your veins. I see that

what you need now is some pure heavenly creature to
drag you out of your apathy."

"Thanks, old chap," observed Lavretsky, "I've about
had enough of these heavenly creatures."

"Shut up, you *cyneec*!" cried Mikhalevich.

"Cynic," Lavretsky corrected him.

"Precisely *cyneec*," repeated Mikhalevich unabashed.

He was still talking even when he had taken his seat
in the tarantass, whither they had brought out his flat,
yellow, surprisingly light portmanteau; muffled in a
Spanish-looking cloak with a rusty brown collar and a
clasp in the shape of two lion's paws, he continued
expounding his views on the destiny of Russia, and waved
his swarthy hand in the air as though scattering the
seeds of future weal. The horses finally started off....
"Remember my three last words," he cried, thrusting his
body out of the carriage and balancing it, "religion,
progress, humanity!... Goodbye!" His head, with the
cap pulled down over his eyes, disappeared. Lavretsky
was left standing alone on the steps, and he gazed intently down the road until the tarantass was no longer
in sight. "I believe he is right," he thought as he went
back into the house, "I believe I am a sluggard." Much
of what Mikhalevich had said had sunk irresistibly into
his heart, though he had argued and disagreed with him.
If a man be good none can resist him.

XXVI

Two days later Marya Dmitriyevna came down to
Vassilyevskoye as she had promised, with all the young
folk. The little girls ran straightway into the garden,
while Marya Dmitriyevna languidly paced the rooms and
languidly admired everything. Her call on Lavretsky she
considered a token of great condescension on her part,
almost a deed of charity. She smiled graciously when
Anton and Apraxia kissed her hand in the time-old way
of manorial servants, and asked for some tea in a listless
drawling voice. To the deep chagrin of Anton, who had
put on white knitted gloves for the occasion, the lady

visitor was served tea by Lavretsky's hired valet who, according to Anton, had no notion of the proprieties. But Anton had his own back at dinnertime: he took up his stand resolutely behind Marya Dmitriyevna's chair and did not surrender his post to anybody. The uncommon sight of visitors at Vassilyevskoye delighted and flustered the old man: it did his heart good to see what fine gentlefolk his master hobnobbed with. Nor was he the only one to be in a state of excitement that day: Lemm too was in a flurry. He was arrayed in a shortish snuff-coloured dock-tailed coat, had drawn his neckerchief taut round his neck and incessantly cleared his throat and made way for people with an air of extreme affability. Lavretsky noted with pleasure that the feeling of intimacy that had sprung up between himself and Liza still continued: she held out her hand to him in a friendly way the moment she came in. After dinner Lemm drew out of his coattail pocket, where he had been fumbling all the time, a small roll of music, and tightening his lips he placed it silently on the piano. It was a romanza he had composed the previous evening to some old-fashioned German words containing an allusion to the stars. Liza sat down forthwith to the piano and began playing it. . . . Alas! the music turned out to be involved and distressingly laborious; the composer had obviously striven to express something deep and impassioned, but had failed; the striving was there but nothing else. Both Lavretsky and Liza felt it, and Lemm perceived it—for without a word he put the music back into his pocket, and at Liza's suggestion to play it again, he merely shook his head, said meaningly "That's that!"—hunched his shoulders, shrank into himself and moved away.

Towards evening the whole company went out fishing. The pond at the bottom of the garden was full of carp and groundlings. Marya Dmitriyevna was placed in an armchair beside the edge, in the shade, a rug was spread for her feet, and she was given the best line; Anton, as an old practised angler, put himself at her disposal. He fussed over the line, baited the hook, slapped the worm, spat on it and even threw in the line with a graceful curve of the body. Speaking of him that day to Lavretsky in her boarding-school French, Marya Dmitriyevna said: *"Il n'y a plus maintenant de ces gens comme ça comme autrefois."* Lemm with the two little girls went further down to a spot near the dam; Lavretsky disposed himself next to Liza. The fish were nibbling incessantly; the carp flashed gold and silver in the air as the lines here and there were drawn in; the little girls emitted ceaseless cries of delight; even Marya Dmitriyevna uttered a delicate little shriek on two occasions. Least of all did Lavretsky and Liza hook in; this was probably because they were paying less attention to the fishing than the others, and allowed their floats to come up to the very bank. The high reddish reeds swished softly round them, the still water shimmered softly, and soft were the voices in which they spoke. Liza stood on a small raft; Lavretsky sat on the bent trunk of a willow tree; Liza wore a white dress girdled with a white sash; her straw hat dangled in one hand, the other was engaged holding up the taut-bent fishing rod. Lavretsky gazed at her clear-cut, somewhat severe profile, at her hair drawn back behind the ears, at her tender cheeks kissed by the sun like those of a child, and thought: "Oh, how sweet art thou, standing by my pond!" Liza stood with her face turned away, gazing at the water with eyes that looked as if they were screwed up or smiling. The lime tree nearby cast its shadow upon them.

"Do you know," began Lavretsky, "I have been thinking a lot about the last talk we had, and have come to the conclusion that you are exceedingly good."

"Oh, I didn't want to give you the impression. . ." Liza started to say, and was overcome with embarrassment.

"You are good," repeated Lavretsky. "I'm a crude sort of fellow, but I can imagine everyone being fond of you. Take Lemm for instance; he's simply in love with you."

Liza not so much knitted as twitched her brows; she always did that when she heard anything disagreeable.

"I felt very sorry for him today," Lavretsky hastened to put in, "with his unfortunate romanza. To be young and inapt is tolerable; but to be old and incapable is a very sad thing. The worst of it is that you don't realise your powers are failing. It is very hard on the old man.... Look out, it's biting.... I hear," added Lavretsky after a pause, "that Vladimir Nikolaich has composed a very nice song."

"Yes," answered Liza, "it's a trifle, but not bad."

"What is your opinion," asked Lavretsky, "is he a good musician?"

"I think he has a great gift for music; but so far he hasn't taken it up seriously."

"Well, and as a man, would you call him good?"

Liza laughed and cast a swift glance at Fyodor Ivanych.

"What an odd thing to ask!" she cried, pulling in her line and throwing it out again.

"Why odd? I ask you about him as one who has just arrived in these parts, as a relation."

"A relation?"

"Yes. I happen to be an uncle of yours, I believe."

"Vladimir Nikolaich has a kind heart," said Liza, "he is clever; *maman* likes him very much."

"Do you like him?"

"He is a nice man; why shouldn't I like him?"

"Ah!" murmured Lavretsky and fell silent. A look of mingled sorrow and scorn flashed across his countenance. His intent gaze disconcerted Liza, but she went on smiling. "Well, God grant they be happy!" he muttered presently, as though to himself, and turned his head aside.

Liza blushed.

"You are mistaken, Fyodor Ivanych," she said, "you shouldn't think.... But don't you like Vladimir Nikolaich?" she asked suddenly.

"No, I don't."

"Why?"

"I believe it's precisely a heart he hasn't got."

The smile left Liza's face.

"You are in the habit of judging people harshly," she said after a lengthy pause.

"I don't think so. What right have I to judge people harshly, when I need indulgence myself? Or have you forgotten that I am a laughingstock?... Ah yes," he added, "did you keep your promise?"

"What promise?"

"Did you say a prayer for me?"

"Yes, I did, and I say a prayer for you every day. But do not make light of it please."

Lavretsky began to assure Liza that the idea of doing so was far from his mind, and that he had the deepest respect for other people's convictions; then he discoursed upon religion, its place in human history, the significance of Christianity. . . .

"One needs to be a Christian," began Liza, not without a slight effort, "not in order to perceive the divine ... and ... the earthly, but because every man must die."

Lavretsky looked up at Liza in surprise and met her gaze.

"What is that word you have just said?"

"That word is not mine," she replied.

"Not yours.... But what made you speak of death?"

"I don't know. I often think of it."

"Often?"

"Yes."

"One wouldn't believe it, looking at you now: you have such a bright, happy face, you are smiling. . . ."

"Yes, I feel very happy now," Liza answered artlessly.

Lavretsky felt an urge to seize both her hands and give them a hard squeeze. . . .

"Liza, Liza," cried Marya Dmitriyevna, "come here. Look at the carp I've caught!"

"I'm coming, *maman*," replied Liza and went up to her, leaving Lavretsky sitting on the willow. "I talk to her as though I had not lived my life already," he mused. Before going, Liza had hung her hat on a twig; Lavretsky gazed at the hat, at its long, slightly crumpled ribbons, with a strange almost affectionate emotion. Liza soon came back and took her place on the raft.

"Why do you think Vladimir Nikolaich has no heart?" she asked after several moments.

"I've told you that I may be mistaken; time will show, however."

Liza became lost in thought. Lavretsky started to talk about his life in Vassilyevskoye, about Mikhalevich,

Anton; he felt a need to talk to Liza, to tell her everything that was passing in his heart; she was such a charming, attentive listener; her rare remarks and observations seemed to him so simple and wise. He told her so.

Liza was astonished.

"Really?" she said. "And I was always under the impression that, like my maid Nastya, I had no words *of my own*. She once told her fiancé: 'You must find it dull with me; you always talk so nicely to me and I have no words of my own.'"

"And thank God for it!" thought Lavretsky.

XXVII

Meanwhile evening was drawing in, and Marya Dmitriyevna declared it was time to go home. The little girls had to be dragged away from the fish pond and were got ready. Lavretsky announced he would see the guests halfway down the road, and ordered his horse to be saddled. As he was handing Marya Dmitriyevna into the carriage, he suddenly remembered Lemm; but the old man was nowhere to be found. He had disappeared as soon as the fishing was over. Anton, with a vigour remarkable in one of his years, slammed the carriage doors and shouted sternly, "Off you go, coachman!" The carriage started off. The back seats were occupied by Marya Dmitriyevna and Liza, while the little girls and the maid sat in the front. It was a warm still evening and the windows on both sides were lowered. Lavretsky trotted abreast of the carriage on Liza's side, his hand resting on the door— he had dropped the reins on the neck of his smoothly pacing horse—and now and then exchanged a few words with the young girl. The glow of sunset had faded; night had fallen, but the air seemed to have grown warmer. Marya Dmitriyevna soon began to doze; the little girls and their maid too fell asleep. The carriage rolled along swiftly and smoothly; Liza leaned forward; the rising moon lighted up her face, the fragrant night breeze fanned her eyes and cheeks. She felt happy. Her hand rested on the carriage door next to Lavretsky's. And he was hap-

py too; carried swiftly along in the still warmth of the
night, never taking his eyes off the sweet young face, listening to the young voice whispering melodiously good
and simple things, he rode half the way before he was
aware of it. Not wishing to wake Marya Dmitriyevna, he
gave Liza's hand a light squeeze and said: "We're friends
now, aren't we?" She nodded; he brought his horse to a
stop. The carriage rolled away, swaying and bobbing up
and down; Lavretsky turned homeward at a walking pace.
The loveliness of the summer night entered his soul;
everything around him seemed so suddenly strange, and
yet so long and so sweetly familiar; a deep peace rested
over everything far and near—and one could see far although the eye could not fathom much of what it saw;
the very peace seemed to be alive with the spring tide
of youth. Lavretsky's horse stepped out briskly, swaying
gently from side to side; its long dark shadow moved
along beside it; there was something strangely fascinating in the tramp of its hoofs, something elating and allur-
ing in the ringing cry of the quails. The stars were lost
in a luminous haze; a crescent moon shone with a hard
radiance: its beams shed a blue lustre across the skies
and fell in patches of pearly gold on the filmy clouds drifting by; the crisp night air drew a film of moisture to the
eye, spread softly throughout the limbs and flowed freely
into the lungs. Lavretsky drank it all in with delight, and
he rejoiced in this delight. "We still have a shot in the
locker," he thought, "we'll show them. . . ." He did not
say who or what. . . . Then he fell to musing about Liza,
thinking that she could hardly be in love with Panshin,
that if he had met her under other circumstances—God
knows what might have happened; that he agreed with
Lemm, though she had no words "of her own". In any
case, that was not true—she did have words of her
own. . . . "Do not make light of it"—came back to Lavretsky's mind. He rode on a long while with his head bent
low, then drawing himself up he slowly pronounced:

And all that I worshipped I have burnt,
And all I have burnt I now worship. . . .

and whipping up his horse he galloped all the way home.

Dismounting, he took a last look round with an involuntary smile of gratitude. Night—kindly, silent night, lay over the hillsides and valleys; from afar, out of its perfumed depths—one could not say whether it was from heaven or earth—there stole a soft and gentle warmth. Lavretsky sent Liza a last silent greeting and ran up the steps.

The next day passed rather tediously. The morning started with a drizzle. Lemm wore a scowl and his lips compressed ever more tightly, as though he had taken an oath never to open them. On his way to bed Lavretsky took with him a batch of French periodicals, which had lain on his table unopened for more than two weeks. He casually broke open the wrappings and ran his eye down the columns of the newspapers, in which there was nothing new. He was on the point of putting them aside when he suddenly leaped out of bed as if he had been stung. In an article in one of the newspapers our old acquaintance, Monsieur Jules, imparted to his readers "sad news": the charming, fascinating Muscovite Lady, he wrote, one of the queens of fashion, who adorned Parisian salons, *Madame de Lavretzki* had died almost suddenly, and the tidings thereof—alack, too true—had just reached his, M. Jules' ears. He was—he went on—a friend of the deceased, one might say. . . .

Lavretsky dressed and went out into the garden; morning found him still pacing up and down the same path.

XXVIII

The next morning, over their tea, Lemm asked Lavretsky to let him have the horses to go back to town. "It's time I started work, that is, my lessons," said the old man, "I'm merely wasting my time here." Lavretsky did not reply at once; he appeared abstracted. "All right," he said at length, "I'll go with you myself." Grunting and irate, Lemm packed his small suitcase without the servants' aid, and tore up and burnt some sheets of music paper. The horses were harnessed. As he came out of his

room Lavretsky slipped into his pocket the newspaper
with M. Jules' article. Lemm and Lavretsky spoke very
little all the way, each was preoccupied with his own
thoughts and glad the other did not disturb him. They
parted rather coolly, too, which is often the case, by the
way, among friends in Russia. Lavretsky drove the old
man to his little house; the latter got out, took his suitcase, and without offering his friend his hand (he held
his luggage in both hands against his chest), without even
looking at him, said in Russian: "Goodbye!" "Goodbye,"
repeated Lavretsky, and told the coachman to take him
to his rooms. He had taken rooms in town in case of need.
After writing some letters and partaking of a hasty
meal, Lavretsky went to the Kalitins. In the drawing
room he found only Panshin, who told him that Marya
Dmitriyevna would soon be coming out and forthwith
entered into conversation with him with the most engaging
cordiality. Until that day Panshin had treated Lavretsky
condescendingly, if not patronisingly; but Liza, in relating to Panshin her visit to Lavretsky, had spoken of him
as an excellent and intelligent man; that was enough: he
had to win over that "excellent" man. Panshin launched
out with compliments, describing how delighted Marya
Dmitriyevna's entire family was with Vassilyevskoye, and
then, as was his wont, passed glibly to his own person,
began to talk about his pursuits, expounded his views on
life, the world and government service, passed a few ut-
terances on the future of Russia, opining that the provincial governors should be kept well in hand; made some
bantering remarks at his own expense, adding that, by
the way, he had been intrusted in St. Petersburg with the
task *de populariser l'idée du cadastre.* He spoke at great
length, solving all difficulties with nonchalant self-assurance, juggling with weighty administrative and political problems as if they were so many balls.

Expressions such as: "That's what I would do if I
were the government"; "You, as a man of intelligence,
will readily agree with me" were for ever on his tongue.
Lavretsky listened coldly to Panshin's grandiloquence: he
did not like this handsome, clever, debonair young man
with his illuminating smile, suave voice and prying eyes.

Panshin, who was quick of apprehension, soon guessed
that his interlocutor was not deriving any particular pleasure from his discourse, and slipped out on some plausible
excuse, deciding in his own mind that Lavretsky might
be an excellent man, but he was cross-grained, *aigri,* and
en somme rather ridiculous. Marya Dmitriyevna made
her appearance attended by Gedeonovsky; then Marfa
Timofeyevna and Liza came in, followed later on by the
rest of the household; later arrived the music-loving
Madame Belenitsyna, a slight little lady with a childishly
pretty tired-looking face, wearing a rustling black gown
and heavy gold bracelets and with a gaudy fan in her
hand; there was her husband too, a chubby florid man with
big feet and hands, pale eyelashes and a set smile on his
thick lips; his wife never spoke to him in public, but at
home, in tender moods, called him her little piggy; Panshin returned; the rooms were full of people and noise.
Such a crowd was not to Lavretsky's taste; he was especially irritated by Belenitsyna who kept staring at him
through her lorgnette. He would have gone away at once
if not for Liza: he wanted to say a word to her in private,
but for a long time could not find an opportune moment,
and had to content himself with following her in secret
delight with his eyes; never had her face looked sweeter
and more noble to him. She showed up to advantage
beside Belenitsyna. The latter was constantly wriggling
in her chair, shrugging her narrow little shoulders, sim-
pering demurely, now narrowing her eyes and then suddenly dilating them. Liza sat still, she looked people
squarely in the face and did not laugh at all. The hostess
sat down to a game of cards with Marfa Timofeyevna,
Belenitsyna and Gedeonovsky, who played a lingering
game, continuously made blunders, blinked his eyes and
mopped his face with a handkerchief. Panshin wore a
melancholy look, expressed himself drily, in gloomy tones
pregnant with meaning—for all the world like a thwarted
genius—but despite the entreaties of Madame Belenitsyna
who flirted with him outrageously, he refused to sing his
song: he felt constrained by Lavretsky's presence. Fyodor
Ivanych spoke little too; the odd look on his face struck
Liza as soon as she saw him: she had a feeling that he

had something to tell her, but was afraid to ask him, she knew not why. At last, as she was going into the next room to pour out tea, she involuntarily turned her head in his direction. He immediately followed her out.

"What is the matter with you?" she said, setting the teapot on the samovar.

"Why, have you noticed anything?" he asked.

"You are not the same today you usually are."

Lavretsky bent over the table.

"I have been wanting," he said, "to tell you a piece of news, but it's impossible now. However, you can read the paragraph marked off here in this article," he added, handing her the newspaper he had brought with him. "Please keep this a secret; I will come tomorrow morning."

Liza was mystified. . . . Panshin appeared in the doorway. She tucked the newspaper into her pocket.

"Have you read *Obermann,* Elizaveta Mikhailovna?" Panshin enquired in a pensive voice.

Liza murmured something and went upstairs. Lavretsky returned to the drawing room and went up to the card table. Marfa Timofeyevna, flushed with annoyance, her cap strings fluttering loose, complained to him of her partner, Gedeonovsky, who, she said, was good for nothing.

"Playing cards, you see," she said, "is not so simple as talebearing."

The delinquent continued to blink and wipe his face. Liza came in and sat down in a corner; Lavretsky looked at her and she looked at him—and both felt almost awestruck. He read perplexity and a kind of secret reproach in her face. He could not speak to her, however much he wanted to; to remain with her in the same room as a mere guest among other guests was too painful: he decided to go away. As he took leave of her he managed to repeat that he would come tomorrow, and added that he trusted in her friendship.

"Come," she answered with the same look of perplexity on her face.

Panshin livened up when Lavretsky had gone; he started to give Gedeonovsky advice, paid ironical attention to Madame Belenitsyna and finally sang his song. But with

Liza he still spoke and looked as before—meaningly and
a little sadly.

Again Lavretsky did not sleep all night; he was not
sad, neither was he disturbed, he was all quiescent; but
he could not sleep. He did not even recall memories of
the past; he simply gazed into what had been his life;
his heart beat heavily and measuredly; the hours slipped
by, but he did not think of sleep. At times the thought
flashed through his mind: "It isn't true, it's all nonsense"
—and then he would stop, bow his head, and again
begin to review his life.

XXIX

Marya Dmitriyevna was none too cordial when Lavretsky called the next morning. "Upon my word, he's made
a habit of coming," she thought. She did not care much
for him as it was, and Panshin, under whose influence she
was, had very insidiously dropped a perfunctory word in
his praise the night before. As she did not consider him
a guest, and did not think it necessary to entertain a relation, almost one of the family, it came about that in less
than half an hour he was walking with Liza in an avenue
in the grounds. Lenochka and Shurochka were running
about within a few paces of them in the flower garden.

Liza was calm as usual, but more than usually pale.
She took out of her pocket the sheet of newspaper folded
up small and handed it to Lavretsky.

"It is terrible!" she said.

Lavretsky did not reply.

"But perhaps it isn't true after all," added Liza.

"That is why I asked you not to mention it to anyone."

Liza walked on a little.

"Tell me," she began, "aren't you distressed? Not at
all?"

"I don't know myself what I feel," said Lavretsky.

"But you loved her before, didn't you?"

"Yes."

"Very much?"

"Yes."

"And you are not distressed at her death?"

"She died for me before this."

"What you say is sinful.... Don't be angry with me. You call me your friend—a friend may say everything. I really feel awful about it.... I didn't like the look you had on your face yesterday.... Do you remember complaining against her the other day?—and she perhaps was dead at the time. It is dreadful. It is as though a punishment had been visited on you."

Lavretsky smiled bitterly.

"Do you think so? At any rate I am free now."

Liza shuddered.

"Please, do not talk like that. Of what use is your freedom to you? You should not be thinking of that now, but of forgiveness...."

"I forgave her long ago," broke in Lavretsky with a deprecatory wave of the hand.

"No, not that," replied Liza flushing. "You misunderstand me. You should be seeking forgiveness...."

"From whom?"

"From God. Who can forgive us if not God?"

Lavretsky seized her hand.

"Ah, Elizaveta Mikhailovna, believe me," he cried, "I have been punished enough as it is. I have atoned for everything, believe me."

"You cannot be sure of that," said Liza in a low voice, "you have forgotten quite recently, when you were talking with me—you were not ready to forgive her...."

They walked on in silence.

"How about your daughter?" Liza asked suddenly, coming to a standstill.

Lavretsky started.

"Oh, you needn't worry! I have sent letters out in all directions. The future of my daughter, as you call ... as you say ... is provided for. Don't worry."

Liza smiled ruefully.

"But you are right," went on Lavretsky, "of what use is my freedom to me? What good is it to me?"

"When did you receive that newspaper?" said Liza, without replying to his question.

"The day after your visit."

"And do you mean ... do you mean to say you did not even shed a tear?"

"No. I was dumbfounded; and where were tears to come from? To cry over the past, when it has all been burned out of my heart? Her misdemeanour did not destroy my happiness, it merely showed me that it never existed. What was there to cry over? Ah well, who knows?—perhaps I might have been more grieved had I received this news a fortnight earlier...."

"A fortnight?" queried Liza. "What could have happened in the last fortnight?"

Lavretsky made no reply, and Liza suddenly coloured deeply.

"Yes, yes, you have guessed," Lavretsky cried suddenly, "during that fortnight I have come to know the value of a pure woman's heart, and my past has receded still further from me...."

Liza was embarrassed and walked slowly towards the flower beds where Lenochka and Shurochka were playing.

"I'm glad I showed you that newspaper," said Lavretsky walking after her. "I've got into the habit of concealing nothing from you, and I hope you will repay me with the same confidence."

"Do you think so?" murmured Liza, stopping. "In that case I should ... but no! That's impossible!..."

"What is it? Tell me, tell me."

"Really, I don't think I ought to.... Well," she added, turning to Lavretsky with a smile, "what's the good of half confidences? Do you know, I received a letter today?"

"From Panshin?"

"Yes.... How did you know?"

"He has proposed to you?"

"Yes," replied Liza, and looked Lavretsky straight and seriously in the eyes.

Lavretsky in turn looked seriously at Liza.

"Well, and what answer did you give him?" he brought out at last.

"I do not know what to answer," replied Liza, letting her clasped hands fall to her sides.

"Why? You love him, don't you?"

"Yes, I like him; he seems to be a nice man."

"You said the same thing in the same words three days ago. What I want to know is, do you love him with that intense passionate feeling we are accustomed to call love?"

"As *you* understand it—no."

"You are not in love with him?"

"No. But is that essential?"

"What!"

"Mamma likes him," went on Liza, "he is kind; I don't see anything objectionable in him."

"Yet you hesitate?"

"Yes . . . and perhaps—because of you, because of what you said. Do you remember what you said the day before yesterday? But this is weakness. . . ."

"O my child!" cried Lavretsky and his voice shook. "Do not play at cross purposes, do not call weakness what is really the cry of your heart, that does not want to give itself without love. Do not take upon yourself such a fearful responsibility to this man you do not love and to whom you wish to belong. . . ."

"I do what I'm told, I take nothing upon myself," Liza started to say.

"Do what your heart dictates; it alone will tell you the truth," broke in Lavretsky. "Experience, reason—all that is dust and ashes, idle show! Do not deprive yourself of the greatest, the only happiness this world contains."

"And you say that, Fyodor Ivanych? You yourself married for love—and were you happy?"

Lavretsky threw up his hands.

"Oh, don't talk about me! You simply can't understand what a young, guileless, atrociously brought up boy can mistake for love!... Besides why should I be unfair to myself? I told you just now that I did not know what happiness was.... It's not true! I was happy!"

"I think, Fyodor Ivanych," said Liza in a low voice (when she disagreed with a person she had a habit of dropping her voice; in addition, she was greaty agitated), "that happiness on earth does not depend on us. . . ."

"But it does, it does, believe me" (he gripped her hands in his; Liza turned pale and looked at him with something akin to fear, but unflinchingly) "as long as we don't ruin our own lives. For some people a love match may be a misfortune; but not for you, with your steady character, your pure heart! I beseech you, do not marry without love, merely from a sense of duty, self-sacrifice, or anything of that kind. . . . It is no better than lack of faith, it is as bad as a marriage of convenience, even worse. Believe me—I have the right to say so: I've paid dearly for this right. And if your God. . . ."

Here Lavretsky suddenly became aware that Lenochka and Shurochka were standing near Liza and staring at him agape. He let go of Liza's hands, saying hurriedly: "I beg your pardon," and turned towards the house.

"One thing only I beg of you," he said, coming back again, "do not make a hasty decision, wait a bit, think over what I have told you. Even if you do not believe me, even if you did decide on a marriage of convenience— you mustn't marry Panshin—he can't be your husband. . . . You promise not to be in a hurry, don't you?"

Liza wanted to answer Lavretsky, but she did not utter a word—not because she had made up her mind "to be in a hurry", but because her heart beat too violently and a feeling akin to terror took her breath away.

XXX

As he was leaving the Kalitins, Lavretsky encountered Panshin; they bowed coldly to each other.

Lavretsky went to his rooms and shut himself in. He was in the grip of emotions he had hardly ever experienced before. Was it so very long ago that he had been in a state of "peaceful stupor"? Had struck bottom, as he had expressed it? What had changed his position? What had brought him up to the surface? A very ordinary, inevitable, though always unexpected contingency—death? Yes; but he was thinking not so much of his wife's death or of his own freedom, as of what answer Liza would give Panshin. He felt that in the last three days he had come to regard her with different eyes; he remembered how, returning home and thinking of her in the silence of the night, he had said to himself: "If only!. . ." That "if only", which he had applied to the past, the unattainable, had now come to pass, though not as he had envisaged it,—but his freedom alone was not all. "She will obey her mother," he thought, "she will marry Panshin; but even if she does refuse him—what difference will it make to me?" Passing the mirror he glanced at his face and shrugged his shoulders.

The day passed quickly in such ruminations; evening set in. Lavretsky went to the Kalitins. He walked with a hurried step, but his pace slackened as he neared the house. Panshin's droshky stood before the porch. "Come," thought Lavretsky, "I mustn't be an egoist," and he went into the house. He encountered nobody indoors, and there was no sound in the drawing room; he opened the door and saw Marya Dmitriyevna playing picquet with Panshin. Panshin bowed to him in silence, and the hostess exclaimed: "Well, this is unexpected!" and frowned slightly. Lavretsky sat down near her and began to look at her cards.

"Why, do you play picquet?" she asked him in a tone of veiled annoyance, and promptly declared that she had played a wrong hand.

Panshin made a count of ninety and began calmly and politely taking tricks with a sedate and dignified countenance. So might diplomats play; probably this was the way he played in St. Petersburg with some high dignitary in whom he wanted to create a favourable impression of his solidity and matureness. "A hundred and one, a hundred and two, hearts, a hundred and three," his voice droned in measured tones, and Lavretsky could not make out whether it had a ring of reproach in it or self-satisfaction.

"Can I see Marfa Timofeyevna?" he enquired seeing that Panshin was about to reshuffle with an air of still greater majesty. Not a vestige of the artist was visible in him now.

"I think so. She is in her room upstairs," replied Marya Dmitriyevna. "You may enquire."

Lavretsky went upstairs. He found Marfa Timofeyevna at cards too: she was playing Old Maid with Nastasya Karpovna. Roska barked at him; but both the old ladies were delighted to see him; Marfa Timofeyevna especially seemed in excellent spirits.

"Ah, Fedya! Welcome!" she cried. "Pray, sit down, my dear. We'll just finish this game. Do you want some jam? Shurochka, get him out the jar of strawberry. Won't you have any? Well, stay as you are; but don't smoke, please; I can't stand your horrid tobacco, and it makes Matross sneeze."

Lavretsky hastened to assure her that he did not have the least desire to smoke.

"Have you been downstairs?" continued the old lady. "Who's there? Is Panshin still hanging around? Did you see Liza? No? She wanted to come here. . . . Why, here she is— talk of angels."

Liza came into the room and, at sight of Lavretsky, she blushed.

"I have just come for a moment, Marfa Timofeyevna," she began. . . .

"Why for a moment?" interposed the old lady. "Why are all you young maids such a flighty lot? You see I have a visitor—sit down and chat with him, entertain him."

Liza seated herself on the edge of a chair, looked up at Lavretsky—and felt that she must tell him the result of her interview with Panshin. But how was she to do it? She felt both embarrassed and ashamed. She had not known him long, this man who seldom went to church and who took his wife's death so calmly—and here she was confiding her secrets to him. . . . True, he took an interest in her; she herself trusted him and was attracted to him; and yet she felt ashamed, as though a stranger had walked into her pure maiden's bower. Marfa Timofeyevna came to the rescue.

"Unless you entertain him," she said, "who will, poor fellow? I'm too old for him, he's too clever for me and too old for Nastasya Karpovna—she'll only be content with the young ones."

"What can I do to entertain Fyodor Ivanych?" said

Liza. "If he likes I can play him something on the piano," she added irresolutely.

"Splendid; that's a clever girl," said Marfa Timofeyevna. "Go downstairs, my dears; when you're finished, come back; I've gone and been left Old Maid; it's a shame, I must get my revenge."

Liza rose to her feet. Lavretsky followed her out. Descending the staircase, Liza stopped.

"It is rightly said," she began, "that the human heart is full of contradictions. Your example should have daunted me, make me distrust marriage for love, but I. . . ."

"You've refused him?" broke in Lavretsky.

"No; but I haven't consented either. I told him everything, all that I felt, and asked him to wait. Are you satisfied?" she added with a quick smile, and touching the banister lightly with her hand ran down the stairs.

"What do you want me to play?" she asked, lifting the lid of the piano.

"Whatever you like," replied Lavretsky, sitting down so that he could see her.

Liza began to play and for a long while did not take her eyes off her fingers. At length she glanced up at Lavretsky and stopped playing—his face seemed to her so strange and striking.

"What is the matter with you?" she asked.

"Nothing," he retorted, "I feel very happy; I'm glad for your sake, I'm glad to see you—please go on."

"It seems to me," said Liza after a pause, "that if he really loved me he would not have written that letter; he should have felt that I could not give him an answer now."

"That's not important," observed Lavretsky, "what is important is that you do not love him."

"Don't! How can we talk like this! I keep thinking of your dead wife, and you terrify me."

"Don't you think, Woldemar, my Lizette plays charmingly?" Marya Dmitriyevna was saying to Panshin.

"Yes," said Panshin, "very charmingly indeed."

Marya Dmitriyevna threw a tender glance at her young partner, but the latter put on a still more momentous and preoccupied air and called fourteen kings.

XXXI

Lavretsky was not a young man; he could not long remain under any illusion as to the feeling he entertained for Liza; he realised finally that day that he loved her. He was not elated at the thought. "Couldn't I think of anything better to do," he communed with himself, "at thirty-five years of age than to be delivering my soul again into a woman's keeping? But Liza is not like *her*; she would not demand degrading sacrifices; she would not divert me from my studies; she would herself inspire me to hard and honest toil, and we would go hand in hand towards a noble goal. Yes," he wound up his reflections, "that's all very well, but the trouble is she hasn't the least desire to go with me. Didn't she say that I terrify her? But she doesn't love Panshin either.... A poor consolation!"

Lavretsky went back to Vassilyevskoye; but he could not stand more than four days of it there—so tedious did it seem to him. He was, moreover, in a state of suspense: the news announced by M. Jules required corroboration, and he had not received any letters. He returned to town and spent the evening at the Kalitins'. It was not difficult for him to notice that Marya Dmitriyevna regarded him with disfavour; but he managed to appease her a little by losing fifteen rubles to her at a game of picquet— and he spent about a half hour almost alone with Liza, despite her mother's admonition the previous evening not to be too familiar with a person—*qui a un si grand ridicule.* He found a change in her—she seemed to be more meditative; she chided him for his absence and enquired whether he would not go on the morrow to Mass (the next day was Sunday).

"Do go," she said, before he could reply, "we will say a prayer together for the peace of *her* soul." Then she added that she did not know what to do—whether she had the right to keep Panshin waiting for her decision any longer.

"Why?" asked Lavretsky.

"Because," she said, "I now have a feeling what that decision will be."

She complained of a headache, and irresolutely holding out the tips of her fingers to Lavretsky, went upstairs to her room.

The following day Lavretsky went to Mass.

Liza was already in the church when he arrived. She noticed him, though she did not turn her head. She prayed fervently, her eyes shone with a gentle light and softly she bowed and lifted her head. He had a feeling that she was praying for him too—and his soul was thrilled with an ineffable tenderness. He was at once happy and a little remorseful. The people standing sedately around, the dear familiar faces, the solemn chanting, the smell of incense, the long slanting rays of light falling from the windows, the very gloom of the walls and vaulted roof—all this touched his heart. It was a long time since he had been to church, it was long since he had communed with God: even now he uttered no words of prayer—he did not pray even without words—but, for a brief moment, with all his soul, if not his body, he prostrated himself in humble homage to the ground. He remembered how in his childhood he had prayed so long in church until he could feel, as it were, a cool touch on his brow: that, he used to think, is the guardian angel receiving me, placing on me the seal of grace. He looked at Liza.... "Thou hast brought me here," he thought, "touch me, touch my soul." She was still praying softly; her face seemed to him filled with joy; his heart swelled once more with tenderness, and he prayed for peace for another soul and forgiveness for his own....

They met outside on the porch; she greeted him with a look of sunny and tender gravity. The sun threw a bright radiance over the young grass in the churchyard and the gay dresses and kerchiefs of the womenfolk; the bells of neighbouring churches pealed on the air; sparrows twittered on the hedges; Lavretsky stood bareheaded, a smile on his face; a gentle breeze played with the strands of his hair and the ribbons of Liza's hat. He helped Liza and Lenochka, who was with her, into their carriage, gave away all his money to the poor and slowly wended his way homeward.

XXXII

Hard days set in for Fyodor Ivanych. He was in a constant state of fever. Every morning he went himself to the post office, impatiently tore open letters and wrappers, but found nothing either to confirm or disprove the fateful rumour. At times he would be disgusted with himself: "Here am I," he thought, "waiting like a vulture for blood, for certain news of my wife's death!" He called on the Kalitins every day; but there too he felt no easier: the mistress obviously sulked at him, received him out of condescension; Panshin treated him with exaggerated courtesy; Lemm affected an air of misanthropy and barely nodded to him, and worst of all—Liza seemed to be shunning him. When she happened to be left alone with him she was in a state of confusion where she had been all trustfulness before; she was at a loss what to say to him, and he felt embarrassed, too. In the space of a few days Liza had become quite different from what he had known her—there was a lurking anxiety, a hitherto unwonted tremulousness in her movements, her voice, in her very laugh. Marya Dmitriyevna, wrapped up as she was in herself, suspected nothing; but Marfa Timofeyevna began to keep an observant eye on her favourite. Lavretsky more than once regretted having shown Liza the newspaper: he could not help being aware that there was something offensive in his state of mind to a pure nature. He also believed that the change in Liza was due to her inner conflict, her doubts as to what answer to give Panshin. Once she brought him a book, a novel of Walter Scott's, which she had asked him to lend her.

"Have you read it?" he asked.

"No, I'm not in a mood for reading just now," she replied, turning to go away.

"Wait a minute: I haven't been alone with you for such a long time. One would think you're afraid of me."

"I am."

"Good heavens, why?"

"I don't know."

Lavretsky said nothing.

"Tell me," he resumed, "have you made up your mind yet?"

"What do you mean?" she said, her eyes downcast.

"You know what I mean. . . ."

Liza suddenly flushed.

"Oh, don't ask me," she broke out warmly, "I don't know anything; I don't even know myself. . . ."

And she was gone.

The next day Lavretsky arrived at the Kalitins' after dinner and found preparations in progress for vespers.

In a corner of the dining room, on a square table covered with a clean cloth small holy images in gilt frames with small tarnished jewels in the nimbus stood leaning up against the wall. An old serving man in a grey frock coat and shoes walked slowly and noiselessly across the room, set two wax candles in the slender candlesticks before the icons, crossed himself, bowed, and quietly left the room. The unlighted drawing room was empty. Lavretsky walked about the dining room and enquired whether it was anybody's Saint's Day. He was told in a whisper that no, vespers was to be held at the desire of Elizaveta Mikhailovna and Marfa Timofeyevna; that it had been intended to bring down a wonder-working icon, but it was away ministering to a sick man thirty versts from here. Soon the priest arrived with the deacons. He was a middle-aged man with a large bald patch, and coughed loudly in the hall; the ladies came filing slowly out of the sitting room and went up to receive his blessing; Lavretsky bowed to them in silence and they returned his bow in silence. The priest tarried a while, coughed once more and enquired in a deep-chested undertone:

"Shall we begin?"

"Please begin, father," said Marya Dmitriyevna.

He started to don his robes. A deacon in a surplice asked in an unctuous voice for a hot ember; a scent of incense arose. Maidservants and menservants came in from the hall and huddled before the door. Roska, who had never been downstairs before, suddenly darted into the dining room: they began shooing her out, but she got scared, began to scurry hither and thither and suddenly sat down in her tracks; a footman picked her up

and carried her off. The service began. Lavretsky snuggled into a corner; his emotions were strange, almost sad;
he could not quite make out what it was he felt. Marya
Dmitriyevna stood in the forefront, before the chairs; she
crossed herself with languid ladylike nonchalance, ever
and anon glancing around and then suddenly lifting her
eyes ceilingward: she was bored. Marfa Timofeyevna
looked anxious; Nastasya Karpovna bowed low to the
ground and got up with a discreet kind of rustle; Liza
stood as if rooted to the spot, without stirring; the rapt
expression of her face alone betrayed that she was praying steadfastly and fervidly. When kissing the cross at the
end of the service she likewise kissed the large red
hand of the priest. Marya Dmitriyevna invited the priest
to tea; he doffed his vestments, assumed a secular air and
crossed to the drawing room with the ladies. A subdued
conversation began. The priest drank four cups of tea,
incessantly mopping his bald head with his handkerchief,
and related, by the way, that Avoshnikov, the merchant,
had made a donation of seven hundred rubles for gilding
the "cumpola" of the church, and imparted a reliable remedy for freckles.

Lavretsky contrived a seat near Liza, but she held
herself rigidly, almost severely aloof and never glanced
at him once. She seemed to be deliberately ignoring him;
a kind of cold and solemn fervour appeared to have taken
possession of her. Lavretsky felt an inexplicable urge to
smile and say something amusing; but there was perplexity in his heart, and he finally went away mystified. . . .
He felt that there was something in Liza which he could
not penetrate.

On another occasion Lavretsky was sitting in the drawing room listening to the specious yarns of Gedeonovsky,
when suddenly, he could not say why, he turned his head
and intercepted an intent questioning look in Liza's eyes. . . .
It was bent on him, that enigmatic look. Lavretsky thought
of it the whole night long. His love was not like a boy's, it
was not befitting for him to sigh and pine, and Liza herself did not inspire emotions of that kind; but love has
its tortures for every age—and he was spared none of
them.

XXXIII

One day Lavretsky, as was his wont, was at the Kalitins'. After a sultry day such a lovely evening had set in that Marya Dmitriyevna, despite her aversion to draughts, ordered all the windows and doors into the garden to be opened, and declared she would not play cards because it was a shame to play in such weather when one should be enjoying nature. Panshin was the only guest. Stimulated by the beauty of the evening and conscious of a flow of artistic sensations, but not caring to sing before Lavretsky, he chose to read some poetry: he recited well, but not too intelligently and with unnecessary finesse, some poems of Lermontov's (Pushkin had not yet made his return to fashion) and then, as though suddenly ashamed of his effusions, began, apropos of the well-known poem *A Reverie,* to reprove and impugn the younger generation; he did not lose an opportunity to prove how he would change everything his own way if he had the power. "Russia," he said, "has fallen behind Europe; we must catch up with her. It is claimed that we are young—that's nonsense; what we lack is an inventive capacity; K—v himself admits that we did not even invent the mousetrap. Consequently, we must perforce borrow from others. We are sick, says Lermontov,—I agree with him; but we are sick because we have only half become Europeans; our only cure was a hair of the dog ... ("le cadastre" thought Lavretsky). The best intellects among us, *les meilleures têtes,*" he went on, "have long been convinced of that; all nations are essentially alike; simply introduce good institutions and the deed's done. I daresay things could be adjusted to prevailing national customs; that's our business, the business of state ... (he very nearly said 'statesmen')—of public officers; but, if need be, you needn't worry—the institutions themselves will remake the national customs." Marya Dmitriyevna nodded her head complaisantly at everything he said. "There," she thought, "what a clever man is holding forth in my drawing room." Liza sat in silence, leaning against the window; Lavretsky too was silent; Marfa Timofeyevna, who was playing cards in the corner with her companion, mut-

tered something to herself. Panshin paced up and down
the room and spoke fluently but in a tone of secret exasperation: he seemed to be upbraiding not a whole generation, but several people of his acquaintance. The first
evening notes of a nightingale that had made its nest in
a large lilac bush in the Kalitins' garden filled the pauses
of his oration; the first stars lit up in the rose-tinted sky
over the motionless tops of the limes. Lavretsky rose and
began to remonstrate with Panshin; a dispute sprang up.
Lavretsky championed the youth and independence of Russia; he was ready to immolate himself and his generation,
but he stood up for the new men, their convictions and
their aspirations; Panshin retorted irritably and sharply,
maintained that intelligent people should change everything, and let himself go to a point when, mindless of his
Kammerjunker status and official career, he called Lavretsky an antiquated conservative, and even hinted—true,
very remotely—at the dubious position he occupied in
society. Lavretsky did not lose his temper, nor did he raise
his voice (it came back to him that Mikhalevich had also
called him antiquated—but a Voltairean); and he coolly
defeated Panshin on all points. He proved to him the im-
practicability of changing things at a bound, of changes
from above born in the overweening minds of official-
dom, justified neither by a knowledge of the mother country nor a genuine faith in an ideal, even a negative one;
he cited his own education, demanded first and foremost
a recognition of the popular wisdom in a spirit of abase-
ment—a spirit without which hardihood cannot challenge error; finally, he did not waive the reproach, which
he considered merited, of reckless waste of time and
energy.

"That's all very well!" exclaimed Panshin, who was
by this time thoroughly annoyed, "now that you've come
back to Russia—what do you intend to do?"

"Plough the land," replied Lavretsky, "and try to
plough it as well as possible."

"Very commendable, no doubt," rejoined Panshin.
"I've been told you have been very successful in that direction; but you must allow that not everybody is fitted
for that kind of pursuit. . . ."

"*Une nature poétique*," threw in Marya Dmitriyevna, "certainly cannot plough the land ... *et puis* it is your vocation, Vladimir Nikolaich, to do everything *en grand*."

This was too much even for Panshin: he looked crestfallen and changed the subject. He tried to turn the talk on the beauty of the starry sky, the music of Schubert—but the conversation flagged; he finally proposed to Marya Dmitriyevna a game of picquet. "What! On such a night?" she remonstrated feebly, but nevertheless ordered the cards to be brought in.

Panshin broke open a new pack with a loud snap, while Liza and Lavretsky, as though of one accord, got up and sat down near Marfa Timofeyevna. They both felt suddenly so happy, that they were even a little afraid of remaining alone together—they were also aware that the embarrassment of the last few days had vanished never to return. The old lady patted Lavretsky stealthily on the cheek, winked slyly, nodded her head several times and said in a whisper: "You have brought that wiseacre down a peg, thanks." A hush descended on the room; the only sound was the faint crackling of the wax candles and the occasional tap of a hand on the table, an exclamation or a count of score—and the song of the nightingale, audaciously loud and sweet, poring in a cascade through the open casement together with the dewy coolness of the night.

XXXIV

Liza had not spoken a word during the dispute between Lavretsky and Panshin, but had followed it closely and was all for Lavretsky. For politics she had very little interest; but the supercilious tone of the worldly official (he had never let himself go like that before) repelled her; his contempt for Russia shocked her. It had never entered Liza's mind that she was a patriot; but she felt at home with Russian people; the Russian habit of mind delighted her; she would unassumingly talk for hours on end with the peasant overseer of her mother's estate when he came to town, and talk to him as an equal, without a trace of superiority. Lavretsky felt all this: he would not have bothered to answer Panshin himself; what he had said was meant for Liza alone. They had not spoken to each other, their eyes had rarely met; but both of them realised that they had become close-knit that evening, that they liked and disliked the same things. On one point only were they at variance, but Liza cherished a secret hope to bring him to God. They sat beside Marfa Timofeyevna and seemed to be following the game; they were indeed following the game—but meanwhile their hearts beat high within them, and nothing was lost on them: for them it was the nightingale sang and the stars shone and the trees whispered softly as if lulled by summer's languor and warmth. Lavretsky gave himself up entirely to the feeling that flooded his soul—and rejoiced in it; but no word can convey what was passing in the pure heart of the maiden: it was a mystery to herself; let it then remain a mystery for all. No one knows, nobody has ever seen nor will ever see how the seed, born to live and flower, swells and ripens in the bosom of the earth.

Ten o'clock struck. Marfa Timofeyevna went upstairs with Nastasya Karpovna; Lavretsky and Liza crossed the room, stood at the open door leading into the garden, looked out into the darkness, then at one another, and smiled; they had a feeling like taking hands and talking to their heart's content. They went back to Marya Dmitriyevna and Panshin who had not yet finished their game of picquet. At length the last king was called, and the hostess rose sighing and groaning from her cushions in the easy chair; Panshin took his hat, kissed Marya Dmitriyevna's hand, observed that some people were lucky to go to sleep if they wanted or enjoy the lovely night whereas he had to sit up till morning over some stupid papers, bowed coldly to Liza (he had not expected to be asked to wait when he made his proposal—and was therefore cross with her) and left the house. Lavretsky followed him. They parted at the gate. Panshin waked his coachman by poking the end of his stick into his neck, took his seat and rode off. Lavretsky did not feel like going home: he walked into the open country, leaving the town behind him. The night was quiet and clear, though moonless; Lavretsky wandered for a long time through the dewy grass; he came across a narrow path; he took it; it led him up to a long fence, to a wicket; he pushed it, half unwittingly; the gate creaked and swung open, as though it had been expecting the touch of his hand. Lavretsky found himself in a garden, took several paces up a lime avenue and suddenly came to a stop in astonishment: he recognised the Kalitins' garden.

He quickly stepped into the dark shadows of a hazel clump and stood a long time without stirring, wondering and shrugging his shoulders.

"This is not mere chance!" he thought.

All was hushed around; not a sound reached him from the house. He walked on cautiously. At a bend in the avenue the whole house suddenly came into view; all was in darkness save for a glimmer of light in two upper windows: in Liza's room a candle was burning behind a white curtain, and in Marfa Timofeyevna's bedroom a little lamp glowed red before the icon casting a soft sheen on the gilded frame; below, the door leading onto the balcony gaped wide open. Lavretsky sat down on a wooden garden seat, propped his face in his hand and gazed at the door and at Liza's window. A clock in town struck the hour of midnight; a little clock in the house shrilly tinkled twelve; the night watchman played a tattoo on his board. Lavretsky thought of nothing, expected nothing; he was glad to feel himself near Liza, to sit in her garden, on the seat she had sat on many a time.... The light in Liza's room vanished. "Good night, my dearest girl," whispered Lavretsky, without stirring from his seat, his eyes fastened on the darkened window.

A light suddenly appeared in a window of the ground floor, moved to another, then to a third.... Somebody was walking through the rooms with a candle. "Can it be Liza? Impossible!" Lavretsky rose from his seat.... He caught a glimpse of a well-known face—Liza came into the drawing room. In a white gown, with braided tresses hanging over her shoulders, she stepped quietly up to the table, bent over it, put down the candle and began looking for something; then turning her face towards the garden she approached the open door and stood on the threshold, a slim white-clad figure. Lavretsky shivered violently.

"Liza!" an almost inaudible whisper broke from his lips.

She started and peered into the darkness.

"Liza!" repeated Lavretsky more loudly and came out of the shadows.

Liza thrust her neck out in alarm and recoiled. She had recognised him. He called her a third time and stretched out his arms to her. She came away from the door and stepped into the garden.

"You?" she murmured, "You here?"

"I ... I ... hear me out," whispered Lavretsky, and grasping her hand he led her to the seat.

She followed him unresistingly; the pallor of her face, her fixed gaze, her every gesture expressed unutterable astonishment. Lavretsky made her sit down and stood facing her.

"I did not think of coming here," he began, "I was drawn ... I ... I ... I love you," he uttered in involuntary dismay.

Liza looked up at him slowly; she seemed only now to have become aware of where she was and what was taking place. She wanted to get up, could not, and buried her face in her hands.

"Liza," murmured Lavretsky, "Liza," he repeated, and went down on his knees at her feet. . . .

A slight tremor shook her shoulders, the fingers of her pale hands pressed still closer to her face.

"What is the matter?" murmured Lavretsky, and he heard a subdued sob. His heart beat madly. . . He knew the meaning of those tears. "Can it be that you love me?" he whispered, and touched her knees.

"Get up," he heard her say, "get up, Fyodor Ivanych. What are we doing?"

He got up and sat down beside her. She was no longer weeping and regarded him attentively with her wet eyes.

"I'm frightened; what are we doing?" she faltered.

"I love you," he murmured once more; "I am prepared to give all my life to you."

She shuddered again as if she had been stung, and lifted her eyes to the heavens.

"It is all in God's hands," she said.

"But you love me, Liza? We shall be happy?"

She dropped her eyes; he drew her gently to him, and her head sank on his shoulder. . . . He inclined his head and touched her pale lips with his own.

*   *   *

Half an hour later Lavretsky was standing at the garden gate. He found it locked and was obliged to vault the fence. He returned to the town and walked through the sleeping streets. A sense of immense unhoped-for happiness filled his soul; all his doubts were at rest. "Begone, dim phantom of the past!" he thought. "She loves me, she will be mine." Suddenly the air above his head seemed to be filled with a burst of exquisite triumphant sound; he stopped: the strains rose still more sublime, sweeping on in a mighty flood of melody—and all the vastness of his joy seemed to speak and sing in the throbbing music. He looked round him; the sounds were floating from two upper windows of a small house.

"Lemm!" cried Lavretsky, and ran towards the house. "Lemm! Lemm!" he repeated loudly.

The sounds died away, and the figure of the old man in a dressing robe, his chest exposed and hair dishevelled, appeared at the window.

"Aha!" he uttered with dignity. "It is you?"

"Christopher Fyodorych, what glorious music! For God's sake, let me in."

Without uttering a word the old man, with a majestic flourish of the arm, dropped the key of the street door from the window. Lavretsky took the stairs at a bound, rushed into the room and up to Lemm; but the latter imperiously waved him to a chair, saying abruptly in Russian: "Sit, listen," sat down himself to the piano, looked proudly and sternly about him, and began to play. It was long since Lavretsky had heard anything of the kind: the tender passionate melody gripped the heart from the very first note; it was all aglow, languishing with the fire of inspiration, joy and beauty; it rose and melted on the air; it spoke of everything that is precious, unutterable and hallowed on earth; it breathed of immortal sadness, and ascended dying to the heavenly spheres. Lavretsky drew himself up and stood pale and chilled with rapture. The music seemed to clutch at his heartstrings, still quivering with the tumult of new-found love; it pulsated with love itself. "Again," he whispered as the last chord died down. The old man threw him an eagle glance, tapped his chest with his hand, saying slowly in his own tongue: "I have done this, for I am a great musician," and he played his wonderful composition again. There were no candles in the room; the beams of a climbing moon fell athwart the windows; the soft air was vibrant with sound; the poor little room seemed a holy place and noble and inspired loomed the old man's head in the silvery twilight. Lavretsky went up to him and embraced him. At first Lemm did not respond to his embrace, he even repulsed him with his elbow; for a long time he sat motionless, with the same stern, almost surly expression and only mumbled twice: "Aha!" At last his transfigured countenance relaxed, and in response to Lavretsky's ardent congratulations he first smiled faintly, then burst into tears, sobbing weakly like a child.

"It is remarkable," he said, "that you should have come just at this moment; but I know, I know everything."

"You know everything?" queried Lavretsky, taken aback.

"You heard what I said," replied Lemm. "Didn't you realise that I know everything?"

Till daybreak Lavretsky could not fall asleep: he sat on his bed all night. And Liza too did not sleep; she was praying.

XXXV

The reader is acquainted with Lavretsky's childhood and upbringing; we will now say a few words about Liza's education. She was ten when her father died; but he had not devoted much time to her. Overwhelmed with

business worries, constantly preoccupied with schemes for
the advancement of his fortune, choleric, brusque and
impatient, he gave money ungrudgingly for teachers, gov-
ernesses, clothes and other requirements of his children;
but he detested having "to dandle the squalling brats",
as he put it; indeed he had very little time to dandle
them—he worked, attended to business, slept little, played
cards once in a while, then back to work again; he compared himself to a horse harnessed to a threshing machine.
"Yes, my life has run out all too quickly," he muttered
on his deathbed with a bitter smile on his parched lips.
Marya Dmitriyevna did not devote very much more time
to Liza, than her husband had done, although she had
boasted to Lavretsky that she had brought up the children
all by herself: she dressed her up like a doll, patted her
on the head before visitors and called her to her face
a clever little girl and a darling, and that was all: a
constant attention was too much for the indolent lady.
During her father's lifetime Liza was in the custody of
her governess, a Mademoiselle Moreau from Paris, and
when he died she was placed into the charge of Marfa
Timofeyevna. Marfa Timofeyevna the reader knows;
Mademoiselle Moreau was a shrivelled diminutive creature with little bird-like ways and bird's brains. In her
youth she had led a very gay life, but in approaching old
age had retained only two passions—sweetmeats and
cards. When she was full-fed, not playing cards or chattering, her face would become like a death mask: there
she would be—sitting, looking, breathing, and yet it was
obvious that her head was innocent of any thoughts. You
would not even say she was kindhearted: there is no such
thing as a kindhearted bird. Whether it was due to a
frivolously spent youth, or to the air of Paris which she
had inhaled from childhood, but she was infected with
a kind of cheap universal scepticism which found vent
in the commonplace expression: "*tout ça c'est des bêtises*". She spoke a solecistic but pure Parisian patois, did
not gossip and had no caprices—what more could one
desire of a governess? She exercised very little influence
on Liza; all the more powerful was the influence on the
child of her nurse Agafya Vlasyevna.

This woman's history was most interesting. She came
of peasant stock; at the age of sixteen she was married
to a muzhik; but she was remarkably unlike her peasant
sisters. Her father had been a bailiff on the estate for
twenty years, had made a lot of money and pampered
her. She was an exceedingly beautiful maid, the queen of
the parish, clever, bold and with a tongue in her head.
Her master, Dmitry Pestov, Marya Dmitriyevna's father,
a quiet modest man, saw her once at threshing time,
spoke to her, and fell passionately in love with her.
Very soon she became a widow; Pestov, though he
was a married man, took her into his house and dressed
her like a lady. Agafya quickly adapted herself to
her new role, as if she had never lived otherwise. She
waxed fair and plump; her arms beneath their muslin
sleeves grew as "floury white" as those of a merchant's
wife; the samovar was never taken off the table; she
disdained to wear anything but silks and velvets and
slept on feather beds. This blissful state of things went
on for five years, and then Dmitry Pestov died; his widow,
who was a merciful mistress, out of regard for the memory of her late husband, was loath to deal harshly with
her rival, the more so that Agafya had always kept her
proper distance; she married her, however, to a cowherd
and banished her out of sight. Three years passed. One
sultry summer day the mistress visited her cattle farm.
Agafya served her such delicious cool cream, was so
demure, neat, cheerful and contented that her mistress
forgave her and admitted her to the house; within six
months she had grown so attached to her that she appointed her housekeeper and gave over to her the management
of the entire household. Agafya rallied, grew plump and
fair once more; she had her mistress' implicit trust. Thus
elapsed another five years. And then Agafya came to
grief again. Her husband, whom she had elevated to the
position of footman, took to drink, was frequently missing
from home and ended by stealing six of the mistress'
silver spoons, which he secreted for the time being in his
wife's coffer. This came to light. He was restored to
cowherd and Agafya fell from her high estate; she was
not banished from the house, but humbled to the position

of needlewoman and made to wear a kerchief on her head instead of a lace cap. To everybody's surprise Agafya meekly bent her head before the storm. She was over thirty at the time, all her children were dead and her husband did not live long. It was time she came to her senses; and come to her senses she did. She became very taciturn and religious, never missed a single matin's service nor a single mass, and gave away all her fine clothes. She spent fifteen years quietly, meekly, staidly, quarrelling with nobody and putting up with everything. If insulted she would merely bow meekly and be grateful for the homily. Her mistress had long forgiven her, and restored her to her good graces, and had even bestowed her own cap as a gift to her; but Agafya would not discard her kerchief and always wore a dark dress; and after her mistress' death she became still more quiet and humble. A Russian is easily prone to fear and affection; but one cannot easily win his respect: it is not yielded soon or without discrimination. For Agafya everybody in the house had a great respect; nobody ever so much as mentioned previous lapses, as though they had been interred together with the old master.

When Kalitin became Marya Dmitriyevna's husband it was his intention to place Agafya in charge of the household; but she could not be persuaded "for fear of temptation"; when he raised his voice at her she bowed humbly and left the room. Kalitin was no fool at sizing up people; he sized up Agafya too and did not forget her. When he moved to town, he gave her, on her own acquiescence, the place of nurse to Liza, who was then getting on for five.

Liza at first was scared by the stern and grave-looking countenance of her new nurse, but she soon got used to her and grew to love her very dearly. She was herself a grave child; she had something of the starkly defined features of her father; only her eyes were not like his; they had a look of gentle regard and kindness rarely to be found in children. She did not care for dolls, her laughter was neither loud nor long, and she bore herself sedately. Hers was not habitually a thoughtful cast of mind, but she never lacked food for thought: after a brief

silence she would usually put a question to a grownup
which showed that her mind had been busy on some new
impression. She stopped lisping very early and spoke
quite clearly when she was three years of age. She feared
her father; her feelings towards her mother were inde-
terminate: she neither feared her nor displayed any signs
of affection for her; she displayed no outward signs of
affection for that matter to Agafya either, though she
was the only person she loved. Agafya was inseparable
from her. The two made an odd sight together. Agafya,
clothed all in black, with a dark kerchief on her head,
her wan face waxlike but still beautiful and expressive,
would be sitting erect, knitting a stocking, while Liza
sat at her feet in a little armchair, likewise engaged in
her little task or listening gravely with upraised clear
eyes to what Agafya was telling her; and Agafya did
not relate fairy tales, but in slow and even tones told
her about the life of the Holy Virgin, the lives of her-
mits, saints and martyrs and holy men and women, told
her how the saints lived in the wilderness, how they sought
salvation, suffered hunger and privation and did not stand
in awe of kings but confessed Christ; how the birds of
the air brought them meat and the beasts of the field
obeyed them; how flowers sprang up where their blood had
been shed. "Wallflowers?" Liza once asked—she was very
fond of flowers.... Agafya spoke to Liza gravely and
humbly conscious, as it were, that it was not for her to be
uttering words so sublime and holy. Liza hung upon her
lips—and the image of an all-powerful omniscient God
stole with a sweet power into her soul, filling it with pure
and reverent awe, while Christ became a near, an intimate presence, something almost kindred; Agafya taught
her to pray as well. Sometimes she would rouse Liza
early at daybreak, dress her hurriedly and steal away
with her to morning service: Liza would follow her on
tiptoe with bated breath; the chill and dusk of early
morn, the cold and vacant church, the very secrecy of
these sudden absences, the stealthy coming back to bed—
all this curious mixture of the forbidden, the strange and
holy thrilled the child to the depths of her soul. Agafya
never chided any one and did not scold Liza for being

fractious. When displeased she was always silent, and Liza knew what that silence meant; with the quick sagacity of a child she also understood when Agafya was annoyed with others—with Marya Dmitriyevna or Kalitin himself. Agafya had care of Liza for over three years, when Mademoiselle took her place; the lightheaded Frenchwoman, however, with her jejune manners and exclamatory *"tout ça c'est des bêtises"*, could not replace her dear nurse in Liza's affections: the seeds had struck root. Besides, though Agafya no longer attended Liza, she was still in the house and often saw her charge, who was still true to her.

Agafya, however, did not get on with Marfa Timofeyevna when the latter came to live in the Kalitins' house. The touchy and self-willed old lady did not like the grave and dignified mien of this former peasant woman. Agafya set out on a pilgrimage and did not come back. There were dark rumours that she had retired to a hermitary of the Raskolniks. But the mark she left in Liza's heart was indelible. She continued to attend mass which she looked forward to as a holiday, prayed with relish, with a sort of restrained and bashful fervour which was a source of secret wonder to Marya Dmitriyevna; Marfa Timofeyevna too, although she never restricted Liza's freedom in any way, tried to moderate her zeal and dissuade her from making too many prostrations—she did not consider it fitting in a girl of noble family. Liza studied well, that is diligently; she was not blessed with particularly brilliant abilities or great intellect; she learnt by dint of hard work. She played the piano well, but only Lemm knew what that cost her. She did not read much; she had "no words of her own", but she had thoughts of her own and went her own way. Not in vain was she her father's daughter: he, too, had never asked people what to do. And so she grew up, quietly, unhurriedly, till she reached the age of nineteen. She was very charming, without knowing it. Her every movement was full of unstudied, somewhat awkward grace; her voice had the silvery tone of untouched youth, the slightest pleasurable sensation brought an engaging smile to her lips, and lit up her eyes with a deep and caressing light. Imbued with a keen sense of duty, a fear of hurting anyone, with a heart kind and gentle, she loved everybody and no one in particular; God alone she loved fervidly, timidly, tenderly. Lavretsky was the first to disturb the even tenor of her life.

Such was Liza.

XXXVI

The next day, a little after eleven in the morning, Lavretsky went to the Kalitins. On the way he met Panshin who galloped past him on horseback, pulling his hat down to his very eyebrows. At the Kalitins' he was not received—for the first time since his acquaintance with them. Marya Dmitriyevna was "resting"—the footman announced; "the mistress" had a headache. Marfa Timofeyevna and Elizaveta Mikhailovna were not at home. Lavretsky strolled about the garden in the faint hope of meeting Liza, but he saw no one. He came back in two hours to be told the same thing by the footman who eyed him askance. Lavretsky thought it unseemly to call a third time in one day, and decided to go to Vassilyevskoye where he had matters to attend to. On the way he made plans, each more sanguine than the other; but when he arrived at his aunt's little village his spirits drooped; he started a conversation with Anton; as luck would have it the old man was full of dismal reminiscences. He told Lavretsky how Glafira Petrovna had bitten her own hand before she died—and, after a pause, added with a sigh: "Every man, my dear master, is destined to devour hisself." It was late when Lavretsky journeyed back to town. The strains of yesterday's music haunted him, and the image of Liza rose to his mind in all its gentle clearness; he was thrilled at the thought that she loved him, and it was with a mind at rest and a feeling of happiness that he rode up to his town house.

The first thing that assailed him on coming into the hall was a smell of patchouli which he loathed; here too stood tall travelling trunks and suitcases. The face of his valet who came running out to meet him struck him as

22*

odd. Without stopping to analyse his impressions he
crossed the threshold of the drawing room. . . . From the
sofa there rose to meet him a lady in a black silk dress
with flounces who, raising a cambric handkerchief to her
pale face, advanced a few steps, bent an immaculately
coiffured perfumed head—and fell at his feet. . . . Then
only did he recognise her: that lady was his wife.

He caught his breath. . . . He leaned up against the
wall. . . .

"Theodore, do not turn me away!" she said in French,
and her voice was like a knife thrust at his heart.

He stared at her vacantly, but nevertheless had a momentary impression that she had grown whiter and more
obese.

"Theodore!" she resumed, lifting up her eyes now and
then and carefully wringing her beautiful hands with
their rosy polished fingernails. "Theodore, I have wronged
you, deeply wronged you—nay, I am a wicked woman,
but please hear me out; I am racked by remorse; I have
become a burden to myself, I could no longer endure my
position; how often I was on the point of appealing to you,
but I was afraid to incur your anger; I have made up my
mind to break with the past . . . *puis j'ai été si malade*—I
was so ill," she added, passing her hand over her brow and
cheek, "I took advantage of the rumours about my death
to give it all up; without resting day or night I hastened
hither; I hesitated long before I could summon up
courage to appear before you, my judge—*paraître dev-
ant vous, mon juge;* but I fought down my tremors,
remembering how kind you always were; I found out
your address in Moscow. Believe me," she went on, slowly getting up from the floor and sitting down on the edge
of an armchair, "the thought of death has often been in
my mind, and I would not shrink from that awful step—
ah, life is merely an insufferable burden to me now!—but
the thought of my daughter, my little Ada, arrested my
hand; she is here, she is asleep in the other room, poor
child! She is tired—you will see her; she, at any rate,
is guiltless before you; oh, I am so miserable, so miserable!" cried Madame Lavretskaya and broke into
tears.

Lavretsky came to himself at last; he moved away from the wall and turned towards the door.

"You are going?" cried his wife in tones of despair. "Oh, how cruel! Without uttering a word, or even a reproach. . . . This contempt is unendurable, it is terrible!"

Lavretsky stopped.

"What do you want me to say?" he uttered in an expressionless voice.

"Nothing nothing," she broke in hastily, "I know that I have no claim to anything; I am not bereft of my senses, I assure you; I have no hope, I dare not hope that you will forgive me; I venture only to beg that you command me what to do, where to live? I will obey your commands, whatever they be, like a slave."

"I have no commands to give you," replied Lavretsky in the same lifeless tones, "you know that it is all over between us . . . now more than ever. You may live wherever you please; and if your allowance is insufficient. . . ."

"Oh, do not utter such dreadful words," broke in Varvara Pavlovna, "spare me, at least . . . at least for this mite's sake. . ." saying which she ran precipitately into the next room and instantly returned with a very elegantly dressed little girl in her arms. Long fair locks fell over her pretty rosy little face, her big, dark, sleepy eyes; she smiled and blinked at the light, leaning a dimpled little hand on her mother's neck.

"*Ada, vois, c'est ton père,*" murmured Varvara Pavlovna smoothing the curls back from her eyes and kissing her, "*prie le avec moi.*"

"*C'est ça, papa?*" lisped the child.

"*Oui, mon enfant, n'est ce pas, que tu l'aimes?*"

This was too much for Lavretsky.

"In what melodrama is there a scene exactly like this?" he muttered and went out.

Varvara Pavlovna stood stock-still for some moments, gave a slight shrug of her shoulders, carried the little girl into the next room, undressed her and put her to bed. She then took up a book, sat down by the lamp, waited for about an hour and went to bed herself.

"*Eh bien, madame?*" queried her maid, a Frenchwoman she had brought with her from Paris, as she was unlacing her corset.

"*Eh bien, Justine,*" she replied, "he's much older, but I believe he is just as kind as he was. Give me my gloves for the night, lay out my grey gown with the high collar for tomorrow; and don't forget the mutton chops for Ada.... I daresay it will be a job to get them here; but we must try."

"*A la guerre, comme à la guerre,*" retorted Justine, and put out the candle.

XXXVII

For more than two hours Lavretsky wandered about the streets of the town. The night he had spent in the outskirts of Paris came back to his mind. His heart was rent with pain and his head, dull and stunned, whirled with the same dark, senseless, furious thoughts. "She is alive, she is back," he whispered in constantly recurring bewilderment. He felt that he had lost Liza. He fumed with rage; this crushing blow had come like a bolt out of the blue. How could he be so credulous as to believe that drivelling article, that wretched rag of a paper? "Well, say I didn't believe it," he reflected, "what difference would it make? I would not have known that Liza loves me; she would not have known it either." He could not shake off the image, the voice, the eyes of his wife ... and he cursed himself, cursed the whole world.

Faint with weariness and pain he came before dawn to Lemm. For a long time no one responded to his knocking; at length the old man's head appeared at a window in a nightcap, looking sour and shrunken and utterly unlike the inspired and impressive visage which twenty-four hours ago had surveyed Lavretsky majestically from the height of its sublime artistry.

"What is it?" asked Lemm. "I cannot play for you every night, I've taken a decoction." Lavretsky's face must have looked peculiar, for the old man cupped his hand to his eyes, gave his late visitor a close scrutiny and opened the door.

Lavretsky came into the room and sank into a chair; the old man stood in front of him, drawing his frayed gaudy dressing robe about him, shivering and gnawing his lips.

"My wife's come," said Lavretsky; he raised his head and suddenly broke into a mirthless laugh.

Lemm looked dumbstruck, but he did not even smile; he only drew his robe closer about him.

"Of course, you didn't know," went on Lavretsky, "I had imagined.... I read in a newspaper that she was dead."

"O-oh, you read that not long ago?" asked Lemm.

"Not long ago."

"O-oh," reiterated the old man, lifting his eyebrows. "And she is here now?"

"Yes. She is at my house; I ... I'm a luckless man." He smiled bitterly.

"You're a luckless man," repeated Lemm slowly.

"Christopher Fyodorych," began Lavretsky, "will you deliver a note for me?"

"Hm. May I know to whom?"

"To Elizave...."

"Ah, yes, yes, I understand. All right. And when has it got to be delivered?"

"Tomorrow, as early as possible."

"Hm. I can send Catherine, my cook. No, I'll take it myself."

"And you will bring me an answer?"

"Yes, I will."

Lemm heaved a sigh.

"Yes, my poor young friend; you are indeed a luckless young man."

Lavretsky wrote Liza a few words: he told her of his wife's arrival, asked her to let him see her—then threw himself down on the narrow sofa and turned his face to the wall; the old man lay down on his bed, tossing restlessly and coughing, and drinking his decoction in gulps.

Morning came, and they both got up. They looked at each other with strange eyes. Lavretsky at that moment felt like doing away with himself. Catherine the cook brought them some bad coffee. The clock struck eight. Lemm put on his hat, and saying that he gave his lesson at the Kalitins' at ten o'clock but would invent a plausible excuse, he set out. Lavretsky flung himself again on the little sofa and grim mirth stirred anew in the depths of his soul. He thought of how his wife had driven him out of the house; he imagined Liza's position, closed his eyes and clasped his hands behind his head. At last Lemm came back and brought him a scrap of paper on which Liza had written in pencil: "We cannot meet today; perhaps tomorrow evening. Farewell." Lavretsky drily and absent-mindedly thanked Lemm and went home.

He discovered his wife over her breakfast; Ada, with her head all in ringlets, in a little white frock with blue ribbons, was eating mutton chops. Varvara Pavlovna rose at once when Lavretsky came in, and stepped forward to meet him with an air of submissiveness. He asked her to follow him into the study, locked the door from inside and began to pace up and down the room; she sat down demurely with folded hands and followed his movements with eyes that were still beautiful, though lightly touched up.

Lavretsky could not force himself to speak for some length of time; he realised that he had no control over himself; he could clearly see that Varvara Pavlovna was not at all afraid of him and merely pretended to look as though she would swoon at any moment.

"Look here, madam," he began at length, breathing heavily and clenching his teeth, "there is no need to deceive each other; I do not believe in your penitence; even if it were sincere it would be impossible for me to go back to you, live with you."

Varvara Pavlovna sat close-lipped and narrow-eyed.

"It is aversion," she was thinking, "it's all over! I am not even a woman in his eyes."

"Impossible," Lavretsky repeated, buttoning his coat right up. "I don't know what made you come here: probably you have run out of money."

"Ah! You insult me," whispered Varvara Pavlovna.

"However, you are still—unfortunately—my wife. I cannot really turn you out . . . now this is the proposal I want to make to you. You may, this very day if you choose, go to Lavriky; live there; there's a good house there, as you know; you will get whatever you need in addition to your allowance. . . . Do you agree?"

Varvara Pavlovna raised an embroidered handkerchief to her face.

"I have told you already," she said with a nervous twitch of the lips, "that I will agree to everything you think fit to do with me; now it's only left for me to ask you—will you at least let me thank you for your magnanimity?"

"Let's do without thanks, please—it's better that way," put in Lavretsky hurriedly. "And so," he went on, making for the door, "I can count on. . . ."

"Tomorrow I will be at Lavriky," murmured Varvara Pavlovna, rising respectfully from her seat. "But Fyodor Ivanych. . . ." (She did not call him Theodore any more.)

"What do you want?"

"I know I have not yet earned forgiveness, but may I at least hope that in time. . . ."

"Eh, Varvara Pavlovna," interrupted Lavretsky, "you're a clever woman, and I'm no fool either; I know that you don't care a scrap about that. I've forgiven you long ago, but there has always been an abyss between us."

"You will find me submissive," rejoined Varvara Pavlovna bowing her head. "I have not forgotten my sin; it would not surprise me to know that you were even glad to hear of my death," she put in meekly, pointing to the newspaper which Lavretsky had left on the table.

Fyodor Ivanych started; the article had been marked in pencil. Varvara Pavlovna regarded him with a look of still deeper humiliation. She was superb at that moment. The grey Parisian gown clung to her lissom, girlish-looking figure; her shapely tender neck encircled in a white collar, the gentle rise and fall of her bosom, the arms bare of bracelets or rings—her whole figure, from her sleek head to the tip of a barely visible shoe, was so elegant. . . .

Lavretsky glared at her in hatred, very nearly cried: "Bravo!" very nearly brought his fist down on her temple, and turned on his heel. An hour later he was on his way to Vassilyevskoye, and two hours later Varvara Pavlovna had hired the smartest carriage in town, put on a simple straw hat with a black veil and a modest mantle, left Ada to Justine's care and repaired herself to the Kalitins: from the information she had elicited from the servants she learnt that her husband visited them every day.

XXXVIII

The day Lavretsky's wife arrived in the town of O— was a cheerless day for him and a dreary day for Liza, too. She had barely gone downstairs and greeted her mother when the sound of horses' hoofs was heard outside, and she saw with trepidation that Panshin was riding into the courtyard. "He has come so early in order to get his answer," she thought, and was not mistaken; after sauntering a while in the drawing room he suggested they should go out into the garden where he demanded to know his fate. Plucking up courage Liza told him that she could not be his wife. He heard her out, standing sideways with his hat drawn down over his forehead; politely, but in a changed voice, he asked her whether that was her last word and whether he had given any ground for her changing her mind, then passed his hand to his eyes, heaved a short fitful sigh and drew his hand away again.

"I did not want to follow the beaten path," he said in a hollow voice. "I thought to choose a helpmeet after my own heart; but obviously it is willed otherwise. Farewell, fond dream!" He made a low bow to Liza and turned back to the house.

She hoped he would leave at once; but he went into Marya Dmitriyevna's room and stayed there close on an hour. On leaving, he said to Liza: *"Votre mère vous appelle; adieu à jamais..."* mounted his horse and set off at a canter from the house steps. Liza found Marya Dmitriyevna in tears: Panshin had apprised her of his fate.

"What have you done to me, what have you done?" was how the distressed widow commenced her plaint. "Whom do you want? Isn't he good enough for you? He's a *Kammerjunker!* He's not a fortune-hunter! In St. Petersburg he could marry any maid of honour if he wanted. Oh dear, and didn't I look forward to it! And is it long since you've changed your mind? This thing could not have dropped from the clouds, this ill-wind's of somebody's blowing. I wonder if that oaf of a cousin's not behind it? A fine confidant you have fished up!"

"And he, poor dear," Marya Dmitriyevna went on, "how respectful he is, how considerate even in his misfortune! He promised not to desert me. Oh dear, I will not get over it! Oh dear, what a splitting headache I have! Send Palasha to me. You will be the death of me if you don't think better of it—do you hear?" And admonishing her several times for an undutiful girl, Marya Dmitriyevna dismissed her.

Liza went to her room. She had scarcely recovered her composure after her interview with Panshin and her mother when the storm broke out anew, from whence she least expected it. Marfa Timofeyevna strode into her room, slamming the door behind her. The old lady's face was pale, her cap askew, her eyes ablaze, and her hands and lips quivering. Liza was amazed: she had never seen her sensible and sober aunt in such a state.

"A pretty pass, madam," Marfa Timofeyevna spluttered in a trembling whisper, "a pretty pass! And where on earth did you learn the likes, my dear!... Give me some water; I can hardly speak."

"Calm yourself, auntie; what is the matter?" said Liza, passing her a glass of water. "Why, I thought you were not too fond of Panshin yourself."

Marfa Timofeyevna deposited the glass.

"I can't drink—I'll knock my last teeth out. Where does Panshin come in? What's Panshin got to do with it? Better tell me, young lady, who taught you to be making appointments at night—eh? What now?"

Liza turned pale.

"Now, don't you start denying it," went on Marfa Timofeyevna. "Shurochka saw it all with her own eyes and told me. I've forbidden her to chatter, but she's not a liar."

"I am not denying anything, auntie," said Liza in a low voice.

"Oh! So that's it, is it, young lady? So you made an appointment with that old meek-faced sinner?"

"No."

"How then?"

"I was going down to the drawing room for a book; he was in the garden—he called me."

"And you went? Fine. Do you love him, or what?"

"I love him," murmured Liza.

"Goodness gracious! She loves him!" Marfa Timofeyevna snatched the cap off her head. "Loves a married man! Do you hear that, eh! Loves him!"

"He told me his wife had died."

Marfa Timofeyevna made a sign of the cross. "May she rest in peace," she whispered, "she was a vain hussy, God forgive her. I see. So he's a widower. He's a cunning blade, it looks. He has no sooner killed off one wife than he goes after another. Sanctimonious snakes! Let me tell you one thing, niece: in my day, when I was young, maids got it hot for pranks such as this. Don't be angry with me, my dear; only fools are angry at the truth. I gave orders not to admit him today. I love him, but this I will never forgive him. A widower, if you please! Let me have some water.... As for sending Panshin about his business, you are a clever girl; but don't go sitting about at nights with that billy-goat's breed, those male creatures; don't break my old heart! You'll find I am not all fondling and petting—I can bite too.... A widower!"

Marfa Timofeyevna went off, and Liza sat down in a corner and burst into tears. She felt wretched at heart; she had not deserved such humiliation. Love had brought her no gladness: twice since yesternight she had been crying. Hardly had this new and wonderful feeling arisen in her heart, than she was already paying such heavy toll and her sacred secret was exposed to the rude touch of alien hands! She felt ashamed and bitter and wounded, but without a vestige of doubt or fear—and Lavrets-

ky was dearer to her than before. She had wavered
only so long as she had not understood her own mind;
but after that meeting, after that kiss, she wavered no
longer; she knew that she loved—and she loved honestly,
earnestly, with an affection that was strong and lifelong
and defiant; she felt that no power on earth could dis-
sever that bond.

XXXIX

Marya Dmitriyevna was greatly perturbed when Varvara Pavlovna Lavretskaya was announced; she was at
a loss whether to receive her or not: she was afraid of
giving offence to Fyodor Ivanych. At last, curiosity pre-
vailed. "Oh well," she reflected, "she's one of the kin,
too," and sinking back in her armchair, she said to the
footman: "Show her in." Several moments passed; the
door opened; Varvara Pavlovna swiftly glided across the
room to Marya Dmitriyevna, and without giving her a
chance to rise from her chair, bent almost on her knees
before her.

"Thanks awfully, dear aunt," she began in a low trem-
ulous voice, speaking in Russian. "Thanks awfully; I
did not hope for such forbearance on your part; you are
as good as an angel."

Having said which, Varvara Pavlovna suddenly seized
one of Marya Dmitriyevna's hands, and pressing it lightly between her lavender gloves raised it unctuously to
her full rosy lips. Marya Dmitriyevna was bewildered
beyond words at the sight of this beautiful, exquisitely
dressed woman almost prostrated at her feet; she did
not know what to do: she would have liked to withdraw
her hand, to offer her a seat, to say something kind; she
got up instead and implanted a kiss on Varvara Pavlovna's smooth scented brow. Varvara Pavlovna was
quite overcome.

"How do you do, *bon jour*," said Marya Dmitriyevna,
"of course, I never expected . . . but, of course, I am glad
to see you. You understand, my dear, it is not for me to
act as judge between man and wife. . . ."

"My husband is entirely right," broke in Varvara Pavlovna, "I alone am to blame."

"That is a very laudable sentiment," rejoined Marya
Dmitriyevna, "very. Have you been here long? Have you
seen him? But, please, sit down."

"I arrived yesterday," answered Varvara Pavlovna,
humbly taking a seat. "I have seen Fyodor Ivanych, I
have spoken to him."

"Ah! Well, and how did he take it?"

"I was afraid my coming so unexpectedly would rouse
his anger," resumed Varvara Pavlovna, "but he did not
deprive me of his presence."

"That is to say, he did not. . . . Yes, yes, I understand,"
commented Marya Dmitriyevna. "He is only a little rough
on the surface, but he has a kind heart."

"Fyodor Ivanych has not forgiven me; he would not
hear me out. . . . But he was so kind as to assign Lavriky
for me to reside at."

"Ah! A beautiful estate!"

"I am setting out tomorrow, in compliance with his
orders; but I deemed it my duty to call on you first."

"Thanks, thanks awfully, my dear. One should never
forget one's relations. Do you know, I am surprised how
well you speak Russian. *C'est étonnant.*"

Varvara Pavlovna sighed.

"I have been abroad too long, Marya Dmitriyevna, I
know it; but my heart has always remained Russian and
I have not forgotten my native land."

"Quite, quite; that's a good thing. Fyodor Ivanych,
however, was not expecting you. . . . Yes, you can take it
from me: *la patrie avant tout.* Oh, what a lovely mantle
that is, may I look at it?"

"Do you like it?" Varvara Pavlovna slipped it quickly
off her shoulders. "It's very simple, from Madame Baudran."

"You can see that at once. From Madame Baudran. . . .
How charming and chic! I'm sure you must have brought
lots of fascinating things with you. If I could only see
them."

"My entire toilette is at your service, dearest aunt. If
you permit, I can show some of the things to your maid.

I have a maidservant with me from Paris—she's a wonderful dressmaker."

"It is very good of you, my dear. But really, I shouldn't like to trouble you."

"Trouble me. . ." rejoined Varvara Pavlovna in a tone of mild reproach. "If you want to make me happy, dispose of me as you would your own property."

Marya Dmitriyevna melted.

"*Vous êtes charmante*," she murmured. "But why don't you take off your hat and gloves?"

"Oh, may I?" asked Varvara Pavlovna, clasping her hands pathetically.

"Why, certainly; you are dining with us, I hope? I . . . I will introduce you to my daughter." Marya Dmitriyevna looked uneasy. "Oh, in for a penny!. . ." she thought. "She is a bit out of sorts today."

"O, *ma tante*, how kind of you!" cried Varvara Pavlovna and lifted her handkerchief to her eyes.

A servant boy announced Gedeonovsky. The old gossip came in lavishing bows and smirks. Marya Dmitriyevna introduced him to her guest. At first he was thrown into a flutter; but Varvara Pavlovna was so bewitchingly respectful that his ears soon began to tingle, and gossip, tittle-tattle and flattery dripped blandly from his tongue like honey. Varvara Pavlovna listened with a restrained smile and gradually joined in the conversation. She spoke modestly of Paris, of her travels, of Baden; she raised a laugh from Marya Dmitriyevna on two occasions, and each time she gave a little sigh as though inwardly reproaching herself for unseemly merriment; she obtained permission to bring Ada with her next time; taking off her gloves she showed with her smooth-skinned hands redolent of soap *à la guimauve* how and where flounces were worn, quillings, lace and rosettes; promised to bring a bottle of Victoria's Essence, a new English scent, and was delighted as a child when Marya Dmitriyevna agreed to accept it as a gift; she was moved to tears at the recollection of the thrill she had when she first heard Russian church bells; "they went straight to my heart," she murmured.

At that moment Liza entered the room.

Ever since the morning, from the moment when, frozen with horror, she had read Lavretsky's note, Liza had been steeling herself for the encounter with his wife; she had had a presentiment that she would see her. She made up her mind not to avoid her, as a retribution for what she called her sinful hopes. The sudden crisis in her destiny had shaken her to the very core of her being; in some two hours her face had become drawn; but she did not shed a single tear. "Serves me right!" she said to herself, suppressing with difficulty and emotion a rush of poignant resentful impulses that appalled her. "Well, I must go!" she thought as soon as she heard of the arrival of Lavretskaya, and she went down.... She stood for a long time outside the drawing room before she could summon up courage to open the door; "I have done her wrong"—with this thought she entered the drawing room and forced herself to look at her, forced herself to smile. Varvara Pavlovna came forward to meet her the moment she saw her, and bowed slightly, but with deference. "Allow me to introduce myself," she said unctuously, "your *maman* has been so gracious, that I hope you too will ... be kind." The expression on Varvara Pavlovna's face when she uttered the last word, her sly smile, the cold yet soft glance, the gesture of her hands and shoulders, the very gown she wore, her whole being roused such a feeling of repulsion in Liza that she was unable to make reply and it was all she could do to hold out her hand. "This young lady cannot abide me," thought Varvara Pavlovna as she squeezed Liza's cold fingers, and turning to Marya Dmitriyevna she murmured: *"mais elle est délicieuse!"* Liza faintly coloured: there was something mocking and insulting in this interjection; but she decided not to rely on her impressions and took a seat by the window at her tambour. Even here Varvara Pavlovna did not leave her in peace; she went up to her, complimented her on her taste and skill.... Liza's heart beat violently and painfully; she tried with all her might to keep her chin up. It seemed to her that Varvara Pavlovna knew everything and was tormenting her in malicious glee. To her relief Gedeonovsky began to talk to Varvara Pavlovna and diverted her attention.

Liza bent over her tambour and glanced at the other furtively. "This is the woman," she thought, "*he* once loved." But she instantly banished the thought of Lavretsky from her mind: she was afraid of losing her self-possession, she felt that her head was gently reeling. Marya Dmitriyevna began to talk of music.

"I have heard, my dear," she began, "that you are a veritable virtuoso."

"I haven't played for a long time," retorted Varvara Pavlovna sitting down promptly to the piano and running her fingers deftly over the keys. "May I?"

"Please do."

Varvara Pavlovna gave a masterly rendering of a brilliant and difficult Hertz etude. She had great force and dexterity.

"A sylphid!" cried Gedeonovsky.

"Remarkable!" Marya Dmitriyevna chimed in. "Well, Varvara Pavlovna," she observed, calling her for the first time by her name, "I avow you have astonished me; you really should be giving concerts. We've a musician here, a German, an eccentric old fellow, but a very knowing musician; he gives Liza lessons: he will be simply crazy over you."

"Does Elizaveta Mikhailovna play too?" enquired Varvara Pavlovna turning her head slightly towards her.

"Yes, she doesn't play badly and likes music; but what is that compared to you? But there is another young man here; there's a man you ought to meet. He's an artist at heart and composes very charming things. He alone would be able to appreciate you fully."

"A young man?" said Varvara Pavlovna. "Who is he? Some poor fellow?"

"Oh dear, no, our foremost ladies' man, and not only here but in St. Petersburg too. A *Kammerjunker*, received in the best society. You have probably heard of him: Panshin, Vladimir Nikolaich. He is here on government business . . . a future minister I should say!"

"And an artist?"

"An artist at heart, and so courteous. You shall see him. He has been coming here very often; I invited him down this evening; *I do hope* he will come," added Marya

Dmitriyevna with a little sigh and a devious rueful smile.

Liza understood the smile, but she was not in the mood to mind it.

"And young?" intoned Varvara Pavlovna.

"Twenty-eight, and extremely good-looking. *Un jeune homme accompli,* indeed."

"A model young man, I should say," observed Gedeonovsky.

Varvara Pavlovna suddenly struck up a boisterous Strauss waltz, opening with such a dazzling strident trill that Gedeonovsky was staggered; in the middle of the waltz she unexpectedly introduced a sad theme and finished up with the aria from "Lucia", *Fra poco....* It dawned on her that gay music was not appropriate to her position. The "Lucia" aria, with emphasis on the sentimental passages, moved Marya Dmitriyevna deeply.

"What feeling!" she observed in an undertone to Gedeonovsky.

"A sylphid!" repeated Gedeonovsky, rolling up his eyes.

The dinner hour arrived. Marfa Timofeyevna came downstairs when the soup had already been served. She greeted Varvara Pavlovna drily, answered her polite talk in monosyllables and did not look at her. Varvara Pavlovna soon realised that there was nothing to be got out of this old lady and gave up trying to entertain her; all the kinder was Marya Dmitriyevna to her guest: her aunt's discourtesy piqued her. Marfa Timofeyevna, however, avoided not only Varvara Pavlovna; she did not look at Liza either, although her eyes were all aglitter. She sat like a stone image, all yellow and pale and tight-lipped and ate nothing. Liza looked calm; indeed, the storm within her had subsided; she felt oddly benumbed, like a person condemned. At dinner Varvara Pavlovna was not very talkative; she seemed to have become diffident again and her face wore a look of demure melancholy. Gedeonovsky alone kept the conversation going with his stories, looking ever and anon uneasily at Marfa Timofeyevna and clearing his throat—he always had an attack of huskiness when he was about to tell a lie in her presence—but she did not hinder him or interrupt. When the dinner was over it turned out that Varvara Pavlovna was very fond of whist; Marya Dmitriyevna was so delighted by this intelligence that she was quite overcome, saying to herself: "Really, what a fool that Fyodor Ivanych must be! Fancy not appreciating such a woman!"

She sat down to a game of cards with her and Gedeonovsky, and Marfa Timofeyevna led Liza upstairs, saying she looked bad and no doubt had a headache.

"Yes, she has an awful headache," said Marya Dmitriyevna addressing herself to Varvara Pavlovna and rolling up her eyes.

"I get such awful attacks of migraine too...."

"Really!" murmured Varvara Pavlovna.

Liza went into her aunt's room and sank limply into a chair. Marfa Timofeyevna looked at her long and silently, then quietly went down on her knees before her and silently started kissing her hands. Liza leaned forward, a flush mounting into her face—and began to weep, but she did not make Marfa Timofeyevna get up, neither did she take her hands away: she felt that she had no right to take them away, to prevent the old lady from giving vent to her remorse and sympathy, from begging forgiveness for what had passed the day before; and Marfa Timofeyevna could not kiss enough those poor, pale, powerless hands, while the silent tears flowed from her eyes and from those of Liza; and the cat Matross purred in the wide armchair among the knitting wool, and the long flame flickered and wavered in the little oil lamp before the icon, while in the next room, behind the door, Nastasya Karpovna stood furtively wiping her eyes with her checked handkerchief twisted into a little ball.

XL

Meanwhile, down below in the drawing room, the company were playing whist. Marya Dmitriyevna was winning and was in a good humour. A servant came in and announced the arrival of Panshin.

Marya Dmitriyevna dropped her cards and began to fidget in her chair; Varvara Pavlovna glanced at her with

23*

a quizzical smile and then turned her eyes to the door.
Panshin entered attired in a black frock coat with a high
English collar buttoned up to the throat. "It was not
easy for me to obey, but you see I have come," spoke his
unsmiling, freshly-shaven face.

"Really, Woldemar," cried Marya Dmitriyevna, "you
always used to come in unannounced!"

Panshin answered Marya Dmitriyevna with his eyes
alone, bowed politely to her, but did not kiss her hand.
She introduced him to Varvara Pavlovna; he fell back
a pace, bowed to her just as politely but with a tinge of
elegance and deference, and seated himself at the card
table. The game was soon over. Panshin made enquiries
about Elizaveta Mikhailovna, heard that she was indisposed, murmured his regret; then he dropped into conversation with Varvara Pavlovna, diplomatically weigh-
ing and enunciating incisively each word and lending
a polite ear to her answers. The solemnity of his diplomatic tone, however, had no effect on Varvara Pavlovna
and touched no answering chord. On the contrary, she
studied him with a jovial regard, talked in a casual tone,
while her fine nostrils quivered slightly as though with
suppressed mirth. Marya Dmitriyevna began to extol
her gifts; Panshin politely, as far as his collar would
permit him, inclined his head, averring that "he was
convinced of it all the time", and led off on a tack that
brought him almost to Metternich himself. Varvara Pavlovna narrowed her velvety eyes and murmuring in an
undertone: "Why, but you are an artist too, *un confrère*,"
added *sotto voce: "Venez!"* with a nod towards the piano.
This one word *"Venez!"* which she had let fall had an
instantaneous, almost magical, effect on Panshin. His
grave mien vanished; his face broke out into smiles, he
brightened up, unbuttoned his coat and repeating: "Not
much of an artist, alas! but you, I hear, are a real artist,"
he followed Varvara Pavlovna to the piano.

"Make him sing his song—about the floating moon,"
cried Marya Dmitriyevna.

"Do you sing?" asked Varvara Pavlovna flashing at
him a swift smile. "Sit down."

Panshin began to plead excuses.

"Sit down," she repeated, drumming her fingers insistently on the back of the chair.

He sat down, coughed, pulled at his collar and sang his song.

"*Charmant*," pronounced Varvara Pavlovna, "you sing very well, *vous avez du style*, sing it again."

She moved round the piano and stood directly facing Panshin. He repeated his song, communicating to his voice a melodramatic tremor. Varvara Pavlovna gazed at him steadily, propping her elbows on the piano and holding her white hands level with her lips. Panshin finished.

"*Charmant, charmante idée*," she said with the calm assurance of a connoisseur. "Tell me, have you written anything for a woman's voice, for a mezzo-soprano?"

"I hardly compose anything at all," said Panshin, "I just do it to amuse myself, you know . . . but do you sing?"

"Yes."

"Oh! sing us something, do!" urged Marya Dmitriyevna.

Varvara Pavlovna pushed her hair back from her flushed cheeks and tossed her head.

"Our voices ought to go well together," she murmured, turning to Panshin; "let us sing a duet. Do you know *Son geloso*, or *La ci darem*, or *Mira la bianca luna?*"

"I sang *Mira la bianca luna* once upon a time," replied Panshin, "but that was ages ago and I've forgotten it."

"Never mind, we will rehearse it in a low voice. Allow me."

Varvara Pavlovna sat down to the piano. Panshin stood beside her. They sang through the duet in an undertone, Varvara Pavlovna correcting him several times, then they sang it aloud and repeated twice: *Mira la bianca lu . . . u . . . una*. Varvara Pavlovna's voice had lost its freshness but she managed it very dexterously. Panshin was shy at first and a little out of tune, but he soon warmed up, and if his performance was not quite irreproachable, he made up for it with shrugs of the shoulders and a swaying of the body and an occasional lifting of the hand like a true singer. Varvara Pavlovna played two or three pieces of Thalberg's and coquettishly "recited" a French ariette. Marya Dmitriyevna could not find words to express her delight; several times she had wanted to send for Liza; Gedeonovsky too was at a loss for words and could only shake his head, when he suddenly yawned and barely managed to disguise it. The yawn was not lost on Varvara Pavlovna; she suddenly turned her back to the piano, murmured: *"Assez de musique comme ça,* let us talk," and folded her arms. *"Oui, assez de musique,"* repeated Panshin gaily and plunged into small talk—light, sparkling, and in French. "Quite like in the best Parisian salon," thought Marya Dmitriyevna, listening to their irrelevant finespun chitchat. Panshin was enjoying himself immensely; his eyes shone, his face was wreathed in smiles; at first, on meeting Marya Dmitriyevna's gaze, he would pass his hand across his face, knit his brows and sigh fitfully; but later he forgot about her entirely, and abandoned himself to the enjoyment of this semi-worldly, semi-artistic parlance. Varvara Pavlovna, it appeared, was quite the philosopher; she had a ready answer for everything; she never faltered, never had doubts on any score; one could see that she had conversed much and often with clever men of every sort and kind. All her thoughts and feelings revolved round Paris. Panshin turned the conversation on literature: it transpired that she, like he, read only French books: George Sand drove her to exasperation, Balzac she respected, though he was tedious, Sue and Scribe, she considered, had a profound knowledge of human nature, and Dumas and Feval she worshipped; at bottom however, she preferred Paul de Kock to them all, but of course she did not even mention his name. Indeed, literature did not interest her very much. Varvara Pavlovna skilfully steered clear of anything even remotely reminiscent of her own situation; of love there was not a mention in her conversation, in fact, its drift was rather one of austerity where the passions were concerned, of disenchantment and humility. Panshin expostulated; she demurred ... but strange to say, while her lips uttered words of stricture, severely condemnatory at times, the sound of these words was stroking and caressing and her eyes spoke ... exactly what those lovely eyes spoke it was hard to say; but their purport was dim and sweet and unforbidding. Panshin tried to fathom their secret meaning, he too tried to make his eyes speak, but he felt all his efforts were in vain; he realised that Varvara Pavlovna as a lioness from foreign parts stood above him, and consequently he was not completely at his ease. Varvara Pavlovna had a habit of lightly touching the sleeve of the person whom she happened to be talking to; these momentary contacts had a most disquieting effect on Vladimir Nikolaich. Varvara Pavlovna possessed the faculty of getting on easily with people; within two hours it seemed to Panshin that he had known her for years, while Liza, the girl he really loved, and whom he had the evening before proposed to, was swallowed up in a mist, as it were. Tea was served; the conversation became still more unconstrained. Marya Dmitriyevna rang for the servant boy and told him to tell Liza she should come down if her head was better. At the mention of Liza's name Panshin fell to discussing self-sacrifice and mooted the point as to whether men or women were more given to self-sacrifice. Marya Dmitriyevna instantly became excited, claimed that women were more prone to self-sacrifice than men, vowed she would prove it there and then, got herself in a tangle and wound up with a rather lame illustration. Varvara Pavlovna picked up a music book, screened herself with it and, bending towards Panshin while taking small bites at a cake, she remarked *sotto voce* with a bland smile on her lips and in her eyes: *"Elle n'a pas inventé la poudre, la bonne dame."* Panshin was somewhat taken aback and astonished at Varvara Pavlovna's temerity; but he did not suspect the measure of derision this unexpected burst of candour contained for his own person; and forgetful of all the kindness and devotion Marya Dmitriyevna had shown him, of the dinners she had given him and the money she had loaned him he replied (wretched man) with the same smile and in the same tone: *"Je crois bien"*—nay, not even so, but *"J'crois ben!"*

Varvara Pavlovna shot him an amiable glance and got up. Liza came in; Marfa Timofeyevna had tried in vain to dissuade her: she was determined to go through with her ordeal. Varvara Pavlovna advanced to meet her together with Panshin, who reassumed the diplomatic look.

"How are you feeling?" he asked Liza.

"I am better now, thank you," she replied.

"We have been having a little music here; it's a pity you haven't heard Varvara Pavlovna. She sings remarkably well, *une artiste consommée.*"

"Come here, *ma chère*," called Marya Dmitriyevna.

Varvara Pavlovna responded dutifully, like a child, and sat down on a little stool at her feet. Marya Dmitriyevna had called her away so as to leave her daughter alone for at least a moment with Panshin; she still cherished a hope that the girl would come to her senses. Besides, an idea had occurred to her which she was eager to divulge forthwith.

"Do you know," she whispered to Varvara Pavlovna, "I want to try to reconcile you with your husband; I won't say that I'll succeed, but I can make an attempt. He has a great regard for me, you know."

Varvara Pavlovna raised her eyes slowly to Marya Dmitriyevna and crossed her hands in a beautiful gesture.

"You would be my saviour, *ma tante*," she said piteously; "I don't know how to thank you for being so good to me; but I have wronged Fyodor Ivanych too deeply; he cannot forgive me."

"But did you ... really..." began Marya Dmitriyevna probingly.

"Don't ask me," broke in Varvara Pavlovna, dropping her eyes. "I was young and frivolous.... But I don't want to excuse myself."

"Well, anyway, why shouldn't we try? Don't despair," rejoined Marya Dmitriyevna, and was on the point of patting her on the cheek when she glanced at her face with misgiving. "She's demure enough," she thought, "but she's certainly a lioness."

"Are you ill?" Panshin meanwhile was saying to Liza.

"Yes, I am not well."

"I understand you," he murmured after a prolonged silence. "Yes, I understand you."

"What do you mean?"

"I understand you," repeated Panshin knowingly; it was the only thing he could find to say.

Liza was disconcerted, then she thought: "Let it be so!" Panshin assumed an air of mystery and fell silent, glancing to one side with a stern expression.

"I believe it has already struck eleven," observed Marya Dmitriyevna.

The guests took the hint and rose to take their leave. A promise was extracted from Varvara Pavlovna that she would come to dine the next day and bring Ada; Gedeonovsky who had nearly dozed off in a corner offered to see her home. Panshin solemnly bowed to everybody, and on the steps outside, when assisting Varvara Pavlovna into her carriage, he squeezed her hand and cried after her: *au revoir!* Gedeonovsky sat beside her; all the way she beguiled the time by resting the tip of her dainty foot, inadvertently as it were, on his; he was flustered and started paying her compliments; she simpered and made eyes at him when the light of a street lamp fell into the carriage. The waltz she had played was ringing in her head, she was tingling with excitement; wherever she was she had merely to conjure up lights, a ballroom, figures whirling to the strains of music—and her blood was on fire, her eyes became strangely blurred, a smile hovered about her lips, and her whole body thrilled with a sense of bacchanalian grace. When she reached home Varvara Pavlovna skipped lightly out of the carriage— could anyone but a lioness do that the way she did it?— faced round to Gedeonovsky and suddenly burst into a peal of merry laughter right under his nose.

"An engaging person," reflected the privy councillor as he bent his steps homeward, where a servant was awaiting him with a glass of opodeldoc. "It's well I am a respectable man.... I wonder why she laughed though?"

Marfa Timofeyevna sat all night at Liza's bedside.

XLI

Lavretsky was a day and a half at Vassilyevskoye and spent most of the time prowling about the neighbourhood. He could not stay long in one place: his heart was racked with grief; he suffered all the torments of ceaseless, violent and impotent passions. He remembered the emotions that flooded his soul the day after his arrival in the country; he remembered the plans he had then made, and was furious with himself. What could have torn him from what he had known to be his duty, the sole task of his future? The thirst for happiness—once again the thirst for happiness! "It seems that Mikhalevich was right," he thought. "You wanted to taste the joys of life a second time," he soliloquised, "you have forgotten that it is a luxury, an unmerited boon even when it comes once to a man. You say it was not complete, it was spurious? Very well, then prove your title to complete and genuine bliss! Look round you—who is there blest with happiness, who is joyful? Take that peasant going to the meadow with his scythe—mayhap he is contented with his fate?...

"Well, would you care to change places with him? Think of your mother: what she asked of life was so infinitesimally small,—and what was doled out to her? It seems you simply boasted when you told Panshin you had come to Russia to plough the land; you have come to go philandering after the girls in your old age. Directly you received news of your freedom you dropped everything, forgot everything on earth and ran like a schoolboy after a butterfly...." The image of Liza rose continuously to his mind amidst these broodings; he dismissed it with an effort, as he did that other plaguing image, those imperturbably roguish, lovely, hateful features. Old Anton perceived that his master was out of sorts; after sighing once or twice behind the door and once or twice in the doorway he finally made bold to go up to him and advised him to take a drink of something warm. Lavretsky shouted at him, told him to get out and then begged his pardon; but this only saddened Anton still more. Lavretsky could not stay in the drawing room; his greatgrandfather seemed to be looking down derisively from the canvas at this weakling of a descendant. "Bah! You poor fish!" his wry mouth seemed to be sneering. "Come," he said to himself, "it can't be that I will let myself go to pieces, give in to this ... scratch?" (Men badly wounded in war always refer to their wounds as "a scratch". Unless he deceived himself man could not live on earth.) "Am I a snivelling boy after all? All right: I had a close glimpse, I almost held in my hands the chance of happiness of a lifetime—and it suddenly vanished; but then in a lottery too, a slight turn of the wheel—and the beggar would become a rich man. If it's not to be, it's not to be, and that's all there is to it. I will set about my business with clenched teeth and force myself to keep quiet; it's not the first time either I've had to take a hold on myself. What made me slink away, why am I sticking here with my head buried in a bush like an ostrich? No nerve to face the music?—nonsense! Anton," he shouted out aloud, "have the tarantass brought round at once. Yes," he reflected again, "I must force myself to keep quiet, I must pull myself together...."

With reasonings such as these Lavretsky sought to ease his pain; but the pain was deep and poignant and even Apraxia, who was bereft not so much of mind as of all emotion, shook her head and followed him sadly with her eyes as he got into the tarantass to go to town. The horses went off at a canter; he sat stiff and motionless, staring motionlessly at the road before him.

XLII

Liza had written Lavretsky the day before asking him to call in the evening; but he first went to his rooms. He found neither his wife nor his daughter at home; the servants told him that she had gone with the child to the Kalitins. The information astonished and infuriated him. "It looks as though Varvara Pavlovna has made up her mind to lead me a dog's life," he reflected, with hatred burning in his heart. He began to pace to and fro, kicking and throwing aside toys, books and feminine things that got in his way; he called Justine and ordered her to clear away all that "rubbish". *"Oui, Monsieur,"* she said with a grimace and began to set the room in order, stooping gracefully and giving Lavretsky to understand with her every movement that she thought him an uncouth bear. He glared balefully at her dissolute but still "piquant" mocking Parisian face, her white oversleeves, her silk pinafore and little cap. He dismissed her at length, and after long hesitation—Varvara Pavlovna not having returned—he decided to go to the Kalitins, not to Marya Dmitriyevna (he would not enter her drawing room, that room where his wife was, for anything in the world), but to Marfa Timofeyevna; he remembered that the staircase from the servants' entrance led straight to her apartment. He decided on this course. Chance favoured him; in the courtyard he met Shurochka who conducted him to Marfa Timofeyevna. He found her, contrary to her usual habit, alone; she was sitting in a corner, without a cap on, her body huddled and her hands crossed over her breast. She was very upset when she saw Lavretsky, got briskly to her feet and began to pace about the room as though searching for her cap.

"Ah, it's you, it's you," she began, avoiding his eyes and fussing about the room, "well, good day to you. Ah, well! There you are. Where were you yesterday? So she's come; yes, of course. Well, it can't be helped."

Lavretsky sank into a chair.

"There, sit down, sit down," continued the old lady. "You came straight upstairs? Why, yes, to be sure. Well? So you came to see me? Thanks."

The old lady paused; Lavretsky did not know what to say to her, but she understood him.

"Liza ... yes, Liza's been here a little while ago," she went on, tying and untying the strings of her reticule. "She is not feeling well. Shurochka, where are you? Come here, my dear; why can't you sit still? I have a headache too. I suppose it's through that singing and music."

"What singing, aunt?"

"Why, they've been at those—now, what d'ye call 'em ... duet things. And all in Italian too: *chi-chi* and *cha-cha*, just like magpies. They'd begin to draw out the notes fit to make all your teeth ache. That fellow Panshin and your better half. And how soon they became thick, no standing on ceremony, just like among relations. Come to think of it, though, even a dog will try to find a home. You can't expect it to perish as long as there's folks as don't drive it away."

"Still, I'd never have believed it," observed Lavretsky, "it wants a lot of nerve."

"No, my dear, not nerve, but calculation. God forgive her! You're sending her to Lavriky, I hear?"

"Yes, I'm putting that estate at Varvara Pavlovna's disposal."

"Has she asked for money?"

"Not yet."

"Well, that'll come soon enough. But I've only just taken a good look at you, my dear. You're not ill, are you?"

"No."

'Shurochka!" cried Marfa Timofeyevna. "Go and tell Elizaveta Mikhailovna—that is, no, ask her. . . . She's downstairs, isn't she?"

"Yes."

"Well, then ask her what she's done with my book. She'll know."

"Very well."

The old lady began pottering about the room again, opening and closing the drawers in the chest. Lavretsky sat motionless. Suddenly light steps were heard on the stairs, and Liza came in.

Lavretsky rose and bowed; Liza stopped at the door.

"Liza, Liza dear," said Marfa Timofeyevna fussily, "where's my book? What have you gone and done with the book?"

"What book, auntie?"

"Gracious me, the book! I didn't call you though. . . . There, it doesn't matter. What's going on downstairs? Here, Fyodor Ivanych has come. How's you head?"

"It's all right."

"You always say: all right. What's going on down there—music again?"

"No, they're playing cards."

"To be sure, she's good at everything. Shurochka, I see you want to go and play in the garden. Run along."

"Oh no, Marfa Timofeyevna. . . ."

"Come, don't argue now, run along. Nastasya Karpovna is out in the garden by herself; go and keep her company. Come, that's a good girl." Shurochka departed.

"Where on earth is my cap? Where has it got to now?"

"Let me look for it," said Liza.

"You sit where you are. I still have the use of my legs. I suppose it's in my bedroom."

Casting a sidelong glance at Lavretsky, Marfa Timofeyevna went out. She had left the door ajar, but suddenly came back and shut it. . . .

Liza leaned back in her chair and slowly put her hands to her face; Lavretsky did not stir from his place.

"So this is how we were to meet again," he broke the silence.

Liza removed her hands from her face.

"Yes," she said in a low voice. "We've been punished all too soon."

"Punished," murmured Lavretsky. "What have *you* been punished for?"

Liza raised her eyes to his. They expressed neither grief nor anxiety; they looked shrunken and faded. There was a pallor on her face and slightly parted lips.

Lavretsky's heart contracted with compassion and love.

"You wrote me: it is all over," he whispered, "aye, it is all over—before it had begun."

"We must forget all that," murmured Liza. "I am glad you came; I wanted to write you, but it is better so. Only we must make the most of these minutes. We must both do our duty now. You, Fyodor Ivanych, must make it up with your wife."

"Liza!"

"I beg you to do that; only so we can make amends . . . for what has happened. Think it over—you will not deny me this."

"Liza, for God's sake—what you demand is impossible. I am prepared to do anything you command me; but to make up with her now!. . . I'll put up with anything. I've forgotten and forgiven but I can't compel my heart to. . . . Why, that's cruel!"

"I am not asking you . . . to do what you say; do not live with her if you cannot; but make it up with her," replied Liza and covered her face again with her hands. "Think of your little daughter; do this for me."

"Very well," muttered Lavretsky through clenched

teeth, "I will do that, I suppose; I'll do my duty that way. But what about you—what does your duty consist in?"

"I know what my duty is to be."

Lavretsky started.

"You're not thinking of marrying that Panshin fellow, are you?" he demanded.

A wan smile flitted across Liza's countenance.

"Oh, no!" she said.

"Ah, Liza, Liza!" cried Lavretsky. "How happy we might have been!"

Liza looked at him again.

"Now you see yourself, Fyodor Ivanych, that happiness does not depend upon us, but on God."

"Yes, because you...."

The door leading into the next room opened quickly and Marfa Timofeyevna reappeared with her cap in her hand.

"I've found it, drat it," she said, standing between Lavretsky and Liza. "Probably mislaid it myself. That's what age does to you, alack! Come to think of it, youth is no better either. Are you going to Lavriky too with your wife?" she added, turning to Fyodor Ivanych.

"With her to Lavriky? I? I don't know," he murmured after a pause.

"Are you going down?"

"Not today."

"Well, you know best; but you ought to go down, Liza. Oh, goodness gracious, I haven't fed the bullfinch yet. Wait a moment, I'll soon...."

And Marfa Timofeyevna hurried out without putting on her cap.

Lavretsky stepped quickly up to Liza.

"Liza," he began in a supplicating voice, "we are parting for ever, my heart is breaking—give me your hand in farewell."

Liza raised her head. She regarded him with dimmed weary eyes.

"No," she murmured, and drew back the hand she had already held out. "No, Lavretsky" (it was the first time she had used this name), "I will not give you my hand.

What is the good? Go away, I implore you. You know
that I love you. . . . Yes, I love you," she added with an
effort, "but no. . . no."

She pressed her handkerchief to her lips.

"Give me, at least, that handkerchief."

The door creaked. . . . The handkerchief slid to Liza's
lap. Lavretsky caught it before it dropped, thrust it
quickly into his pocket, and, turning round, met Marfa
Timofeyevna's gaze.

"Liza, darling, I believe your mother's calling you,"
said the old lady.

Liza got up at once and went out.

Marfa Timofeyevna resumed her seat in the corner.
Lavretsky began to take his leave.

"Fedya," she said suddenly.

"Yes, auntie?"

"Are you a man of honour?"

"What do you mean?"

"I am asking you—are you a man of honour?"

"I hope so."

"Hm. Pledge me your word that you are a man of
honour."

"Have it your way. But what is it all about?"

"I know what it is all about. And you too, my dear, if
you'll give the matter a thought—you're no fool, you
know—you'll understand what I'm aiming at. And now,
my dear, goodbye. Thank you for coming to see me; and
remember, you have given your word of honour, Fedya;
come, kiss me. Ah, my dear boy, it's hard for you, I
know; but then it's not easy for anyone. I used to envy
the flies once—there, I thought, they're having a good
time out of life—until one night I heard one of the
fellows whining in the spider's clutches; no, thought I,
they have their troubles too. It can't be helped, Fedya.
Now don't forget your pledge. Go now. Goodbye."

Lavretsky went down the back stairs and had reached
the gates when a manservant overtook him.

"Marya Dmitriyevna would like to see you," he said
to Lavretsky.

"Tell her, my man, that I can't just now. . ." Fyodor
Ivanych began.

"The mistress told me to say it was very particular," went on the servant. "She told me to tell you she was alone."

"Have the visitors gone?" asked Lavretsky.

"Yes, sir," rejoined the servant with a grin.

Lavretsky shrugged his shoulders and followed him.

XLIII

Marya Dmitriyevna was sitting alone in her boudoir in a Voltairean armchair, and sniffing Eau de Cologne; on a little table at her side stood a glass of orange-flower water. She was agitated and seemed to be somewhat apprehensive.

Lavretsky came in.

"You wanted to see me," he said, bowing coldly.

"Yes," replied Marya Dmitriyevna, taking a sip of water. "I heard that you had gone straight up to my aunt; I gave orders to ask you in—I wanted to have a talk with you. Sit down, please." Marya Dmitriyevna drew a deep breath. "You know," she went on, "that your wife has come."

"I know that," rejoined Lavretsky.

"Well, then, that is, what I wanted to say is: she came to see me, and I received her; that is what I wanted to see you about, Fyodor Ivanych. I, thank God, enjoy the esteem of everybody, and nothing on earth would induce me to do anything that was not respectable and proper. Although I anticipated that it would displease you, I couldn't find the heart to refuse her, Fyodor Ivanych; she's a relation after all—through you; now, put yourself in my position; what right had I to shut my doors on her—don't you agree?"

"You have no reason to be worrying over that, Marya Dmitriyevna," replied Lavretsky. "You did the right thing; I am not in the least angry. I haven't the slightest intention of debarring Varvara Pavlovna from the society of her acquaintances; I did not look in today simply because I did not want to meet her—that is all."

"Oh, how glad I am to hear you say that, Fyodor

Ivanych," cried Marya Dmitriyevna, "though I must say I always expected it of your generous nature. As to my worrying—that is not surprising, for I too am a woman and a mother. And your wife, you know ... of course, I cannot be your judge—I told her so myself; but she is such an amiable person, she is really so delightful. I don't see how one can help liking her."

Lavretsky smiled ironically and toyed with his hat.

"And this is what I wanted to say to you besides, Fyodor Ivanych," rattled on Marya Dmitriyevna, moving up closer to him, "if you could have seen how modestly she carries herself, how respectful she is! It is really quite touching. And if you could have heard in what terms she speaks of you! I'm entirely to blame, she says; I didn't appreciate him, she says; he's not a man, she says, he's an angel. Indeed, that's what she says—an angel. She is so contrite.... 'Pon my word I've never seen such contrition in all my life!"

"Excuse my curiosity, Marya Dmitriyevna," murmured Lavretsky, "I'm told Varvara Pavlovna has been singing here—did she sing while she was being contrite, eh?..."

"Oh, it's a shame to talk like that! She sang and played the piano only to please me, because I insistently begged her to, almost commanded her. She was looking sad, so sad; now, thought I to myself, what could I do to divert her—and then I'd heard that she had such a wonderful talent! I assure you, Fyodor Ivanych, she is utterly crushed, ask Sergei Petrovich if you like—a heartbroken woman, *tout-à-fait*, really, you know!"

Lavretsky only shrugged his shoulders.

"And then what a little angel is that Ada of yours, what an adorable child! She is so sweet, such a clever little thing; and she speaks French marvellously; and understands Russian too—called me auntie. And you know, she's not the least shy like most children of her age, not at all. And how she resembles you, Fyodor Ivanych, it's most extraordinary. The eyes, the eyebrows ... well, just the image of you. I'm not particularly fond of little children, I must confess, but I've simply lost my heart to your little girl."

"Marya Dmitriyevna," Lavretsky ejaculated, "may I ask you, what is your object in telling me all this?"

"My object?" Marya Dmitriyevna took another sniff at the Eau de Cologne and a sip of water. "Well, I am telling you this, Fyodor Ivanych, because ... I am a relation of yours, after all, I take a warm interest in you. ... I know your heart is of the best. Listen, *mon cousin*, I am at any rate a woman of experience and will not speak at random: forgive her, forgive your wife." Marya Dmitriyevna's eyes suddenly brimmed with tears. "Just think: her youth, her inexperience ... perhaps a bad example: she hadn't the kind of mother who could have set her right. Forgive her, Fyodor Ivanych, she has been punished enough."

The tears trickled down Marya Dmitriyevna's cheeks; she did not wipe them away: she liked a cry. Lavretsky sat as if on thorns. "My God," he thought, "what torture, what a day this has been!"

"You do not answer," Marya Dmitriyevna began again, "how am I to take it? Can you really be so cruel? No, I will not believe it. I feel that my words have convinced you, Fyodor Ivanych, God will reward you for your generosity, and now receive your wife from my hands. ..."

Lavretsky instinctively got up from his chair; Marya Dmitriyevna rose too, and moving swiftly behind a screen, reappeared leading Varvara Pavlovna by the hand. Pallid and lifeless, with downcast eyes, she seemed to have relinquished all thought and volition of her own—and delivered herself utterly into Marya Dmitriyevna's hands.

Lavretsky recoiled.

"You were here all the time!" he exclaimed.

"She is not to blame," broke in Marya Dmitriyevna hurriedly, "she would not stay on any account, but I commanded her to remain; I put her behind the screen. She assured me this would only make you angrier; I would not even listen to her; I know you better than she does. Come, take your wife from my hands; come, Varya, don't be afraid, go down on your knees" (she gave a tug at her arm), "and my blessings. ..."

"Wait a minute, Marya Dmitriyevna," interjected Lavretsky in a low but terrible voice. "I daresay you are fond of affecting scenes" (Lavretsky was not mistaken: Marya Dmitriyevna still retained her schoolgirl's passion for theatrical effects); "they amuse you, but they may be very painful to other people. However, I am not going to talk to you: in *this* scene you are not the principal character. What do *you* want of me, Madame," he added, turning on his wife. "Haven't I done what I could for you? Don't tell me you haven't laid this plot; I won't believe you—and you know that I cannot believe you. What then do you want? You're a clever woman—you do nothing without a motive. You must understand that to live with you as I lived before is out of the question; not that I am angry with you, but because I am not the man I was. I told you that the day after you came back, and you no doubt agree with me now in your heart of hearts. But you want to reinstate yourself in the world's opinion, it is not enough for you to live in my house, you want to live with me under the same roof—isn't that so?"

"I want you to forgive me," said Varvara Pavlovna without raising her eyes.

"She wants you to forgive her," repeated Marya Dmitriyevna.

"And not for my sake, but for Ada's," whispered Varvara Pavlovna.

"Not for her sake, but for Ada's," re-echoed Marya Dmitriyevna.

"Very good. Is that what you want?" uttered Lavretsky with an effort. "Very well, I consent to that too."

Varvara Pavlovna threw him a keen glance, and Marya Dmitriyevna exclaimed: "There, God be thanked," and pulled Varvara Pavlovna again by the arm. "Now receive from my hands. . . ."

"Wait a minute, I tell you," Lavretsky interrupted. "I agree to live with you, Varvara Pavlovna," he went on, "that is, I will take you to Lavriky and live there with you as long as I can stand it, then I'll go away and come down from time to time. You see, I don't want to deceive you; but do not ask me more than that. You would laugh yourself were I to take our good cousin on her word and fold you to my bosom, and start assuring you that . . . that what has been has not been, that the felled tree can blossom again. But I see: one must bow before the inevitable. You will not understand these words the way I mean ... but never mind. I repeat, I will live with you ... no, that I couldn't promise. ... I will be reconciled with you, I will regard you as my wife again...."

"Give her at least your hand on it," said Marya Dmitriyevna, whose tears had already run dry.

"I have never deceived Varvara Pavlovna yet," retorted Lavretsky. "She will take my word for it. I will see her off to Lavriky; and remember, Varvara Pavlovna, this arrangement will be considered void as soon as you leave Lavriky. And now, with your leave, I will go."

He bowed to both ladies and hurried out.

"You're not taking her with you," called out Marya Dmitriyevna.

"Let him be," whispered Varvara Pavlovna to her, and promptly fell on her neck, lavishing terms of gratitude, kissing her hands and calling her her benefactress.

Marya Dmitriyevna accepted her blandishments indulgently; but at bottom she was displeased with Lavretsky, with Varvara Pavlovna and with the whole scene she had devised. It did not turn out nearly as touching as she had expected; Varvara Pavlovna, she thought, should have flung herself at her husband's feet.

"How is it you didn't understand me?" she queried. "I kept on telling you: down!"

"It's better so, dear auntie; don't worry—everything went off splendidly," Varvara Pavlovna assured her.

"True, he's as cold as ice," observed Marya Dmitriyevna. "You did not cry, to be sure, but then I cried my eyes out to him. So he wants to shut you up in Lavriky. Does it mean you won't even be able to come and see me? All men are so hardhearted," she concluded with a knowing shake of the head.

"But then women can appreciate goodness and generosity," murmured Varvara Pavlovna, and slipping down on her knees before Marya Dmitriyevna, she flung her arms round her portly waist and pressed her face against her. Her face wore a furtive smile, and the tears began to ooze once more from Marya Dmitriyevna's eyes.

When Lavretsky got home he shut himself up in his valet's room, flung himself on a sofa and lay like that till morning.

XLIV

The next day was Sunday. The church bells ringing for matins did not wake Lavretsky—he had not closed an eye all night—but they had brought back the memory of that other Sunday when he had attended church on Liza's request. He got up hastily; an inner voice told him he would see her there today as well. He let himself quietly out of the house, leaving a message for Varvara Pavlovna, who still slept, that he would be back for dinner, and strode off to where the plaintive monotony of the bells seemed to be luring him. He arrived early; there was hardly a soul in the church; a deacon was reading the hours in the choir; his deep-chested drone, arrested by an occasional cough, rose and fell. Lavretsky took up a place near the door. Worshippers came in one by one, stopped, crossed themselves, bowed on all sides; their footsteps resounded in the quiet, empty church, reverberating hollowly under the vaulted roof. A decrepit little woman in a threadbare cloak and hood stood on her knees near Lavretsky, offering up fervid prayers; her toothless, yellow, shrunken visage was tense with pious emotion; her red eyes gazed fixedly upward at the holy figures on the iconostasis; every now and then she thrust a bony hand from under her cloak and with a slow sweeping movement made a broad and rigid sign of the cross. A peasant with a bushy beard and grim face, ruffled and rumpled, came into the church, dropped precipitately on his knees and began to cross himself apace, flinging back and tossing his head after each prostration. His face and every one of his gestures were expressive of such poignant grief that Lavretsky was tempted to accost him and ask what his trouble was. The peasant started back fearfully, sullenly, and stared at him.... "My son died," he blurted out, and resumed his prayers.... "What can supplant the solace of the church for these people?" thought Lav-

retsky, and tried to pray himself; but his heart was weighed down and embittered, and his mind was running on
other things. He was waiting for Liza, but Liza did not
come. The church began to fill with people, but still she
did not come. The service had started, the deacon had
already read the gospel, the bell had been rung for the
last prayer; Lavretsky shifted his position—and suddenly
he caught sight of Liza. She had been in the church before he arrived, but he had not noticed her; huddled between the wall and the choir, she had not moved or looked
around. Lavretsky did not take his eyes off her all
through the service: he was bidding her farewell. The
congregation began to disperse, but she still tarried; she
seemed to be waiting for Lavretsky to leave. At length
she crossed herself for the last time and went out without turning her head; she had a maid with her. Lavretsky
followed her out and caught up with her in the street;
she walked quickly with head bent and a veil drawn over
her face.

"Good morning, Elizaveta Mikhailovna," he said loudly with forced casualness. "May I escort you?"

She said nothing; he walked on by her side.

"Are you satisfied with me?" he asked her, dropping
his voice. "You have heard what happened yesterday?"

"Yes, yes," she replied in a whisper, "that is well."

And she walked on faster.

"Are you satisfied?"

Liza only nodded her head.

"Fyodor Ivanych," she began in a steady but faint
voice, "I wanted to ask you—please do not come to see
us any more, go away as soon as possible; we can see each
other later—some other time, in a year perhaps. But
now, do this for my sake; do as I ask, I beseech you."

"I am ready to obey you in everything, Elizaveta
Mikhailovna—but must we part like this? Will you not say
one word to me?. . ."

"Fyodor Ivanych, you are walking now by my side . . .
but you are already so far, far away from me. And not
only you. . . ."

"Speak out, I implore you!" cried Lavretsky. "What
do you mean?"

"You will hear of it, perhaps.... But come what may, forget ... no, do not forget me, think of me."

"Can I forget you?..."

"Enough, goodbye. Do not follow me."

"Liza," began Lavretsky.

"Goodbye, goodbye!" she repeated drawing her veil still lower and darted forward almost at a run.

Lavretsky gazed at her retreating figure, then turned back down the street, his head bowed. He almost collided with Lemm who was also walking with his hat tipped over his nose and his eyes on the ground.

They looked at each other in silence.

"Well, what do you say?" Lavretsky brought out at length.

"What can I say?" rejoined Lemm gloomily. "I say nothing. Everything is dead and we are dead (*Alles ist tot und wir sind tot*). You are going to the right?"

"Yes."

"And I go to the left. Goodbye."

*   *   *

The next morning Fyodor Ivanych started out with his wife for Lavriky. She rode ahead in a carriage with Ada and Justine; he behind, in the tarantass. The pretty little girl could not tear herself away from the window all through the journey; everything filled her with wonder: the peasant folk, the huts, the wells, the yokes over the horses' heads, the tinkling bells and the innumerable rooks; Justine shared her wonder; Varvara Pavlovna laughed amusedly at their remarks and exclamations. She was in a good mood; before setting out she had cleared up the situation with her husband.

"I understand your position," she had said to him, and from the look in her shrewd eyes he gathered that she understood his position perfectly, "but you must at least give me credit for being an easy person to live with. I will not thrust myself on you or hinder you; all I wanted was to secure Ada's future; that's all."

"Well, you have achieved all your ends," observed Fyodor Ivanych.

"There's only one thing I dream of now: to bury myself forever in seclusion; I shall always remember your generosity. . . ."

"Pah! Have done. . . ." he interrupted.

"And I shall know how to respect your independence and peace of mind," she went on completing the phrase she had prepared.

Lavretsky made her a low bow. Varvara Pavlovna understood that her husband was inwardly grateful to her.

On the evening of the next day they arrived in Lavriky; a week later Lavretsky went to Moscow, leaving his wife five thousand pocket money—and the day after his departure Panshin, whom Varvara Pavlovna had asked not to forget her in her retirement, came upon the scene. She made him extremely welcome, and till late in the night the lofty rooms of the house and the garden without resounded with music and singing and gay French speech. For three days Panshin enjoyed the hospitality of Varvara Pavlovna; when taking his leave he pressed her beautiful hands in his own, and promised to come again shortly. He was as good as his word.

XLV

Liza had her own little room on the second floor of her mother's house, a clean airy chamber with a white bed, pots of flowers in the corners and before the windows, a small writing table, a bookshelf and crucifix on the wall. This nook was known as the nursery; Liza had been born in it. On returning from the church after meeting Lavretsky, she tidied up her room more thoroughly than usual, dusted everything, went over all her copybooks and letters from girl friends and tied them up with ribbons, locked all the drawers, watered the flowers, touching each blossom with her fingers. All this she did leisurely, silently, with a look of rapt and gentle solicitude on her face. Then she stood still in the middle of the room, gazing slowly round, and going up to the table over which hung the crucifix, she went down on her knees, placed her head on her clasped hands and remained motionless.

Marfa Timofeyevna came in and found her in this posture. Liza had not noticed her entrance. The old lady went out on tiptoe and coughed loudly several times. Liza got up quickly and wiped her eyes which glistened with bright unshed tears.

"Ah, I see you have been tidying up your little cell again," observed Marfa Timofeyevna and bent low over a young rose plant, "how lovely it smells."

Liza looked pensively at her aunt.

"What was that word you said?" she whispered.

"What word, eh?" the old lady put in quickly. "What do you mean? This is terrible," she cried, suddenly flinging off her cap and sitting down on Liza's little bed, "it is more than I can endure! I've been on tenterhooks for four days now; I can't go on pretending that I don't notice anything—I can't bear the sight of you getting paler and pining away and weeping, I can't, I can't!"

"Why, what is the matter with you, auntie?" murmured Liza. "I am all right. . . ."

"All right!" cried Marfa Timofeyevna. "You tell that somebody else, not me! All right! Who has just been standing on her knees? Whose lashes are still wet with tears? All right! Take a look at yourself, what have you gone and done with yourself—look at your face, look at your eyes! All right, indeed! Don't I know what it's all about?"

"It will pass off, auntie, in time."

"Pass off, but when? Good Lord in heaven! Could you have loved him that bad? But he is an old man, Liza dear. Well, I admit he is a good fellow, he doesn't bite; but what of that? We're all good people; the world is large enough, there is enough and to spare of that kind of stuff."

"I tell you it will pass off, it has passed off already."

"Listen to me, Liza darling," Marfa Timofeyevna said all at once, making Liza sit down beside her and stroking now her hair, now her kerchief, "it only seems to you now in the heat of the moment that your grief is inconsolable. Ah, my dearest, only death knows no medicine! You only just say to yourself: 'I won't give in, no fear!' and you'd be surprised how easy it comes off your chest. Just grin and bear it a little."

"Auntie," replied Liza, "it has passed already, it is all over."

"All over! All over indeed! Why, just look how pinched your poor little nose is, and you say it is over! A fine way of getting over it!"

"Yes, it is over, auntie, if you will only consent to stand by me," said Liza with sudden animation, flinging her arms round Marfa Timofeyevna's neck. "Auntie dear, be a friend to me, help me, don't be angry, try to understand. . . ."

"Why, what's that, what's that, my dear girl? Don't scare me like that, please; I shall begin to scream, don't look at me like that; tell me quickly, what is it?"

"I . . . I want. . ." Liza hid her face on Marfa Timofeyevna's bosom. "I want to go into a convent", she whispered.

The old lady almost bounded off the bed.

"Cross yourself, Liza, my dear, you don't know what you're saying! Good God, what a thing to say!" she stammered when she had finally found her tongue. "Lie down, darling, take a little nap; all this comes from sleepless nights, sweetheart."

Liza raised her head; her cheeks flamed.

"No, auntie," she said, "don't speak like that; I have made up my mind, I have prayed, I have sought counsel of God; it is over, my life with you is over. Such a lesson was not for nothing, and it is not the first time I have been thinking of this. Happiness did not come my way; even when I had hopes of happiness my heart was heavy with foreboding. I know all—my own sins and others' and how papa made his fortune; I know all about it. Prayers, prayers must wipe this all off. I am sorry for you, sorry for mother and Lenochka; but there is no help for it; I feel that life here is not for me; I have bidden farewell already to all and everything in the house for the last time; I am answering a summons; my heart is sick with pain, I want to shut myself away for ever. Do not hold me back, do not try to dissuade me, but help me, or else I will go alone. . . ."

Marfa Timofeyevna listened to her niece aghast.

"She's ill, she's delirious," she thought, "we must send for a doctor, but which one? Gedeonovsky was praising one the other day, but he's such a liar—perhaps this time he was telling the truth?" But when it dawned on her that Liza was not ill and not delirious, when she, Liza, constantly returned the same answer to all her expostulations, Marfa Timofeyevna was alarmed and distressed beyond words. "But you do not realise, my darling," she began to remonstrate with her, "what the life in those convents is like! They will feed you, my sweet, on horrible green hemp oil, they will give you coarse, rough underwear to put on, send you out in the cold; you'll never survive it, Liza darling! It's all Agafya's doing this is—it's she who had led you astray. But then she first had her taste of life, she'd lived for her own pleasure; you've got to live too. Let me at least die in peace; then you can do as you please. And where did you ever see anybody going into a convent because of a goat's beard—God forgive us—because of a man? Well, if you feel so bad about it, go on a pilgrimage, put up prayers to some saint, have a service sung, but don't go putting a black hood on your head, my darling, my sweet child. . . ."

And Marfa Timofeyevna burst into bitter tears.

Liza consoled her, wiped away her tears, wept herself, but was not to be shaken in her resolve. In her despair Marfa Timofeyevna resorted to threats—she said she would tell her mother everything, but all in vain. Liza yielded at last to the old lady's earnest pleading and agreed to postpone her intentions for six months; but a pledge was extracted from Marfa Timofeyevna in return that, should Liza not change her mind during that period, she would help her and secure Marya Dmitriyevna's consent.

*   *   *

With the first spell of cold weather Varvara Pavlovna, despite the promise she had given to bury herself in seclusion, removed to St. Petersburg where, having provided herself with funds, she rented a modest but charming set of apartments found her by Panshin, who had left O— prior to her. During the later part of his sojourn in O— he had entirely forfeited Marya Dmitriyevna's good graces; he suddenly stopped calling on her and was almost a permanent fixture at Lavriky. Varvara Pavlovna had enslaved him, nothing more nor less; no other word can describe the illimitable, irrevocable and absolute power she had over him.

Lavretsky spent the winter in Moscow, and in the following spring the news reached him that Liza had taken the veil in the B— convent in one of the remotest parts of Russia.

EPILOGUE

Eight years passed. It was spring again.... But let us first say a few words concerning the fate of Mikhalevich, Panshin and Madame Lavretskya, and take leave of them. Mikhalevich, after many vicissitudes, found his true vocation: he obtained a position as senior usher in a government school. He is quite content with his lot, and his charges "adore" him, though they mimick him behind his back. Panshin has moved high up the official ladder and is aiming at a directorship; he walks with a slight stoop, doubtlessly through the weight of the Vladimir Cross he wears around his neck. The official in him has gained indomitable ascendancy over the artist; his still young-looking face has grown sallow, his hair thin and he no longer sings, nor sketches, but secretly dabbles in literature: he has written a comedy in the style of a proverb, and as nowadays all authors invariably "delineate" something or somebody, he has delineated therein a coquette, and reads it in private to two or three devoted ladies of his acquaintance. He has not, however, embarked on matrimony, although he had many fine opportunities of doing so. For this Varvara Pavlovna is to blame. As for her, she resides permanently in Paris, as before: Fyodor Ivanych gave her a promissory note on himself, thereby securing his ransom and immunity from another surprise invasion. She has grown older and stouter, but is still attractive and elegant. Everybody has his beau ideal; Varvara Pavlovna found hers in the dramatic works of Dumas fils. She assiduously frequents the theatre where consumptive and languishing camelia ladies are portrayed on the stage, to be Madame Doch seems to her the height of human bliss; she once declared that she would desire nothing better for her own daughter. It is to be hoped that fate will spare Mademoiselle Ada such bliss: from the rosy chubby child she was she has become a weak-chested pale little girl; her nerves are already bad. Varvara Pavlovna's admirers have diminished in number, but still make a showing; some of them she will probably retain to the end of her days. The most ardent of them these days is a certain Zakurdalo-Skubyrnikov, a retired guardsman of the whisker-wearing clan, a man of thirty-eight, of extraordinarily vigorous physique. The French habitués of Madame Lavretskaya's salon call him *"le gros taureau de l'Ukraine"*; Varvara Pavlovna never invites him to her fashionable evening parties, but he unquestionably enjoys her good will.

And so ... eight years passed. Once more the skies suffuse the radiant joys of spring; once more spring smiles upon the earth and upon men; once more under its caresses the world is turning to blossom, to love and song. The town of O— has changed little in these eight years; but Marya Dmitriyevna's house seems to have grown younger; its newly-painted walls are cheerfully bright and the panes of the open windows reflect shimmering crimson in the rays of the setting sun; from these windows the light and happy sound of clear young voices and incessant laughter is wafted into the street; the whole house seems to seethe with life and brim over with gaiety. The mistress of the house has long since gone down to the grave: Marya Dmitriyevna died two years after Liza took the veil and Marfa Timofeyevna did not survive her niece long; they lie side by side in the town cemetery. Nastasya Karpovna too is no more; the faithful old woman had been

going every week for several years to pray over her
friend's grave.... Her time had come as well, and her
bones were laid to rest in the damp earth. But Marya
Dmitriyevna's house did not fall into strangers' hands, did
not pass out of the family, the nest was not ruined: Lenochka, grown into a slim beautiful girl, and her fiancé—a
fair-haired officer of the hussars; Marya Dmitriyevna's
son who had just married in St. Petersburg and had come
down for the spring with his young wife; his wife's sister,
a sixteen-year-old schoolgirl with rosy cheeks and limpid
eyes; Shurochka, also grown up and winsome—such was
the youthful household to whose gay laughter and chatter
the walls of the Kalitins' house resounded. Everything in
the house had changed, everything fitted in with the new
inmates. Clean-shaven grinning servant lads, full of quips
and cranks, had replaced the staid old servants of former
days; where Roska used to waddle in dignified corpulence
two setters were frisking madly and gambolling over the
sofas; the stables now housed lean amblers, spiriter carriage horses, mettlesome outriders with plaited manes and
saddle horses from the Don; the breakfast, dinner and supper hours were all mixed and muddled and things were
run in a "new-fangled way" as the neighbours put it.

On the evening in question, the inhabitants of the Kalitins' house (the oldest of whom, Lenochka's fiancé, was
twenty-four) were engaged in a simple, and, judging from
their merry laughter, an exceedingly amusing game: they
chased about the rooms trying to catch each other; the
dogs followed suit and barked excitedly and the canaries
in their cages hanging above the windows rent the air,
adding to the general uproar with the piercing racket of
their frenzied twittering. At the very height of this ear-
splitting fun a mud-bespattered tarantass drove up the
gates and a man of five and forty in a travelling cloak
stepped out of it and stood stockstill in amazement. He
stood for some time without stirring, cast an observant
glance over the house, went through the gate into the
courtyard and slowly mounted the steps of the porch. He
encountered nobody in the hall; suddenly the door of the
living room was flung open and out rushed a flushed Shurochka, while in hot pursuit came all the yelling and

shrieking young horde. They pulled up, subdued at the sight of a stranger; but the bright eyes that surveyed him looked just as kindly and the fresh faces still smiled. Marya Dmitriyevna's son went up to the visitor and asked him in friendly tones what he wanted.

"I am Lavretsky," the visitor said.

He was answered by a burst of cries—not that these young people were so delighted at the arrival of a distant, almost forgotten relation, but simply because they were all agog to raise a din and rejoice on any provocation. Lavretsky was instantly surrounded: Lenochka, as an old acquaintance, made herself known first, declaring that she certainly would have recognised him in a short while, and introduced the rest of the company, calling each one, even her betrothed, by their pet names. They all trooped through the dining room into the drawing room. The wallpaper in both rooms was new, but the furniture remained intact. Lavretsky recognised the piano; even the embroidering frames by the window were the same, standing in the same position and, it seemed, with the same unfinished embroidery in them as eight years ago. They made him sit in a comfortable armchair; all sat around politely in a circle. Questions, exclamations and narrations followed one another in quick succession.

"It's a long time since we've seen you," Lenochka remarked artlessly, "and Varvara Pavlovna too."

"Naturally!" her brother put in hastily. "I carried you off to St. Petersburg and Fyodor Ivanych has been living all the time in the country."

"Yes, and mother has died since then."

"And Marfa Timofeyevna," Shurochka murmured.

"And Nastasya Karpovna," Lenochka observed, "and Monsieur Lemm...."

"What? Lemm is dead too?" Lavretsky enquired.

"Yes," replied young Kalitin, "he went away to Odessa; they say someone lured him away; and he died there."

"Do you know whether he left any music?"

"I don't know. I doubt it."

All were silent and exchanged glances. A cloud of melancholy flitted across the young faces.

"Matross is alive, you know," Lenochka said suddenly.

"And Gedeonovsky too," her brother added.

At Gedeonovsky's name, there was a burst of merry laughter.

"Yes, he's alive, and still the same old liar," Marya Dmitriyevna's son went on, "and can you imagine it, this here madcap" (he pointed to the schoolgirl, his sister-in-law) "put some pepper in his snuffbox yesterday."

"You should have heard him sneeze!" Lenochka cried, and her voice was drowned in another peal of irrepressible laughter.

"We've recently had news of Liza," young Kalitin observed, and a hush fell again on all, "she is all right, her health is a little better now."

"Is she still in the same convent?" Lavretsky asked not without an effort.

"Yes."

"Does she write?"

"No, never; but we get news through other people." A sudden profound hush followed; "a sweet angel is passing," everybody thought.

"Would you care to go into the garden?" Kalitin enquired. "It's very nice now, though we've let it run a bit wild."

Lavretsky went out into the garden and the first thing he caught sight of was the garden seat, that same garden seat on which he had once spent with Liza those fleeting moments of unforgettable joy; it had grown black and warped, but he had recognised it, and his heart was gripped by an emotion that was exquisitely sweet and bitter— a feeling of poignant sadness for youth that had vanished, for happiness once possessed. He strolled down the avenues with the young people; the lime trees looked hardly any older or taller, but their shade was thicker: all the bushes, however, had shot up, the raspberry bushes had grown sturdily, the hazels were a rank overgrowth and everything was redolent of the freshness of the woods, the scent of grass and lilac blossoms.

"This is just the spot for puss-in-the-corner," Lenochka cried suddenly, as they emerged into a small grassy enclosure among the lime trees, "there are just five of us, too."

"What about Fyodor Ivanych?" her brother observed. "Or don't you count yourself?"

Lenochka coloured slightly.

"But would Fyodor Ivanych, at his age. . . ." she began.

"Please go on with your games," Lavretsky hastened to interpose; "take no notice of me. I will feel all the better for knowing that I am not in your way. And there's no need for you to entertain me; we old folk have an occupation which you know nothing of yet, and which no entertainment can replace—memories."

The young people listened to Lavretsky with affable politeness tinged with amusement—as though a teacher were giving them a lesson—and then suddenly scattered, making for the green patch; four of them took up positions under the trees, one stood in the middle, and the fun began.

And Lavretsky retraced his steps to the house, went into the dining room, drew near the piano, and touched one of the keys: a faint but clear note vibrated on the air, and touched an answering chord within his heart: it was the opening note of that inspired melody with which Lemm, poor Lemm, had so delighted him on that memorable and happy night so long ago. Then Lavretsky passed into the drawing room and stayed there for a long time: here, where he had so often seen Liza, her image rose more vividly before him; he seemed to feel her presence around him; but his grief for her was agonising and not easy to bear; it had none of the quietude which death brings. Liza was alive, somewhere far away and out of reach; he thought of her as of the living and he could not trace the features of the once beloved girl in that dim pallid vision clad in the guise of a nun and moving amid the curling vapours of incense. Lavretsky would not have recognised himself either, had he been able to see himself with the eyes with which he mentally regarded Liza. During these eight years he had at last turned the corner of his life, which many men pass without turning, but without which no one can wholly remain an honourable man: he had really ceased to think of his own happiness and self-interest. His spirit was quelled and—to be frank—he had grown old not only in face and body, he had grown old in heart; to keep a young heart in old age, as some people say, is difficult and almost absurd; he may well be content who has not lost his faith in goodness, tenacity of purpose and the will to act. Lavretsky had the right to be content: he had really become a good husbandman, had really learnt to plough the land and he laboured not in his own interests alone; he had spared no pains to secure and strengthen the well-being of his peasants.

Lavretsky went out into the garden, sat down on the familiar garden seat, and on this dearly beloved spot facing the house where he had vainly reached his hands out for the last time to grasp the coveted goblet frothing and sparkling with the golden wine of delight, he, a lonely homeless wanderer, looked back on his life, while the joyous shouts of the young generation who had already taken his place came floating to him across the garden. He felt sad at heart but without bitterness or distress: he had much to regret, nothing to be ashamed of. "Play, rejoice, grow, vigorous youth," he thought, and there was no gall in his reflection; "your life is before you, and for you life will be easier; you will not have to seek out paths for yourself like we did, to struggle, fall and rise again amid the darkness; we had our hands full trying to survive—and how many of us did not survive!—but you have a duty to perform, work to do—and the blessing of us old folk be with you. For me, after this day, after these experiences, there remains but to take my last leave of you—and, in view of the approaching end and a God who waits, to say with sadness but without envy, without dark feelings: 'Welcome, lone age! Burn out, useless life!' "

Lavretsky quietly rose to his feet and quietly went away; nobody heeded him; nobody detained him; the sounds of merriment rang out louder than ever in the garden behind the green wall of lofty lime trees. He got into his carriage and bade the coachman drive home and not to hurry the horses.

*   *   *

"And the end?" perhaps the disappointed reader will ask. "What happened afterwards to Lavretsky? and Liza?"

But what is there to tell of people who though still living have retired from the world and its strife, why come back to them? Lavretsky, it is said, paid a visit to the remote cloister where Liza had taken refuge, had seen her. Stepping down from choir to choir she walked close past him; she passed with the even, meekly hurried gait of a nun and did not glance at him; only the eyelashes quivered slightly and the emaciated face bent still lower and the fingers of her clasped hands entwined with the rosary were pressed still tighter. What were they both thinking, what were they feeling? Who can know? Who can say? There are such moments in life, such feelings. . . . One can but point to them—and pass on.

THE END

REQUEST TO READERS

Progress Publishers would be glad to have your opinion of the translation and design of this book. Please send all your comments to 21, Zubovsky Boulevard, Moscow, U.S.S.R.

TO BE PUBLISHED IN 1974

Progress. Russian Classics Series

PUSHKIN A. *Selected Works.* In two volumes

This two-volume edition of selected works of Russia's great poet Alexander Pushkin (1799-1837) will give the readers an idea of scope and versatility of his genius.

The first volume contains new translations of the poems *The Gypsies* and *The Bronze Horseman,* his dramas in verse *Mozart and Salieri* and *The Stone Guest,* the drama *The Water Nymph,* and Russian folk tales in Pushkin's rendering.

The second volume contains Pushkin's prose: *The Tales of Ivan Belkin,* the psychological short novel *The Queen of Spades,* and the historical novel *The Captain's Daughter.*

The introduction was written by the prominent Soviet poet Alexander Tvardovsky.

The two volumes are lavishly illustrated.

TURGENEV I. *Three Short Novels* (Collection)

The works of Ivan Turgenev have not aged in the course of the century which has passed since their writing and are still popular the world over. *Asya, First Love* and *Spring Torrents* belong to his most popular short novels. They raise the eternal theme of love. Probably no other writer had ever handled this delicate problem and traced its complex connections with the other aspects of life with Turgenev's tact and skill. As always with Turgenev, love is not simply a blessed gift from heaven, but a dramatic experience fraught with trials.